"I'm not the kind of person men want to marry."

"You're not?" Kyle's eyes did a head-to-toe scan of her. "Why?"

"I'm not pretty," Sara admitted, embarrassed. "I don't know anything about fashion or how to dress. I certainly don't know anything about love or, uh, romance. I've never even dated."

"Sara, not every man is concerned about glamour or looks. Not that you have to worry. You're a very beautiful woman." He touched her arm as if to reinforce his words. "But what matters most is that you have a generous, tender heart that cares for people. That's the most attractive thing about you."

Inside her heart the persistent flicker of admiration she always felt for him flared into a full-fledged flame. But Sara didn't know how to respond. If she wasn't careful, his kindness would coax her into confessing the ugliness of her past, and then he'd see that she wasn't any of those things he'd said.

LOIS RICHER

North Country Hero
&
North Country Family

HARLEQUIN® LOVE INSPIRED®CLASSICS

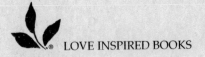

LOVE INSPIRED BOOKS

Recycling programs for this product may not exist in your area.

ISBN-13: 978-1-335-23255-7

North Country Hero & North Country Family

Copyright © 2019 by Harlequin Books S.A.

The publisher acknowledges the copyright holder of the individual works as follows:

North Country Hero
Copyright © 2013 by Lois M. Richer

North Country Family
Copyright © 2014 by Lois M. Richer

www.Harlequin.com

Printed in U.S.A.

CONTENTS

Lois Richer loves traveling, swimming and quilting, but mostly she loves writing stories that show God's boundless love for His precious children. As she says, "His love never changes or gives up. It's always waiting for me. My stories feature imperfect characters learning that love doesn't mean attaining perfection. Love is about keeping on keeping on." You can contact Lois via email, loisricher@gmail.com, or on Facebook (loisricherauthor).

Books by Lois Richer

Love Inspired

Rocky Mountain Haven

Meant-to-Be Baby
Mistletoe Twins

Wranglers Ranch

The Rancher's Family Wish
Her Christmas Family Wish
The Cowboy's Easter Family Wish
The Twins' Family Wish

Family Ties

A Dad for Her Twins
Rancher Daddy
Gift-Wrapped Family
Accidental Dad

Visit the Author Profile page
at Harlequin.com for more titles.

NORTH COUNTRY HERO

For Jehovah hears the cries of his needy ones
and does not look the other way.
—*Psalms* 69:33

I wrote this story after losing my father last September.

I dedicate this book to his memory.

I love you, Dad.

Chapter One

"I've already told you, Marla. I don't want to get involved with this 'Lives Under Construction' place."

The anger in the man's voice and the mention of her new employer piqued Sara Kane's interest so much, she stopped reading her book on the northern lights.

"Yes, Marla," he said with a weary sigh. "I know you told me I need to get involved, that you believe it will facilitate my recovery. And I will get involved. Eventually. But I told you I'm only going back home to Churchill to settle things. I'm not looking to get involved and I'm certainly not staying."

Sara suddenly realized she was listening in on someone's private cell phone conversation. Shame suffused her, but it wasn't as if he was whispering!

Sara tried to refocus on her book but couldn't because he was speaking again.

"Fine," he agreed with some exasperation. "I promise you I will touch base with Laurel Quinn while I'm there, since you've already told her I'm coming."

Did that mean this man knew Laurel? Maybe he, like her, was one of Laurel's former foster kids, Sara mused.

"But touching base is all I'm going to promise you, Marla. You've been a wonderful therapist, and I appreciate everything you've done for me. But I have to stand on my own two feet now." Though he barked out a laugh, Sara heard an underlying bitterness. "Two feet—get it? That was supposed to be a joke."

Sara didn't understand what was so funny, but then that wasn't unusual. At twenty-two, there were a lot of things she didn't understand. But she would. She was going to Churchill, Canada, to work, but while she was there she intended to do all the things she'd missed during the ten miserable years she'd been in foster care.

First on her to-do list was finding her birth mother.

"I don't know what my future plans are, Marla. That's what I need to figure out." The man's voice suddenly dropped. "Everything I loved doing is impossible now."

The words brimmed with such misery, Sara had to force herself not to turn around and comfort him.

Don't give up, she ached to tell him. *Life will get better.*

"You're breaking up, Marla. I'll call you after I get to Churchill. Bye."

Churchill, Manitoba. Her new home.

A wiggle of satisfaction ran through Sara. This was her chance to start over. This was her opportunity to figure out how to be like everyone else instead of always being the oddball, and how to have the life she'd dreamed of for so long. Most of all, it was her opportunity to find the love she craved.

For Sara, Churchill would be a beginning. But for the man in the seat behind her, it sounded as if Churchill was going to be an ending. She couldn't help wondering why.

The train rumbled along. People went to the dining car to eat their dinner. Forewarned by Laurel, Sara had brought along a lunch so she could save her money. The thermos of homemade soup was warm and filling. She'd just sipped a mouthful when *he* rose behind her. His hand pressed the seat back near her head, dragging on it as he stood. A moment later he walked past her down the aisle, paused politely for a woman with a child to precede him, then followed her into the next car. Sara's curiosity mushroomed.

When the angle of his body and the dim overhead lights didn't give her a good view of his face, Sara decided she'd pay more attention when he returned. That way she could ask Laurel about him when they arrived in Churchill.

But though she waited long hours, the man did not return. Frustrated that her formerly fascinating book on the northern lights no longer held her attention because *he* kept intruding into her thoughts, she finally exchanged that book for another in her bag, a romance about a hero determined to find the love of his life, who'd disappeared five years ago.

Yet even that couldn't stop Sara's mind from straying back to *him*. He was returning to Churchill. Because someone he loved had lived there, someone he'd had to leave behind? For a while she let the romantic daydream she'd been reading become his story. What would it be like to be loved so deeply that someone actually came to find you?

The train seemed to hum as it rolled along the tracks. Outside, darkness began to drape the landscape. Weariness overcame Sara. She leaned back to rest her eyes and again her thoughts returned to him. She'd heard deep longing in his voice when he'd mentioned settling things, as if he ached for someone.

Sara didn't understand a lot of things, but she understood that feeling.

She ached, too, for somebody to love her.

Maybe, just maybe, she could find the love she sought in Churchill.

"Churchill, Manitoba. End of the line."

Kyle Loness grimaced at the prophetic nature of the conductor's statement. This seemed like the end of the line for him, for sure.

He peered out the window, waiting for everyone else to leave before he rose and reached for his duffel bag. The bed in his sleeper hadn't afforded much rest. Now the bag's extra weight dragged on him, making his bad leg protest as he went down the aisle to the door. He winced at arrow-sharp stabs of pain. Though it felt as if there were still glass shards in his calf from the explosion, he knew that was a mirage.

He knew because there were no nerves below his knee. In fact, there was no leg. A prosthesis allowed Kyle to walk. Yet the phantom pains were very real, and for a moment, just before he stepped onto the platform, he wished he'd downed another pain pill.

"Can I help you?"

The whisper-soft query came from a young woman dressed in clothes clearly inadequate for this place. Her long caramel-brown hair flew every which way, tormented by a gust of icy wind off Hudson Bay. Her gray-shot-with-silver eyes blinked at him, wide and innocent-looking between the strands. She shuddered once, before steeling herself against the elements.

"Thanks, but I'll manage." Kyle immediately regretted his gruff refusal as surprise flickered across her face. But she said nothing. She simply nodded once and waited for him to move.

To prove he was fully capable of maneuvering, Kyle stepped down too quickly. He would have toppled onto the platform if not for the woman's quick reaction. She stepped forward, eased her shoulder under his arm and took most of his weight as he finished his ungainly descent.

While Kyle righted himself, his brain processed several fleeting impressions. First, she seemed too frail to survive Churchill. Her thin face looked gaunt and far too pallid in the blazing sun. The second thing Kyle noted was that she jerked away from him as soon as he was stable, as if she didn't like him touching her.

Well, why would she? He wasn't exactly hunk material, especially not since a roadside bomb had blown off his leg and scarred most of the rest of him.

"Thanks," he mumbled, embarrassed that he'd needed her assistance.

"You're welcome." She didn't smile. She just stood there, watching him. Waiting.

Kyle turned away, pulled up the sliding handle of his suitcase and leaned on it. He needed a moment to regroup before negotiating the long walk through the old train terminal and down the street toward his dad's house.

Except—his breath snagged in his throat—his dad didn't live there. Not ever again.

A knife edge of sorrow scraped his already-raw nerves. Kyle sucked in a breath and focused on getting out of here.

There were taxis in Churchill—two of them. But he

was pretty sure both would have been commandeered by the first people off the train. He could wait for them to come back, but the thought of doing so made him feel as though he couldn't rely on himself. He'd grown up learning how to be independent and he wasn't about to give that up, despite his disability.

Kyle felt the burn of someone staring at him and knew it was her. The woman's scrutiny puzzled him. Once they glimpsed his ugly scars, once they realized he was handicapped, most people—especially women—avoided looking at him. She didn't. His surprise ballooned when her fingers touched his sleeve.

"May I know what happened?" she asked in that whisper-soft voice.

"I was in Afghanistan. I lost part of my leg." The words slipped out automatically. He steeled himself for the mundane murmur of *I'm sorry,* which everyone offered.

It never came.

"I'm so glad you're safe now," she said.

The compassion in her eyes stunned Kyle as much as the brief squeeze she gave his arm.

"God bless you."

God? Kyle wanted to snort his derision. But her sincerity choked his reaction. Why shower his frustration with God on her? It wasn't her fault God had dumped him.

"Thanks." Stupid that her fleeting touch should make him feel cared for.

Alone. You're alone, Kyle. Get on with it.

They were the only two people left on the platform. Kyle led the way inside the terminal. She held the door for him but he refused to say thanks again. He didn't want her help. Didn't need it. Coming here was all about taking back control of his life. About not being dependent.

On anyone.

"Hey, Kyle."

"Hey, Mr. Fox." Kyle added the traditional Native greeting in Cree then waved his hand at the stationmaster he'd known since he'd moved here when he was ten. He ordered himself not to wince when the old man ogled his scarred face. *Get used to it,* he told himself. Folks in Churchill weren't known for their reticence.

"What was that?" The young woman stood next to him, her head tilted to one side. "Those words you said?"

"That was Cree, a Native language. It means something like 'How goes it?'" Kyle kept walking, pausing just long enough to greet his former schoolteacher in French before moving on.

"How many languages do you speak?" the woman asked.

"A few," he admitted.

As a toddler, Kyle's first words were in French, thanks to his European mother. Then as a child, while his father consulted for the military, he'd become fluent in both Pashto and Dari. After that, learning a new language had come easily. In fact, his knack for languages was what had changed Kyle's status from reservist to active duty, and sent him to Afghanistan two years ago.

"It must be nice to speak to people in their own language." The woman trailed along beside him, held the station door open until he'd negotiated through it, then followed him to the waiting area out front.

"Yeah." He glanced around.

The parking lot was almost empty. Trains came to Churchill three times a week—often not on time, but they came. Natives of the town were used to the odd schedule and disembarked quickly after the seventeen-hour ride from Thompson, anxious to get home as fast as they could.

Tourists usually took longer to figure out the lay of the land. Local businesses got them settled, signed them up for some excursions if they could and fed them. Churchill made a lot of money from tourists. Except that somehow Kyle didn't think the woman behind him was a tourist, he decided after taking a second look. It seemed as though she was looking for someone.

So who was she?

Once Kyle had known all the town regulars. But he hadn't been home in two years, and a lot of things had changed. Things like the fact that his dad was never again going to stand beside him while they watched a polar bear and her cubs play among the ice floes in the bay.

Dad was gone and Kyle was damaged goods—too damaged now to scout the back country, climb the rocky shore or do anything else requiring intense physical effort. He wasn't even sure he could manage the walk home.

He paused to reconnoiter while his hand massaged his hip, as if it could short-circuit the darts of pain now shooting upward.

"Is something wrong?" Her again. Her quiet question was neither intrusive nor demanding. Just a question.

"Nothing's wrong." Kyle grimaced. Again he sounded sharp, irritated. He didn't mean to, but the rawness of the place matched his mood. Still, he'd better get rid of that chip on his shoulder. This woman was not his enemy. "I'm fine. Thanks."

"Okay." That calmness of hers—where did it come from? What made her so accepting, so gentle in the face of his irritation?

None of your business. Stop thinking about her.

But he couldn't because the soft slap of her sneakers against the pavement told Kyle she was right behind him.

"Are you following me?" he asked, turning to stare at her.

"Sort of." The wind had tinted her cheeks pink, but now the color intensified into a rose blush. "Someone was supposed to pick me up." She checked the plain watch around her too-thin wrist.

Kyle thought he glimpsed the faint white mark of a scar, but then it was gone as she shifted her small overnight bag from one arm to the other.

"I'm late and they're not here."

"Stay here. They'll come to the station for you. Everyone in Churchill knows when the train comes in." He studied her again, curious about this waiflike woman. "Who are you waiting—?"

"Sara!" The yell came from a blond-haired woman who screeched her van to a halt, jumped out and rushed over from the parking lot. "I'm so sorry I'm late." She flung her arms around the younger woman in a bear hug. "Welcome."

"Thank you." Those silver-gray eyes grew shiny.

Tears? Why? he wondered.

"You must be Kyle Loness. Marla told me you were coming." The new arrival laid a brief hug on him, too, then laughed. "Welcome to you, too, Kyle."

Oddly enough the embrace felt good, even though it knocked Kyle slightly off balance.

"Thanks. I'm guessing you're Laurel Quinn." He smiled when she slid an arm around Sara's waist and planted a hearty kiss on her cheek in the same way his mom had done to him before cancer had sapped her strength. "You're the woman who's starting the youth center, right?"

"That's me. I see you know Sara." Laurel glanced back and forth between them.

"Uh, not really," he said, suddenly too aware of the younger woman standing silent, watching him. "We just got off the train together."

"Well then, Sara, meet Kyle Loness. Kyle, this is Sara Kane. She's going to be our cook at Lives Under Construction." Laurel beamed as she proudly said the name.

"Lives Under Construction," he repeated, remembering his conversation with Marla. "What exactly is that?" he asked, and immediately wished he hadn't. He didn't want to get involved.

"It's an alternative approach to serving time for young offenders," Laurel told him.

"Here?" He glanced around, struggling to put together the few pieces Marla had given him. "You've made Churchill your base?"

"Yes. It's perfect. The boys can't run away because there is no place to run to. With our quarters outside of town, it won't be easy for them to create much mischief, either." Like him, Laurel didn't miss Sara's shudder. "It's cold out here and Sara's not dressed for this wind. Why don't you come with us, Kyle? You can see my project for yourself. I'll drive you home later."

Home. The word made his stomach clench.

"Kyle?" Laurel frowned at the long silence. Her gaze slipped to his leg. "Okay?"

"Yeah, sure."

But it wasn't okay at all. He'd had the prosthesis on for too long. His stump was shooting pins and needles to his hip. He'd never make the walk to his dad's house in this condition. Might as well take the proffered ride and see what Laurel had created. There was nothing waiting for him at home, anyway. Not anymore. "I'd like to see your Lives Under Construction."

He didn't tell her he was also coming because he was curious about Sara, and her role in Laurel's center for troubled youth.

They walked together to Laurel's battered vehicle. Kyle took a second look at Sara, who shivered as the wind toyed with her coat. Ms. Kane didn't look as though she could survive a group of young offenders or the rigors of cooking for hungry teens.

Actually, she looked as if she needed another hug.

Don't get involved.

Despite the warning in his head, Kyle wondered what Sara's story was. He'd first spotted her yesterday when they'd boarded the train. During the ride he'd seen her twice more and thought she'd seemed a little tense. But she'd visibly relaxed the moment Laurel appeared and now gazed at her with a mix of neediness, adulation and hope.

Sara grabbed his bag and put it in the back of Laurel's van with her own small satchel. "You take the front." She waited until he had, then crawled into the seat behind. She remained silent as Laurel talked about her project. She didn't lean forward to hear. Obviously she knew all about the plans for Lives Under Construction. But then she'd have to if she was cooking there.

"We get our first six boys later this week." Laurel

steered out of the parking lot and took a right turn. "A mix of twelve-and thirteen-year-olds."

Churchill's only highway ended about fifty miles out of town. Kyle knew they wouldn't go that far. Only the odd inquisitive tourist did that.

"None of these kids are model citizens." Laurel shrugged. "They wouldn't be in the system if they were."

He remembered that Marla had said Laurel was a former social worker. So of course she would know about the legal system as it related to kids.

"How long will they be here?" The pain in his leg was letting up but his mouth was dry from the medication he'd taken earlier. Kyle swallowed with difficulty, congratulating himself when it seemed no one had noticed the squeak in his voice.

Until Sara leaned forward and handed him an unopened water bottle. Whoever she was, this woman saw too much. Intrigued by Sara but also by Laurel's project in spite of his determination to remain detached, Kyle took a sip.

"Thanks," he muttered.

"You're welcome," Sara said.

"I have been given a one-year license." Laurel's pride was obvious. "If nobody messes up, the kids will be here for that long. I hope to get them excited about their education."

"Local school?" he asked, curious in spite of himself.

"Yes. As much as possible, I want them to become part of the community." Laurel hit the brakes to swerve around a red fox that raced across the road. She must have seen his grimace of pain as his shoulder bounced off the door frame. "Sorry."

"It's okay. Spring always brings them out." Kyle

glanced around, noting the many signs of spring. New birth, new life. His dad's favorite season. His heart pinched.

"This is spring?" Sara hugged herself tighter into her thin coat. "It can't be more than a few degrees above freezing outside!"

"That's warm for Churchill in May." Kyle twisted to look at her. "Enjoy it. When it gets hot, the bugs come out. That's not fun."

A tiny groan pushed through Sara's bluish-tinted lips before she subsided into silence.

When they finally pulled into the drive of a building that dated back to World War II, Laurel pointed out the renovations she'd incorporated into the old army barracks.

"It will do to begin with. Later I hope to expand and add on." She pulled open the heavy door. "Come on in. I'll give you both the grand tour. Then we'll have coffee."

Having gained respite from his pain during the car ride, Kyle followed Laurel and Sara into the massive structure, proud that he wasn't limping too badly and therefore wouldn't garner anyone's sympathy. He'd had enough sympathy for a lifetime.

"I'm impressed with what you've accomplished here," he told her, admiring the changes in the old building. It came as a relief to end up in the kitchen. He sank gratefully into a chair. "Really impressed," he added, noting the professional-looking kitchen. He was also aware that Sara had arrived before them and was now busy at the kitchen counter.

"Me, too." Laurel grinned.

"So this is your dream, to help at-risk kids. Marla said it's been a long time coming." He pulled his gaze

away from the silent Sara and wondered at her defer-
ence to Laurel.

"Yes, it is my dream." Laurel's blue eyes grew misty.
"This is a big answer to my prayers."

"Really?" She'd prayed to come to Churchill? Kyle
bent forward to listen.

"Really." Her smile had a misty quality to it. "Just
after our son was born, my husband was killed in a car
accident. I was a single mom, alone and with a child to
support." Her voice caught. "Brent was killed when he
was sixteen, a victim of gun violence on the streets. His
killer was thirteen. He'd been in the system for years,
learned more violence with each visit."

"I'm so sorry," Kyle murmured, aghast.

"So am I." Laurel reached out and squeezed his fingers. "But Brent's death spurred me to a new goal. To
create a place where young offenders could learn new
ways instead of sinking deeper into violence. So here
I am, almost fifty years old, starting a new career."
She smiled.

"I'm glad." Kyle thought he'd never seen anyone who
looked more at peace.

"Coffee?" Sara murmured from behind him.

Kyle tried to ignore the citrus scent that floated from
Sara's hair directly to his nostrils as she reached to set a
cup in front of him. Brief contact with her hand ignited
a spark that shot up his arm. Confused and irritated by
the burst of reaction he did not want to feel, he edged
away, shifting positions at the battered table.

"Thanks." He couldn't help the huskiness in his voice.
He did not like the reactions Sara evoked in him.

When he'd been injured, his fiancée had flown to his
side in Kabul. Repulsed by the extent of his injuries,

she'd dumped him and left on the next flight. That still burned. No way was he going to let himself get involved again. Besides, he was only back in town to close this chapter of his life.

"You're welcome." Sara handed Laurel a brightly colored mug of steaming brew then sat across from Kyle in a prim position, feet together, back ramrod straight.

Sara hadn't poured a cup of coffee for herself. Instead, her long, thin fingers wrapped around a glass of plain water. Here in the kitchen, under the bright fluorescent lights, Sara might have passed for a teenager, except her serious eyes and the hint of worry lines around them told him she was older. Those eyes said she'd seen the rough side of life.

If Laurel had been a social worker, was Sara one of her "cases"? His questions about the younger woman mounted, matching the hum of the printer working overtime in Laurel's office around the corner. He studied Sara more closely. She didn't wear makeup. But then she didn't need it. She had a natural beauty—high cheekbones, almond-shaped eyes and wide mouth, all visible now that she'd scraped back her hair into a ponytail.

The room's silence forced Kyle to refocus. He realized that Laurel had asked him his plans.

"I'm inquiring because Marla suggested you might be willing to give us a hand. I thought perhaps you could teach my boys what living in the North Country means." Her smile flashed. "I've heard you're the best tracker these parts have ever seen."

Sara's unusual eyes widened and refocused on him.

"Was, maybe." Kyle grimaced at his messed-up leg then frowned at her. "Who told you about my tracking?"

"Everyone in town talks about you, Kyle. They're so

proud of your service overseas." She went on to list all the things she thought he could teach her young offenders.

"Wait." Kyle had to stop her. "I wish you success, Laurel. But I can't take that on right now. Even if I could still do what I once did. Which I can't."

"I see." She didn't say anything more, nor did her face give away her thoughts.

Sara's forehead furrowed in a frown as if she had a question. But she didn't speak.

"And as for plans, I don't have any firm ones yet." He took a gulp of his coffee, glanced at his watch and knew he had to leave now, while the pain was still manageable. "I'm taking things one day at a time."

Just then a low, menacing rumble filled the room, followed by a loud pop.

"Oh, it's that dratted printer again. I'm beginning to wish I'd never seen the thing. It's become my worst nightmare." Laurel jumped up and raced to her office.

Sara's wide eyes met his. "Excuse me." She followed Laurel. It seemed as if she was eager to get away from being alone with him.

Kyle decided there was no point in sitting in the kitchen by himself. He walked to the office and paused in the doorway behind Sara, slightly shocked by what he saw. Two computers took up most of the floor space. They lay open, as if someone had been tinkering. A half-destroyed keyboard sat on top of a file cabinet beside a hard drive with six screws taped to it. In the corner, an assortment of cords and cables spilled out of a tattered cardboard box. He couldn't decide if someone was tearing apart PCs or putting them together.

"Can we do anything?" Sara asked after exchanging a tiny smile with Kyle.

"I have no idea what's wrong this time," Laurel said, glowering at the now-silent printer. "I suppose I'll have to call Winnipeg and get another sent out." She exhaled. "That will take at least three days."

"I can clean things up," Sara offered. "But I'd be no help with fixing anything electrical."

"I might be. My dad tinkered with computer stuff and I often helped him." The words poured out before Kyle could stop himself. "Want me to take a look?"

"Would you?" Laurel stood back. "It's jammed," she explained.

"Yeah, I see that." Kyle hid his grin as he eased past Sara. He pulled over an office chair and sank onto it, bending to examine the innards of the machine. With painstaking slowness he eased bits and pieces of paper free. After a moment of watching him, Sara brought a trash can so he could throw out the scraps. "Thanks."

She didn't smile, simply nodded. But those gray-silver eyes of hers followed every move he made between quick glances at the monitor. Since it was filled with an error message, Kyle couldn't figure out what was so captivating. He refocused on the printer, removing the ink cartridge and resetting it after he'd lifted out the last shredded bit of paper.

"She has quite a stack of paper here. Do you suppose she's printing a book?" he teased, winking at Sara.

"Sort of." Sara picked up one of the printed sheets and read it. "It looks like a list of rules and procedures at Lives Under Construction. Is there one for each boy?" she asked Laurel.

"Yes. I was hoping to have them done before the boys get here."

"Don't worry." Sara reached out and squeezed her

fingers. Kyle noticed a smile flit across her lips. "I'm sure Kyle can do something. Can't you?" She looked at him with a beseeching gaze that made him want to fix this fast. Why was that?

"It's a good printer," he told them. "But it's touchy about loading in a lot of paper."

"I think I know what that means. You're not supposed to print more than a certain number of sheets at a time and then refill. Right?" She raised her eyebrows, waiting for Kyle's agreement.

"Yes. That would be a good idea. But for now this thing needs a new part before it will work again." He stood too quickly and clasped the corner of the desk to balance. A millisecond later Sara's hand was on his elbow, steadying him.

There it was again, that lightning-bolt reaction to Sara's touch. Kyle eased out of her grasp as fast as he could without looking rude.

"I suppose a new part will take forever to get here and cost the earth." Laurel sighed.

"Not necessarily. My dad used to have a printer like this." Kyle smiled at the memory. "Dad was a pack rat. I'm pretty sure the old printer is still in a closet somewhere. I could see if it's still there and strip the part for you, if you want." He didn't look at Sara. The flare from her touch still lingered on his skin.

"But you've just come home," Laurel said. "I'm sure you're tired."

"I'm fine." Not quite true but Kyle wasn't going to tell her that.

Laurel glanced once at the printer, her longing obvious. "Look, Kyle. I appreciate it, but—"

"Laurel, let him try," Sara urged.

"She's right," Kyle agreed, surprised by Sara's mothering tone. "Let me take a look at home first. If I can't find anything, then you'll have a better idea of your next step."

"See? That makes sense." Sara grinned at him as if they shared a secret and when she did, his heart began to gallop.

Kyle tried to ignore the effect this stranger was having on him.

"You're right. Thank you, Kyle." Laurel stepped forward and hugged him. "You are a godsend."

"I doubt that." He glanced toward the kitchen. "Do you mind if we finish our coffee before we leave? I haven't had coffee that good since I left home."

"That's Sara. She can make anything taste wonderful." Laurel led the way to the kitchen.

Kyle stood back but Sara, her cheeks now pink, motioned for him to precede her. Once he was seated, she poured fresh coffee. Then she sat with folded hands, listening intently as he and Laurel chatted, though she never offered her own opinion. Very aware of the way Sara kept glancing toward the office, Kyle figured she must be impatient to check her email so he finished his coffee quickly, almost scalding his tongue.

It was time to go home. Time to stop avoiding the truth.

Back in Laurel's car, Sara again sat in the rear seat but this time she leaned forward to listen as Kyle described Churchill's landmarks. Ten minutes later they arrived at his father's house.

"I'm sure you'd like a few moments alone," Laurel said. "I have some things to do downtown. We'll come back in half an hour. Will that give you enough time, Kyle?"

A lifetime wouldn't be enough to reconcile losing his father but all he said was "Yes. Thanks." He climbed out awkwardly.

In a flash, Sara exited the car and lugged his bag to the door.

"Will you truly be all right?" she asked, her somber gaze holding his.

"I'll be fine." He wanted to be upset at her for lugging his suitcase out, but her compassion was genuine so he forced himself to smile. "I'm used to managing."

"Okay." She opened her mouth to say something more, but apparently thought better of it because she turned around and climbed back into Laurel's car without another word.

Kyle waited until the battered SUV rumbled away. Then he faced the house.

Home. He was finally home.

He squeezed his eyes closed against the loss that burned inside.

Why didn't You take me instead? he asked God. *I'm useless, but Dad wasn't. He was needed around here. What am I supposed to do now?*

Kyle stood there, waiting. But no answer came.

He was all alone. He'd better get used to it.

He was strong, he was knowledgeable and he was kind enough to help when asked. But Kyle Loness made Sara daydream and she couldn't afford that.

Because of Maria.

"Sara? Are you awake?" Laurel shifted the van into Park then turned to frown at her. "Oh, you are awake."

"Yes." Sara shoved away thoughts of Kyle.

"Well, I'm going to be about fifteen minutes. Then

we'll pick up a few groceries before we go back to Kyle's. Do you want to wait for me in the car?" she asked as she climbed out.

"No." Sara followed her onto the sidewalk. "I'd rather walk a bit. I need to stretch my legs."

"Okay. Stick to the main street. I remember your skewed sense of direction," Laurel teased. "Don't get lost on your first day in Churchill."

"I'm better at direction now than I was." Sara blushed, embarrassed by the reminder of her first faux pas after she'd left foster care. "I won't get lost."

She waited until Laurel had entered the building before heading toward Kyle's house.

The thing was, no matter how Sara tried, she couldn't seem to forget about him, and not just because he was so good-looking. Good-looking? Her brain scoffed. Kyle Loness was heartbreakingly handsome. Tall and muscular, the faint shadow of a beard defined the sharp jut of his jaw. Sara supposed he grew it to hide the scar that ran from the outside corner of his eye straight down past his jawbone, which, in her opinion, did nothing to diminish his good looks. And when he'd looked at her with his cornflower-blue eyes, a funny little shiver wiggled inside her, just like the heroines in the romantic novels she loved. How silly was that?

But it wasn't only his good looks that drew her. The image of Kyle working on Laurel's printer had been burned into her brain. Obviously he knew about computers. And she didn't. But she could learn, if someone would teach her. Someone like—Kyle? Maybe he could help her find her family.

Sara scanned the street ahead and saw him standing where they'd left him. Her silly heart resumed the pattering that had begun when he'd stepped off the platform and stumbled into her arms. She tried to quell it by reminding herself that Kyle Loness would find little interest in her. Why would he? Sara knew nothing about men.

Is it only his computer knowledge that intrigues you?

Of course it was. He might look like a romance hero but Sara knew nothing about romance, men or relationships.

Confused by her thoughts, she refocused on Kyle, who seemed lost in thought. Then he straightened, stepped toward the house and jerked to a stop. In a flash Sara realized why. Kyle had forgotten about the stairs and was now trying to figure out how to maneuver them to get into his house.

She had a clear view of his face. The pain lines she'd glimpsed on the train when he'd hobbled to his seat this morning had now etched deep grooves on either side of his mouth. He bit his bottom lip, grabbed the railings on either side and basically dragged himself upward, inch by painful inch, increasingly favoring his injured leg. His chiseled face stretched taut with concentration as he fought his way upward. She held her breath, silently praying for him, only exhaling when he finally conquered the last stair.

When Kyle paused, chest heaving with his efforts, Sara wanted to cheer. The sun revealed beads of perspiration dotting his face. For a moment he seemed to waver, as he had when he'd stepped off the train and again earlier, in Laurel's office. Sara took an automatic step forward to help, but froze when he reached out and turned the doorknob.

This was his homecoming. He wouldn't want her there.

She didn't belong. Again.

Hurt arrowed a path through her heart. She squeezed her eyes closed.

Focus on why you're here, Sara. You're here to help the kids. To figure out God's plans for your future and to make up for Maria.

For years Sara had tried not to think about the little girl. But now, as she fingered the scar at her wrist, the memories burst free of the prison she'd locked them in.

She'd been twelve when she tried to escape her foster home, unaware that her foster sister had followed her onto the busy street—until she heard Maria's cry when the car hit her. Sara had rushed to the child, cradling her tiny body as life slipped away, unaware of the shards of headlight glass that dug into her wrists, left behind by the speeding car.

Sweet, loving Maria had died because of her.

In shock and overwhelmed by guilt, Sara had been too scared to tell police the real reason she'd run, so after she'd relayed all she remembered about the car that had hit Maria and received stitches on her wrists, they'd taken her back to her foster parents, the Masters. The couple used Maria's death to convince Sara that if she tried to leave again, her foster siblings would pay. After that, there'd been no need for the Masters to lock her in the basement each night.

Sara's overwhelming guilt kept her in their abusive home. She had to stay to protect the other kids, as she hadn't protected Maria. She'd stayed until her new social worker—Laurel—uncovered the Masters' perfidy.

Almost eighteen, Sara had finally been removed from their care. But she hadn't gone home because she didn't have a home anymore. All she had were faded memories of her mother sitting on the sofa crying and her father stoically staring straight ahead while strange people took her away from them. She'd never known why it had happened and she'd never seen her family again.

Now she needed answers.

Blinking away her tears, Sara watched Kyle disappear inside his house. She waited a moment longer, then walked back to Laurel's car, puzzling over why she'd felt compelled to ensure Kyle had made it inside his house.

"Because I saw how lost he looked," she whispered to herself. "Because he needs help. Because... I don't know."

"There you are." Laurel's gaze rested on Sara's hand as it rubbed her scar. She moved closer, touched a fingertip to the tear on Sara's cheek then wrapped an arm around her shoulder. "You've been thinking about the past again. Oh, my dear Sara. You're free. God has something wonderful in store for you. Don't let the past drag you down."

"No, I won't." Sara dredged up a smile, hugged her back then walked beside her to the grocery store. But as they strolled down the aisles, she thought of Kyle inside his empty house.

They had something in common. Both of them had lost their families and neither of them could just forget about it.

Maybe, somehow, she could help him get over his loss.

Maybe if she did, he'd teach her how to use a computer.

Maybe then she'd finally find her family.

Chapter Two

Kyle rubbed his eyes, unable to dislodge memories evoked by the familiar aroma of his home. Tanned leather and Old Spice—it smelled of Dad, of happiness, of moments shared together. All of which were gone.

Emotion rose like a tidal wave. He fought for control.

When Kyle was younger, Churchill had been a fantastic adventure he'd embraced. Now it was just another problem in his life.

But for a moment, as the midmorning sun warmed Kyle through the window, the sensation of being loved enveloped him. He relaxed into that embrace. Comfort erased the pain of loss that dimmed everything in his world these days.

Home—without his dad? He closed his eyes and wept.

Moments later, footsteps treading up his stairs shattered his privacy. He rubbed his shirtsleeve across his face. The computer part. Of course.

"Come on in," he called before they could knock.

Laurel preceded Sara into his kitchen. "Do you need

more time?" Laurel scanned his face, then the empty tabletop.

"I haven't looked yet." He tore his gaze from the wall where a family photo hung. It had been taken six months before his mom's death. "I was just sitting here—remembering."

"You can help us out another time, when you're more rested," Laurel said in a gentle tone.

"I'm fine." Kyle didn't want to give Laurel any more chances to draw him into her program at Lives. He'd do this one thing for her now and then get on with his own life. He opened a door that had once been a pantry and nodded. "Yep, just as I thought."

A small squeak of surprise made him glance over one shoulder.

Sara's eyes were huge. She met his gaze, looked back at the shelves and said, "Oh, my."

Finding her understatement hilarious, Kyle chuckled as he dug through his father's accumulation of computer parts. "I told you Dad was a pack rat."

"No luck, huh?" Laurel asked when he drew back from the cupboard.

"Not yet." Kyle motioned to Sara. "Could you help me for a minute? I think the printer is on the bottom of this shelf. If you could hold up this box while I free it, I wouldn't have to waste time unpacking all this junk."

"Okay." She moved beside him and followed his directions exactly.

With a tug Kyle freed the printer, but in doing so brushed against Sara. Assailed by a host of reactions, from the fragrance of her hair to the way one tendril caressed her cheek, to the fierce look she gave when he had to yank on the cord to free the end, he realized that asking for Sara's help had been a bad idea.

He moved away, eager to put some distance between them and hopefully end his heart-racing response to her.

"Thanks." He set the printer on the table and opened it.

"If you explained how to reinstall it, I wouldn't have to drag you back out to Lives. Maybe I could do it myself," Laurel said.

Kyle lifted his head and arched one eyebrow. From what he'd seen in her office earlier, Laurel Quinn's aptitude did not lie in computers.

"Yeah." Her face turned bright pink under his look. Laurel laughed. "You're right. I haven't got a clue."

"I can do it in a matter of a few minutes," he told her as he lifted out the part she needed. He deliberately didn't look at Sara. "But you will have to bring me back home after, and I know you're busy."

"I've got almost everything ready to greet the first two boys, Barry and Tony." Laurel's eyes shone with expectation. "I'm hoping that while you and I are busy with the printer, Sara will start some of her fantastic cinnamon buns for tomorrow."

"I can do that." Sara, cheeks pink, looked away from Kyle. What was that about?

"I've got what we need." He held up the tiny relay switch. "I'm ready to go."

"Oh, Laurel, I just remembered. We'll need to move those groceries so there will be enough room for everyone," Sara said quickly.

Too quickly? Kyle searched her face. A puzzled Laurel opened her mouth, but Sara grabbed her arm and pulled, insistent. Frowning, Laurel stepped outside.

"Come out when you're ready, Kyle," Sara said, her voice a bit forced. "We'll meet you at the car."

And that was when Kyle got it. Sara knew the stairs gave him problems. She was keeping Laurel busy so he could navigate without feeling as if they were watching him.

Her thoughtfulness eased the knot of tension inside.

Sweet, thoughtful Sara. Why couldn't he have met someone like her first?

Kyle shut down the wayward thoughts. He'd ruled out romance in Afghanistan the day he'd been dumped, and he wasn't going to change his mind now. Anyway, Sara couldn't care about him. How could she? He was a ruined shell with nothing to offer a woman. He couldn't even figure out his own future.

Kyle shrugged on his jacket, shoved the printer part in his pocket and stood. He'd get this done and then move on to his own business. Sara was nice, sure. But there was no point in pretending her kindness was anything more than that.

Self-consciously he tromped down the stairs and walked to the car. Once again, Sara was seated in the rear seat, so Kyle sat in front. Once again, he filled in the drive's silences with facts about Churchill. And once again, after he got the printer running, Sara served him her delicious coffee along with a sandwich and some kind of lemon cookie that melted in his mouth. As Kyle ate, he quashed his yearning to linger, to get drawn in by the warmth of Sara's smile and forget the emptiness that awaited him at home. He couldn't afford to forget that. His future wasn't here in Churchill. God had made sure of that.

So finally he pushed back his chair, thanked Sara

for the lunch and asked Laurel to take him home. Sara walked with them to the car.

"I'm glad to have met you, Kyle," she said, hugging her arms around her thin waist, revealing the scars he'd noticed earlier. "I'll be praying for God to bless you with a wonderful future."

"Thanks." He wanted to tell her asking God for anything was pointless but he didn't. Instead, as they drove away, he voiced the other question that plagued him. "What is Sara's story, Laurel? Why is she here in Churchill? She looks like she'll blow away in the wind."

"You'll have to ask Sara. Suffice it to say that she deserves happiness and I hope she'll find some here. She's a wonderful person." Laurel smiled at him. "So are you, Kyle. Anytime you want to fill in a few hours of your day, feel free to drop by. Lives Under Construction can always use another hand."

"I know Marla told you I'd be interested in doing that," Kyle admitted. "But the truth is, all I want to think about right now is cleaning up my dad's place."

Laurel patted his shoulder then swung the van into his driveway. "After you've had time to grieve, please visit us, even just for another cup of Sara's coffee."

"I'll think about it," Kyle said, knowing he'd do no such thing. He climbed out of the car. "Thanks again. See you."

Kyle waited till Laurel's car disappeared, then braved the stairs again. Inside, the house seemed empty, lonely. He flicked up the thermostat and sat down in his father's recliner in the living room. A notebook lay open on a side table. He picked it up.

"Two weeks until Kyle comes home. Yahoo!" His

father's scrawl filled the page, listing things they'd do together. Kyle slammed the book closed.

Why? his heart wept. *Why did You take him before I could see him again?*

Suddenly he heard Sara's words in his mind.

I'll be praying for God to bless you with a wonderful future.

Well, Sara could pray all she wanted, but whether God granted her prayers or not, nothing could make up for the loss of his dad.

With a weary sigh he rose and thumped his way to the kitchen, where he sat down to deal with the stacks of mail someone had dropped off. For a moment, he wished Sara was here with him. Somehow he thought that smile of hers and the calm way she approached life would make facing his not-so-wonderful future a whole lot easier.

But of course, imagining Sara in his house was just a silly dream. And Kyle was well aware that it was time he let go of dreams and face reality.

"Laurel, what's an ATV?" Sara shifted to allow the flames of the fireplace to warm her back.

"All-terrain vehicle. Like those big motorized bikes we saw this afternoon. Why?" Her friend stopped working on her sudoku puzzle to glance up.

"Kyle mentioned an ATV."

"Well, we have an ATV here," Laurel told her. "But I'm not sure you should try riding it without some lessons."

"I'm sure I can walk anywhere I need to go. I'm looking forward to it." Sara loved to walk. In the time since she'd been released from the Masters' home, she'd discovered the freedom of going wherever she wanted, of turning around, of changing direction without having every movement scripted for her. That freedom was precious. Sara ignored Laurel's next remark about winter being too cold for much walking. "Tell me about Kyle's father."

"His name was Matt, ex-military," Laurel said. "I knew him a little—a very nice man, full of laughter. He and Kyle ran a tourist business together. Matt couldn't go overseas when Kyle got hurt because he'd had a heart attack. He didn't want his son to know. I think the hardest thing for Kyle to accept is that his dad isn't here with him."

"There's a kind of reverence in his voice when he mentions his father." Also an echo of utter loss that Sara couldn't forget. "He must have loved his dad very much."

Laurel stayed silent for a few moments "Sara, you're not comparing the love they shared with— Well, you don't think of your foster father as your dad, do you? Because the Masters are not in any way part of who you are. They tried to ruin you, but you were too strong. Now your heavenly Father has other plans for your future."

"I wish I knew what they were." Sara wanted to escape the misery she'd endured. But at night, when the darkness fell, those horrid feelings of being unloved returned.

Actually, they never quite left her. That was why she needed to find her birth family—to make newer, better memories.

"Hang on to the truth, Sara," Laurel told her.

"The truth?" Sara wasn't sure she knew what that was anymore.

"You are the beloved child of God. But you have to trust Him and be patient for His work to erase what the Masters did." Laurel got up to press a kiss against the top of her head. "I love you, too."

Sara squeezed her hand. But she waited until Laurel was busy making hot chocolate before she slid a sheaf of papers out of her pocket and studied them.

To find your birth parents we must have these forms signed and returned along with the fee and a copy of your birth certificate. This will initiate a search of our records.

So many times Sara had wondered about the mother who only came back to her in fragmented dreams. Who was she? Why had she put Sara into foster care? Why had she never come back? Didn't she love Sara? Didn't her father care that his daughter might need him?

In the past, Sara had come up with a thousand reasons why her parents had never come to retrieve her—fairy tales, happily-ever-afters, like the romance stories she loved reading.

But now she needed the truth. She wanted to find her parents, embrace them and let their love erase the past. She wanted to have what Kyle had lost—people who loved her always.

She wanted a forever family.

"Here you go, sweetie."

"Thanks." Sara hurriedly tucked her papers into her pocket before accepting the gigantic mug from Laurel. Laurel was as close to Sara's ideal mother-fantasy as anyone had ever been, but even Laurel couldn't fill her need for her mother's love.

"Enjoy it." Laurel smiled. "Savor this time alone because once the boys arrive it's going to get mighty busy." She sat in the chair across from Sara, her face serious. "Are you sure cooking here won't be too much for you?"

"I'm sure." Sara cupped her hands around her mug.

"Let me tell you a bit about each boy so you'll be prepared." Laurel gave a brief history, ending with the youngest and in Sara's eyes the most vulnerable boy, Rod.

"I think I'll like Rod." Sara knew she'd like all of the boys. Kids were easy to love.

"I'm not telling you about them because I expect you to get involved with their programs," Laurel said.

"Oh?" Sara frowned, confused.

"I hired you to cook for us because I know how great you are at it." Laurel leaned forward. "But I want you to be free to do other things."

"Like what?" Sara already had a to-do list. Finding her family was first.

"Sara, you lost most of your childhood being a servant to the Masters. All the years you should have been a kid were spent making sure the other foster kids were okay."

"I had to do that," Sara said simply.

"You shouldn't have had to," her mentor insisted. "You're twenty-two. Have you ever taken time to think about yourself?"

"I managed." Sara didn't like to dwell on the past.

"Oh, my dear, you managed wonderfully. But now you have this time in Churchill and I want it to be your time. I want you to enjoy your life, find new interests.

Make new friends." Laurel's voice softened. "I want you to focus on your future."

Sara thought about Kyle, alone in his house with that awesome yard. Rod would be arriving tomorrow. The sprout of an idea pushed down roots in her mind. She tucked it away until she could consider it more thoroughly.

"I will focus on my future. But I need you to do something for me, too, Laurel." Sara paused to assemble her thoughts. "I know I'm going to love it here. But I will only stay till Christmas. By then I believe God will have shown me what he wants me to do with my future."

"Well..." Laurel inclined her head.

"No, I mean it. I know myself, Laurel. I'll love it here, I'll get too comfortable and I'll want to stay. But you must ignore that, even if I ask you not to. You have to find someone else to take over for me after Christmas. Promise?" She leaned forward, her gaze intent on Laurel.

"If you insist," Laurel finally agreed.

"I do. I thought about this a lot while I was going to cooking school. Our minister said that in order to be the person God intends us to be, we must discover what He wants us to do." She leaned back, smiled. "That's what I am going to do while I'm here in Churchill. I'm going to search for God's plan for my future. So you cannot let me talk you into my staying."

Laurel studied her for a long time before she nodded. "All right."

"Now, what kind of things should I do while I'm here?"

"There's a pool at the recreation center attached to the school. You could take swimming lessons," Laurel told her. "Also, the school holds classes for anyone who wants to upgrade their education. You might want to look into that."

"Yes, I do." Sara didn't feel compelled to explain. Though the Masters had claimed Sara was home-schooled, Laurel had revealed their lies.

Laurel understood how awkward and geeky Sara felt, how much she wanted to shed her "misfit" feelings and be like everyone else. That was why she read so much. But sometimes it wasn't enough to just read about something. Her reaction to Kyle was a prime example. Nothing she'd read had prepared her for the instant empathy she felt for him.

"I'll pray that God will reveal His plans to you, Sara, so you'll be able to figure out what He wants for your future."

Sara already knew what she wanted in her future. She wanted her family reunited.

"Could I take computer classes?" Sara asked.

"Why not? You'll probably have to wait till fall for the new sessions, though. We'll phone and check tomorrow. I'll pray that God will reveal His plans to you so you'll be able to figure out what you want for your future." Laurel drew her into a hug.

She already knew what she wanted; she wanted her family reunited. But she closed her eyes and let her spirit revel in Laurel's embrace. Somehow that triggered thoughts of Kyle. Hugs were new to her, but he was used to them. He'd had parents who loved him and showed it. She'd seen it in the photos on his kitchen wall. He came from a tight-knit happy family.

"I'm going to bed now," Laurel said, releasing her. "You must be tired after that long train trip."

"Oh, no. Riding on that train was like being rocked to sleep." Sara could remember being rocked. Barely.

Laurel kissed her forehead. "Goodnight, sweetie."

"Goodnight, Laurel." Sara followed her, stepped into the room Laurel had given her earlier and gazed around. Her room. Space that belonged to her and her alone.

For now she had a home, just like Kyle.

Sara marveled at how far she'd come today. She loved Churchill from the moment she'd stepped off the train. Rough and wild, but brutally honest. Everyone seemed friendly—except for Kyle. An image of him sitting in his kitchen—exhaustion, agony and utter loss etched on his face—filled her thoughts. Sara could excuse his brusqueness because he'd been hurting, body and soul.

What she couldn't excuse was the way she'd stared at him so admiringly.

"Stop thinking about him," she scolded herself. "This isn't a fairy tale. He's a wounded veteran who lost his father. He's none of your business."

To dislodge Kyle's face from her mind, Sara curled onto the window seat, seeking the rolling ribbons of northern lights her book had talked about. But Laurel said the approach of summer meant it would stay light well into the night, that Sara wouldn't see the lights for months.

The northern lights, learning the computer—it seemed as though everything had to wait till fall. But she would only be here till Christmas. Would she find her family by then?

She had to. As soon as possible.

Reading had always been her escape as well as her education, but Sara now knew book knowledge wasn't the same as actually living and experiencing. She was short on experience. That was why she always felt as if she was a step behind everyone else. But she would catch up; she would learn about love and families and all the things other people took for granted.

She tugged the papers from her pocket and began to fill them out. Tomorrow she'd visit Kyle, not only to discuss the idea she'd had earlier to help Rod, but because she didn't want to wait until fall to learn how to use a computer. Maybe she could persuade Kyle to do an exchange—she'd clean his house or maybe cook him something and he'd teach her how to use a computer to search for her family.

Because her family *was* out there. Somewhere. Sara just had to find them. Then she would finally have somebody who loved her, somebody she could love back. She'd have the circle of love Kyle had always known to support her in doing whatever God asked of her.

"Please help me." The prayer slipped from Sara's lips as she peered into the growing gloom. "Please?"

Chapter Three

"Thank you." Kyle paid the delivery boy, hefted the box of groceries onto the counter and closed the door. "Finally," he muttered.

He grabbed the tin of coffee, opened it and started a fresh pot of brew. While he waited impatiently he unpacked the rest, bumping into several pieces of furniture in the crowded room as he stored his supplies.

It wasn't long before exhaustion dragged at him, caused by staying up too late to open the cards and letters full of sympathy from those who'd known his dad. Kyle turned, swayed and grabbed the back of a kitchen chair to keep from toppling over. He needed to sit, and fast. But first he poured himself a cup of too-strong coffee.

"Better," he groaned, savoring the rich taste. "Much better." But not as good as the coffee Sara had made him.

Kyle pushed that thought away.

The prosthesis ground against his skin—his "stump," he corrected mentally. There weren't enough calluses to protect the still-raw tissue, even after almost three months. He sank onto a chair, rolled up his pant leg and undid the brace that held the prosthesis in place. The relief was immediate. He reveled in it as he sat there, sipping his coffee. Unbidden, memories of the day he'd been injured filled his thoughts. To distract himself, he booted up his dad's laptop and checked his email.

A tap on the window drew Kyle's attention. Sara Kane stood watching him. He waited to see the revulsion his fiancée hadn't been able to hide. He searched for the disgust and loathing that had swum through her eyes when she'd seen his damaged limb. But Kyle couldn't find it in Sara's dark scrutiny and wondered why.

What could he do but wave her in? While she entered, he closed the computer and set it on his dad's desk.

"Good morning. I brought you some cinnamon buns." Her gaze moved from the computer to him. She closed the door behind her and set a pan on the table. Her gaze held his. "You didn't answer the doorbell."

"It's been broken since we moved in here. Dad was always going to fix it but—" Kyle realized he was rubbing his leg and quickly dragged his hand away. He was about to pull down his pant leg when she spoke.

"I could help you," she whispered. "If you want help."

"I don't." *Stop acting like a bear, Kyle.* "Thank you but I'll be fine, Sara." He didn't want her here, didn't want her to see his ugliness. "Don't worry about me."

Her solemn gaze locked with his but she said nothing.

"How did you get here?" He clenched his jaw against a leg cramp then gulped another mouthful of coffee, hoping that would help clear his fuzzy head.

"Laurel. She had to stop in town before picking up

the boys from the airport. I wanted to ask you something so I told her I'd walk over here from the post office."

Kyle watched as Sara filled the kettle with water and switched it on. A moment later she'd found a basin under the sink and added a towel from the bathroom.

"What are you doing?" Kyle demanded through gritted teeth as waves of pain rolled in. He'd refused to take any pain reliever last night, knowing he had to learn to manage it or risk becoming addicted. And he couldn't afford that. He couldn't afford to become dependent on anyone or anything.

"Hot water will ease your soreness." Sara kept right on assembling things.

"Are you a nurse?" Kyle clamped his jaw together more tightly. Couldn't she see he wanted to be alone?

"If I say yes, will you let me help you?" she asked in a soft tone.

"No."

"I didn't think so." A flicker of a smile played with the corner of her lips but Sara kept right on working.

The woman had guts, Kyle admitted grudgingly as she added cold water to the basin, tossed in a handful of salt and set it on the floor in front of him. Because he craved relief, he didn't object when she poured boiling water from the kettle into the basin. Steam billowed up as she knelt in front of him. She dunked the towel, thoroughly soaked it then wrung it out. A moment later she wrapped the steaming towel around his stump and held it there, her hands gentle but confident.

Kyle almost groaned before he flinched away. No one outside the hospital staff had ever touched that ruined, angry part of him.

"Is it too hot?" She waggled her fingers in the water and frowned. "It doesn't feel too hot."

Actually it felt a lot like a warm hug.

"Kyle?"

He studied the top of her caramel-toned head. Somehow Sara's tender touch eased his yearning to be enveloped in his father's arms, something he'd craved during his intensive rehab and the weeks of therapy that followed.

"Kyle?" His name rushed from her lips, urgent. "Is it okay?" Her eyes were wide with—fear?

Why would she be afraid?

"It's fine," he groaned.

Liar. It is light years better than fine.

"I'm glad." A sweet smile lit up her entire face.

In the quietness of that moment Kyle couldn't help but compare Sara's response to the decimating reaction of the woman who'd claimed to love him. When she'd glimpsed his shattered limb in the veteran's hospital she had turned away and raced out, never to return.

Clearly, as he'd noticed several times, Sara was made of stronger stuff. His curiosity about her rose.

But Kyle didn't ask questions because the longer Sara's calm gaze held his, the more his muscles relaxed. She rinsed the cloth three times, each time reapplying and holding it in place until it cooled. Finally the knot of pain untied and slid away. He sighed his relief.

"The water's too cool now," Sara murmured. "I could heat more?"

"No. Thank you." Kyle felt half-bemused as he realized his whole body felt limp, as it had when he'd come out of the anesthetic after each of his surgeries.

"Where did you learn to do that?" His curiosity about the strength in such a delicate-looking woman grew.

"My fos—brother used to get banged up. Hot salt-water cloths always helped him."

Sara's slight hesitation before she'd said *brother* and the way she stumbled over *banged up* intrigued Kyle. What story lay hidden beneath those few words?

"It's a great remedy." The way she'd knelt in front of him to care for him humbled Kyle. "Thank you," he said, and meant it.

"You're welcome." She rose in one fluid motion and glanced at the pan of rolls she'd left sitting on the table.

His father's favorite line from Milton's *Paradise Lost* flickered through Kyle's mind. "Grace was in all her steps, heaven in her eyes, in every gesture dignity and love." He'd never known anyone but his mom who'd so perfectly fit the description.

Until now.

"I'll just slip these buns into the oven to warm. You can rest for a while, then, when you're ready to eat, they'll be waiting." Sara tightened the foil around the container and placed it inside the oven.

It struck Kyle then that he was doing what he'd vowed not to. He was letting someone do things for him. He was letting himself become dependent.

"What did you want to ask me?" The question was perfunctory. He didn't want to hear. What he really wanted was for this disturbing woman to leave him alone.

Sara took her time dumping the basin, washing it out and storing it.

"Come on. I can't be that unapproachable," he prodded with a smile.

"Yes, you can." Sara looked straight at him, unsmiling. "But I'll ask anyway. I want to use something of yours."

"Use something—of mine?" That sounded as if she'd made it up on the spur of the moment. Maybe she was only here because she felt sorry for him. Kyle's gut burned. "Like what?"

"That." She pointed out the grimy window that overlooked his backyard.

Kyle followed her pointing finger. He couldn't figure out what she meant at first. There was nothing in the backyard. Except—

"I'd like permission to use your greenhouse, Kyle," she said.

"My mom's greenhouse." Past memories, very personal memories, of the joys he shared inside that greenhouse built inside his head but he suppressed them. Kyle was suddenly irrationally annoyed at the way Sara kept pushing her way into his world. All he wanted was to be alone. "What could you possibly want that for?"

"Last night Laurel told me some of the boys' histories so I'd understand why they're at Lives." She sat down. A tiny line furrowed her brow as she studied her hands. "I'm not sure I'm allowed to discuss them."

"I'll keep whatever you want to tell me confidential," Kyle promised, curiosity mounting.

"Laurel says one of the boys is quite withdrawn. Rod." She peeked through her lashes at him. "But he did very well when he was involved in a program at a tree nursery."

Kyle waited, surprised by her earnest tone.

"Of course, there aren't any tree nurseries here in Churchill," Sara said, "but I thought that if he could get involved in growing something, it might help. We don't have the capability at Lives. But I remembered seeing your greenhouse when we were here yesterday. If Rod could grow fresh herbs, I could use them in my cooking. Laurel said we'd share whatever we grew with you." Her silver-gray eyes never left his face. "If you agree to let us use the greenhouse, that is."

"I see." Kyle studied the glass structure. "The roof might not be stable, you know. I'd have to have it checked, maybe repaired."

A disappointed look flickered across her face. "You're saying no?"

"I'm saying I don't know." Kyle didn't want to reveal any sign of weakness, and having her see his injured leg made him feel weak, so he strapped on his prosthesis, rolled down his pant leg then slid his feet into a pair of his father's moccasins. "Let's go out and take a look."

"Okay." Sara pulled on the thin jacket she'd shed when she first came inside.

"You'll freeze if that's all you have to wear until summer gets here," he warned.

Sara chuckled, her smile brimming with something he couldn't quite define. All Kyle knew was that little seemed to faze this woman. A twinkle in those gorgeous eyes told him she'd faced much worse than cold weather, and come out on top.

"I'll be fine, Kyle."

He had a strong feeling that Sara Kane would be fine, though he couldn't have said why. Perhaps it was the resolute determination in her manner. Sara Kane wouldn't give up easily. He admired that.

"Open that cupboard. There should be a jacket in there, a red one." He didn't tell her the coat was special. He simply watched as she drew out his mother's red parka. "Try it on."

Sara shrugged into the coat. Her transformation was spectacular. A bird of paradise—she looked magnificent, delicate and incongruous in this land of icy winds and frozen tundra. The color lent life to her, enhancing subtle undertones in her hair and making her skin glow with a beauty Kyle had almost missed.

"I don't think any of our guests ever looked as good as you in that."

"Your guests?" She pulled the faux-fur collar around her ears and studied herself in the mirror, seemingly bemused by what she saw.

"Dad and I ran a guiding company," he told her. "There are gloves in the pockets, I think."

"Guiding? What does that mean?" She pulled on the gloves and bent her fingers experimentally, as if she expected the gloves' thickness to impede movement.

"Guiding tourists to see the local sights," he explained. "The northern lights, whale watching in a Zodiac, ATV treks into the wilderness or jaunts to see the polar bears—we did it all." Bitterness oozed between his words, rendering his tone brittle and harsh, but even though he heard it, Kyle found it impossible to suppress his sense of utter loss.

"Polar bears." Sara's eyes were huge. She peeked over her shoulder as if expecting one to pounce from the bedroom.

"Churchill is famous for its polar bears. But it's late in the season. When the ice goes out they leave to hunt seals. This year it's very early but the ice is almost gone. Global warming, I suppose." Kyle hated the fear pinching her pretty face. He rushed to reassure her.

"But even if some bears are still hanging around, you don't have to worry. There's a town patrol that does a good job of keeping tabs on the bears' whereabouts. Sometimes you'll hear gunshots—pops," he modified when her eyes expanded even more. "The noises deter the bears. I didn't hear any on the way here yesterday or so far this morning, so it should be okay."

"Uh-huh." Sara inhaled and thrust back her shoulders as if she were about to venture into battle.

"Listen, Sara." Kyle leaned forward. "Before we go outside I want to tell you something."

"Okay." It looked like she was holding her breath.

"Churchill is very safe." He grabbed his jacket off the hook near the door. "But we tell this to everyone who comes here to prepare them. Just in case."

"In case." She gulped. "Right."

"It might seem counterintuitive to you, but if you do happen upon a bear, do not turn your back on him and do not run." *Gently. Don't terrorize her, Kyle.* "Either of those actions will make you look like prey to him."

"Which I will be," she pointed out in a whisper, her face now devoid of all color.

"Well, yes." He had to smile. "But what you want is to look like his adversary. Make yourself as tall as possible. Put your arms in the air and wave them. Yell as loud as you can. But do not run." *Why did he suddenly feel he had to protect her?* "Bears love the chase."

"Okay." She trembled, her alarm visible.

Kyle had wanted Sara to be cautious. Instead he'd alarmed her.

Her eyes lost their silver sheen and darkened. She looked petrified.

Way to go, Kyle.

"I'd offer to drive you back, but I don't think I could drive, even if Dad's old truck was running. He cracked it up just before—" He swallowed, forced himself to continue. "Anyway, I don't have transport."

"I'm sure I'll be fine." Sara didn't look fine. She looked like someone who had dredged up her last ounce of courage to face the lion's den.

"Yes, you will be," Kyle agreed. "Now let's go take a look at Mom's greenhouse." He rose, ignored the twinge of pain in his hip and followed her outside, embarrassed by his slow progress down the stairs and Sara's obvious attempt to ignore it.

Kyle didn't intend to be in Churchill long, but by the time he reached the bottom step he'd made up his mind to hire someone to build a ramp. Dragging himself up and down these stairs sucked the energy out of him, not to mention that it made him feel like some kind of spectacle.

"Okay?" Sara opened the gate to his backyard.

"Just dandy." He chose his steps over the uneven ground carefully. What a fool he'd been to wear these soft leather slippers and risk injuring himself again.

"The structure looks good," Sara said, her head tilted to one side like a curious bird as she peered at the glass roof. "Of course, I don't really know anything about greenhouses."

"A friend wrote that he'd check on things till I could get home. It looks like he's made sure everything is still solid." Kyle pressed against the metal frame. Nothing swayed. "I brought the key. Let me check inside."

The door swung to with a loud creak. Inside, the glass was dingy with years of dust. Debris covered parts of the floor.

"Oh, my." Sara stared like a deer caught in head-lights.

"After Mom passed away, Dad and I never used this for anything much but storage. I should have cleaned it out." Kyle pulled away the cobwebs. "It's filthy."

"It won't take long to clean." Obviously recovered, Sara pressed the toe of her shoe against a stack of plastic bins. "What are these?"

"I don't know. Dad must have packed them." Kyle turned a pail upside down and sat on it. Then he opened the top bin. A bundle of bubble wrap lay inside. He lifted it out and slowly unwrapped it. A notebook fell out.

Instantly Kyle was a kid again, rushing home from school to find his mom in here, scribbling in her gardening journal while Dad teased her about her addiction to roses. Kyle gasped at the overwhelming pain.

"Kyle, what's wrong?" Sara hunkered down in front of him. Her hand covered his. "Are you in pain?" she asked ever so gently.

"Yes." For once he wasn't ashamed to admit it. His heart ached so deeply he felt as if life had drained out of his body. He fought to be free, but the ache blemished his spirit like a scab on a scar.

"Can I help?"

"I'm okay." Kyle inhaled, forced away the sadness. "This is my mom's journal. I didn't realize we still had it." He flipped through the pages, chuckling at the funny drawings his mom had made. "She was always trying to produce a new breed of rose."

"Under these conditions?" Sara lifted one eyebrow in surprise.

"Yes. Look." He held up the book to show the sketch.

"This was going to be her Oliver rose—named in memory of her high school friend. But the Oliver rose couldn't take Churchill's harshness. He was too weak."

He was suddenly aware of Sara, crouched behind him, peering over his shoulder.

"I can't read her writing."

"No one could." He cleared his throat. "Listen. 'My dear Oliver is a wuss. One chilly night without the heater and he's lost all his leaves. Pfui! A weakling. And a reminder of what God expects of us, a stiff backbone that weathers life's challenges. I want a rose that will use the negatives of life to get tough and still bloom. I'll wait and try again next year. But I fear my Oliver rose is finished.'" Kyle smiled. "She always spoke of her roses as if they were people."

"It sounds like she had a sense of humor," Sara said.

"A wicked one. Listen to this." Kyle read her another passage about a yellow rosebush a friend had sent them. His laughter joined Sara's. "I remember that bush. Coral Bells. It lasted year after year, no matter what adversity it encountered. My mother put Oliver next to it to give him some gumption. But it didn't help." He closed the book, suddenly loath to continue revealing these precious memories. "I wonder what else is in this box."

To hide his emotions, Kyle tugged out layers of old newspaper, aware that Sara still crouched beside him, neatly folding each piece of paper he tossed on the ground. Below the paper lay trophies from school sports, local awards he and his father had won for their business, a book filled with clippings and letters from past customers—he kept pulling them out until finally the box was empty.

"Garbage." Kyle refused to be swamped by memo-

ries again while Sara watched. "I should chuck them."
He set aside the plastic box and began working on the
second bin. But it, too, was filled with childhood me-
mentos that only served to remind him of things he
could no longer do.

At the very bottom lay a series of Sunday-school
awards and a big ribbon with *top place* printed on it in
silver letters, from the championship quiz team he'd
once led.

"More garbage." Bitterness surged that God hadn't
been there when Kyle had needed Him, despite his faith
and despite the many pleas he'd sent heavenward. "No
need to keep any of this."

But Sara was already rewrapping each item and laying it carefully back into the container.

"Looks like this is the last one Dad got around to
packing." Kyle paused, needing breathing space so he
could face whatever came next without revealing to Sara
how affected he was. "My father the pack rat must have
needed room in the house."

"I think he wanted to keep your special things safe
for you," Sara said, her voice firm yet soft. "So you
wouldn't forget your history."

"Maybe." He yanked off the last lid and tossed away
the flat sheet of plain brown paper lying on top.

And stared at the contents.

Sara's fingers curved around his shoulder.

He felt stupid, awkward and juvenile. But he could
do nothing to stop the tears. They rolled down his hot
cheeks and landed on his wrinkled shirt in a trickle that
quickly became a river.

Kyle lifted out the familiar wooden box, letting the

satin smoothness of the wood soak through to his hands, waiting for it to thaw his heart.

"Kyle?" Sara's gentle voice bloomed with anxiety. But she said no more, waiting patiently until he finally pulled his emotions under control. "What is it?"

"A seed box," he told her. His index finger traced the letters he'd carved on the lid years earlier. "It was a Christmas gift Dad helped me make for my mom when I was twelve." He lifted open the top, slid out one of the drawers, brushed a fingertip against the velvet lining inside.

"It's beautiful." Sara leaned forward to examine the surface. "Is it rosewood?"

"Yes," he said, surprised by her knowledge. "I had to order the wood specially. I thought we'd never get it done in time." The laugh burst from him, harsh and painful. "Actually, I guess we didn't."

"What do you mean?" Sara sounded slightly breathless.

"Mom had barely put her seeds in this when she was diagnosed with breast cancer. By planting time she was too sick to come out here anymore." He snapped the lid closed and thrust the box inside the bin. "She was so sure God would heal her. She said over and over, 'Trust in God, Kyle. He'll never let you down.'" Fury burned inside, a white-hot rage that could not be doused. "Well, He did. He let me down twice. And I will never trust Him again."

He rose and made his way to the door, not caring about his awkwardness. All he wanted was to get away, to hide out until he found a way to deal with his anger.

"Do whatever you want in here, Sara. You're welcome to it. Just don't ask me to help you." With that,

Kyle stepped outside. He stood there, eyes closed as he inhaled the fresh, crisp air into his lungs and blew out frustration.

You're starting over, he reminded himself. *Forget the past.*

Behind him he heard Sara close the greenhouse door with a quiet click. Desperate to be alone, he headed for the stairs to the house. He almost cheered when behind him a horn tooted and broke the strained silence. Kyle glanced over one shoulder at Sara.

"It's Laurel," she said. One hand went to the zipper of the red coat.

"Keep it. You might need it." He held her gaze, nodding when her eyes asked him if he was sure.

"Thank you." She hesitated then lifted her chin. "And thank you for letting us use the greenhouse. Enjoy your cinnamon buns."

"Thanks." He watched her walk to Laurel's van. She opened the door then turned to face him.

"God bless you, Kyle," she said in the softest voice. "I'll stop by tomorrow."

"That's not necess—" Kyle's words fell on emptiness. Sara was gone, the van driving away.

Kyle stomped into the house, fuming. He didn't want her here, checking on him, blessing him. He wanted to be alone, to become totally self-sufficient.

Yet as he sampled the sticky sweetness of the cinnamon buns, Kyle almost welcomed the thought of someone else, someone whose presence would stop him from being engulfed by bitterness at what he'd lost.

He stopped himself. His plan for the future did not include staying here or becoming dependent. It certainly could not include getting mesmerized by a pair of silvery-gray eyes. He would never allow himself to be that vulnerable again.

For now, Kyle was home. He'd take the rest of his life one step at a time.

But if Sara did come back, he'd try to find out more about her, like what had made her stare so longingly at his dad's laptop when she'd seen it lying on the desk.

And why she seemed so certain God would bless him.

Chapter Four

"Have a wonderful day, Rod," Sara said as the tall, quiet boy shuffled his backpack over his shoulders, the last of the six boys to leave. "Enjoy your first day of school. And don't forget we're going to the greenhouse this afternoon."

Rod nodded, staring at her for several minutes. "You're sure it's okay?"

"Pretty sure." She patted his shoulder at the sound of Laurel tooting the van's horn. "You'd better go."

He gave her another of those silent, soulful looks before he left.

"Arriving near the end of the year like this can't be easy for him, for any of them," she mused aloud. "But surely they'll be okay, won't they, Lord? Laurel said the school agreed to hold summer courses to get them up to speed and ready for a new term in the fall. Please help them all use this opportunity."

Feeling a bit self-conscious about talking aloud, Sara refocused, wrinkling her nose at the stack of dishes.

"What a mess. I think I'll leave cleanup until after I finish prepping for dinner." Humming to herself, Sara

retrieved a box of apples from the storeroom then realized there wasn't enough counter space.

"Okay, then. Cleaning it is." As she got to work
washing and scrubbing away the remains of breakfast,
she sang a praise chorus she'd learned at the church
she'd attended in Vancouver. She'd barely made a dent
in the mess when a small, delicate hand covered hers.

"Oh!" She jerked away in surprise.

"I'm sorry. I didn't mean to startle you." The very
proper English voice came from a tiny woman dressed
in trim jeans and a fitted white blouse. Her silver hair
had been caught in a knot on the top of her head, revealing periwinkle-blue eyes that sparkled like stars
when she smiled. "I'm Lucy Clow. And this is my husband, Hector."

"It's very nice to meet you." Sara blinked. "I'm afraid
Laurel is—"

"On her way to school with the boys." Lucy nodded.
"She knew we were coming." She lifted the scraper
from Sara's fingers. "Let me do this. Hector and I are
here to help." The loving glance she gave the tall, bald
man made Sara wish someone would look at her like
that.

"I do have a few things planned for today," Sara admitted. *Including cleaning Kyle's greenhouse this afternoon.* Having met Rod, she was confident he would
enjoy working there. "Would you like a cup of coffee
before you start?"

When Hector cleared his throat, Lucy chuckled.
"Hector's hinting that he needs a good cup of coffee
before he starts work on Laurel's computer room."

Computer room? Laurel hadn't mentioned setting
up a computer room.

The thought of it brought Sara a burst of anticipation. But she reminded herself that having a computer and being able to use one were two different things.

She'd wanted so badly to ask Kyle about teaching her when she'd been to his house the other morning. His computer had been sitting right there, but she'd hesitated because he'd been in such pain when she arrived. Besides, wasn't asking for use of the greenhouse enough for one day?

"I've just made a fresh pot." She poured two cups. "I thought Laurel would need it when she returns."

"I can imagine." Lucy laughed. "Those poor boys are probably nervous about their first day." She sipped her coffee then set it down and got to work, her hands moving with lightning-quick speed as she rinsed and stacked plates.

Hector, too, seemed in a rush as he quickly drank his coffee.

"Please relax and enjoy your coffee, both of you. And, Lucy, it's very kind of you to help me while Hector's working, but don't feel you must. This is my job."

"Laurel says you're very good at it, too." The blue eyes twinkled. "I am *not* good at cooking, as Hector will tell you. But I'm very good at cleaning." Lucy stacked the dishwasher deftly. Sara had never used one before and she hadn't quite mastered loading it properly. "I like cleaning, don't you?"

"Not so much." Sara began washing the apples. "I won't refuse your help because I want to get going on these apples for pies."

"Those boys will love homemade apple pie, won't they, Hector?" Lucy's husband nodded but said nothing.

"You live in Churchill?" Sara began paring the apples.

"We do now." Lucy turned on the dishwasher then picked up a knife and joined Sara. "We used to be missionaries to the Inuit in a community much farther north than Churchill. We're retired from that now, but we believe God can still use us." She winked at Hector. "Since we don't have children, folks in Churchill are our family. So that makes you our family, too—Sara, isn't it?"

"I should have introduced myself. Yes, I'm Sara Kane." She was dumbfounded by the enthusiastic welcome these strangers offered. "It's nice to meet you."

"You, too. This project is so worthwhile," Lucy said in a more serious tone. "Each of us is under construction throughout our lives as God works on us, but it's doubly true for these young boys. What an appropriate name Laurel chose."

"Yes." Sara frowned. She hadn't thought about her life as being under construction but Lucy was right. It was.

"Why don't I finish peeling these apples while you start your pastry?"

Hector interrupted to thank Sara for the coffee then disappeared. Apparently he'd already received his instructions about Laurel's computer room. Lucy continued to work, humming while her knife whizzed over the apples.

After lining five pie plates, Sara had a small amount of pastry dough left. An idea occurred. After searching the cupboards, she finally found an individual-size foil dish and spread dough in that, too.

"Making a pie for someone special?" Lucy asked in a coy voice.

"Oh. No." Sara blushed. As if she'd have someone

special in her life. "It's— I thought I'd make one for Kyle Loness. He's just arrived home and—"

"Yes, we heard. So sad that his father wasn't here to see him." Lucy closed her eyes. Her lips moved but no sound was audible. When she opened her eyes and found Sara watching her, she smiled. "I like to remind God of His needy kids."

Besides Laurel, Sara had never met anyone so open about their faith.

"Hector and I organized a cleanup of Kyle's yard last week but we didn't touch the greenhouse. We intend to stop by on our way home and ask him if we can help with that, too." Lucy finished paring the apples then asked if she could prepare vegetables for dinner.

"I thought we'd have carrots for dinner."

"Great." Lucy looked delighted by the chore. "I'm sure Kyle will love your thoughtfulness," she said. "As I recall, his mom's pie was always first to go at the church socials."

After yesterday, the last thing Sara wanted to do was revive more of Kyle's memories of his mother. Too late now, she ignored her hesitation and listened to Lucy describe her life as a missionary as she finished. Then she slid all the pies into the big, old-fashioned baker's oven. But she hesitated only a moment before she set the smallest pie inside the oven. If Kyle didn't want it, someone else would.

Sara's thoughts wandered to the handsome veteran. How was Kyle this morning? Was his leg still hurting him? The part inside of her hadn't felt like a misfit when she'd tried to ease his pain. She'd felt useful, as if he needed her.

"Sara?"

She suddenly realized Lucy had asked her something. "Sorry?"

"I was just being nosy, wondering how you'd met Kyle." Lucy winked.

"We arrived in Churchill on the same train," Sara explained as she bagged the rest of the apple slices and packed them into the freezer. A quick cleanup then she assembled the ingredients for peanut butter cookies. Laurel had told her people would often drop in and that Sara should be prepared to offer a snack or even a meal at a moment's notice. Time to start building a larder reserve.

"Kyle was always such a gentleman," Lucy mused. "He's the kind of man who isn't afraid to open a door or lend you an arm if the ground is rough. A real hero type. I don't know why more young men don't understand how attractive that is."

"Kyle is nice," Sara murmured, her cheeks burning under Lucy's scrutiny. "He's agreed to let me use his mother's greenhouse for a project with one of the boys."

Lucy's eyes widened. "Kyle hasn't allowed anyone to touch that greenhouse since his mom's death—"

Lucy was interrupted by noises from the front hall.

Laurel's laughter echoed to them, followed by a rumbled response lower than Hector's voice. To Sara it sounded like Kyle. Immediately her pulse began to flutter. Had he come to take back his offer about the greenhouse? Laurel bounded into the room. When she saw Lucy she wrapped the tiny woman in a hug.

"Bless you and Hector for coming so quickly. I appreciate it." She turned to Sara. "You met Lucy, right? Isn't she a wonder?"

"Yes, she is," Sara agreed with a smile for the vibrant senior. "I've appreciated her help."

"I knew you would." Laurel waited as Lucy excused herself to answer her cell phone in another room then said, "Kyle's taking off his coat. He agreed to look at my computer to see if he can get rid of the gremlin that's taken over."

"That's nice," Sara said, hearing the breathlessness in her voice. It was nice that Kyle was here. *Nice?* Sara scoffed at herself. She was getting good at understatement.

He walked into the kitchen.

"Good morning, Kyle." Sara pretended her stomach hadn't turned into a jellied mush.

"Hi." His response emerged in a low growl. A tic at the corner of his mouth told her he was hurting and wanted to sit.

Sara pretended she needed to check the oven so she could move closer to him. "Are you okay?" she whispered.

"For now." His smile seemed a little forced.

"I haven't told him yet, Sara," Laurel said, her grin stretched across her face, "but I'm hoping that by the time Kyle gets the kinks out of my laptop, I'll have persuaded him to get some of those old desktop computers running for the boys."

"I suspected you wanted more when you asked me about my dad's stock of parts," Kyle said, his smile wry. "Marla didn't tell me you were so devious."

"That's because she doesn't know. Yet." Laurel chuckled then sniffed. "Something smells very good, Sara. How long before whatever's in that oven is ready to eat?"

"I'm baking apple pies. They won't be finished for a while." A flutter of nervousness wrapped around Sara's stomach as she met Kyle's gaze. A new thought occurred to her. Maybe he felt she'd been too forward when she applied the hot cloths to his leg. Did he think she'd been too presumptuous? And why did it matter so much? "There's fresh banana loaf. I made it before breakfast for the boys' lunches."

"Perfect. But we're not having coffee yet. Kyle has to earn his snack first." Laurel linked her arm in Kyle's so he had to leave the room with her.

"What a taskmaster you work for, Sara," he complained as he left.

Sara was still chuckling when Lucy returned and asked what was so funny.

"You see, such a gentleman," Lucy said after Sara's explanation. She nodded her silver head. "He didn't even refuse her."

"I don't know many people who can refuse Laurel." Sara slid a sheet of her cookies in the second oven. Then she set a large pot on the stove, adding a chicken and some of the vegetables Lucy had prepared.

"What's that for?" Lucy asked.

"Soup for lunch. You will be staying, won't you?"

"We'd love to," Lucy replied promptly. "In fact, I just reminded God that Hector will want lunch in a couple of hours and I have nothing at home."

Sara couldn't help laughing. When had she last felt so lighthearted? *Lucy feels like family, God—but I still want my own.*

By the time the cookies were cooling, her side ached from laughing at Lucy's stories. Then Kyle appeared in the doorway and Sara's breath snagged in her throat. She was glad his attention was focused elsewhere.

"Good morning, Mrs. Clow." His tone was grave, solemn.

"For goodness' sake, Kyle." The diminutive woman rushed up to him and wrapped her arms around his waist. "After all these years can't I finally be plain old Lucy?"

"I don't think you could ever be plain old anything," Kyle murmured, a hint of tenderness softening his usually harsh tone.

"I'm so glad you're home safe and sound, my dear boy." Lucy's voice brimmed with emotion. "So glad. Hector and I prayed for you every day."

"Thanks." As Kyle awkwardly patted her back, his eyes met Sara's. He was obviously uncomfortable with Lucy's effusive hug but he made no effort to shift away.

Sara loved that though Kyle was not a "toucher," he tolerated Lucy's embrace without complaint, even gently hugging her back before Lucy finally drew away.

Lucy was right. Kyle was exactly what most women would want in a man.

"Before she got caught on the phone, Laurel said I'm to tell you we need coffee," he said to Sara.

Sara studied Kyle for a moment, noting the way he rubbed his temple. He looked tired.

"She insists those computer relics she tore apart can be reassembled into working computers." He rolled his eyes. "She must think I'm a magician."

"Laurel does have a way of coaxing more from you," Lucy agreed. "But since it's to help these precious boys, I can't complain."

"I shouldn't, either," Kyle mumbled. "Lives Under Construction is an excellent project. It's just—"

His gaze met Sara's and she immediately understood that he'd planned to do other things today. "I guess I'll have to learn to be flexible," he said with a shrug.

"With Laurel we all have to learn that," she agreed.

The corners of his lips tipped up in the tiniest smile, but it made a world of difference to Sara. Suddenly the day seemed much brighter. But why? Kyle should be nothing to her, just a means to the greenhouse, that was all. And yet, because he smiled at her, her heart beat more rapidly. To hide her reaction she took out the banana loaf and began slicing it.

"Something smells wonderful." Kyle's face tilted up, his nose in the air.

"Apple pie, just like your mom's." Lucy beamed. "Sara even made you your own special one. Isn't that sweet?"

Sara gulped, embarrassed that she'd drawn attention to the fact.

"It's very kind of you to think of me, Sara," Kyle said after a pause.

"It's nothing. I'm trying to use up some old apples is all," Sara rushed to explain. "I didn't know you were coming here today. I thought I'd drop it off when Rod and I go to the greenhouse this afternoon."

"About that—"

"I've explained it to him," she said, desperate to prevent Kyle from telling her he'd changed his mind. "He's eager to get started with our plan. After school we'll clean all that glass."

"Uh-huh." Kyle glanced at Lucy as if he wanted to say something.

"I didn't know you were thinking of allowing people to use the greenhouse, Kyle." The blue in Lucy's gaze intensified.

"I wasn't," he admitted. "But as you said, if it's to help this Lives project, we shouldn't complain."

Sara smothered a laugh at the way Kyle had deflected Lucy's comment, but she doubted the former missionary would be silenced so easily. She gulped when his attention turned to her.

"As I told you, Sara, no one's been in the greenhouse for a while," Kyle reminded. "Hector's agreed to check it out after lunch. You and Rod will have to wait until he gives the okay."

"That will be fine." His slight smile and the way his gaze held hers for an infinitesimal moment sent a tingle straight to that needy spot inside Sara. Thankfully the timer beeped. She broke the electric connection that seemed to hum between them by turning away to mix up some biscuit dough to go with her soup. What on earth was wrong with her?

Laurel and Hector arrived and took their place at the table.

"I love how your baking smells fill the whole place." Laurel accepted her coffee with a grin. "It gives Lives exactly the homey atmosphere I want for the boys."

Embarrassed by her praise, Sara busied herself filling cups. By then the only seat left at the table was beside Kyle.

She did not want to sit there.

She wasn't sure why except that being around him somehow made her feel awkward, as if she had an upset stomach or was off balance.

Feeling out of place, Sara checked on her pies then began cleaning the mixing bowl and utensils she'd used.

"Sara, come and join us. You deserve a break." Lucy's smile made her blue eyes look guileless. "There's a space for you beside Kyle."

Sara tried to refuse, but it was easier just to sit down beside Kyle. She was far too aware of him sitting next to her, shifting frequently just like her.

It came as a relief when everyone finally finished and rose to leave. But Sara jumped up too quickly and bumped against Kyle.

"I'm sorry," she exclaimed, cheeks burning when he grasped the table edge to balance himself. "I'm so clumsy."

"It wasn't you. It was me," he said, wincing. "I haven't quite got the hang of this new leg they gave me. My therapist insists I checked myself out of therapy too early, so it's my own fault."

"Can I help?" she offered, shy but unwilling to let him hurt if she could somehow assuage it. Besides, everyone had gone. If he refused her help, no one would see her embarrassment at being rejected.

"How? More hot salt cloths?" he teased.

"If they'll help, yes," she said steadily, meeting his gaze head-on, though her face grew warm under his stare.

Kyle looked at her for so long that she began to wish she hadn't made the offer.

"Never mind. I should—"

He cut her off. "I don't think I've ever known anyone like you, Sara Kane."

"Is that a good thing or a bad thing?" she whispered.

Kyle chuckled. It was the first time she'd heard true mirth in his voice.

"Time will tell, Sara." With that he left for the computer room, his gait odd and uneven but determined.

Sara had no idea what he'd meant.

"Are those pies in danger of burning?" Lucy asked from the doorway, breaking into her reverie. Sara hurried to open the oven as Lucy flipped her phone closed. "I think Kyle likes you," she said.

"I hope so. I could use a friend." Sara turned away to concentrate on her work but inside a bubble of happiness rose. She hoped Kyle liked her, she hoped it with every fiber of her being, because she was beginning to like him a lot. Friendship was okay, wasn't it?

Friendship with a man? In a flood of uncertainty her feelings took a tumble. She wasn't good at relationships. She certainly didn't know how to be friends with a man like Kyle. He was an acquaintance but that was all he was. That was all he could be, because she didn't have anything to offer him, even if she was interested.

Sighing, she lifted out each golden sizzling pie and set it on a cooling rack.

"Now what can I do?" Lucy asked.

"You've already done so much."

"I don't mean with kitchen work." Lucy's hands rested on her shoulders. Gently she eased Sara around to face her. "Tell me what's troubling you."

"What you said about Kyle—him liking me, I mean." Sara gulped. "I don't know what to do about it. I've never had a man as a friend before. It scares me. Maybe I'll do something stupid to offend him. Or maybe, when he gets to know me, he'll regret it. I haven't been anywhere or done anything important, like him. All I can do is cook."

Shame suffused her. How dorky she sounded, like a stupid, dumb kid.

"And you cook extremely well, Sara." Lucy brushed a hand over her hair. "But why would you think Kyle would reject friendship with you? Has he done or said something—"

"No, not at all," Sara interrupted, ashamed that she had somehow made Lucy think ill of Kyle. "It's just— I've been praying God would give me some friends. I've never had any, you see. I just didn't think someone like Kyle would want to be my friend." Lucy seemed to understand.

"I think you're going to find a lot of friends in Churchill, my dear. I would be honored to be your first." She held out her hand.

"Thank you," Sara said as she folded Lucy's hand in hers, thrilled that this woman thought of her as a friend.

Could You help Kyle think of me like that, too, God?

"Isn't there something you'd rather do than watch me fiddle with this mess?"

Kyle glared at Sara, wondering why she hung around when it was clear this computer was not going to function properly without a major overhaul.

"I want to learn about computers," Sara said.

He raised his eyebrows at her.

"I don't know anything about them." She bit her bottom lip, something he now recognized as a habit she employed when embarrassed. "It sounds stupid for somebody my age, but I don't even know how to operate one. Where I grew up, we didn't have computers."

"Oh." He cursed his insensitivity.

"I'm hoping you get one of these running soon so Rod can show me how to use it." Sara lowered her lids, hiding the expression in her eyes.

"Rod?" Kyle soldered two wires together and tested the connection. "Isn't he the boy you want to work with in the greenhouse?"

"Yes. Apparently he's very good on computers. He plans to set up a web page in memory of his uncle." Sara frowned, her silvery eyes darkening. "That is what it's called, right? A web page?"

"Uh-huh." Kyle held his breath and pressed the on switch. He clenched his fist at the popping sound as sparks sprayed across his workbench. "Piece of junk." He smacked his fist in the center of the circuit board. "This is hopeless."

"You can't make it work?" Sara's face fell as if she'd lost her best friend.

"I'm good but I'm no magician." Kyle wished he didn't feel responsible for those gray clouds in her eyes. "There's a reason people get rid of old computers, you know." He rubbed his eyes with one hand and the knot in his shoulder with the other. Then he glanced at his watch. "I'd better get home. I can't do any more today."

"You've been at this a long time," Sara agreed.

Kyle looked up, and found he couldn't make himself look away from her. The sun poured in the window, amplifying her simple beauty, holding him spellbound. When she smiled his breath caught in his throat—until he realized her smile was directed at someone else.

"Come in, Rod," she said. "I want you to meet Kyle. He owns the greenhouse. He's also trying to fix these computers for you."

"Hey." Rod nodded at Kyle, glanced at the array spread over the workbench and shook his head. The thirteen-year-old made a face. "Wasting your time. They're pieces of junk."

Kyle let out a shout of laughter. "I agree with you wholeheartedly, buddy."

"So?" Rod stared at him.

"There's nothing here worth salvaging." Kyle shifted under those intensely dark eyes.

"Uh-huh." Life seemed to drain out of Rod.

"Sara said you're planning to set up a web page. About what?"

Kyle wasn't sure why he was asking. He had his own life to figure out. But there was something about this kid that gnawed at him. He seemed so totally deflated over the loss of the computers.

"It's uh, personal. You know?" Rod shrugged.

"Yeah, I know about personal." Kyle hated showing his disability in public but his leg was bothering him something fierce. He'd been seated for too long. He tried to rise, grabbed the side of the bench for balance and forced himself upright, grateful when Sara's hand supported him.

"Kyle was injured in Afghanistan," Sara explained.

Kyle's anger bubbled up. He wondered why she'd said that. He glared at her but she was watching Rod so he did, too, and was stunned by the grief that covered the boy's face. A long silence ensued.

"My uncle died there." Rod stared at the floor. After a moment, he lifted his head and glanced at Sara. At her nod he continued. "He was like a father to me. I want to create a web page in his memory, so other soldiers can check in and remember their friends who died," he said.

Stunned by the boy's selflessness, Kyle glanced at Sara. Her silver eyes sparkled with unshed tears.

"I don't want to forget him," Rod murmured. "Nobody should forget the people who died so we can be free." His hands clenched at his sides. "A guy at school said the best thing would be to forget my uncle, the war and everything. He said we should get on with life and that my uncle was a loser. One day I couldn't take it anymore so I beat him up."

Kyle's gut tied in a knot. He was suddenly aware that his hands were fisted and that every muscle in his body had tensed. Anger gripped him. Suddenly, helping Rod set up his web page was very important.

"We'll get a computer running for you, Rod," he said. "Don't worry."

"Thanks." The boy's sadness seemed to melt away. "Some of the other guys need it to stay in contact with their families. Letters aren't as good as email."

"I hear you," Kyle said, remembering the many emails he'd shared with his dad. He lifted his head, and caught Sara studying him with that beautiful smile and his heart did something funny. "I am going to make sure Lives Under Construction gets a computer lab," he assured her before he could stop himself.

"I believe you will, Kyle," she said with complete faith. "I trust you."

I believe you will, Kyle.

I trust you.

Was it possible that she truly meant those things? Could she believe in him and trust him?

Kyle was astonished by what those simple words did to him. And in that moment, he resolved not to let down sweet Sara Kane.

Chapter Five

"Thanks for helping me, Teddy." Kyle couldn't stifle his grin as his father's best friend carried the last carton from the train station and set it inside the truck bed.

"Absolutely my pleasure." Teddy Stonechild slammed the truck gate closed. "Do we need to stop somewhere else?"

"Nope. We'll go straight to Lives," Kyle told him. A heady delight filled him as he imagined how Sara would react to his surprise.

"Uh, listen, Kyle." Teddy sat in the truck, waiting for him to fasten his seat belt, a troubled look on his face. "It might not be the best idea for me to go along with you."

"What do you mean?" Kyle frowned at him. "You've only been back in Churchill a day. You haven't seen what Lives Under Construction is like now that the boys are here."

"True. But when I was here before I, well, I kind of made an enemy of Laurel Quinn." Teddy shrugged. "It wasn't intentional and I'd take it back if I could, but that isn't going to happen."

Kyle frowned. Teddy liked everyone.."How did you make an enemy of Laurel?"

"I mentioned my, uh, concerns about her project to the town council earlier this year." Teddy looked sheepish as he explained. "Well," he said defensively, "you know how often I've stayed here. I feel like part of the community and that's how they treat me. So I told the truth."

"You dissed her project? Publicly?" Kyle winced.

"That's not all." Teddy's face turned bright red.

"What else?" Kyle asked cautiously.

"I guess I came on a little too strong with my objections. She had to, well, jump through some extra hoops before they granted approval." Teddy looked totally abashed.

"That's not like you." Kyle frowned. "You usually welcome everyone who comes to town."

"And I tried to welcome her. But something about Laurel Quinn and her plan got under my skin," Teddy admitted. "She doesn't seem like a good business manager," he defended.

"Given the job she's trying to do, I'm not sure the business part matters as much as helping those kids. She's not the CEO of your hotel chain, you know." Kyle shrugged. "Anyway, that's in the past. Just promise me that today you'll keep your issues to yourself," he said.

"Of course." Teddy looked offended. "It's a moot point now, anyway. The place is up and running."

"And doing good work," Kyle added.

"So you've said." Teddy gave him an odd sideways look. "I heard you're letting the cook use your mom's greenhouse." Teddy had always had a soft spot for Kyle's mother.

"Her name is Sara and yes, I have agreed. She's using it to help a kid named Rod. They're going to grow herbs or something."

"Sara, huh?"

"Sara Kane." Kyle's face burned at Teddy's narrowed scrutiny. Funny how his heartbeat accelerated just saying her name. "I decided to let them use it until I sell the place and move on."

"You're still determined to do that?" Teddy asked.

"Yes. There's nothing for me here now. I can't do the things I did and I won't become dependent on others." The grimness of his future sucked away Kyle's joy. "You know what my injuries mean. I can never have kids, never be a father. It's too hard to be here and know that. I'll leave and find something else."

"Doing what?" Teddy frowned at him.

"I haven't quite figured that out yet." Kyle clamped his mouth shut until they drove into the yard site. He did not want to think about leaving Churchill right now.

"Kyle, hello." Sara met them at the door, wearing his mother's red jacket. His heart gave a thunk but it wasn't sadness, more like appreciation. She looked good.

"Leaving?" he asked.

"I was going to do some more work on the greenhouse," she said. "Lucy and Hector brought us some used bikes, so I can ride to your place now. It won't take as long." She smiled at Teddy. "Hello. I'm Sara."

Kyle introduced them.

"Nice to meet you," Teddy said in his usual affable tone. "Is Laurel here?"

"She's out, I'm afraid." Sara watched him unload three boxes from his truck. "Is that a delivery for her?"

"Sort of." Kyle held the door open for Teddy. "It's

this way," he said, walking toward the computer room. "If you'll bring in the rest, I'll begin unpacking."

"Sure." Teddy left for another load.

"What is all this, Kyle?" Sara watched as he slid his box knife under the tape and ripped open the box. He felt her freeze when she read the side of the box. "Are those—?"

"Computers." He grinned as he lifted out a tower. "Six of the latest models. All Teddy and I have to do is get them operational and you guys are set."

"Six computers? But how did you get them?" Sara's silver-gray eyes stretched wide.

"I ordered them a couple of days ago. They arrived on the train this morning." He didn't understand her hesitation or the worried look she gave him.

"But Laurel says we're on a very tight budget." She bit her bottom lip. "I'm sure she can't afford—"

"Don't worry," he said, anxious to ease her obvious distress. "These are paid for."

"How? Laurel never mentioned—"

"I paid for them. Or rather, Dad did. He left some money he said should be used for a good cause. I think this is a good cause and I know he'd agree." He winked at her, wanting to share the joy that bubbled inside at being able to give. "Plus it will save me spending more frustrating hours on those relics of Laurel's."

Sara simply stared at him, as if she didn't believe he was serious.

"Can you hold this box so I can slide out the tower?" Kyle waited for her to shrug out of the red jacket, then with her help, lifted out the monitors and towers. Teddy arranged the units on the tables Hector had built, and then carried out the empty boxes.

Eager to get everything up and running, Kyle began connecting the systems, only too aware of Sara's intense scrutiny over his shoulder.

"Can you show me how to do that?" she said after he'd connected the first one.

Kyle was about to refuse her help, to say he could manage it alone, when he glimpsed the longing in her eyes. Again he wondered why a computer held such fascination for her.

"Please?" she asked.

"It's pretty easy. It's all color coded. Put the red plug in the red socket." He waited until she did that. "Now the green one to green. Now yellow."

With each step, Sara's smile widened. Kyle had never seen anyone find such pleasure in so simple a thing.

"There are no more colors," she told him. "Is it ready to go now?"

"No." He laughed at her frown. "That's only the first step. We still have to connect the speakers and then I have to program each computer."

"Oh." Disappointment dimmed her joy. "How many days will that take?"

"Days?" Kyle shook his head. "A few hours, maybe. Tell me what you know about computers, Sara."

"Nothing." She shrugged, looking embarrassed.

"I'll give you a crash course," Kyle said, suddenly feeling bad for her. "Computers are machines that have to be told what you want them to do. So I'm going to install programs that will do that. When I'm finished, they'll be ready to use."

"It sounds kind of complicated." Sara frowned.

"Well, I think making apple pies and soup and stew is complicated. Each of us has our own thing we're familiar with." Kyle continued explaining, but it wasn't long before he recognized Sara was totally lost.

He was feeling a little lost himself with that fresh lemon scent of her hair assailing his nostrils.

"Never mind. Once I get these running you'll understand better," he said, aware that Teddy sat silently listening across the room.

"I won't bother you. It's not fair for me to take up more of your time. Anyway, Rod has promised he will help me learn computers."

Kyle felt oddly disappointed but before he could puzzle out his feelings, Sara gasped.

"What's wrong?" Teddy asked, surging to his feet.

"The time," she said. "I must prepare lunch. You and Kyle will stay?"

Kyle opened his mouth to refuse but Teddy beat him to it.

"We'd love to stay for lunch." He grinned. "Kyle promised he'd feed me but he's not a very good cook. He says you are."

"That's nice of him." Sara's gaze met Kyle's then skittered away.

"Apple pie is my favorite," Teddy hinted.

"I'm afraid there isn't any left." Sara chuckled at Teddy's dejected expression. "But I'll think of something else for dessert today." She walked to the door, her steps quick and light. "We'll eat when Laurel returns. Let me know if you need anything."

"Thank you." Kyle waited until her footsteps died away before he turned back to the computer he'd been working on.

"Nice lady," Teddy mused.

"Very nice." Kyle struggled to focus his brain on booting up the computer and off Sara.

"What girl her age doesn't know about computers?" Teddy asked.

"I don't know. Something to do with her being in foster care, I think." Kyle scratched his head, trying to sort through the bits and pieces he knew about Sara and drawing a blank. "She hasn't told me much and I don't like to ask. Whenever she mentions the past, she gets this sad look as if it's painful to talk about."

"You should ask her. If it's painful, maybe it would help her to talk about it," Teddy said.

"Yeah," Kyle agreed. But the thought of such a personal conversation put a lump in his throat. He had a hundred questions rolling around his brain. As if he needed to think some more about Sara Kane. What he needed was to get back to his own life, not get more involved in hers. "I'm expecting some calls this afternoon about listing the house, so I have to get this finished and get home. Okay?"

"Sure. As long as we get to eat Sara's lunch before we leave." Teddy rose. "I'll go outside and load up some of that junk from the renovations. I can haul it away this afternoon."

Despite Kyle's best efforts to remain focused as he worked, every so often Sara's face pushed its way into his mind until he acknowledged that he needed to know more about her. But how?

Rod wanted to create a website for wounded warriors to meet and share experiences. Personally Kyle had no desire to rehash his hellish memories, but maybe if he helped the boy, he could figure out why

Sara Kane was so different from any other woman he'd ever met.

And maybe then he'd be able to figure out why he found her so appealing.

"I have never tasted anything so delicious, Sara. Thank you." Teddy accepted a third helping of lasagna, giving Sara a rush of satisfaction.

"I'm glad you like it." Her gaze rested on Laurel. Her boss had thanked Kyle effusively for the computers and then fallen strangely silent for the rest of the meal, very unlike the usually garrulous Laurel. In fact, every time she looked at Teddy, her blue eyes shot daggers at him.

"It is very good lasagna," Kyle agreed quietly. "Especially with the spinach."

"My way of sneaking vegetables into the boys. Would you like some more?" It was obvious to Sara that Laurel and Teddy had some issues between them, but since she didn't know anything about relationships, she doubted she could help.

"I've eaten plenty, thanks." Kyle's gaze slid from Teddy, to Laurel, then to her. "You're still intending on coming to the greenhouse this afternoon?"

"As soon as I finish cleaning up from lunch. Rod said he'd join me there. He has last period of class free and we want to get started." Sara knew they were just making conversation to cover the silence between the others, but the greenhouse was a connection between her and Kyle, making them cohorts of a sort. She liked that. "It's warmer today. I think I'll plant some lettuce seeds."

"Fresh lettuce, huh? That will be nice." Laurel glared at Teddy. "Not having to buy lettuce should cut our expenses, improve our bottom line."

Teddy bristled. "Look, Laurel, I didn't mean—"

"Excuse me. That's my phone." Laurel cut off Teddy's explanation and bolted from the room.

Kyle glanced at Sara and raised his eyebrows. Sara nodded. Something was definitely wrong between these two.

"I got some help with the expenses from Lucy, too," Sara said brightly, trying to lift the dark mood of the room. "Not only did she scrounge up those bikes for us to use, but her friend donated some rhubarb. I made a crisp for dessert."

"It sounds wonderful, but I guess I'm not as hungry as I thought." Teddy pushed away his plate. "I'll take that with me and eat it for dinner tonight. I should get going now."

"Of course. I'll wrap it up." Sara glanced at Kyle.

"I'd love some rhubarb crisp," he said. "But since Teddy's eager to get going and I caught a ride with him, maybe I could take some with me, also."

"Certainly." Sara wrapped generous portions for each man then walked them out. "I can't thank you enough for the computers, Kyle. I know the boys will be thrilled. And thank you, Teddy, for all your help, too."

"Rod can show you how to get online tonight," Kyle told her as he shrugged into his jacket. "You'll be an expert in no time."

"I'm not sure about that," she said. "But I'll try." Both men waved, climbed in Teddy's truck and drove away.

Sara closed the door and went to clean the kitchen. She found Laurel sitting at the table, her head in her hands.

"What's the matter?" Sara asked. She sat down, waiting for her friend to explain.

"It's that man," Laurel burst out. She lifted her head. Her face was red, her mouth pinched together in a tight line.

"Teddy? I could tell that there was something wrong between you two. But he's been such a help. He cleaned up that pile of garbage outside," she began.

"I don't care that he cleaned it up," Laurel snapped.

Sara had never seen Laurel so flustered. "I'm sorry, but I don't understand."

"I'm not sure I understand myself," Laurel admitted. "Teddy and I got off on the wrong foot. He's one of those men who has to be right, the kind who thinks he knows everything." She shook her head. "Forget it. I'm acting like a kid."

Sara was totally confused about relationships in general but this one in particular. By the time she thought of something to say it was too late.

"I have paperwork to do before I pick up the boys. I should get going," Laurel said as she left.

"See you later, then." Sara, totally muddled by Laurel, dragged on the coat Kyle had lent her and climbed on one of the bikes, wishing she had a clue how to help her friend. "Lord, I'm going to need some help to figure out this relationship business," she prayed as she rode into town.

By the time she arrived at Kyle's she was breathless from pedaling so hard because she couldn't rid her brain of thoughts of polar bears pursuing her. But a rush of joy bubbled inside her when she saw Kyle sitting in the sunshine.

"I thought you'd be having a nap after all your work this morning." She climbed off the bike, propped it up and walked into his yard. To her surprise, Kyle followed her into the greenhouse.

"I got tired of sorting through Dad's stuff so I thought I'd give you a hand out here."

"That's very nice of you, Kyle, but I didn't expect you to work on this. Rod and I can do it."

"I know you can." His now-familiar grin flashed. "I just need something to do, something physical," he amended. "I'm used to being on the go."

"By all means then, clean to your heart's content." In the warmth of the greenhouse, Sara took off her jacket and got to work, trying to ignore the fact that less than six feet away Kyle scrubbed and polished. She wasn't sure if she should talk to him or leave him be, but after a while, curiosity got the better of her. "Is there a lot of stuff you have to go through?"

"The usual accumulation, I guess." He rubbed particularly hard on one spot where Sara could see no dirt.

"It must be wonderful to look at his things and enjoy memories of happy times," she said.

"Not really." Kyle's voice sounded hard. "I look at his snowshoes and remember that I can't do that with him anymore. I can't do it by myself, either."

"No, you can't do that again. Yet. But you're alive," she said as gently as she could. "You can build new memories."

"How?"

"I don't know," she admitted honestly. "You'll have to ask God."

"Not gonna happen." He set down his cloth. "God and I don't talk."

There was a finality there that Sara couldn't argue with.

"Here comes Rod," Kyle said. He opened the door and greeted the boy. "I'll leave the two of you to finish. I'm going to tinker on my old ATV and see if I can get it ready to be sold."

"Thanks for your help." A part of her heart pinched as

she watched Kyle walk away, broad shoulders bowed. He wasn't even going to try to use the machine. He was just going to let it go, let the past die as if it had never been.

Sara whispered a prayer. "Please help him."

Then she lifted her head and smiled at Rod. "I'm glad you're here," she said. "There's a lot of dirt that's accumulated."

Rod seemed to know what to do and they worked together for some time. Sara had no idea how long they'd been at it when Kyle yelled. When she saw him lying on the ground, her heart flew up into her throat. She dropped everything and ran.

"What's wrong? Did you hurt yourself?" When he simply lay there without answering, she demanded, "Kyle, what are you doing?"

"Admiring the clouds." He frowned at her. "What do you think I'm doing? I'm trying to figure out if I've broken something." He grunted as he sat up. "I might have left some bones intact," he muttered as he stretched. Rod held out a hand and Kyle grabbed it, using the boy's strength to leverage himself upright. "Thanks," he said.

Rod simply nodded then walked back inside the greenhouse.

"This thing is a heap of junk." He kicked his foot against one tire and winced. "I need a cup of coffee."

"We should go." Sara turned but froze when Kyle grabbed her arm.

"What I meant was, would you like a cup of coffee, too?" His gaze met hers and held.

"I guess I could. If you're sure you want me to."

"I'm sure, Sara. I'd like it very much." The sincerity in his voice convinced her he wanted company.

She checked her watch. She had time before she

needed to start on dinner. "It's a lovely day. We could have it outside."

"If you want." Kyle wore a strange look. "Would you mind making it? Some things never change and I'm still lousy with coffee."

"So that's why you invited me." She laughed at his guilty look. "Just for that I should refuse."

"Please don't." He stood there, waiting, then lifted his eyebrows. "Please? I'd owe you one really big favor."

Like teaching her about the computer?

"Okay." She glanced toward Rod, thinking to ask if he wanted something to drink, but his attention was totally on the system that ventilated the greenhouse. Men. With a huff, Sara went inside. A moment later she had to laugh. As if she knew anything about men or how they thought.

It did feel nice to be needed, especially by Kyle because he always seemed so determined to be independent. It wasn't that she felt sorry for him. Kyle wasn't the kind of man who generated sympathy. It was more that she wanted to hear him laugh again, see joy fill his face.

Sara gulped at the strange sensations filling her. They made her nervous so she concentrated on the process of making the coffee, but in doing so she found the kitchen terribly confining. How could Kyle even get around? Everything seemed to be in the wrong place, in the way. A peek out the window told her Kyle and Rod were engaged, so Sara made her decision.

While the aroma of coffee grounds filled the room, she pushed and shoved, using every mite of strength she could summon. Five minutes later, she stood back, pleased with her efforts.

"How's that coffee— Oh." Kyle stood stock-still, taking in her changes.

"You don't like it," she guessed, watching emotions flicker across his face. "I'm sorry. I'll put it back, I promise."

"Wait. I think I can actually get around now." Kyle walked to the fridge, opened the door and shut it. He reached up to a cupboard and then pulled open the bottom drawer. "It works like a real kitchen should. It's the way it was when my mom was alive."

Sara flinched. Why hadn't she left well enough alone?

"This room came alive with her personality. She baked for everyone, everything." Kyle half smiled at Sara, lost in his memories. "After she died, Dad and I used it more as an office. He brought that armoire down here so he could do books for the business, but it should go back upstairs. It's too big for here."

Loath to break into his reminiscences, Sara waited several moments. He finally looked at her as if suddenly remembering where he was.

"The sun's gone, so we'll come in for coffee. Can you fill two of those yellow mugs? There's soda in the fridge for Rod. I'll call him."

Sara set his filled mug and Rod's soda on the table. When Rod and Kyle were seated, Sara sat, too, so Kyle wouldn't guess her mug was filled with water. Though she loved the scent of it brewing and enjoyed making it for others, she just didn't enjoy the taste.

"This is great coffee." Kyle savored a mouthful as he glanced around the room. "You know, maybe I should hire you to help me smarten the rest of the house up. That might help it sell faster."

Sell?

The bottom dropped out of her world. Sara set down her yellow cup and leaned back.

"You're selling your home?" she asked, trying to hide her surprise and shock.

"Yes, of course. I can't live in Churchill anymore," Kyle said in a matter-of-fact tone. "I'll clean up the place and hope to get a good dollar. Then I'll move."

Sara stared at her hands, devastated. She'd begun to think of Kyle as a friend, a very good friend. She'd even let herself daydream that maybe, perhaps, one day he could become more than that. Of course that was only a dream; it would never happen. But she had thought that with time she could help him break free of his bitterness toward God. Now he was saying they wouldn't have that time together.

Sara didn't want to examine the reasons why she found that depressing. She only knew she had to try to stop Kyle from leaving, not for herself but because she cared about him, and running away from his home, where his memories were etched into the Canadian north like long-ago carvings in the rock, wouldn't heal his hurting heart. Kyle had lived, loved, laughed and done everything here and she wanted him to do it again.

She wanted the very best for him. That was more important than any silly romantic daydreams. How could leaving be the best for him? And how could she deal with the sense of loss that even now enveloped her?

As Sara studied the man she'd come to respect and admire, her head and her heart swirled with questions about Kyle Loness. None of which she had answers to.

Chapter Six

Kyle hadn't expected the call for help to come so soon.

"Whatever Sara did, the computer is totally whacked." Rod's voice gave little away.

"What's on the screen?" Kyle asked hopefully.

"It's black. Don't tell her I said this," Rod mumbled, "but Sara is about as good with a computer as I am with pie dough. She was checking out a website, last thing I knew. A few minutes later she yelled. By the time I got there her computer was dead."

"You don't know what she was doing?" Kyle clung to a fragment of hope that he wouldn't have to go out again today. His leg was aching and he'd hoped to relax.

"I haven't got a clue. I can usually figure out computer stuff but this time I'm stuck. Whatever she did, it shut down the system." Rod didn't sound hopeful.

"Are you in the computer room now?"

"Yes." Rod's flat tone held no hope.

"Let's try something." Kyle led him through several steps. Nothing worked. Finally he agreed to go to Lives.

"Please don't tell Sara I called you," Rod urged. "She really wants to get on the internet. But I'm afraid she'll try again on another computer and maybe knock out the entire network if you don't help me figure out what's wrong."

"I'll see if Teddy can drive me over." Kyle was curious about what was behind Sara's need to understand computers and get online. "Do you know why she's so eager to use the internet?"

"She's trying to find out about her family." A pause, then, "She's coming. I have to go." Rod hung up before Kyle could say any more.

He called Teddy, who reluctantly agreed to a second visit to Lives. While he waited for his ride, Kyle mused on what he'd learned.

Sara was a foster child. Now she was trying to find her family. That made sense if she'd been removed from her home as a young child. It might also explain why she was so curious about his past. Kyle remembered her appreciation of his home. Was that why she'd looked so devastated when he'd told her he was selling this place?

Because she didn't have a home of her own?

He recalled another of his father's favorite quotations, this time from Robert Frost. "Home is the place where, when you have to go there, They have to take you in." Though he'd moved around as a kid, Kyle had always had a home.

Apparently Sara had not enjoyed the same security.

Hearing the low growl of Teddy's engine outside, Kyle tugged on his coat and walked out of the house. Sometime yesterday, Hector had managed to build a ramp, making it much easier to leave the house. Kyle made a mental note to buy the man dinner as thanks as he climbed inside the truck.

"What's the emergency?" Teddy demanded.

"Sara killed one of the computers."

"Already?" Teddy's eyes widened.

"Yes, but you can't say anything," Kyle insisted. "I'm going to pretend we stopped by to make sure everything's okay with them. You good with that?"

Teddy shrugged.

"Apparently Sara is upset. She blames herself for the crash."

"Is Laurel going to be there?" Teddy asked in a low tone.

"I imagine so." Kyle studied his friend. "Is that a problem?"

"Not as long as I don't run into her." Teddy grimaced. "I know what you're going to say."

Kyle inclined his head to one side, curious to see if Teddy knew him as well as he thought.

"You'll say let it go. I'm trying." Teddy tossed him a sideways glance. "May I suggest you do the same?"

"I don't know what you're talking about." Kyle stared out the window. "I'm not the one who's feuding with the woman who runs Lives."

"To clarify, I'm not exactly feuding with Laurel Quinn, but that isn't what I meant." Teddy was silent until they turned into the driveway of Lives. "I meant that chip on your shoulder."

"You're seeing chips where there aren't any." Kyle grasped the door handle but Teddy's grip made him pause.

"You're going to tell me you're not mad at God or at that woman who dumped you?" Teddy nodded when Kyle didn't respond. "That's what I'm talking about. You have to let it go."

"You expect me to accept that God chose to kill my father two weeks before I was to come home?" Kyle barked a harsh laugh. "I should pretend that's okay with me?"

"You're making it sound like God reached out and struck him dead," Teddy argued. "Your dad had a heart attack, Kyle."

"Which God could have prevented. At least until I got home. But He didn't." Kyle exhaled.

"It was hard for me to accept your father's death, too," Teddy said. "But ultimately I am not in charge of the world. God is. As His child, I accept that He knows what He's doing."

"That's a cop-out." Kyle shoved the door open and awkwardly climbed out.

"Is it?" Teddy walked with him to the door. "I don't understand astrophysics or space sciences. Does that mean it's a cop-out if I accept it when they tell me there is no life on the moon?"

"It's not the same."

"Sure it is." Teddy's lips lifted. "I'm telling you, buddy, if you don't knock that chip off your shoulder, you'll miss what's right in front of you."

"Which is?" Kyle asked, though he wasn't sure he wanted to know.

"Sara." Teddy's smirk said it all.

The door opened before Kyle could respond.

"Hi, Laurel," he said.

"Wow!" Laurel grinned at him. "Your sense of smell must be incredible." She shot a glare at Teddy but stood back to allow them both to enter.

"My sense of smell?" As soon as he said it, Kyle knew what she was talking about. The aroma of freshly made popcorn filled the room, combined with—caramel?

"Sara's just made some special popcorn for our

movie night. You're welcome to join us. I'm sure the movie will be to your taste—action adventure with lots of car chases. The guys chose it."

"Sounds great." Kyle walked to the door of the family room and smiled at the group of boys. Then he turned back to Laurel. "Actually we just came to check if the computers are working properly. Sometimes there are hiccups with new systems."

"That's very kind of you. Boys, this is the man who kindly donated those new computers for you to use." She waited until the yells of "thanks, man" ended. "Do we have an issue with the computers?" she asked, glancing around the room.

Kyle waited but no one said anything, including Rod, who seemed intent on staring at the floor. A moment later, Sara stepped forward, wearing a red-checked apron and holding a wooden spoon in one hand.

"I broke one," she admitted with a red face.

"Good thing we stopped by, then," Kyle said with a warning glance at Teddy. "I'll go check it out."

"Need any help?" Laurel asked.

"Uh—" He struggled with an appropriate way to refuse Laurel's offer.

"I wasn't talking about me." She laughed self-deprecatingly. "I thought maybe Rod could help you. He seems to be the most computer literate among us."

Rod didn't say anything. But he rose to lead the way toward the computer room. Laurel, after a sideways glance at Teddy, flopped down in a chair in the family room.

"I'll stay here. I'm partial to Sara's special popcorn." Teddy flopped down in the chair Rod had just vacated. "Actually I'm partial to anything Sara makes."

The boys hooted with laughter as Sara's cheeks pinked even more.

"Save me some," Kyle said before he left.

Rod was waiting for him in the computer room. "It's this one," he said, taking the chair in the next station.

Kyle tested the connection, the switch and several other possibilities before typing in commands. Nothing happened. "Huh. That's weird."

"It's ruined, isn't it?" Sara stood behind them, her hands twisting together.

"No, Sara, I'm sure it's not." Kyle was touched by the concern in her eyes.

"Then what's wrong with it?" She didn't wait for an answer. "I knew I shouldn't have used it. Rod thought I'd be fine, but I have no idea what I'm doing. I've ruined your lovely gift and now the boys will suffer." Tears glittered in her lashes.

"Sara." Kyle waited until she looked directly at him. "It's not broken. Computers get glitches. Sometimes they refuse to do something. Stop worrying. We'll figure it out."

"Okay." A flicker of relief lightened her gray eyes.

"Now, can you tell me what you were doing?" he asked. "Do you remember?"

"I was looking at—do you call it a page?" She waited for his nod. "Rod said if something was underlined it meant there was more information. So I clicked on a word. A bunch of things started flashing on the screen. I couldn't stop them no matter how often I clicked on the back arrow." She turned to Rod. "I remembered you told me that's how I should get back to where I was. It didn't work. I touched a key and everything went black."

Rod nodded. His gaze met Kyle's.

"You thinking what I'm thinking?" Kyle asked.

"A virus. But how did it get around the protection?" Rod frowned.

"What's a virus?" Sara asked.

Rod explained while Kyle worked. But no matter what he tried the computer did not respond.

"Maybe this machine's a dud," Rod mused.

"Let's open it up." With Rod's help, Kyle removed the back. He was too conscious of Sara watching every move, her soft lemon scent filling his nostrils. Maybe that was why he missed the most obvious solution.

"Look." Rod pointed to the loose cord connection.

"I don't understand how that happened. Or why it suddenly became an issue." Kyle reset the component and pressed the power button. The computer immediately hummed to life. Once the normal screen was visible, Kyle ran a diagnostics test. Everything seemed to be fine. "Now you try using the internet," he said to Sara. He rose from his seat.

Sara backed away. "I'll ruin it," she said.

"It wasn't anything you did. It was a loose connection. That's fixed now." He smiled at her. "Go ahead and try it."

"Do you mind if I leave?" Rod asked. "I want to see the movie."

"Yes, go, Rod. Please. You've spent enough time on me." Sara grimaced.

"Go, Rod. I'll teach her." Kyle knew he was doing what he'd told himself not to do. He was getting involved. But Rod said Sara wanted to find her family. He couldn't walk away from that. "Okay. Tell me what you want to know."

"It's silly." She avoided his gaze.

"Nothing's silly. The internet is loaded with information. Let's find what you need."

"I want to find my family," she said after studying him for a minute.

"Okay, then." Kyle pulled up a chair beside her, trying to ignore the soft feelings her look of gratitude caused. He couldn't ignore her beauty so easily and got caught up in the stare from her lovely silver-gray eyes.

Time lapsed until Kyle realized his thoughts had strayed to her full pink lips, imagining what kissing them would be like. He coughed, straightened and forced himself to focus. "Let's start with a search on last names. Go ahead."

Each time she tried to give up, he refused to let her. Gently, tenderly he repeated the steps that would lead her to find what she wanted. He returned her grin when at last her search returned results. "See? You can do it."

"With your help. Thank you for being so patient." Her smile blazed away his shadows.

Kyle basked in that smile for a few minutes before he got his senses under control by reminding himself of his intent. He was leaving Churchill. He was going to find a place where he could do something he loved. The fact that he had no idea exactly what that something might be nagged at him. But Kyle ignored it, just as he ignored the flutter of awareness that rushed through him when Sara hit the wrong keys and, to redirect her, he covered her hand with his without thinking about what he was doing.

"There's not much here," she said, obviously disappointed.

"Now we have to go a step deeper," he told her, hating that sad tone in her usually musical voice. "Can you add anything to the information you've already given?"

"My mother's name is Sophia," she said, apparently unaware of the effect she had on him.

The lemon scent of her hair, the softness of her skin when her hand brushed his, the little gasps she made when something new filled the screen all contributed to breaking his concentration.

"Should I type in her whole name?"

"Can't hurt to try." He waited while she did. "That's what searching the web is about, Sara. Keep putting in information, asking questions. Eventually you'll find something that will lead you to the next step."

"Yes, I see." She gazed at him. "Thank you, Kyle."

That sweet smile, those incredible eyes—Kyle suddenly knew that it wasn't going to be easy to remain uninvolved.

Sara Kane was a very lovable woman.

But he'd met lovable before and it had let him down. He'd learned that lesson and faced the shame of it. No way was he going to repeat the experience.

Don't get involved, he told himself.

You already are, his brain mocked.

He ignored that little voice and concentrated on showing Sara everything she needed to know.

"I did it, Laurel." Sara felt like crowing with triumph. She slid the last pan of apple strudel in the oven.

"Hmm? Did what?" Laurel blinked at her as if she hadn't heard a word.

"You're tired. You should have slept in," Sara told her. "Teddy said that's what Saturdays are for."

"Maybe Teddy can afford to sleep in. He doesn't

have this place to run. Not that he wouldn't like to," she added in a cranky voice. "He's always trying to boss me around." Laurel's forehead creased in a frown.

"Really?" Sara frowned. "I didn't notice that. Well, he's being helpful. What's wrong between you two, anyway?"

"He tried to stop Lives," Laurel said, her face tightening. "He talked to town council about it without consulting me first." She shook her head. "Whenever I look at him I remember that and the gossip his interference caused. It makes me furious."

"Well, I think he's over that. He's a nice man and he's trying to help us. So is Kyle." Sara blushed at Laurel's searching glance. "Last night he helped me search for my mother online. I even learned how to send an email," she said, proud of her accomplishments.

"Good for you. You got a response to that letter you sent about your mom. Wasn't that helpful?"

"Not really. They said the records are sealed unless I get her permission. But how can I get her permission if I can't find her?" Sara shook her head. "It's very frustrating."

"I'm sure it is. But don't give up. Maybe with Kyle's help, you'll find her or your father." Laurel yawned again. "I'm going to work outside today. Teddy told me all that scrap metal someone left behind can be sold. We could use the money."

"I've been thinking." Sara paused, unsure about offering her opinion.

"About what?" Laurel said. "You're a part of Lives, Sara. I appreciate your input."

"Well, I was wondering if we should have an open house. To show people in Churchill what we're about." She hesitated then explained. "When I was coming back from the greenhouse the other day, I heard some women talking. They think the kids are dangerous. Maybe if they saw what Lives looks like, they'd feel more at ease, even offer to help us occasionally."

"If people think that, it's Teddy Stonechild's fault." Laurel's tone was blistering. "He fostered so many rumors about this place, I had to keep reassuring them to get them to even consider allowing me to open. I suppose he's complaining about my management again."

"I doubt that, but it doesn't matter, Laurel. What matters is how we get the town's support." Sara thought for a moment. "We could do it next Saturday, offer coffee and stuff that I'd bake. Nobody could take offense if they're sitting around chatting."

Laurel was silent.

"It was just an idea. You probably have something else in mind." Sara shrugged.

"It's brilliant. You are a genius." Laurel hugged her so tightly she squeezed out Sara's breath. "Can you make enough pies?"

"Why pies?" Sara asked.

"Because the men will come for sure if there are pies." She chuckled then sobered. "But will this interfere in your work in the greenhouse? I know that's important to you."

"Rod and I have planted a few seeds," Sara explained. "But we're waiting until it warms up a bit. Kyle's mom wrote the best planting time is the first week of June."

Laurel gave her a speculative look. "You're fond of Kyle, aren't you?"

"I like him. Is that what you mean?" At Laurel's silence, Sara looked up from her work.

"Actually I was wondering if you and he were romantically attracted to each other."

Sara stared at her. Then she began to laugh.

"What's so funny?" Laurel demanded. "Women are attracted to men, you know."

"It's funny because no one would be attracted to me." Sara rolled her eyes. "I don't know anything about men, but I would think they'd be attracted to girls who know things, who understand and enjoy the same things they do."

"Sweetie, you are beautiful and smart. And you know plenty of things, which is why you run this place as well as you do."

"That's nice of you to say." Sara tucked away the compliment.

"I'm not being nice," Laurel said firmly. "I'm being truthful. In my experience, men like women who enjoy life. That's you, Sara. You enjoy everything."

"Cooking for those you love—what's not to like?" Sara asked in all seriousness, surprised when Laurel exploded with laughter. "Anyway, you're wrong about Kyle. He isn't attracted to me. He's not even going to stay in Churchill. He's going to sell his home."

"Really?" Laurel asked.

"Yes." Sadness filled Sara. "He doesn't think he can stay here and still have a full life. I wish he'd see all the things he can do instead of all the things he can't."

"Maybe you can show him."

"I'd like to," Sara said, studying her friend. "But how?"

"I don't know. Maybe if you got him to try some of the things he used to love."

"That's too big a step right now," Sara said, certain

that Kyle wouldn't even consider it. "But maybe if I could get him talking—" She fell into thought.

"You're planning something, aren't you?" Laurel smiled. "I know that look."

"I'm planning to have guests tomorrow. A Sunday lunch after church, like roast beef and mashed potatoes. And pie," she added with a twinkle. "Perhaps lemon?"

Laurel smiled. "And who are we inviting to this meal? Lucy and Hector?"

"Of course." Sara smiled. "After all their help, that would be natural. And Teddy, of course."

"Oh, why him?" Laurel's face lost its mirth.

"You can hardly deny he's been a great help to us," Sara reasoned. "Just removing that pile of junk makes Lives look so much better. You said it yourself—we'll take all the help we can get."

"But that's not the reason, is it?"

"Of course not." Sara spared a moment to imagine her friend with someone special in her life.

"You're not—" Laurel hesitated. "You're not trying to matchmake, are you? Because I am in no way interested in Teddy Stonechild."

"I wouldn't dream of playing matchmaker." Sara covered her burning cheeks with her hands. "I don't know anything about that," she admitted.

"Then…" Laurel raised one eyebrow.

"My thought is that if we could all get together over a meal, perhaps the boys would ask some questions of Kyle and he would tell us what it was like to be raised here."

"Sounds reasonable," Laurel agreed. "But what's the point?"

"If Kyle could speak about the past, share his best

memories of living here," Sara said, "maybe it would spark some desire to stay here."

"Why does it matter to you so much, sweetie?" Laurel's lips curved in a smile.

"Because he doesn't have anywhere to go," Sara burst out. "Kyle's running away from here and from his anger at God over his father's death. But he doesn't know where to go and he doesn't realize that life won't be any easier for him away from Churchill. When he sells his house he'll have nothing left of his past or his family. I don't want him to give that up without counting the cost."

Laurel whistled.

"What?" Sara asked.

"I'm amazed by your ability to see the hurt in people's hearts." Laurel hugged her close. "I've known psychiatrists who couldn't have diagnosed Kyle's hurt as well as you."

"I just don't want Kyle to keep blaming God," Sara said, embarrassed by the praise.

"As I said, a very clever woman." Laurel let her go. "Sunday lunch is what we'll have. And next Saturday is going to be the grand opening at Lives Under Construction. Tomorrow we'll ask our friends to help us put on a day like Churchill hasn't seen for a long time. We'll invite anyone who wants to come."

"Do you think Kyle will come?" Sara asked anxiously.

"I think you'll probably have to persuade him," Laurel answered honestly.

"Then that's what I'll do. But I'll pray for help." Sara couldn't keep the smile she felt inside from showing.

Feeling positive about her plans, Sara decided to try her hand at another internet search. She logged in as Kyle had shown her then typed in her mother's name and a bunch of—what did he call them?—hits, a bunch of hits appeared.

"Please help me find her," she prayed. But an hour later, she was no further ahead. She clicked off the screen. Maybe tomorrow she'd ask Kyle if there was a way to narrow the search even more.

It occurred to Sara then that she was running to Kyle with a lot of her problems. But that was only temporary. She'd soon learn how to search on her own.

In the meantime, she was going to use every interaction with him that she could to try to get him to rethink his anger at God and his future. After all, she was concerned about him and his insistence on self-reliance. She felt he used it to isolate himself. He needed her help.

Really?

Or was it that she needed to help him to satisfy the longing in her heart to see him whole, healed and fully engaged in life.

And then he'll leave, her head reminded her. A pang of loss shot through her but Sara focused on something else, something that chewed at her.

Why did helping Kyle matter so much?

In the silence of the kitchen Sara searched her heart. She couldn't help but acknowledge that helping Kyle eased that longing in her heart to be special to someone.

It wasn't only friendship she felt for Kyle. But what exactly was it?

Chapter Seven

"So that's what we're planning." Sara cupped her mug of hot chocolate, head tilted to one side as she waited for his response.

"A grand opening, huh?" Kyle finished filling the little peat pots lined up on the greenhouse shelf. Then he picked up his own mug. Sara followed him outside to the two chairs he'd placed in a patch of sun beside the house. The warmth told him summer was definitely on the way.

"Well?" she prodded.

"A grand opening is a good idea," he admitted. Funny how he'd learned to discern the nuances in Sara's voice; she sounded nervous.

"God is blessing us at Lives. We want the community to share that. So would you like to take part in our opening?" Sara asked.

Blessing? God was blessing Lives? Given that Kyle had witnessed a major plumbing issue while he was enjoying Sunday lunch today, he was of the opinion that God had messed up in the blessings department. But he wasn't about to argue with Sara. He was weary of hearing her harp on the subject of God's goodness.

"Why me? I don't have anything to do with Lives."

"You've had a great deal to do with it, and you're welcome to have more." Her smile teased him. "As much as you want."

"Sara, I'm happy for you to use the greenhouse and I'm glad if the computers are of some help and I was happy to talk about my experiences living here with the kids the other day at lunch. I hope it helped them."

"I think it did," she said, eyes shining. "The way you talk about tracking animals, going on expeditions, even watching the polar bears and their cubs, that was amazing. I think we all felt like we were right there with you."

"That's nice," he said, feeling trapped. "Thank you for saying that. But I've got to get ready to move." She was getting too close. That intense silver-gray scrutiny of hers saw too much and that made Kyle antsy. "I have a lot to sort through."

"I can help you," she offered.

A heartfelt no almost spilled from Kyle's lips, but he didn't say it. It would seem as though he was throwing her generosity back in her face, and he couldn't bring himself to do that. Yet he desperately wanted Sara to understand he could manage alone.

"Where would you start?"

"I don't know." Kyle weighed the negatives of letting her help. She'd be in his space again. And she'd leave her mark there. Even out here, in the fresh air, he was still inundated with that lemon scent of her hair.

He ignored the voice in his head telling him to reject her offer.

"In the living room?" he suggested.

"Okay." She drained her mug then jumped up, obviously excited. "I've got two hours before I have to get back. We can get a lot accomplished in that time."

"Sure." Kyle led the way inside, certain he'd lost his mind in agreeing to let her help. "Where would you like to start?" Sara asked, her lips tipped up in an eager smile.

Kyle glanced around the room, which bulged with the paraphernalia of his father's life, and again felt grief's familiar weight.

"Let's start with the magazines," Sara suggested.

He checked to see if she sensed he was about to recant. But as usual, Sara was focused on the job to be done. Again his curiosity about her past bubbled up. What made her so driven? He was going to ask but Sara was all business.

"The hospital would love these magazines for their waiting room. We'll throw out the oldest ones."

"I'll do that." Kyle could deal with magazines and newspapers, even if they were of the hunting and fishing variety, which his father had loved.

"Okay. I'll collect all the knickknacks so you can decide which to keep." Sara placed the objects on the square glass coffee table where Kyle had colored as a child, humming as she worked.

Kyle knew the song. *This is the day that the Lord hath made*. It was from Psalms.

"Your father must have loved animals." She held up the intricate carving of a walrus in her palm. "This is exquisite."

"When I was a kid, a chief of a Native tribe gave it as a gift after Dad rescued his daughter."

Kyle was surprised when she recognized the artist.

"I saw his work in a Vancouver gallery," Sara explained. She gazed at him in that starry-eyed fashion of hers. "He's one of Canada's foremost sculptors. You were so blessed to live here, Kyle."

Blessed? As a kid, maybe. Not so much now, he thought.

"I think God puts us where we can learn so that when we are in hard places, we have something to fall back on. Don't you?"

Kyle pinched his lips together as he loaded the last of the magazines into a box.

"I love to hear Lucy's missionary stories." Sara dusted each item and the crevice where it had lived. "Her stories remind me over and over that God is always with us."

Kyle couldn't stop the rush of words that tumbled out. "I don't believe that."

"I guess it's hard to believe when things seem really bad." The cloud in her eyes dimmed Sara's joy, but just for a moment. The shadows disappeared as quickly as they'd come. "But it's true. The Bible tells us that."

"And you believe everything the Bible says?" he demanded.

"Don't you?" a wide-eyed Sara asked.

"Not anymore." Kyle grunted when his shin bumped into one of the three recliners in the room. "This should have been trashed long ago."

"I guess your dad loved it." Sara hummed "Heavenly Sunshine" now.

"My mom used to sit in this old chair," he mused to himself. "She loved to knit here, in front of the window."

"Then there's your answer," Sara said. "The chair probably helped your dad remember the good times with her. Sometimes God uses memories to comfort us."

"Sara, stop!" Kyle yelled. Her response infuriated him. "Stop telling me how good God is, how wonderful God is, how much He cares for us. I don't want to hear it."

She looked as if he'd slapped her. Tears welled in her amazing eyes. She made no attempt to rub them away. "I'm s-sorry, Kyle," she stammered.

"So am I. But I can't take it anymore." He moderated his voice but wouldn't back down. "I can't hear about God's goodness while I'm emptying out this house my father loved."

"Kyle—" She reached out a hand.

"No." He jerked away from her and almost lost his balance, which made him even angrier. "You believe anything you want, but you can't convince me that God did the right thing by letting my dad die. Don't even try."

Sara turned away and pretended to clean another shelf, but he knew by her sniffing that she was weeping.

The next few minutes seemed like hours. Sara worked but not with the joy she'd shown before. Before she'd seemed tough, resilient and strong enough to weather anything, but she didn't look strong now. She looked beaten.

He'd done that to her.

That was when it dawned on Kyle that Sara's gutsy exterior hid a deep vulnerability. Why was that? What in the past had hurt her?

He had a hunch it had to do with her foster-care years and made a vow to find out, but not now. He'd hurt her now.

If you hurt someone, Kyle, you have to make it right. His father's voice shamed him.

"Sara, I'm sorry," he said, trying to coax her to face him. "I wasn't trying to hurt you or demean your faith."

He swallowed the lump in his throat. "It's just—I'm not where you are right now. I don't know if I ever will be again. I feel betrayed."

"God doesn't betray us, Kyle. Not ever." She moved to the side table where his father's Bible lay open. She fingered the pages for a few moments. When she finally spoke she said, "God is good. He cannot be otherwise. From what I've heard of your father, I believe he knew that. I also believe he is at peace with God. All his questions have been answered."

"Well, mine haven't," Kyle snapped back.

"God is ready and willing to listen to your questions, Kyle." She lifted her head to study him. "All you have to do is ask them." She touched his arm with the very tips of her fingers and then got back to work.

As Kyle watched her, a new thought crept into his brain. What would it be like to have Sara nearby to confide in? How would it feel to know she was there for him all the time?

Kyle immediately rejected that. He'd resolved not to allow any involvement in his life. He wasn't going to be staying in Churchill, anyway.

But even if he did, what would Sara get out of a relationship with him?

The answer hit hard—a life with a cripple.

Kyle was older than Sara, but it was the kind of age that came from much more than just years. Besides, he had a hunch she was running from something herself.

In that moment Kyle realized that maybe *he* could help *her*. He'd been selfish, self-involved and thinking only of himself. He'd willingly accepted every time she offered help, but what had he given back to her?

"I have to go now, Kyle. But I was wondering…"

Sara bit her bottom lip in hesitation. Then, before his eyes, her resolve moved in. "Will you take part in our grand opening ceremonies?"

"Just a small part," he finally agreed. He owed her that at least, for making her weep.

"Great!" She threw her arms around him and hugged him, then quickly pulled away, almost costing him his balance. Her sunny smile sent a shaft of warmth straight to his heart. "See you tomorrow."

Kyle said goodbye to her, but it was long after Sara Kane had left his house. Half-bemused by the rush of yearning she'd left behind, he slowly boxed up the trinkets she'd laid across the table, keeping only three that were precious to him. He hauled the magazines to the trash and put the newer ones on the back step. He'd ask Teddy to take those to the hospital, as Sara had suggested.

But even an hour later, the question foremost on Kyle's mind just wouldn't go away.

Who is Sara Kane?

He could have found a way to ask her, but it seemed intrusive. Besides, he didn't want to know more about this disturbing woman. She was in his thoughts enough without adding to it. Besides, what if it included a man who'd hurt her? How could he respond to that? Or what if he did ask her and she mistook his question? What if she thought—well, the wrong thing. Like he was interested in her or something.

Aren't you?

Kyle's brain swirled with a thousand reasons why it would be a bad idea to ask Sara about her past. And for every reason the question hung in his brain, his need to know grew.

Who was Sara Kane?

Ignoring the work he'd hoped to do before the real-estate agent's visit on Tuesday, Kyle finally sat down at his dad's desk and booted up his laptop. The cursor blinked at him, waiting. His little finger hovered over the enter key. One click, that was all it would take to find out more about her. One click.

Sara's expressions—happy, sad, excited, worried, troubled—all of them passed through Kyle's mind. Sara, who worked so hard to make others happy. Sara, who always tiptoed lightly around others' feelings. How had she become that way?

Kyle wasn't aware of the passage of time until suddenly, as the moody shadows of the evening filled the room, he knew he couldn't do it. He couldn't pry into her past. Not yet.

He'd win her trust and learn her story the old-fashioned way: by talking to her himself. Lives' grand opening offered the perfect opportunity.

"I can't believe I agreed to cut the ribbon."

Kyle studied the throngs of people who'd shown up for the grand opening of Lives Under Construction.

"The persuasion of a woman is a powerful thing," Teddy agreed. "Especially if that woman has an innocent, vulnerable look like our Sara."

"Our Sara?" Kyle frowned.

"Haven't you noticed?" Teddy asked. "The whole town's adopted her. You're not the only one who cares about her."

Kyle took a second look at his friend's face. Something unspoken lingered under those words, some hint that suggested there was more to his appearance here today than a simple favor.

"I do care about her—as her friend."

"Did I say differently?" Teddy smiled the smug grin Kyle hated.

"No. You implied it." He glared at the big man. "You think I'm doing this because I've got some kind of a crush on Sara Kane?"

"There's that chip on your shoulder again." With a look that said he'd been maligned, Teddy moved to greet one of the town's council members.

Kyle knew Teddy was hinting that he was getting involved.

"You look good," Sara said as her eyes scanned him, taking in every detail. "I'm sure you look amazing in your uniform, too." Surely she hadn't overheard his conversation with Teddy.

"It's—uh, at the cleaners." *Stupid.* There was no dry cleaner's in Churchill. He licked his lips and swallowed nervously.

"Do all these people bother you?" She patted his arm, her sunny smile warming him. "Don't worry. Once we get started it won't take a minute for the mayor to declare Lives is officially open. Then you can disappear if you want."

"Sure." Kyle didn't explain his worry that the mayor would make some reference to him being a veteran and draw attention to his damaged leg. "It's a pretty good turnout."

"Curiosity is a powerful motivator," she murmured, again revealing her insightful nature. "I only hope I have enough food."

"Are you kidding?" Kyle had seen the long tables with their pristine white cloths and the trays of edibles. "You've got enough to feed an army."

"Thank you, Kyle." Her smile flashed as she touched his arm again. "You always know how to cheer me up."

"Any news about your mom?" He asked mostly to get his focus off the tingle of her touch. When the joy leeched from her face, he wished he'd kept his mouth shut.

"No. I haven't been able to find anything." The glow in her silver-gray eyes dimmed. "I don't know what else to try."

"Maybe when this is over, we could take another stab at it," he offered. Then he wondered why he'd made the gesture. He didn't want to get more involved in Sara's life. He'd deliberately stayed away from Lives this past week as much as possible for just that reason.

But the sadness on her face made him want to help.

"Are you sure you wouldn't mind, Kyle?" The sparkle returned to her eyes, picking up the glints of silver in the scarf she wore knotted at her neck. Her voice was full of hope. "Really?"

"I wouldn't mind," he told her, mesmerized by her gorgeous smile.

"Thank you."

"Sara, I have to ask. What happens if you can't find your mother?"

"Then I look for my father." She fixed him with her gaze. "I have to find my family, Kyle. It doesn't matter where they are or what happened to them, or why they left me. I have to find them."

"Good for you." He saw Laurel marshaling the various dignitaries to get them on the little platform. Kyle had to get up there before things started. He wasn't about to let the entire town see the gimp stumble, or even worse, trip. "I'll talk to you later," he said.

"You will." Sara's eyes held his for a moment before he drew away.

Because she was watching, Kyle forced himself to walk without the limp that usually accompanied his steps. He made it to the platform and negotiated his way onto it without mishap. Jubilant, he stood exactly where Laurel told him to and faced the crowd. Thankfully her speech was short.

"I'm delighted to welcome you here today. Our children are our future. But how can they build that future unless they learn to reject the violence that is so pervasive in our world? Our goal at Lives Under Construction is to show those who come here that there is a better way, a way that they will find if we stand beside them, guiding them, showing them love for themselves and for others. Thank you."

The mayor then stepped forward and gave his short speech with no mention of Kyle, to his relief. Then the president of the chamber of commerce announced, "I hereby declare that Lives Under Construction is officially open."

On cue, Kyle stepped forward and snipped the ribbon held by the dignitaries. A burst of clapping ensued.

"Please join us in celebrating our grand opening," Laurel said, indicating the tables of tea, coffee and punch, which the boys manned.

People began chatting with their neighbors. Laurel thanked Kyle for his help then hurried away to make sure her students were doing their jobs properly.

"Good work, Kyle," Sara said, grinning. "You could be a professional ribbon cutter."

"Yeah," he said, wondering if that was all he was good for now. Caught in his thoughts, he stepped off the platform onto a bit of spongy rock moss he'd specifically avoided earlier. His knee buckled and in a flash, Kyle was flat on his backside with the whole world watching.

Furious with himself, he struggled to rise but his prosthesis inhibited his movements.

Without a word, Sara slid her arm under his shoulder and around his back. "Lean on me, Kyle," she murmured.

Pain radiated through his hip and down to his stump. He could hardly breathe for the agonizing spears that shot through his body. Somehow Sara managed to get him upright. He felt rather than saw her motion with her hand. A moment later three of the boys clustered around him, shielding him from the onlookers.

Then Kyle heard shy, quiet Rod say in a loud voice meant to carry, "There's pie, lots of it. Lemon and apple and chocolate."

The crowd shifted like a school of fish, their interest in Kyle forgotten.

"Inside," Sara said to the boys. "Let's use the side entrance. It's closer and we don't have to go through the crowd."

"I'm going home," Kyle argued, furious at his weakness. "Get Teddy."

"Teddy's holding court, creating a diversion. Use it," Sara ordered. Her implacable expression brooked no discussion. "Use us to walk, Kyle."

"Wonderful idea," he puffed, trying to spare her his weight and unable to do even that. "Wish I could do it. But thanks to God, I can't even walk anymore."

Sara glanced at him but said nothing more until he was inside and seated on a chair in the computer room. She got his leg straightened and resting on a stool, then sent the boys back outside, except for Tony, their newest arrival, who'd flown in just yesterday. She ordered him to bring ice and a towel. When he'd left and the two of them were alone, Sara clamped her hands on her hips and glared at him.

"You blame everything on God, don't you, Kyle?" He'd never heard her voice so harsh.

"He could have—"

She didn't let him finish.

"Yes, yes. God could have kept your father alive, He could have saved you from losing your leg and He could have kept my family together." Sara bent, placed her hands on the arms of the chair Kyle was sitting in and leaned forward until her face was within inches of his. "But He didn't."

"Exactly." He leaned back, thinking he'd proven his point.

But Sara was just getting started.

"So what are you going to do now?" she demanded. "Spend the rest of your life blaming Him?"

"I don't have any rest of my life," Kyle snarled. "My life is over."

"Really?" Her fingers slid around his wrist. "There's still a pulse."

"My life is over, Sara," he repeated. "Why can't you accept that?"

"Because it isn't true." She drew another chair forward and sat in it, facing him but farther away, for which Kyle was thankful. Her nearness, as usual, did odd things to his heartbeat. "I'll accept that your life *as you knew it* is over. Now it's time to reinvent yourself."

"As what? A cripple who can't even stand up in public? As the guy everyone feels sorry for? Embarrass myself like that again?" He clenched his jaw and shook his head. "Sorry, can't do that. Won't do that."

"That isn't what I meant and you know it. But a little embarrassment isn't the worst thing that could happen to you." She took the ice and towel Tony brought, made a pack and placed it on the exact spot where the pain was the greatest.

As the chill penetrated the pain, Kyle wondered how she knew exactly where to put the ice pack.

"I've got to get back out there," she said. "Laurel is counting on me to keep the food coming. Can we talk about this later?"

"I doubt it." He tried not to show how much pain he was in. "If I ever imagined, even for a minute, that I could be a contributor to this community, that dream was smashed out there. I can't even stand up."

"We all trip at some time in our lives. Maybe you should let yourself lean on us while you try harder." Sara's amazing eyes held him in their grip for several moments. Then she rose, smoothed her plain black skirt and straightened her shoulders. "Stay here. Tony will get you whatever you need. I'll see you later."

Furious at her intimation that he'd given up too easily, Kyle waited until she was almost out the door before he spoke again.

"You want me to start over, Sara? Well, I'm going to do exactly that. Just as soon as I sell the house."

Sara paused for one infinitesimal moment then kept walking.

Anger seared through him. Why couldn't she understand? Why couldn't anyone understand what he'd lost?

"Help me get out of here," he said to Tony, but the boy shook his head.

"I haven't been here long but I know one thing. Sara says you stay then you stay," he said. "Want to play checkers?"

Kyle wanted to explode at him. But what good would that do? He shook his head.

Tony watched him for a moment then sat across from him. "Can I ask you something?"

"I suppose." Why had he ever agreed to come here today?

"At school they told us there are polar bears around here." Tony studied him. "Did you ever see one?"

"Sure." Kyle shrugged. "My dad and I used to take tourists to see them. The ice is pretty much gone from the bay now, so most of the bears are gone, too. I don't think you have to worry about running into one."

"I'm not worried. I'd like to run into one. I want to know what they're like."

Kyle frowned. "Why?" he demanded.

"My grandmother was Inuit. She's gone now, but she used to tell us stories about Mother Bear. I wish I'd listened better." Tony's expression was filled with sorrow. "I thought I hated being part Inuit but it's like hating a part of myself. You know?"

"Yeah, I know." He adjusted his ice pack. "My dad knew a lot of the old stories."

"Can you tell me some of them?" Tony begged.

Seeing the keen interest on the boy's face, Kyle launched into the first story that came to mind. As he began, he was besieged by memories of the intonation of his father's voice. But then the power his father had infused into the story took over and he strove to do justice to the moral of the tale.

For the first time in months, some of the joy Kyle

had felt before he'd left home for Afghanistan surged back, and he tried to share that with Tony.

But when Tony had to go, Kyle was left in the room on his own. And the self-doubts assailed him. Was that all he was good for now, storytelling?

It wasn't enough. With a pang of frustration he realized this afternoon had served one good purpose. It had shown him more clearly than ever before that he was fooling himself to cling to Sara's assurance that he could resurrect some kind of life in this place.

By listening to her, he'd clung to hope like a crutch. But today the crutch had been wrenched away when he'd embarrassed himself by showing the entire town that he could no longer even stand on his own. Surely Sara would have to admit that. There was no way he could forge a future here.

Look at me. I was totally dependent on Sara to get me out of there. Now I have to wait for Teddy to get me home.

"No," he said out loud. "I will not live like that, dependent on others, no matter what anyone says, not even Sara."

But as he said it, Kyle suddenly realized the gap there would be in his life, a gap only Sara could fill.

And that scared him more than anything the military had put him through.

Chapter Eight

"I can't thank you all enough," Laurel said as she scanned each firelit face. "Without you, I don't know if we could have done it."

"To Laurel and her very successful grand opening," Sara said, lifting her glass of punch. She leaned over and clinked the rim against Kyle's. "Today was a total success."

"Hear, hear," Teddy said. "I don't know how you came up with the idea, but it was a great one."

"Sara might not think so tomorrow," Laurel said, brushing aside his compliment. "That crowd almost ate us out of house and home."

"Close." Sara chuckled as a rush of pride filled her. "There are only four tarts, two pieces of fudge and three pieces of pie left over."

"Anyone like another hot dog before we move on to what's left of dessert?" Teddy asked. When the others groaned and patted their stomachs, he grinned. "I guess I'll just have to eat this one myself then," he said.

"I love campfires," Tony said. "Kyle knows lots of

good stories. We could make them into campfire stories."

"What makes a campfire story?" Sara felt a rush of heat rise up her neck to her face as boys and adults alike turned to stare at her. Determined not to show how embarrassed she was that she couldn't share such a simple thing, she shrugged. "I lived in the city. We never had campfires."

"I don't suppose a lot of city kids do get to sit around a fire anymore," Kyle said thoughtfully. "I suppose you'll count this fire as another of those blessings you're always talking about."

"Depends on your story," she shot back with a wink. Immediately she felt self-conscious. Was it being too familiar to wink at a man?

But Kyle only grinned at her, so she relaxed.

After hearing Tony extoll Kyle's virtues as a storyteller, everyone was eager to hear him tell more about the North, this place they now called home.

Good, Sara thought. *That's exactly what I want. If Kyle can dig up happy memories of the past, maybe he'll finally let go of some of his sorrow.*

"What kind of story are you going to tell us, Kyle?" she asked.

"Me?" Kyle glared at her. "Why not Teddy?"

"I'm not a true northerner," Teddy protested. "I'm just a visitor who loves this place and keeps coming back. You have more experiences in your little finger than I'll ever know. Why not share some?"

"About what?" Kyle frowned.

"About polar bears," Sara said before anyone else could suggest a topic. "Lucy told me one was hauled off to polar bear jail yesterday, though I'm not sure exactly what that is. Can you tell us, Kyle?"

The other boys chimed in on the question. Everyone looked toward Kyle for an explanation. He turned his head to shoot Sara a look she interpreted to mean he'd have preferred to remain silent. Eventually he gave a resigned sigh and explained.

"The jail is a building in a compound on the outskirts of the town. It's divided into cells in which they put bears who have roamed too close to town." Kyle stopped as if he'd finished explaining, but the boys wouldn't let him get away with such a meager explanation.

"Come on, Kyle," Tony said.

"Yeah, tell us more than that," another insisted.

"Guess we won't have to worry about a visit from a bear tonight," Kyle said with a grin. "It's too noisy. All right." He held up his hands. "It's a specially designed jail. The goal is to keep the bears isolated from human contact and reintroduce them back into the wild, but away from Churchill. The wildlife service doesn't want to hurt them, but it does want to protect both those who live here and the bears that pass through and use the Hudson Bay to migrate."

"Migrate to where?" Rod seemed totally enthralled.

"You want their migration schedule? This is going to take a while," Kyle muttered.

"We're not going anywhere," one of the boys said. Then he grinned. "Because there's nowhere to go."

Sara hid her smile as the boys burst into laughter at the joke. She was delighted the kids weren't allowing Kyle to stop. She fell under the spell of his words when he related the bear's phases from the birth of a cub to its journey to adulthood.

She could listen to him forever.

By the time Kyle finished, Sara was certain each boy would soon be on the internet, searching for more information on polar bears. She had a hunch they would have tried tonight but Laurel insisted it was too late and they'd have to wait till tomorrow.

The newly informed boys willingly lugged dishes and carefully stored their refuse, conscious now that they must not leave anything that would attract wildlife. They now wanted to be part of the bears' protection. Sara whispered a prayer of thanksgiving as she loaded the dishwasher and cleaned the counters.

She startled when she noticed Kyle standing in the shadows and automatically checked his eyes to gauge whether he was in pain. But his expression was closed and she couldn't tell. So she asked, "Anything wrong?"

"Nothing except that I can't leave. Teddy's in Laurel's office showing her some computer accounting program he brought her, so I can't go home yet."

"At least they're not arguing about something. That seems like progress, don't you think?"

He shared her smile. "Maybe a little. But I need to get home."

"Why?" She chuckled. He was so easy to talk to, and so much fun to tease. "You don't have a curfew, do you?"

"No." A glimmer of a smile tugged at his lips. He leaned one hip against the chair rail that projected halfway up the wall.

Sara couldn't help admiring him. He was so handsome, so…in control.

"I'd planned to help Rod with graphics for his web page this evening, but I guess that will have to wait for another day." He studied her. "How's the search for your mom going?"

After a moment, Sara said, "I did find something I wanted to ask you about."

She'd debated whether to bother Kyle again. Not that her questions seemed to irritate him. He'd been patient and understanding. But after that confrontation in his living room, Sara felt she was taking too much of his time.

"Well, I'm here now." He waited. "Go ahead and ask."

"It would be easier to explain if I showed you. Would you mind taking a look?"

There was a trace of hesitation before he said, "Sure."

"Thanks. I appreciate it." Sara led the way to the computer room, glad that the boys weren't there. She needed for this to be private.

Once the computer had booted up, she clicked on the site she'd previously saved. "I'm not sure what this message means."

"It's just someone trying to sell something. It's nothing." His hand covered hers on the mouse as he clicked it. Sara gasped at the contact, hoping he didn't notice how flustered she was. A new page was now visible.

Kyle leaned over her shoulder to read the screen. He caught his breath. "Sara, this is from eight years ago. Maybe you shouldn't—"

"What?" She turned her head. His face was mere inches from hers and her heart raced.

"Nothing." His face closed up.

"It's about a tornado in Ontario," she said, turning back to read the screen. "My mother's name led me here so there must be something about her, but it keeps changing so I can't get where I want to go. See?"

"Let me sit there for a minute, would you?"

Sara traded places with Kyle, admiring the way his capable hands flew over the keys while she waited. Part of her wanted to read whatever it had to say about her mother, but another part, a part she kept pushing away, was afraid to read it.

She'd told herself she'd been too busy getting ready for the grand opening, that she hadn't had the time or energy to get back on this site. But her need to find her mother outweighed that tiny fear crouched deep inside. Maybe her mother had moved to Ontario. Maybe there was information about her new address. Maybe she'd finally find her mother and the rest of her family.

Hope built fast and furious until her brain urged *Hurry. Hurry. Hurry, Kyle.*

"Okay." Kyle rose and stepped to one side, his voice devoid of all emotion. "Click on it again," he told her.

"But what if—"

"Are you afraid to see what's there?" he demanded.

"Yes. A little," she admitted. "But I still want to know." She frowned at him. "I want to know the truth, whatever it is."

"Then click on it," Kyle ordered.

Not understanding why he sounded so harsh, Sara clicked the mouse and watched the page refresh.

"I don't see my mother's name or anything about her on here," she said. "In fact, this isn't quite the same. It looks like some kind of newspaper article now."

"It is. The *Scarborough Tribune*. Scroll down. You may find something near the bottom." Again he sounded angry and she didn't know why.

After a sideways glance at his face, Sara could feel tension grip Kyle's body. She saw his fist clench against his thigh as if to prepare for something. She wanted to ask him what was wrong but didn't. It had been a long day. Maybe his leg hurt?

"What are you waiting for, Sara?"

"Oh, sorry. I'm holding you up, aren't I?" She scrolled down, scanning paragraphs for the name she wanted. At the bottom of the page she saw it. Eagerly she read the information under the heading "Twister."

And stopped.

"Oh, please, God, no." Her breath snagged in her throat. Her heart beat like a lead mallet in her chest. Hot tears rolled down her face and Sara was utterly powerless to stop them.

Among the dead was a forty-nine-year-old woman, Sophia Kane, believed to be traveling through the area when the tornado struck. Next of kin have yet to be notified.

"Sara." Kyle's fingers closed around her shoulders, turning her face away from the computer screen so she could see only him. "I'm so sorry."

"She's dead, Kyle. All this time I've been dreaming about how we'd connect and how she'd tell me she'd always loved me and wanted me back and—she's dead?" She looked at him, silently begging him to make it better and knowing he couldn't. No one could. "Why didn't I know? Why didn't I feel it? Shouldn't you know when your own mother dies? Shouldn't there be a bond that's broken and you know they're gone?"

"I didn't know when my dad died," he murmured. "I was closer to him than you were to your mom and I didn't know, so don't feel guilty." His arms drew her up. He rose with her and held her close, pressing her against him.

"I feel—stupid, like I should have known," she sobbed.

"How could you know?" Kyle's fingers threaded through her hair, smoothing back the strands. Though he wiped the tears from her cheeks repeatedly, more kept coming.

Desperate to feel connected to someone, Sara slid her arms around Kyle's neck and hung on as a storm of grief battered her heart.

Nothing in her world felt secure anymore. Nothing but Kyle.

What would she do when he left?

And yet he wasn't really hers to hang on to. What man would ever want someone like her, someone without a base, a heritage, even a history? Someone who didn't know anything about loving or being loved?

No man would want a woman like her. But for now, for a few moments, she clung to Kyle as the knowledge that she'd never hear her mother's voice again, never see her face or feel her love, swamped her.

"I know how much it hurts, Sara." His breath grazed the tip of her ear as he whispered the words. "I only wish I could make it better for you."

"You are." She tucked her head under his chin, wondering how she'd go on, alone. "Thank you for being here, Kyle."

If only he could stay, be the one she could turn to. Always.

In sudden clarity, Sara knew her feelings for this man were changing, but to what? She was confused by the crazy joy that exploded inside when he held her. She had to distance herself. Now.

Accepting the tissue Kyle pressed into her hands, she gently pulled away from him.

"I'm sorry for soaking your shirt," she murmured.

"My shirt doesn't matter." He pressed the damp strands of hair back from her face. "What will you do now, Sara?"

"Do?" She frowned at him. "I'll keep looking for clues, of course. I still haven't found my father."

Kyle seemed astonished. "You want to go on searching?"

"If it was your family, wouldn't you?" she demanded.

"Maybe not right after I'd received this news," he said. "You're one gutsy lady, Sara Kane."

"The way you say it, I'm not sure if that's a good thing or a bad thing," she said, forcing a laugh but unable to dismiss the respect in his words.

Kyle's stare made Sara uncomfortable. If she wasn't so clueless about men, she might have thought that was admiration glimmering in his eyes. But why would Kyle admire her? She'd never been anywhere or done anything special. She wasn't a hero like him.

"I meant is as a compliment, Sara." Said like that, she couldn't doubt his sincerity.

"Well, thank you." She blushed and backed away. The look in his eyes made her stomach flutter nervously. What was wrong with her? "I guess Teddy is probably looking for you. You must want to get home. Is your leg giving you pain?"

For some reason that question seemed to irritate him. "My leg is fine," he said.

"Good." She didn't know what else to say.

"Can I ask you something, Sara?"

Surprised, she nodded.

"What do you think about Rod's website idea?"

The question surprised her. She stared at him, watching as he leaned back on his heels. But he was watching her, his gaze unsettling as he watched her print off the page about her mother then shut down the computer.

"It seems to help him accept his uncle's death. Maybe it would help others if they could get online and talk to someone who's gone through what they have." She tilted her head to look at him. "Did you find it helpful to share your sorrow over your mother's death?"

"I didn't talk to anyone. Why do people always assume you'll feel better if you talk?" he demanded in a cranky tone.

"Because a sorrow shared is a sorrow beared, or something like that." She frowned. "I can't remember exactly how Lucy put it but it made sense at the time."

A laugh burst from him.

"What's so funny?" She walked to the door and waited for him to catch up.

"You're just like Lucy. For as long as I can remember she's always tried to ease someone else's load, too. It's—admirable," he said after a tiny pause.

"The Bible says we're supposed to share one another's burdens," she reminded him.

"I knew you'd say that." Kyle's broad shoulders shook with laughter again. He stopped in front of her and tilted her chin up so he could look into her eyes. His own sparkled with amusement.

"Are you laughing at me?" she said, feeling foolish and sort of offended at the same time.

"Admiring you," Kyle corrected. "If there's one thing

I can count on with you, Sara, it's that you will always, somehow, someway, bring the discussion back to God."

"Don't you think God's worth thinking about?" She didn't expect him to answer. Kyle had become an expert at dodging her questions whenever he didn't want to reveal his thoughts.

Sara said nothing as she led him to the kitchen and poured them both a glass of juice and set them on the table.

"I do think about God, Sara." Kyle's voice emerged in a low whisper. "I think about Him a lot. I think about what He was doing when my parents died and when I lost my leg. Where was He when your mother died?" His eyes burned into her.

Sara held his gaze, silently praying for words that would help him shed his anger, words that would lift him up and enable him to see possibilities. She could hear Teddy and Laurel arguing as they came down the hall, and knew she had only a second or two before they arrived. So she said the only thing she could think of.

"I can't be angry at God," she murmured. "He has a plan for my life. I just don't know what it is yet."

It hurt to see pity fill Kyle's face. Sara didn't know what to say, how to make him understand, so she said nothing. Soon after that the men left and Laurel went to bed, leaving Sara alone.

She wandered into the living room and sank down on the floor in front of the huge picture window that looked out across the tundra.

The full moon lit the world in front of her so brightly it looked like early morning. As a hush descended on the building, Sara thought back on her conversation with Kyle. How she longed for him to let go of his pain and renew his faith.

"Show me how to help him, Lord. Make me a blessing."

As she prayed, she couldn't stop replaying those moments in the computer room with him. His comforting embrace had soothed the pain of her mother's loss but it had also reenergized her yearning to be loved.

"Kyle needs Your help, God. He's getting himself tied up in anger and loss and losing sight of all You've given him."

As usual, thoughts of Kyle made her heart race. Just being near him brought all sorts of odd reactions she'd never felt before. She hardly dared think it, but could this be love?

Sara didn't know. Anything she knew about love came from the books she'd read. But these feelings inside her weren't like anything she'd read about. What was love, anyway?

It was affection, fondness for another hurting soul. She certainly felt all of that for Kyle. He was her friend, so of course she cared about him.

She pulled Laurel's Bible near and turned to 1 Corinthians 13. Carefully with great thought, she read the entire passage.

"That's it exactly," she whispered in wonderment. Her fingers traced the words again.

If you love someone, you will be loyal to him no matter what the cost. You will always believe in him, always expect the best of him, and always stand your ground in defending him.

The words felt right and true when applied to what was inside her heart.

"So do I love Kyle, God? And if I do, what do I do about it?"

* * *

Across town, in the darkness of his family home, Kyle couldn't settle. He knew his unease had to do with Sara. That unsettled him even more.

She was utterly beautiful, inside and out. She loved reaching out to everyone, spreading compassion on everyone. There seemed no end to her pluck and Kyle was embarrassed by his growing need to know how this delicate woman, who had grown up in the difficult world of foster care, had acquired her tender heart.

Ask her, his brain ordered. Guilt rushed over him as he remembered the many times he'd rebuffed her questions. He hadn't been willing to share his past with her. How could he now pry into hers?

The laptop sat in the corner, waiting to answer his questions with a few keystrokes. Kyle knew exactly how to coax answers from it in a very short space of time. And yet...

Part of him rebelled at such a blatant invasion of her privacy. The other part argued that if he knew what made her the way she was, maybe he'd be able to show her that dependence on God was not going to help her.

Finally, he opened the laptop, booted it up and initiated his search.

Ten minutes later Kyle was reeling, stunned by the depravity of foster parents who'd kept Sara imprisoned as their personal slave, preying on her neediness and innocence for years. The ugly details filled him with anger, shock and a thousand questions. Why had she stayed, and how had enduring such horror left Sara with her deep and abiding inner joy and faith in God?

He shut down the computer. Tomorrow he'd ask her. Kyle tossed that idea away as quickly as it had come.

If he asked Sara why she was so positive God was on her side after she'd suffered so much, she'd know he'd been prying into her life. She'd also sing God's praises to him yet again, and he did not want to hear that. Bitterness welled up inside at the betrayal of faith he and Sara had both suffered.

But Sara doesn't feel betrayed, an inner voice whispered.

He wanted—no, needed—to help her. Why not go to Lives more often? He could say Rod wanted help with his website or ask Tony, the would-be mechanic, to help rebuild his old ATV. Whatever the excuse, Kyle would talk to Sara and find a way to help her.

The message light flashed on the phone. Kyle pushed the button. Elation rushed in when the Realtor asked to show the house.

Except, if it sold right away, he'd never find out how Sara—

"First you have to get the offer," he said aloud. "And when you do, Sara and Lives Under Construction cannot come into it. You aren't staying here. You're leaving."

Funny how saying that aloud cast a pall over him.

Kyle hobbled to his room. Amazingly, he hadn't taken a pain pill all day. Not even after he'd fallen flat in front of the entire town, which didn't seem so terrible now. In fact, his public humiliation lost all significance when he compared it to Sara's miserable childhood and the added indignity of having that ugliness repeated in the tabloids during the court case.

All Kyle had to do was watch his step, but Sara— how could she get over the things she'd gone through? She hoped finding her family would heal her past but Kyle wasn't so sure.

The memory of her sobbing against his shoulder made him feel helpless.

If only he could—

No! He needed to forget about the tenderness Sara roused in his heart. He had to erase memories of that tickle of delight that shimmied down his arm when his hand brushed her hair. He must obliterate the rush of joy he felt when she laughed. Sleep vanished as he remembered every heart-stirring detail of the day with her.

She can't be more than a friend, his brain reminded. *Nothing more.*

Kyle's last thoughts before he finally found sleep were of silver-gray eyes and the sound of gently amused laughter.

A beautiful face, and an even more beautiful heart.

Chapter Nine

On June 21, Sara went to the beach after dinner.

Since it was the longest day of the year she intended to stay awhile—daylight now lasted well into the wee morning hours. She sat on a bench, backed by the massive, smooth boulders that surrounded Hudson Bay, mesmerized by the elegant dips and dives of gigantic whales floating in the bay.

Silently she pleaded with God to lead her to her father.

"Sara?"

She turned her head. Kyle stood several feet away, breathing heavily from the effort of making his way out to her.

"May I join you?"

"Sure." She studied his careful progress toward her, noting how he avoided the lichen-covered bits of rock, which might be slippery.

"What are you doing?" he asked.

"Enjoying this." She moved her arm to include the panorama before them. "It's nine o'clock at night yet still as bright as this morning. I can't get over it."

"All part of living in the North," he said with a grin.

"And you're not the only one enjoying the light." He pointed out the lawn chairs dotting the crest of the hill above them. "When summer arrives in Churchill, we don't like to miss a day."

She smiled at the *we*. So he still considered himself a Native. Good. Maybe he'd finally realize how much he was needed here.

Kyle sat beside her, his shoulder brushing hers. Unnerved by his touch, Sara turned her attention back to the bay and pointed.

"See those whales? They're black. But I read that Churchill whales are white."

"There are two main types of whales that come here," he explained. "Beluga whales are a gray-white. They go into the Churchill river to have their babies." He pointed. "They come right alongside a boat, so close you can pet their heads."

"Really?" She sighed. "I would love to do that."

"I used to do it in a kayak," he murmured, his gaze on the horizon, deep in thought. After a moment he spoke again. "Those—" he pointed toward the bay "—are the big guys. They also come here to give birth but because of their size, they have to stay in the bay where the water's deeper."

"Laurel said something about there being a fort here?" She leaned back, thrilling to the sound of his deep voice and the way his whole manner grew more animated when he spoke about the town.

"Of course. Prince of Wales Fort," Kyle told her. "Originally called Eskimo Point. Dad and I used to do a boat tour there.

"The fort was built by the Hudson's Bay Company in 1717 to protect and control their interests in the fur trade. It has forty-two cannons with more across the river at Cape Merry. It's a protected heritage site now."

Sara hugged her arms around her waist and imagined Churchill long ago. "This place has so much history. Everywhere you look there's evidence of people pulling together, of families building their homes in a new and unfamiliar land. I'm going to miss the community's closeness when I leave at Christmas."

"What's stopping you from staying?" he asked, one eyebrow arched.

"I took Laurel's job for six months to give me time to make some decisions about my future. I'm kind of like you, Kyle." She smiled at him, but because looking at him made her catch her breath, she refocused on the bay. "Churchill is a great place to get away from—everything."

"I guess."

"But I can't stay here, much as I love it. I need to figure out what God has planned for me in the world and get busy at it."

"You can't do whatever it is here?" His voice held unasked questions.

How could she explain her belief that she needed to learn how to fit in with people, how to function on her own without Laurel or anyone else's support? She couldn't say that.

"I can't stay without a job and that ends at Christmas." She smiled at his puzzled look. "Laurel was my social worker but she's become a sort of mother to me. I had an isolated childhood. She agrees that I need to go back to the city where I used to live and rebuild my life."

"But surely if you wanted to stay—"

"If it was part of God's plan for me, I would, but I

believe staying here would be too easy. It's too comfortable for me here. I wouldn't have to change and grow as much." She struggled to explain what she meant. "I need to change who I am and how I see the world."

"I don't think you need to change anything. I think you'll fit in perfectly well wherever you go."

"Thank you." Flustered by his compliment, she kept her gaze forward. It would be hard to leave Lives, but especially hard to leave Kyle. "Besides, Laurel's already recruiting someone to take my place."

"Maybe she thinks there aren't enough single men here." He eased his leg into a more comfortable position.

"Why would that matter?" Sara asked in confusion.

"Well, if she's concerned about your future, she probably wants you to meet somebody, fall in love, get married and have kids."

Rattled by his searching glance, Sara blushed.

"You don't want to get married and have a family?" A sharp edge to his question made her look at him.

"I'd like that more than anything," she told him. "But I doubt it will happen."

"Why not?"

"Because…" It felt funny to be discussing this with Kyle. But he was sitting there, waiting for an answer, and she couldn't lie. "I'm not the kind of person men want to marry."

"You're not?" His eyes did a head-to-toe scan of her. "Why?"

"I'm a misfit." Sara avoided his eyes. "I'm not really good at anything important."

"I doubt the kids would say that come breakfast time." His eyes crinkled when he smiled.

"Anybody can cook." She shrugged that off.

"I can't." He kept his gaze on her. "Why else wouldn't someone want to marry you?"

"I'm not pretty," she admitted, embarrassed by his continued probing. "I'm not normal. I don't know anything about fashion or how to dress. I certainly don't know anything about love or, uh, romance. I've never even dated."

Kyle was silent for a long time. Sara could feel the intensity of his stare cutting across any pretense she might have offered. So she sat silent, embarrassed and ashamed.

"Sara, not every man is concerned about glamour or looks. Not that you have to worry. You're a very beautiful woman." He touched her arm as if to reinforce his words.

"You don't have to say that," she whispered. "I know I'm not pretty."

"Have you looked in a mirror recently?" He barked out a laugh. "Your eyes are amazing. Your face could be on a magazine. On top of all that you're an awesome cook." His voice lowered to a serious tone. "But what matters most is that you have a generous, tender heart that cares for people. That's the most attractive thing about you. Caring for people is what you do best. It's why the boys care about you so much."

"Thank you for saying that, Kyle," she whispered, more embarrassed than ever by his fulsome praise. "It's very kind of you."

"I'm not being kind." His loud voice drew the attention of some passersby. "Listen to me, Sara. I got myself engaged to a woman who was all of the things you think are so important. But when I lost my leg, she took off without even saying goodbye. She was disgusted by me."

The pain darkening Kyle's eyes made Sara long to hug him, but before she could console him, he continued.

"You have more beauty in your little finger than she had in her whole body, Ms. Kane. And whatever you say, I think you know more about love than most people."

Kyle thought she knew about love? Inside her heart the persistent flicker of admiration she always felt for him flared into a full-fledged flame. But Sara didn't know how to respond. If she wasn't careful, his kindness would coax her into confessing the ugliness of her past and then he'd see that she wasn't any of those things he'd said.

"You don't believe me," he said in a flat tone.

She smiled at him then turned to gaze over the water and said, "You said you used to kayak. Can't you do that anymore?"

"No." No room for explanation there.

"How do you know?" She didn't flinch under his glare. "I just wonder how you can be so sure you can't do it if you haven't tried. Did you sell your kayak?"

"No. But I intend to." His jaw thrust out as he stared straight ahead. "The past is over, Sara."

"Perhaps. But it seems to me that you're giving up too easily on the future." She knew he didn't want to hear that, but he didn't say anything so she kept speaking. "I read about Zodiacs. Maybe you could use one of those. What is it, anyway?"

"A kind of inflated boat," he said with a frown.

"I saw this in the grocery store." She pulled a pamphlet from her pocket. "It's a Zodiac ride to see the belugas. I'm going to do that as soon as I save up enough money."

"You'll have to do it before fall," he told her. "They migrate south and the river freezes."

"Then I will," she assured him. "I am going to do that."

They sat shoulder to shoulder in a companionable silence for a long time.

"I should get going." Sara loathed ending the time she'd spent with Kyle. She'd never had a friend to talk to like this, but tomorrow morning would come early and for as long as she was here, she had no intention of shirking her job. She hesitated to offer her help, wondering if Kyle felt less manly when she did. "How did you get here?" she asked instead.

"I wondered when you'd ask." Kyle's eyes sparkled. "I have transport. Over there." He pointed and she saw a giant yellow machine. "It's my old ATV. Tony helped me get it running. Now I can get around on my own." His face changed. "At least until the snow flies. Or until I sell the house."

"Will that happen soon?" She couldn't help the flutter of worry that Kyle would leave before he realized he still had a lot to give to Churchill, before he realized he didn't have to leave here to have a future.

Or was she worrying that he would leave before she did?

"I've had two showings but so far no sale." He walked beside her across the beach. "Two more days and school will be out for the summer. Then what will the boys do?"

"They'll have summer school, but I don't know what else Laurel has planned." Sara pushed her bicycle toward Kyle's ATV. "She wants to teach them more about Churchill but she hasn't been here long enough to really know the history."

"They can see Canada Day celebrated in true Churchillian style on the first of July." Kyle leaned one hip against his machine. "They'll learn a lot about this place from that."

"Are there fireworks?"

"We don't have fireworks in summer. It's too bright at night. We save them for New Year's Eve." He grinned as if he remembered happier times. Then his face changed. "Any news about your dad, Sara?"

"No." Sara tried to hide her worry. "I found a couple of sites but I think they refer to someone else with the same name."

Why can't I find him, Lord? Don't You want me to have a family to love?

Over and over Sara had reassured herself with Scripture that God is a God of love, that He wants the best for His children. But in spite of that, doubt had begun to root.

She glanced at Kyle's house and thought again of the sweet family he'd been given, of the love that had filled his home and his youth. Why couldn't she have that?

"I could take a look now," Kyle offered. "If you want."

"I'd like that." She had to duck her head to hide her delight at spending more time with Kyle.

"Let's go." His grin made his scar less noticeable. At Kyle's nod Sara began pedaling up the gravelly incline and onto the street. She rode back to Lives, conscious of the sputtering motor behind her.

When they pulled into the yard, the boys ended their basketball game and crowded around Kyle's machine, inundating him with questions.

"One at a time." He made a point of telling the boys to ask Tony their questions, since he was the one who'd helped him fix the ATV.

As Sara watched the proud boy stretch taller, a tiny

thrill rushed through her. Kyle's generosity proved he
was a man who cared, whether or not he acknowledged it.

"Got anything for snacks, Sara?" the oldest boy,
Barry, asked. "We're starving."

"As usual." She grinned. "I made fresh doughnuts
this afternoon. I hid them in the oven. Help yourself."
She looked at Kyle. "I suppose you want some, too?"

"Fresh doughnuts?" He nodded vigorously. "I definitely want some."

"Hot chocolate and doughnuts," Sara confirmed.
"Let's go." She hurried inside, prepared the cocoa then
sat at the table, relishing the laughter and teasing. This
was what she longed for—her own home, her own family.

Finished, the boys thanked her, cleaned up then
headed to their rooms. Kyle had disappeared, too, but
when she carried her mug of tea into the computer
room, she found him studying Rod's website.

"What do you think of it?" she asked.

"He's getting a ton of hits. Apparently a lot of ser-
vicemen and women want to talk about what they endured over there. I didn't expect that. Most of the guys
I worked with kept it inside."

"Like you?" She smiled when he frowned at her.
"But that doesn't help."

"Do you know a lot about keeping ugliness inside?"
he asked, blue eyes darkening.

"I know something about it. I—I didn't have a very
good childhood, Kyle, but the memories got easier when
I spoke to my pastor about it. He helped me understand
that I'm not a victim, I am a survivor. That's been important to me in letting go of the past."

"That's why you're always talking about how good
God is?"

"Sort of." There was an intensity in Kyle's tone that told Sara this was an important moment, so she said a prayer for words to help him understand.

"There wasn't much goodness where I grew up. I watched as the kids who lived with me ached for someone to love them, someone to tell them it was going to be okay."

"I have a feeling you did that for them," he said thoughtfully.

"If I could." Sara leaned forward. "The thing is, everybody goes through stuff, Kyle. Maybe they don't have abusive foster parents like me, or lose a limb as you have, but everyone has something they have to deal with. If we don't face it, it will forever color our future, so I try to face it every day. When I do, I grow stronger."

"I guess you were right."

"I was?" She blinked.

"You keep saying people feel better after talking to someone about their issues." He waved at the screen. "These folks do seem to find relief in sharing. Some of the things I've read on Rod's site—" Kyle shook his head. "I feel ashamed that I've bellyached so much about my lot."

"The point isn't who's suffered more." She touched his arm and looked straight into his eyes. "What's so great about Rod's site is that it allows each of you to see that you're not alone, that others suffered and that there are people who care that you were willing to sacrifice for your country. That's how God is. He never leaves us alone."

To her surprise, Kyle didn't argue. He stared into her eyes for several moments as if he was thinking about what she'd said.

For Sara, that connection went right to that secret place inside where she hid her feelings. Afraid that Kyle would see just how much she'd begun to care what he thought of her, she focused on the computer.

"So this is what I've found about my dad. It must be someone else with the same name." She frowned when he made no response. As he studied the page, his brows drew together. She moved the cursor to change pages.

"Wait." He put his hand on hers and guided the mouse to a line before clicking. A list of names appeared. "Is this birth date right?"

"Yes, but I can't get it to reveal anything else. What am I doing wrong?"

"Wait a minute." He put his hand over hers on the mouse and pressed. The screen changed. "Try again."

She did and her father's name appeared in the center of the screen. A frisson of hope flickered inside until she noticed something. "Kyle, this is a list of obituaries, isn't it?"

"Let me see." He leaned closer, studied the screen then looked at her, sadness filling his eyes. "Yes."

"This is dated eleven years ago." She couldn't believe it. "He's dead. My father is dead?" All this time, all the searching, for nothing? She peered at the page. "He died when I was eleven," she whispered.

"I'm sorry." Kyle stared at her. "Are you all right?"

"I don't know." Sara struggled to express what was going on inside. "I don't really have any strong memories of him. A feeling of being carried, a vague image of his face, that's all." She caught her breath. "But I never thought, I never imagined—" Tears spilled from her eyes and tumbled down her cheeks. "I'm an orphan," she whispered.

"Sara, please don't cry." Kyle's arms went around her and he drew her against his shoulder. "You have friends here," he whispered. His fingers threaded through her hair as he spoke, his soft, gentle tone matching the cadence of his words. "You have people who love you, Sara, who care about you. You're not alone."

"Yes, I am." She drew away from him, dashed her knuckles across her eyes and let the full weight of this new knowledge impact her heart. "I have no mother, no father. No one." The words whispered from her in a wrenching sob.

"Neither do I."

Kyle's stark response stunned Sara. She looked into his deep blue eyes. In that moment she understood the sense of total aloneness Kyle had been dealing with ever since he'd stepped off the train.

How could she have so cavalierly insisted he get on with his life? Compassion rose up in a wave and she leaned forward and wrapped her arms around him.

"I'm sorry, Kyle. I'm really sorry."

"You're sorry for me?" He sat frozen for a moment before he lifted his hands, slid them around her waist and drew her close. "Thank you." His breath brushed the tip of her ear.

She marveled at the strength of his arms around her, at the security she felt.

"It's like you can't wake up from a dream. You don't know where to turn, what to do next. It feels so…" She paused. "Empty."

Kyle said nothing, simply hugged her closer. His lips brushed over her cheek.

No man had ever kissed her like that before. An explosion of emotion rose inside, feelings of wonderment, sweet and tender. An emotion akin to reverence swept over her when he finally drew away.

"It must be doubly hard for you," she realized aloud. "I didn't really know my father. I can't imagine how you deal with being here, seeing and touching all the things your dad loved. I didn't consider that. I'm sorry."

"Don't be sad for me, Sara." Kyle leaned back, using the pad of one thumb to erase the tear marks from beneath her eyes. "Anyway, you're not alone, like me. Aren't you always telling me you have God to bless you?"

"Yes." Sara frowned. "But you're not alone, either, Kyle. You have the entire community just waiting to support you."

There was a long pause while he studied her. Then he leaned forward and kissed her cheek.

As she followed him to the door and waved goodnight, a voice in the back of her mind whispered, *You have me, Kyle. I'm here and I care about you.*

After he'd driven away and she was left alone, staring at the half-lit sky, Sara touched her cheek. This was love; she was certain of it. The tenderness that was flickering to life inside her had to be the real thing. For the first time in her life she felt she was important to someone, to Kyle.

Did he need her as much as she needed him? She wondered if being Kyle's friend would salve the ache in her heart to be loved.

Chapter Ten

Kyle's revelation started on Canada Day, when it seemed everyone he spoke to knew or had been inspired by Sara Kane.

"Sara made the Canada Day cake."

"Sara's put together a treasure hunt for the little kids."

In the days that followed, songs of Sara's generosity filled his ears every time he stepped out of the house. Everyone in town knew Sara.

"The talent show is Sara Kane's doing," an old friend told him.

"She encouraged town council to arrange it," the mayor confided. "We couldn't get anyone to participate until some of the boys from Lives agreed to take part to raise money for our new fire hall."

Someone came by to donate more soil for "Sara's plants." A local business offered to repair Laurel's ratty van for "Sara's boys." Even town council had chimed in, promising that come fall, transportation would be provided for "Sara's kids," thus freeing Laurel from four daily trips into town.

Kyle found rich irony in realizing Sara had even drawn

him into the summer activities at Lives, though he'd intended to remain detached. The box kites he'd helped the boys build, the ones they were now flying, were her idea.

"I always wanted to fly a kite," she'd said. And somehow Kyle just had to make that dream come true.

Now as Kyle watched Rod show Sara how to turn her brilliant yellow kite out over the cliffs, he found he couldn't look away. Her eyes flashed, her cheeks bloomed and her hair streamed behind her in carefree abandon. She gave a whoop of joyful triumph as she leaned into the wind and let the kite soar. Kyle thought he could watch her forever and that bothered him.

He was getting too fond of Sara Kane. After today he'd have to work harder on keeping his distance.

"This was a great idea," Sara said. Having handed the kite to Rod, she flopped onto their blanket on a sun-warmed rock. "It's a perfect day. Look at the boys. They're having so much fun. *I* had so much fun."

"I'm glad." Kyle lowered himself awkwardly beside her. "But I'm not sure I can do much more of this," he said sotto voce, aware that the boys were mere feet away reeling in their kite string. "I'm not good on this kind of terrain."

"I realize you've put yourself out to do this with us," she said. "I wouldn't have had a clue how to teach them to fly a kite. I appreciate your help."

"My pleasure." And it was.

Kyle enjoyed every encounter with her. But more than that, he now realized that as much as Sara and Laurel tried to make Lives as homey as possible, the boys were missing out on the maturing experiences his father had provided to enrich his own life, experiences that required a male perspective. He wasn't the right man to do that for them. But until someone else came along, who else was there?

Of course, being around Sara was no hardship.

"What's the worst part?" she asked.

"I can manage the beach, pretty much," he qualified. "But these rocks are something else."

"I've been praying for you, Kyle." Sara smiled and placed her hand over his. "And I believe God will help you do whatever you set your mind to."

"I hope so." For once he wasn't going to argue. When she removed her hand from his, some of the warmth drained out of the day. "I don't want to make a spectacle of myself."

"Would it matter so much?" Her stare was intense.

"To me, yes."

"I read a verse this morning. 'Happy is he whose hope is in the Lord his God, which made heaven and earth, the sea, and all that therein is: which keepeth truth forever.' It's from Psalms 146." Her silver-gray eyes shone with confidence. "God didn't abandon you, Kyle. I'm more certain of that than ever. He has plans for your life. You just have to keep your hope focused on God."

While Kyle studied Sara's face, a tiny part of his hardened heart melted. But he couldn't afford to get soft, certainly not about Sara, who so desperately wanted a family.

He couldn't give that to her, even if a relationship between them was possible.

And it wasn't. He was leaving Churchill. Soon.

Kyle turned away from her and stared across the bay. Tiny ripples toyed with the glassy surface. As usual, Sara's words challenged him.

In fact, it was the way she'd so quickly found solace

in God after learning of her father's death that compelled him to seek out the new minister in town.

"You have an error in your thinking, Kyle." Rick Salinger hadn't used fancy phrases or tried to pretend that he was anything other than a young pastor in a small, isolated community.

"I do?"

"God doesn't leave us, not even when we try to push Him away. He stays and He waits for us until we're ready to hear what He has to say. No matter how long it takes. Because He loves us."

"Kyle?" Sara's hand on his arm roused him from this morning's early conversation.

"Yeah?" Kyle raised one eyebrow, surprised by the concern on her face. He thought about telling her of his visit to Rick this morning but changed his mind. For now he needed to think about it on his own for a while. "Sorry. What did you say?"

"Do you want to eat lunch now?"

Since the boys were trying to outdo each other in running their kites higher, he decided to use the opportunity to talk to her. "First I want to ask you something."

"Okay." She stopped lifting dishes out of the basket, folded her hands in her lap and waited.

"What will you do about your family now that you know your parents are...gone?" He hesitated to say it, not wanting to hurt her.

"I'm not sure." Now she was the one who stared across the bay. "The thing is, Kyle, I think I might have a brother."

"What?" He blinked at her statement. "You *think?*"

"I know it sounds odd. Listen, and I'll try to explain. For many years I've had nightmares about a child crying and calling for me. At least I thought it was a night-mare." Her hands clenched.

"I'm listening, Sara," Kyle encouraged.

"I was almost thirteen when I was taken to the Mas-ters' home to live. I had been in other foster homes by then, but none were as bad as the Masters'." She gulped. "It got worse the longer I was there. I guess somewhere along the way I blanked out my past."

Her face lost all life, all sparkle. It seemed to Kyle that the light he'd seen shining from inside her ear-lier had been snuffed out. She inhaled, peering straight ahead. Her voice emerged flat, emotionless.

"After six months, I made up my mind I wasn't going to stay."

"But how…" He felt confused.

"I decided to run away."

Kyle stayed silent, hoping she'd finally tell him about her past.

"It was bad." Sara clamped her lips together, clearly summoning all the courage she could find. "Anyway, I decided to leave. I waited until everyone was asleep, then I climbed out the kitchen window and ran. I made it two blocks."

Totally unnerved by the gray tone of her skin, Kyle wanted her to stop. But he knew Sara needed to get this story out.

Sara believed talking about things healed you. Kyle wanted her healed, so he wrapped an arm around her shoulder. She was shivering.

"Tell me the rest," he said softly as he draped his jacket over her shoulders.

"She followed me."

"Who followed you?" Shaken by the dead sound of her voice, Kyle grasped her icy fingers and held on.

"Maria." Sara hiccupped a sob and buried her face against his neck. "She was the sweetest four-year-old you've ever seen. She said I was her big sister." Her voice choked. Tears flowed down her pallid cheeks. "She died because she followed me. I didn't know it but I should have. She was always following me. I killed her."

"No, you didn't." Kyle saw the boys heading for them. They were frowning, clearly worried about Sara. He shook his head, grateful when they backed off. "You loved Maria as if she was your own baby sister." He knew it was true. Sara's big heart couldn't help but enfold a needy child.

"Yes, but—" She stopped.

"Tell me."

"She was running across the road to catch up, I think." She stopped again.

"All of it, Sara."

She inhaled. "I heard a thud, the sound of glass breaking and I heard her call my name. I couldn't figure out— I went back." Sara's hand on his tightened like a vise. "When I got there, Maria was lying in the street, her beautiful hair spread around her. She said she hurt and asked me to hold her. I didn't know if I should move her, but I couldn't just leave her like that."

"Of course you couldn't," Kyle agreed.

"I heard someone calling the police, but Maria kept begging me to hold her. So I cradled her head on my lap." Sara gulped. "She smiled and said thank-you before she drifted off. The ambulance was just arriving when she opened her eyes. She said didn't she make a good snow angel. And then she died."

"Oh, Sara." Kyle couldn't imagine any thirteen-year-old having to deal with such a tragedy. Clearly the guilt still clung. "I'd give anything to erase that memory from your mind." Kyle simply sat there, holding her as she wept.

"Maria died because of me and all anyone was worried about was these silly cuts." Sara's fingers rubbed the scars on her wrists as if she could erase them. "The worst thing was Maria died for nothing. I was too afraid to tell the police why I'd left so they made me go back to the Masters'. After that they locked me in the basement every night so I couldn't run away. They didn't need to do that. Believe me, I wasn't going anywhere."

Rage burned inside Kyle like an inferno. But he kept it in check because Sara needed him.

"I didn't even get to go to Maria's funeral," she whispered.

"She knew you loved her." He held her wrists so she couldn't rub the scars anymore. "You did your best, Sara."

"Did I?" She stared at him, her face filled with ragged emotion. "I never tried to leave again. I couldn't stand the thought of another child being hurt because I wasn't there to protect them."

"I read about you on the internet." Compassion for her and the need to be honest in the face of what she'd just revealed forced his confession. "I read how you kept the other kids safe, how you fed them, made sure they did their schoolwork, washed their clothes. You were the best mother they could ever have had."

God had allowed this—atrocity? Kyle's brain simply could not accept that, but this was not the time to say that to her.

"I tried to care for all of them." She dragged her hair

off her face as she drew away. "I loved them as much as I could."

"I know." Kyle knew beyond doubt that big-hearted Sara would have showered each child with all the pent-up affection she possessed. She would have protected them, gone to bat for them, had probably even taken their punishment.

"They left, you know. One by one the other kids all left the Masters'." She blinked her spiky lashes and stared into his eyes. "But no one ever came for me."

"Oh, Sara." Kyle had never felt more helpless.

"That's why I needed to find my parents, to ask why they never came back. Now I'll never know." She found a tissue, wiped her eyes and blew her nose. "Maybe someday God will help me find out."

"Sara, how can you still believe in God? How can you trust Him when He didn't get you out of there?" Kyle couldn't have stopped the question if he'd wanted to. Something inside him ached to know what made her so secure in her faith. Some intangible longing made him wonder if he could ever feel that secure in God again.

"God put me there, Kyle." Her wide eyes held his, full of certainty.

"Huh?"

"God put me at the Masters'." She smiled, her heart in her eyes. "If Maria hadn't stopped me from leaving, who would have protected the other kids? Who would have made sure they had a birthday surprise and a Christmas treat? Who would have held them when they were sick and loved them when their parents couldn't?"

"Someone, anyone else?" he snarled, angered by her words.

"No." She reached out and linked her fingers with

his. "God gave me a precious opportunity to love those kids." Her laugh at his appalled look echoed around the bay.

"How can you say that?"

"It's not what I'd have chosen," she admitted. "It was miserable and painful and I didn't see it at the time, but I now realize that's why God didn't send my parents to get me. My foster sisters and brothers needed me."

A thousand emotions raced through Kyle: anger, admiration, fury, but most of all a rush of affection. Who wouldn't love this woman?

"Anyway, my past doesn't matter." She slid her hand from his and began to unpack the picnic basket. "I was trying to tell you about…my brother."

"Okay." He waited.

"I thought the dreams were about Maria, but I've finally realized it's not her face I see, it's the face of a little boy with eyes like mine. He holds up his arms, asks me to pick him up. His name is Samuel." Sara's face grew pensive. "I think he's my brother and I intend to find him."

Kyle sat in stunned silence as she called the boys and handed out plates of food. He ate his own sandwich in a bemused fog, trying to absorb what he'd learned, yet not quite ready to deal with the emotions that surged inside.

"Weren't we supposed to go fishing this afternoon, Kyle?"

He blinked back to awareness and saw Barry and Tony standing in front of him. Barry held several rods and reels out from his body as if they were lethal weapons.

"Where did you get those?"

"Lucy and Hector." Tony grinned. "I think they must

have some secret source because they keep coming up with stuff for us."

"Their source is God," Sara said calmly. "They pray and God supplies."

"After lunch, we'll see about fishing," Kyle promised.

By the time everyone had finished lunch, he'd been sitting too long with his injured leg in the wrong position. While Sara and the boys cleaned up, Kyle rose, attempting to straighten his knee. A rush of agony surged through him. He overbalanced and would have fallen. But Sara was there, her shoulder strong enough to brace him as he sat again.

"I want you boys to take our lunch things up to Kyle's house and put them in the greenhouse," she said. "I don't want any polar bears getting a whiff of food and stopping by for a visit."

"Kyle said there aren't any here now," one of the boys said. "They've gone till fall."

"The sooner you've finished putting the basket away, the sooner you can fish," she said. "And when you've caught enough fish for dinner tonight, I might be persuaded to give you each a slice of peach pie I made this morning."

"I'm amazed the legal system hasn't thought of using peach pie as a motivator," Kyle muttered, trying to suppress his laughter as the boys hurried away.

"Whatever works." Sara winked at him and extended her hand. Once she'd helped him stand, Kyle eased away from her.

"Thank you for covering for me. It would have been very embarrassing if the kids had seen me land on my kisser."

"You're not going to do that," she assured him. She

threaded her arm through his elbow. "While the boys are busy, let's try walking across these rocks. We don't have to hurry."

"I don't think I can—"

"This way." She tugged on his arm just enough to let him know she wasn't giving up.

By the time the boys returned, Kyle was in his favorite fishing spot on the beach and though he'd stumbled and miscalculated his way several times, the boys were none the wiser thanks to Sara's unobtrusive help. Though Kyle's leg ached at the strain of this new activity, his dignity was intact.

Kyle taught the boys to cast, to reel in and to remove the fish they caught. He couldn't remember when he'd enjoyed fishing more. The boys were apt pupils, full of questions and eager to listen to his stories.

It seemed natural for him to return to Lives with them, show them how to clean the fish, and share their dinner.

"That was delicious, Sara." He pushed his plate away, replete.

She pretended to bow. "I never cooked wild meat until someone donated it here, but it made me wonder if sometime you'd show the boys how to hunt? Lucy says Hector has bows and arrows they could use."

"Archery takes a long time to learn," Kyle said. "It's a difficult skill to master."

"Well, they have the time to learn it," she shot back. She disappeared and returned a moment later, bearing the promised pies.

Kyle was amused by the silence that fell while those pies were devoured.

"A guy at school was telling us about sled dog races

they have here in the winter," Barry said when everyone had finished seconds. "Do you know about those, Kyle?"

"How about we gather around a campfire to listen to Kyle's story *after* we do cleanup?" Laurel suggested.

Amidst some good-natured grumbling, the boys made the kitchen shipshape while Kyle and Sara built a fire outside.

"Barry's crazy about animals," Sara told him as she chewed on the stem of a straw. Her forehead pleated in a frown. "He wants to be a vet but he's afraid he'd fail the training. I'm searching for a way for him to work with animals so he could build his confidence."

"Your concern to get each of the boys involved in something unique to them makes me think you run this place as much as Laurel does," Kyle teased, delighted when her cheeks turned a bright pink. "I'm not kidding, Sara. You have great insight into what makes these boys tick, more than a lot of professionals would have."

"You just get them to open their hearts," she said. "Then you can see what they really need."

"That's probably easy for you," Kyle mused. "You seem like a natural mother." Maybe not the best thing to say, knowing how much she longed for a family of her own, he thought. "I know a fellow who raises sled dogs. I could ask him if Barry could help out."

"Would you?" Her eyes shone as if she'd been given a prize.

"Sure," he promised.

"I have another favor to ask." Sara glanced over one shoulder as if afraid someone would overhear. "Rod's thirteenth birthday is the day after tomorrow. He really wants to be like his uncle, who I gather was a live-off-the-land man who knew all about nature and survival."

"My kind of guy."

"But far from my realm of experience." She had that gleam in her eye. "I wondered if you'd be willing to arrange some games for the boys that afternoon."

"Games? Such as?" While Kyle admired Sara's determination to help these kids, he recognized that he was getting more involved by the minute.

"I don't know much about games," she said, a frown appearing. "Maybe you could take them on a hike. Anything to make the day special for him."

"Not a hike, but I'll think of something. You take care of the birthday cake."

"Deal." She held out her hand to shake on it. From her cheeky grin an observer would have thought he'd given her the moon.

"What about you?" he asked. "Are you close to getting your Zodiac ride to see the belugas? They'll be gone in a few weeks, you know."

"Haven't had time yet," she demurred and turned away.

Rod had obviously overheard because he pulled Kyle aside later.

"I don't think Sara will ever go for that ride," the boy confided.

"Why not?" Kyle frowned.

"She keeps using the money she's saving on other people." Rod sighed. "Sara ordered some shoes for an old woman she met at church who can't afford the special ones she needs."

"I see." Kyle waited, knowing there was more Rod wanted to say.

"The guys and I figured we'd pool our allowances and treat her, but we aren't going to have enough to pay for her trip before the whales go. Anyway, the tour operator always says he's booked up."

Sara returned and the conversation ended.

But as the evening progressed, Kyle kept glancing across the fire at Sara, thinking about what Rod had told him. He pushed those thoughts away as he told the boys stories. Her face beamed as she listened to him talk about the sled dog races held in Churchill every winter.

Sara the giver, the dreamer of possibilities. He'd seen the yearning in her eyes whenever he spoke about the belugas and knew she desperately wanted to fulfill at least that one dream. But even for something so important to her, she was willing to do without so others could have.

What a woman.

As he drove home later, Kyle reflected on the pleasure he'd enjoyed today. He'd never imagined he could get around the beach so easily, let alone reel in a massive sea-run trout as he had in the old days. But he'd landed Tony's twenty-two pounder with no difficulty—once he figured out how to balance himself to counteract the fish's weight.

In fact, the entire day had been a learning experience about his abilities outdoors. The more he tried, the more he'd wanted to try. Except the water. He dreaded the water. The boys had coaxed him to join them for a swim, but Kyle had no desire to plunge into water only to realize he could no longer swim. He'd even had a few anxious moments while the boys were splashing around, worrying that if they got into trouble, he wouldn't be able to help.

Okay, water sports were out. But the rest of it? Thanks to Sara, he was doing just fine.

Kyle stood in his yard, looking out over the bay, and

smiled. It wasn't just the birthday party he'd promised to help with. Sara had also coaxed him into teaching the boys wilderness survival techniques, starting tomorrow.

Sara Kane gave a lot. Wasn't it about time somebody made sure her dream came true?

The very thought of climbing into a Zodiac and taking it on the river filled Kyle with trepidation. But today, thanks to Sara, he'd grasped there were some things he could still do. He wouldn't tell her until he was absolutely sure, but as soon as he could get Teddy to help, Kyle intended to start training. If he worked hard enough, he might be able to show Sara the belugas before they left.

He went inside and arranged a time and place with Teddy. But as daylight finally waned, Kyle still wasn't ready to sleep. His brain kept mulling over what Sara had said about God putting her in that foster home.

Kyle switched on his computer. He intended to email whatever contacts he could find to learn why Sara had been removed from her home so many years ago. And while he was at it, he'd start a search for this brother, Samuel. Maybe Sara's longing for a family didn't have to end.

Funny how he'd begun to wish he, too, had someone to share his life with.

At 2:00 a.m., just before he shut down his computer for the night, he shot off one last email to Pastor Rick to ask for another appointment.

Kyle had a lot of questions about God. Maybe it was time to get some answers. He owed Sara that much.

Chapter Eleven

"You did a good job with the tomatoes, Rod." Sara smiled as the boy's shoulders lifted with pride. "It's kind of sad to pull up such productive plants. Next year—" She let the words die away, suddenly aware that she wouldn't be here next year.

And neither would the greenhouse.

Yesterday she'd learned Kyle had received an offer on his house. A pang of sadness at his departure left her feeling down.

"Might as well pull them up. September days are too short for growing," Rod muttered.

Sara could tell by his stare into space that his focus wasn't on removing the tomato vines. "Is anything wrong?" she asked.

He worked for a while longer then faced her. "Can I ask you something?"

"Of course." She smiled to encourage him.

"How do I get a girl to notice me?" Rod asked. A faint pink tinged his cheeks.

"Um, I think that's something you should talk over with Laurel," Sara hedged, feeling totally inept. What did she know of relationships? She'd never even had a crush on a boy before she'd started this crush on Kyle. But Kyle was more than a crush.

"I did ask Laurel." He made a face. "She told me I'm too young. As if I'm thinking about running away to get married. It's just that there's this girl and I like her. But I doubt she even knows I'm alive."

"Have you talked to her?" Sara asked, sending a desperate plea heavenward for help.

"I said hi a couple of times." His face turned redder.

"Maybe next time you see her you should say something more." Desperately aware she didn't have the answers he needed, Sara vowed to search the internet tonight.

This time she would not ask Kyle for help. That was too embarrassing.

"Say something like what?" He scowled. "'I like you?' That sounds dorky."

"Yeah, it does. Maybe you could say you think she's pretty. Or compliment her on what she's wearing." Sara saw the front door of the house open and sighed with relief. *She* didn't have to ask Kyle, but Rod could. "Maybe Kyle could help you with this. Why don't you ask him? A lady at church told me he used to be very popular in school. And he was engaged once."

"Yeah, but Tony told me his fiancée dumped him when he got hurt. That would stink." Rod's forehead wrinkled in thought. "But at least Kyle would know what I should do if this girl gives me the brush-off. Thanks, Sara."

"Good. Maybe don't mention his broken engagement. It might still bother him." She continued pulling tomato vines as Rod pushed open the greenhouse door and welcomed Kyle inside. She didn't want Kyle to know she'd been talking about him.

That was getting to be a habit.

"Harvest is over, huh?" He fingered one of the tomatoes Sara had placed in a basket to take back to Lives.

"'To everything there is a season,'" she quoted, unable to suppress a smile when he rolled his eyes. "Well, it's true."

"Yes, it is. And this season is your birthday. Happy birthday." Kyle's blue eyes met hers and held.

"Thank you," she stammered. "But how did you know?" she asked.

"I'm not telling. But there will be no more work for you today. Right, Rod?" He high-fived the boy.

"Right." Grinning, Rod took the vines from her hands and then hugged her. "Happy birthday, Sara."

"Thank you." She returned his hug, amazed that he allowed it. "But it's just another Saturday. There are chores to do—"

"Nope." Kyle caught her hand and drew her from the greenhouse, closed the door firmly and stood in front of it. "Today's special."

As if on cue, the other five boys, Laurel, Lucy and Hector came around the corner of the house, singing at the top of their lungs. Their grins grew when a couple of passersby stopped and chimed in.

"Thank you all," Sara said when they were finished. Though embarrassed to be the focus of attention, she treasured their kindness. "You shouldn't go to all this fuss."

"We haven't yet begun to fuss," Kyle assured her. "Get in Laurel's van. We're going for a ride."

With everyone's eyes on her, Sara did as she was told, insisting on sitting in the backseat so Kyle would be more comfortable in the front. The boys were in high spirits, laughing at her and teasing about the sudden approach of old age, distracting her so well that she was surprised when they arrived at the Churchill River.

"The belugas are still here," she whispered as she got out of the van, mesmerized as always by the silent gray shapes gliding through the water.

"Not for long. Another week, maybe." Kyle grinned when Teddy Stonechild climbed out of his truck and gave him a thumbs-up. "So this is your birthday gift, Sara. We're going for a ride on the water so you can see belugas, moms and babies, up close."

"Really?" She stared at him. "But the man who does the tours said—"

"Forget him. Kyle's giving us our own tour. Happy birthday, Sara." Teddy hugged her then motioned to the boys. "Come on, guys."

In short order Kyle launched two inflated boats in the water and started their motors. *Loness's Tours* was printed on the sides of the boats in black lettering. So these were what Kyle and his father had used in their business.

"We'll split into two groups," Kyle directed. "Sara, you'll be with me in that one. Teddy and Laurel will go in the other. We'll split the boys between us." He directed the others into the boats, chuckling when Lucy adamantly refused to go.

"I like my feet on solid ground," she insisted. "I'll watch from here." She plopped onto the tailgate of Teddy's truck.

"Hector?" Kyle grinned at the other man's eager nod and held the boat steady while he boarded.

"Kyle, it's very kind of you," Sara murmured, pausing beside him before she got into the Zodiac. "But are you sure? I know you don't like the water—"

"I didn't," he agreed. His gaze held hers. "But since a certain woman said she wanted to see the whales up close and personal, I've been practicing in the water for a couple of weeks. But if you're worried, you can go with Teddy."

"I'm not worried, Kyle." She grasped his hand and climbed into the dinghy. "I trust you."

Time stopped while his blue eyes searched hers. Sara stared back, willing him to see into her heart, to see the feelings for him that, despite her determination to weed them out, kept growing.

"Having second thoughts, Sara?" Tony called.

"As if!" Sara broke eye contact with Kyle as she took her seat.

After ensuring life jackets were fastened, Kyle climbed in with an ease that surprised her. He sped up the motor, drove to the middle of the river and positioned the boat where he wanted. Teddy followed. Then they cut the motors so that the hush of the afternoon took over.

Sara gasped as the whales swam toward them, curious to see who was in their territory. Beside them, smaller whales crowded their mothers in their eagerness to get close.

"They come here to feed, give birth and molt their skin. They'll be leaving to go south now that the babies are able to take the journey. The males, the bulls, are over there." Kyle pointed. "We won't go near because they're hunting. They swim round and round like that to draw the fish into their circle. Watch."

Sara gasped when all at once the males plunged into the middle of the circle, somehow avoiding each other as they dove after the fish they'd corralled. She felt the boat move as Kyle sat beside her.

"Let your hand trail in the water," he suggested. His breath felt warm against her ear.

The belugas looked huge next to their puny boat. After witnessing the hunt, Sara feared the mothers and babies would go into the same feeding frenzy and cause their craft to upset. She gazed into Kyle's eyes and knew beyond a shadow of a doubt that he wouldn't let anything happen to her. She dipped her fingers into the chilly water. Almost instantly a cool wet nose pushed against her hand.

"Oh, my." She gasped, freezing for a moment before she slid her hand along the baby whale's back as it swam past. Her heart in her mouth, she skimmed her fingertips over its tail fin. The boys mirrored her actions and soon they were surrounded by whales eager to have their heads, their snouts and their blowholes touched.

"It's amazing. To think God created such wonder as this."

Sara turned her head to thank Kyle and found his lips inches from hers. Suddenly she couldn't say anything, could only feel the press of his strong shoulder against her back and the gentleness of his hand where it rested against her waist.

Is this love? I never dreamed I could feel so light, so happy.

Was this odd tingling, this desire to lean an inch closer and press her lips to his—was that love?

Sara didn't know. She only knew that Kyle's gift of this incredible afternoon meant he'd taken time to re-learn what he'd feared he'd never do again. And he'd done it for her. Did that mean he cared about her, even the tiniest bit?

"Thank you, Kyle," she whispered. "This is the best birthday gift anyone could have given me."

"I'm glad. But the day is just beginning." He grinned before moving back to his seat by the motor. With infinite patience he waited until each boy had his fill of touching the incredible beings.

More than once Sara caught herself staring at Kyle, admiring the proud way he held himself, the agility he'd regained.

"Now we could go over to the Prince of Wales Fort and take a look around, if you want."

Kyle grinned when she and the boys whooped their answer.

He gunned the motor, speeding them across the river. Sara turned her head into the wind, loving the brisk, refreshing air that tugged her hair back, and allowed the heat of the autumn sun to warm her.

"Couldn't have picked a better day for a birthday," Teddy called as they moored the Zodiacs. "Good work, Sara."

She laughed at Teddy, but her breath caught in her throat as Kyle teetered on the edge of the dock, almost losing his balance as he dragged the Zodiac to a drier landing area. He caught her stare and grinned.

"Don't worry. I practiced this part a lot," he joked. He held out a hand to help her disembark. The others surged toward the fort, leaving them to trail behind. "Come on. It's an old place but it's interesting."

Sara listened with rapt attention as Kyle showed her the weathered remains of a rough stone dwelling house, the men's barracks, the storehouse, the stonemason's and carpenter's workshops, a tailor's room and a blacksmith's shop.

"Each of them had a huge part in making this settlement viable," he said. "I've always admired their courage in staying."

"And in bringing their families here," she mused. She touched his arm. "I can't thank you enough for this gift, Kyle."

"You already have." He tucked her arm in his. "Come on. I want to show you the view across the river to Cape Merry."

Sara went eagerly, not even trying to suppress the thrill that walking next to him, hearing the rumble of his voice, watching him move with confidence and assurance, brought.

She sent a silent prayer of thanksgiving that Kyle was finally healing.

Kyle stood on his back step and soaked in the pleasure of having a crowd of happy people in his backyard. It had been too long since he'd laughed so hard.

"Was today worth all your training?" Teddy asked between bites of his hot dog.

"Do you expect me to say you were right to keep pushing me?" Kyle grinned. "You were right," he admitted.

"Of course I was," Teddy said smugly. "Sara seems to be enjoying the day."

"I hope so. She deserves it." Kyle ignored the hint in Teddy's tone.

"Yeah, she does. She's a nice lady. You could do worse," Teddy hinted.

"I did, remember?" Kyle shot him a glare. "I'm not getting involved with Sara. Marriage isn't for me. I think I've proven that. And it's doubly out of the question now. You know why."

"Because you made a bad choice and got dumped?"

"That's not the only reason, though it's a good one."

"Because you can't have kids?" Teddy shook his head. "Doctors don't know everything, Kyle. Didn't you see what happened today? Sara couldn't stop staring at you. She came alive because of you, because of what you did."

"I haven't got anything to offer, Teddy. I don't have a job. I won't have a home. I haven't even got Dad's affairs settled yet." When Sara sent him a quizzical look from the breakfast trays, Kyle smiled back automatically. "Besides, she's leaving after Christmas."

"I certainly hope you've got enough guts not to let her leave." Teddy strode away.

"Something wrong?" Sara handed him a cup of coffee. "He seems upset."

"Teddy likes to give advice. He doesn't like it when I refuse to take it."

"Listen, Kyle. I've been wanting to tell you something all day." She paused, licked her lips and allowed a faint smile to crease her lips. "I might have found my brother. Samuel."

Kyle could hear her hesitation and knew she was afraid her hopes would be dashed again. He hated seeing fear dim her gorgeous eyes. He wanted to chase the shadows away, watch her laugh again.

"Are you sure it's him?"

"Not yet." She grinned. "I checked Facebook for his name and found him. I asked Rod to friend him—is that how you say it?"

"Yes. And?" Kyle wanted to hear all of it.

"His birthdate, his coloring and especially his eyes all make me think he's my brother." Her face glowed. "He looks a bit like me, Rod says."

"Oh." A sudden urge to protect Sara overtook Kyle. What if this guy was some kind of creep? He didn't say that, however, because he knew Sara would tell him to trust God.

"He doesn't say anything about being adopted and he uses the same last name as me, so I do think it's him." She could hardly contain her excitement. "Isn't it wonderful?"

"It is," he agreed. "So what will you do?"

"I'm not sure." Sara's gorgeous eyes dipped to avoid his.

"Today is your day. Anything is possible." Kyle tipped up her chin and stared into her eyes.

"Do you really think so?" she whispered.

"Yes." How desperately he wanted her to finally achieve this dream. Kyle had to ensure she didn't let fear dissuade her. "You've come this far," he said in a very gentle tone. "Don't give up now. Trust God. Isn't that what you're always telling me?"

"Yes." Her smile was tentative.

Kyle brushed his fingers against her cheek. "You've been a warrior since you came here. That's what we all love about you."

"Really? I don't know."

Kyle nodded.

"If I need help," she began.

"I'll be there. All you have to do is call," Kyle assured her.

"Thank you." Her voice came whisper soft.

For a moment, it seemed as if they were in a world of their own. Communication, unspoken but nevertheless full of meaning, flowed between them.

Kyle understood that disappointment from her past

searches for her family had left her feeling insecure, afraid to try again.

He also understood that she could not turn away from this chance to meet the last member of her family if it was at all possible.

Most of all, Kyle understood that he wanted Sara to have everything her heart desired.

"You're a strong, fiercely courageous woman who has God on her side," he whispered as Rod walked toward them. "Don't change it now."

She held his gaze. Nothing changed and yet, in the fraction of a second, everything did. Hesitation, fear—whatever it was—drained away. She stood straight and tall, her head held high.

"I'm going to do it," she told him. She reached out and squeezed his hand. "Thank you."

"Anytime."

"Excuse me, Sara. I need to talk to Kyle. Privately." Rod waited as Sara let go of his hand. She nodded once then walked away.

Kyle hated to have that moment end. He turned to Rod, stuffed down his frustration and asked, "What do you need?"

"The cake? You said I should find you about this time. Remember?"

Kyle nodded. Turning, he moved as fast as he could up the ramp and inside his house.

Rod met him at the top. "So what should I do?"

"Follow me." Kyle led him into the kitchen. "Open the fridge."

Rod did and whistled as he lifted out a massive cake. "Wow!"

"Sara said she'd never had a birthday cake. Imagine." Kyle shook his head. "A woman like Sara should have a cake to celebrate her birthday. So I ordered a big chocolate one."

"There's enough for seconds. Maybe even thirds," Rod enthused. He inserted the candles and Kyle lit them.

"Okay, I'll go first. Then you come behind me with the cake and please, don't drop it," he told the boy.

"If it's chocolate, no worries, mate. I don't waste chocolate." Rod followed him, waiting inside the house until Kyle called for attention. Right on cue, Rod stepped through the door while Kyle led everyone in singing "Happy Birthday" as Rod carried the massive cake to Sara and set it in front of her with a gallant flourish.

Sara's eyes grew huge as the flames sputtered in a tiny draft off the water. "You did this?" she asked, looking directly at Kyle.

"He didn't make it, so it's edible." Teddy joked.

"You had to have a birthday cake," Kyle said quietly.

"Blow out the candles, Sara," Laurel urged.

"Make a wish first," Tony insisted.

Kyle couldn't break away from Sara's silver-gray stare. It felt as if she spun a web about him, holding him in its grasp until she squeezed her eyes closed. A hush fell on the group as she took a deep breath, opened her eyes and blew out all the candles.

Everyone cheered. As she cut slices of cake for the clamoring group, Kyle suddenly knew that he wanted someone in his life, someone to share everything with, someone to be there for the tough spots and the happy ones.

Not just someone. Sara. He wanted Sara, with her shining face, beautiful smile and gentle heart.

And just as surely as that sweet knowledge came to

him, he knew he could never have that relationship with Sara, even if he dared ask her.

How could he subject this caring, giving woman to a lifetime of being shortchanged because he couldn't do anything she wanted or needed? He'd had to practice like crazy just to be able to get those Zodiacs on the water. He needed help all the time. How could he ever be the kind of husband a wonderful woman like Sara deserved?

It was more than being disabled and Kyle knew it. Below all the doubts about his ability to ever be "normal" again lay a fact that no amount of physical therapy, exercise or prayer could change. It was what kept him from losing himself in his dreams of happily-ever-after. It was what restrained him from becoming dependent on Sara's quick-flash smile to cheer him, or the steady encouragement she offered. It kept him from getting snagged in the "can do it" attitude Sara Kane bequeathed on everyone.

Sweet, loving Sara wanted a family. And according to what the doctors had told him about the bomb blast he'd survived, the shrapnel had pretty well made sure Kyle couldn't give her one. Not ever. That was why he couldn't reconcile God and love. That was why he still fought to understand why. That was why he had to leave this place and start over somewhere else.

"Kyle?" Sara stood before him, arm outstretched, holding a big slice of her cake. "Are you okay?" she asked, head tilted sideways.

"Yes." He took the cake. "Thanks."

"This has been a wonderful day."

"Good," he said, irritated by the longing to pull her into his arms. "Just enjoy it."

"I am." She frowned. "Was it very difficult to relearn the skills you needed with the boats?"

"Yes," he said. "And no. It wasn't that hard after I made up my mind I was going to do it. Getting to that stage was a little more difficult."

"I told—"

"Do not even think about saying 'I told you so,'" he warned.

"Okay." She chuckled and his glower evaporated. "Can I ask you something else instead?"

"You can ask," he said slowly.

"If I wrote to my brother, do you think he'd be mad or would he want to talk to me?" She waited eagerly for his answer.

"Sara, I can't tell you that. I don't know him. I don't know how he'd react." The light went out of her face.

"I know. I just thought maybe—" She shrugged and stopped.

Kyle wasn't going to let it go at that. She deserved more from him.

"I'll tell you this. You'll never know unless you write him and ask," he said, watching the way she ducked her head to hide her gaze from him. "I'm guessing you have an address for him?"

"Yes. But what if he doesn't want to talk to me? What if he has another family now?" She was full into her what-ifs. It hurt Kyle to listen to the anxiety in her voice.

"What if he's thrilled to hear from you and wants to see you as soon as possible?" he countered. "What if he's been looking for you ever since you were kids?"

"You think?" Eagerness lit up her lovely face.

"You never know."

As the day cooled and the sun lowered, the party

came to a close. Sara was the last to say good-night. Kyle froze when she threw her arms around his neck and hugged him.

"I don't know how I can ever thank you for such a wonderful birthday," she murmured into his ear.

The sweet softness of her embrace, the quiet whisper of her voice, the feeling that he'd finally come home— all of these overwhelmed Kyle in a rush. Slowly, almost of their own accord, his arms lifted to encircle her waist. Her cheek brushed his, like a whisper of velvet, and all he could do was stand there.

Her lips grazed the corner of his mouth where his scar cut through, then she drew away. "Thank you, Kyle."

"My pleasure" was all he could manage as he watched her slip away.

Long after everyone had gone, Kyle stood in his backyard alone, remembering that moment and wishing, praying, it could happen again.

Why tempt me with something I can't have? Why am I here? What do You want from me?

When no answer came, he went inside, picked up his phone and dialed Pastor Rick. Maybe talking would help, maybe it wouldn't. But a desperate need to understand God ate at him.

"I'm making the first move," he muttered as he stared at a tiny ribbon of green light that was winding its way across the eastern sky. "The rest is up to You."

Chapter Twelve

Sara stood transfixed as the bugler played "The Last Post" during the November 11 Remembrance Day ceremony. The touching observance honoring those who'd fought and died to save Canada drew her tears. This date had never struck her as deeply as it did today, especially with Kyle at her side.

During the Veterans Day lunch that followed, Kyle, seemed unusually silent, as if sobered by memories of friends he'd lost. Later, Sara drove him to his house in Laurel's van, unsure of how to break the silence.

"Who taught you to drive?" he asked when she'd parked in front of his place.

"Laurel. I didn't want to learn, but she insisted. And I'm glad she did. I'll need that skill when I leave."

He glanced at her as if to say something then quickly looked away.

"The for-sale sign is still up," she said in surprise.

"The first offer fell through." Kyle didn't sound especially bothered about that, for which Sara was glad. It meant he wasn't eager to leave, didn't it?

"Thanks for coming with me today." He reached out

for the door handle then paused. "Are you busy this afternoon?"

"No." His hesitant demeanor surprised Sara—Kyle was never hesitant. "What do you need?"

"A…friend." He glanced at her over his shoulder. "A good friend. I want to scatter my dad's ashes today."

"Kyle, I'm honored you'd ask me to do that with you." She laid a hand on his arm, meaning every word. A little thrill ran through her that he felt close enough to her to share this farewell to his beloved father. "Do you want to go right away?"

"Yes." He studied her. "But you'll need warmer clothes. The jacket is okay but—"

"I have my snow pants in the van," she said. "I should order a new coat and return this one of your mother's—"

"I gave it to you. Keep it," he said. "Come on. You can put on your snow pants while I get my ski suit on."

"Okay." She trudged through the snow behind him. Once inside she blinked in surprise at the emptiness of the kitchen. "It feels so big in here."

"I guess you haven't been in here in a while. I've taken out a lot of stuff." He grinned. "When you first came here and moved stuff around, it made me realize how much room there could be."

"You've done a great job," she said, sliding her fingers across a highboy. "I didn't notice this before. It's lovely."

"Yeah. Mom insisted we bring it back with us after our term in Pakistan. It cost a fortune but Dad had given it to her for Christmas one year and she wouldn't leave it behind."

"Did you like living there?" she asked, studying the intricate work.

"Yes. I had a lot of friends and there was always something interesting to do." He found his outdoor gear.

"It must have been hard to move here," she murmured, thinking of the little boy who'd left behind everything familiar.

"With Dad in the military, I was used to moving. Plus my parents always made relocating sound like a big adventure." He paused, his gaze faraway. "Churchill feels like home." Kyle roused himself after a minute and shrugged. "I'll go change out of my uniform."

"I'm glad you wore it to the ceremony. You look really good in it," she told him, shyly determined to let Kyle hear her admiration. "You represented your part of the forces so well. The whole service was wonderful. I've never seen anything like that before," she murmured.

"You've never been to a Remembrance Day service?" he asked, one eyebrow raised.

"Last year I went by myself but it wasn't like today." Feeling childish, she kept her eyes downcast. "I never understood it. My foster parents never talked about people who served to keep our country safe."

"Why doesn't that surprise me?" Kyle muttered before he disappeared into his room to change clothes.

Sara stared after him for a moment, wondering how much he'd learned about her life in the foster home when he'd looked her up online.

After a moment, she shrugged it off and pulled on her snow pants. This day was about Kyle's dad, not her wretched past. She stared at the lean, angled face of the man in the picture on the wall and wished she'd known Matt Loness.

God, I don't have many weeks left here. Please help me help him, she prayed silently.

When Kyle emerged from the bedroom he wore jeans, thick socks and a flannel shirt.

"Ready?" he asked as he dragged on his snowsuit.

"Yes." She zipped up the red jacket he'd lent her. It still felt like a warm hug, but it was nothing compared to being in Kyle's arms. Pushing away her longing, she pulled up the hood. "Will we walk?"

"No. I want to go up on the cliffs and I'm not sure how much I can handle in all this snow. I thought we could take the snowmobile if you don't mind riding behind and holding this." He lifted a small black box off the table. "I can put it in my knapsack if you'd rather not—"

"I'd be honored." Her smile died when she saw him pull a small handgun out of a metal safe. "What's that for?"

"Bears. Just in case. I have a whistle, as well." He tucked both in his pocket. "Shall we go?"

She followed him outside. A snowmobile sat at the side of his house. It started with one pull.

"Tony got this old thing running. He's got a great future as a mechanic if he wants it," Kyle said over the roar of the motor. He helped her straddle the seat.

While Sara clasped the box with both hands, Kyle slid a helmet on her head, fastened it then put on his own. She made herself small, trying to leave enough room for him to sit in front of her, but she was soon glad of his broad back as, a moment later, they went gliding over the snow toward the cliffs.

Filled with trepidation at first, Sara gradually relaxed and found she loved the ride, even when she had to grab hold of Kyle with one hand to keep from falling off. The world seemed like a downy white quilt spread around them. She wondered how far they'd go.

Once on the cliffs, Kyle slowed down as if he was

trying to find exactly the right spot. Finally he stopped the snowmobile on a huge, wind-hardened drift that overlooked the bay. He climbed off then held out a hand.

"Dad loved to come and sit here in the summer. He called it his thinking spot. I think this will do." Once she'd stepped off, he removed his helmet and set it on the seat. Then he took the box from her. "I'm going to walk closer to the edge but you don't have to come."

"Of course I'm coming." Sara removed her own helmet before following, matching her steps with his. When he faltered on a rough patch, she slid her arm through his and pretended she needed his guidance.

"This is the place," Kyle said when they'd gone about a hundred yards.

Sara caught her breath at the vista. Below her the land dropped away to water, which shone like polished glass. Tufts of snow jutted up in icy peaks covered by froth.

"I'm guessing we'll have an early freeze-up this year," Kyle said.

"Is that good?"

"I guess it depends on your viewpoint," he said. "The tourists like to see the polar bears but when the ice locks in, the bears leave. Don't let that ice fool you, though. It's not thick yet. At these temperatures it will take about another week before it's safe to walk on."

Sara glanced around. She'd seen polar bears many times since she'd first arrived. Though she marveled at their beauty, she was in awe of the strength and the power of their massive jaws.

"Relax. I haven't seen any signs," he said with a half smile. "You're safe."

"Polar bears make me think of that verse, 'Fearfully and wonderfully made,'" she told him.

But Kyle's attention was on the small box. He took off his gloves and tucked them under his arm before lifting the lid.

The afternoon seemed to suddenly still. A hush fell. Sara could hear the crackle of the ice and little else. The skies were turning that leaden gray tone that she'd learned meant snow was imminent. Everything seemed to wait.

"Well, Dad," Kyle finally said very softly, "I brought you back to the place you loved the most. I know you're happier now that you're in heaven with Mom, but—I miss you." The last three words burst out of him as if he could no longer contain them. He blinked his eyes hard then murmured, "Goodbye, Dad. I love you."

Sara held her breath as he lifted his arm and slowly tipped the box. A zephyr wind skipped across the snow from behind them. It caught the ashes and carried them in a trail out over the water, where they disappeared and became part of the landscape. She tipped her head up as huge fat snowflakes began to tumble from the heavens.

When she looked at Kyle, he looked bereft, utterly sad and totally alone.

"Your father would have loved hearing what you said," she told him.

"How do you know?" His voice cracked as he dashed away a tear.

"What father wouldn't love a tribute like that from his beloved son?" When he'd pulled on his gloves, Sara again slipped her arm through his, wanting to show him that she was there for him, to ease his pain if he'd let her.

"I miss him." Those three words emerged in a cracked

and strained voice. He pulled her tightly against him and buried his face in her neck. "I miss him so much."

"I know." Sara held him, feeling the sobs heave his chest and knowing this release had been a long time coming. She smoothed his hair with her gloved fingers and waited. When he finally quieted, she eased his head up so she could see his face. "But your father is still with you. You carry him inside your heart, Kyle."

He looked at her for a very long time.

"Only you would say that." He leaned forward and pressed his icy lips against hers, asking, giving, loving.

Stunned at first, Sara did her best to respond, to show him how special he was to her. She knew nothing of the proper way to kiss a man. But she knew that she loved kissing this one. She only knew it felt right to melt into Kyle's arms, to express all that he had come to mean to her. So she kissed him back as her heart overflowed with love.

"How do you do it, Sara?" Kyle asked as he at last drew away, his arms still circled around her. "How do you always know exactly the right thing to say to make me feel better?"

"Do you feel better?" she asked timidly.

"Yes, I do." He brushed his lips against her forehead and let them rest there, lost in his thoughts. Some moments later he said, "Dad was spared pain and suffering. He died in a place he loved among those he loved. And they loved him." He lifted his head. His thumbs pressed her tousled hair off her face. "It would be selfish to wish he'd stayed. And you're right, he is in my heart. Even after I leave here, that won't change." His arms dropped away and it was like a frigid arctic air mass had moved in.

"Do you have to leave?" Sara peered up at him, wishing, praying he'd say no.

"I can't stay in Churchill." He turned and led the way to the snowmobile. "What would I do?"

"What you have been doing," she said. "Work at Lives helping the kids, being a part of the community."

"And live on what?" He handed her a helmet. "Laurel can't afford to pay me even if I was qualified to work with the boys. Which I'm not."

"She's working on a grant to add positions at Lives," Sara told him. "Maybe—"

"I can't live here anymore, Sara."

She swallowed hard but she could not stifle the words. "You belong here," she pleaded, praying he'd agree.

"Maybe once, but not anymore." He drew a ragged breath. "It's too hard to know I'll never be able to take guests snowshoeing, to know that I will never be able to take anyone hunting or teach them to track. It's killing me to see everything I've always loved and know I can't do it anymore."

"Why can't you?" she demanded. "You took us in the Zodiacs."

"It took me ages to figure out how to do that," he said.

"You don't have time?" Sara wasn't giving up no matter how he glared at her.

"I had Teddy to help me that day," Kyle growled. "I can't expect him to come running every time I need help."

New insight dawned in Sara's mind.

"That's what your decision to leave is really about, isn't it?" She shook her head, amazed she hadn't seen it before. "You feel you'll become dependent if you let someone help you."

"Yes, that's it. Okay?" His angry outburst echoed around them. "I can no longer rely on me. And I hate that."

He glared at her so fiercely, Sara should have been frightened. Instead, her heart wept.

Oh, Kyle, if you only understood how much joy it gives others to help you. Especially me.

"Get on the snowmobile, Sara," he said, his voice resigned. "I want to go home."

"Of course you do," she said, facing him. "Because it *is* home. And home is where you belong, Kyle. It's where we all belong." She forced a smile. "By the way, just so you know, no one can completely rely on themselves. Everyone needs God in their lives."

She knew from his obstinate look that she couldn't change his mind so she climbed on behind him and wrapped her arms around his waist, praying for him as they glided over the snow.

At his house Kyle jerked the machine to a halt and pulled off his knapsack. "Thanks for coming," he growled.

"Wait a minute." She pulled on his arm, forcing him to stop. "We have some things to talk about."

"What things?" Kyle went up the ramp and inside with Sara behind him. He shucked off his outdoor clothes then flopped into a chair.

"You kissed me," she began haltingly.

"Yeah." He looked at her and her heart began to race at the flash in his blue eyes. "That shouldn't have happened."

Her heart stopped. "Wh-why?"

"It was a reaction thing. I was—upset and you comforted me and—" He shrugged.

"I was in the right place at the right time. Is that what you're saying?" She glared at him.

"Sara, I cannot have a relationship with you."

Why wasn't she smarter? Why didn't she know the right words to say?

"Why can't you have a relationship with me?"

"I'm a crippled guy who hasn't figured out how to handle life on his own, let alone with someone else. I'm trying but I have a long way to go before I'll be able to fully trust God again." He rose and began pacing, a flicker of anguish tightening his mouth.

"Look at me. I can't even carry two cups to the table without worrying if I'll spill one."

"And you think that matters?" She got up, carried her own cup to the table and sat down again. "Independence is a great thing, Kyle, until you shut everyone out. Please don't shut me out. I care about you. I—I love you."

There, she'd bared her heart. Saying the words had terrified her. She'd never opened up to anyone as she had to this man. But though she was scared of his reaction, she was also proud of her feelings, glad that her heart had chosen him.

"Sara." Kyle sat down then shook his head. "You can't."

She was suddenly angry. "Why?"

"Because you've never had a relationship, have you?" He nodded when she shook her head. "You don't know what love is."

"Really?" She glared at him. "Wasn't it you who told me, not too long ago, that I knew more about love than most people?" She shook her head at him. "Forget the condescension, Kyle. I may be inexperienced, but I do know what's in my heart. I love you. You're just going to have to deal with it."

Kyle stared at her for a moment, obviously surprised.

Sara held his gaze, refusing to back down. Finally he spoke.

"I wasn't trying to hurt you. I was trying to say that you might be mistaken."

"I'm not."

"Sara, you're leaving in a month and a half." A desperate pleading filled his voice. "You've got a chance to live the life you want. You'll find someone special, someone who can love you the way you need."

"Someone like you," she whispered, her heart plummeting at every word.

"No." Kyle shook his head. "Someone the opposite of me." He sighed, rubbed his knee. "If I were going to have a relationship, I'd want it to be with someone like you, Sara. But I can't."

"Because you're afraid you'll get hurt again?" Her boldness amazed her.

"Because I have nothing to give anyone."

Sara sat very still, taking in all that Kyle had just said, trying to understand the truth that lay behind his words and fend off the deep hurt he'd caused. Finally she said, "My brother hasn't answered my letter yet. I guess he's like you. He doesn't want me, either."

"I'm sorry." He moved, as if he'd enfold her in his arms again then stopped himself. "Give him time. I'm sure he'll change his mind."

"Like you will?" she asked. He didn't answer. "I don't think God is going to give me my family, Kyle. I don't think it's His will. The thing is, I can't figure out what His will for me *is.* I thought I'd find it here. That's why I came. I was so sure—" She dashed away her tears as she stared out the window at the snowmobile covered in fresh snowflakes.

"Sara, please talk to me," Kyle said in a low, intense voice.

She smiled at him even as her heart wondered how she'd manage when he was no longer there to talk to. When she was alone.

"What are you thinking?"

"That I now understand the allure of that machine," she murmured. "That ride today—it must be wonderful to get on and go be alone in the wilderness with your thoughts."

"Would you like to learn to drive it?"

"What?" Sara stared at Kyle. "Are you serious?"

"Why not?" He shrugged. "Might come in handy someday."

"I'd love it."

He rose. "Come on. Let's go have your first lesson. I doubt you'll need more than one."

It felt good to move, to break, to escape the tension her admission of love had brought to the room. But the thought of driving that powerful machine terrified her. Heart in her throat, Sara pulled on her warm clothes and followed Kyle outside. The snowmobile sat there, big and intimidating, but offering a whole new world to explore.

"You start it like this." He made her repeat the process several times then listed the rules and made her repeat them back to him.

The entire time Sara struggled to keep her focus off the way Kyle's hand felt covering hers, the way his smile lit up the blue in his eyes, the way his broad shoulders behind her made her feel safe, protected when he took his seat behind her. He was so gentle, so tender and patient. She had to keep reminding herself that this was the man who had just said he could never love her.

"I think you're ready. Head that way." He pointed toward the cliffs where they'd been earlier.

Sara felt his shoulders shake when she pushed the throttle too hard and the machine jerked forward. Embarrassed, she bit her lip and tried again. After several attempts, she soon had the knack of slowing for bumps and crossing trails. Bit by bit she revved the engine to move faster. Okay, he'd said he couldn't love her. But he couldn't stop her from treasuring these precious moments alone with Kyle in this vast, white wilderness.

He directed her past the grain terminal and out of town. Unsure of their destination, Sara followed his directions. Soon they were in the middle of nowhere with only shrubs and the river distinguishing the landscape. Lost in the beauty, she was startled when Kyle asked her to stop.

"Did I do something wrong?"

"No. You did fine," he assured her. "I need to stand for a few minutes." He winced as he tried to stand.

"Wait." Sara climbed off and held out a hand. He hesitated. She debated a moment then said, "Helping someone else makes the other person feel useful, you know."

Finally he grasped her hand to leverage himself upright.

Sara took off her helmet and tipped her face into the falling snowflakes. "I think this is the loveliest place on earth," she whispered and turned to find Kyle directly in front of her.

"Wait till it hits minus-forty degrees," Kyle said, his lips mere inches from her ear.

Sara wanted so badly to feel his arms wrap around her, to be loved. But Kyle didn't want that. Apparently neither did God. She stepped away from him, needing the space to assemble her troubled thoughts.

Sara had overheard Laurel hiring a new cook on the phone this morning. Now, standing here in the snow, she suddenly realized she'd changed her mind, that she wanted to stay on at Lives, at least for as long as Kyle was here. Maybe if she was here long enough he'd change his mind.

But she'd given her promise that she would leave before the New Year began, insisted Laurel not let her change her mind. How could she now make a fuss and force everyone to change their plans?

"See over there, that cove in the river? That's where my buddies and I used to come to fish." Kyle stood beside her, his head bare. "And over there, where the hill rises, we'd haul deadwood over to make a fort. There aren't many trees in Churchill, most grow along the river. We'd shinny up the largest ones and pretend we were settlers sighting French ships in the bay."

"That sounds like fun," she murmured.

"It was. That rock with the oddly shaped top? That's Top Hat Rock. And that is an abandoned stone house." He grinned. "We had a lot of fun playing hide-and-seek there."

Sara could see it in her mind, a younger Kyle, happy and carefree.

"What are you thinking?" he asked.

"That I envy you."

"Why?" His eyes grew dark and stormy. "Because your past was so miserable? I'm sorry, I shouldn't—"

"Don't." She put her fingers over his lips, relishing this bit of intimacy. "Don't be sorry that you had a wonderful home and family that loved you. Don't ever be sorry that you knew such blessings. Anyway, that isn't what I meant." She withdrew her fingers slowly, knowing that she had no right to touch him like that, no matter what her heart wanted.

"Then what?"

"I meant I envy you because you've done so much, seen so much." She smiled. "You know so many things that I haven't got a clue about."

"You've driven a snowmobile." He flashed his devastating smile. His soft voice soothed. "You live what you believe and you pass it on to everyone around you. You fit perfectly wherever you go, Sara."

"Thank you for saying that, Kyle." She tilted her head to one side and smiled. "So I guess you'd agree that God has blessed both of us?"

Sara watched carefully for some sign of anger. She didn't find it. Instead, after a long pause, Kyle nodded, his gaze on something far ahead, which she couldn't see.

"I guess maybe He has," he murmured. "Come on. It's time to go back before it gets dark. Try to remember as many landmarks as you can in case you get lost someday."

"I doubt that will happen," Sara said as she climbed on the machine and drove them back. As she drove, she offered a prayer of thanksgiving that at last Kyle had begun to reconcile his faith. Had he finally begun to see God as the Giver of Life, maybe even of his future?

But even though she was delighted for him, Sara was suddenly struck by the pain his rejection brought, and struggled not to feel devastated. But the man she loved didn't want her in his future. There was no escaping that.

When will You bring love into my life? When will You show me what You want me to do? When will I get Kyle out of my heart?

The silence of the blanketed land offered no answers.

They hit a soft spot and dipped. Sara gripped the handlebars, bracing herself. The snow came harder now, with gusts of headwinds that buffeted them and made visibility difficult. She paused once when Kyle tapped her shoulder.

"You're doing really well, Sara. I just wanted to mention something."

She nodded.

"You see how it's beginning to storm? When the wind really gets going it will be much harder to see. Storms up here can cause white-out conditions."

"It's almost that now," she said, peering through the whirling snow.

"It can get much worse than this. Lots of people get lost in it. Do you remember rule number one?"

"If you get lost, stop, dig a snow fort and take refuge inside while you wait for someone to find you," she repeated, almost yelling to make herself heard above the wind.

"Exactly." He nodded and pointed to the right, showing that she'd gone off track. "Go that way. We're almost home."

Almost home?

Where is my home, God? Sara asked over and over. She heard only one word in her heart.

Trust.

Chapter Thirteen

Kyle caught himself whistling a Christmas carol as he drove his sled to Pastor Rick's. Their talks were helping him finally shed the anger that had clung to his shoulders ever since his father had died. But he wasn't there yet. He said that to Rick.

"Let go and keep your mind open," his new friend advised. "God has a plan, even if you don't know what it is yet. In the meantime, the help, encouragement and role modeling you do for the boys at Lives are making a difference. You realize, don't you, that it's because of your dad that you find it so easy to teach them survival skills?"

"How do you figure?"

"Because that's what your father did for you, Kyle. He taught you to figure things out, to find a way to do what you want." Rick's grin was irrepressible. "Isn't that how you figured out how you can snowshoe with your bad leg?"

"Yeah, I guess it is. Dad always used to say that if you wanted something enough, nothing could stop you." Kyle grinned.

"That's his legacy to you," Rick said. "Strength, grit and determination. You were entrusted with that so you could pass it on to these kids. They need to know that their past isn't going to hold them back, that if they want to and are willing to work at it, they can change their lives."

"I think Sara's pretty well drummed that into them, but I'm happy to do what I can to help out."

"How is Sara? I missed her at church on Sunday," Rick said.

"That might be my fault." Even as he said it, a ton of guilt rose in Kyle. "I think she's avoiding me."

"Why?" Rick listened as he explained what had happened the day he'd spread his father's ashes.

"I had to reject her," Kyle told him.

"Why? From what you've told me, I thought you had feelings for her." Rick inclined his head. "What's wrong with that."

"Nothing can come of it."

"Because you don't want to get involved? Because you don't want to take a chance on loving again, in case you're rejected?" The way Rick said it sounded silly.

"Sara wouldn't reject me because of my leg," Kyle told him and knew it was true. "She's not like that."

"So the issue is—you don't want to take any risks with her, just like you didn't want to take any risks with God. And look how that turned out." Rick shook his head. "You're looking for guarantees, Kyle, and in this life there aren't any. You're going to have to decide what's important to you. If Sara is important then I suggest you figure out a way to make amends." He shook his head. "I don't know a woman in the world who wouldn't be hurting if they got the rejection you described."

They spent a while praying, then Kyle left, troubled

by the words he'd said to her, the way he'd spurned her. He still didn't think a relationship between them was possible, but he needed her friendship.

"And I gave Teddy advice about Laurel," he muttered to himself as he drove to Lives. "Practice what you preach, dummy."

The first thing he was going to do was apologize to Sara. But it turned out not to be that easy. He found her in the kitchen, stirring a pot that gave off the most delicious aroma. How to begin?

"What's that?"

"The filling for chicken pie. I'm making one for Christmas morning—" The last word came out on a wail. Sara sank into a kitchen chair, weeping so loudly Kyle thought his heart would break.

With great difficulty he knelt in front of her, pushed her hair back and peered into her eyes, panicked by her tears and the hopelessness he heard in her voice. "Sara? What's wrong?"

Silver eyes brimming with tears, she looked at him and laid a hand over her heart. "It hurts so badly, Kyle. How can I make it stop?"

"What happened?" He waited as she reached into her apron pocket and pulled out a crumpled piece of paper. Without saying a word she held it out.

Kyle unfolded it. Slowly he read the harsh, condemning words her brother had written, damning claims that Sara had abandoned him to suffer growing up with no one to watch out for him as a big sister should. When Kyle came to Samuel's demand to be left alone, to his insistence that he wanted nothing to do with his sister, a gut-wrenching ache tore through him. The last link to Sara's precious family had been severed.

"It's okay, Sara," he murmured, touching her hand.

"It is *not* okay, Kyle." She snatched back the letter and shoved it into her pocket. "Samuel is my brother, my last living link with our family. How can I just let him go?"

The last word emerged on a sob that shook her. Kyle's heart wrenched at her grief when she stared at him through tear-glazed eyes.

"How will it ever be okay?" she mourned.

With great difficultly, Kyle rose. He leaned over and drew her into his arms.

"I don't know, Sara," he murmured. "Only God knows." She fit perfectly in his arms and suddenly Kyle longed to have the right to be the one to comfort her forever.

Because he loved her.

The knowledge sucker punched Kyle. He didn't say a word; he couldn't have.

He'd cared about Sara Kane for so long…but love?

He rolled it around in his brain, tried to downplay it, but the truth would not be silenced. This woman had taken root in his heart. She belonged there.

Except—how? He could never tell Sara how much she meant to him, never hold her like this again, certainly never let her guess how he felt. Sara deserved so much more than he could offer.

She was going to leave here. Kyle would pretend it was for her good, because it was. Wasn't it better that she go believing that he didn't care for her than to add another burden to her already heavy load?

Kyle pushed away everything but his concern for this precious woman. She was alone. Here, now, there was no one but him to comfort her, to help her through this. He couldn't back away, he couldn't ignore her suffering. He had to do something. He lifted his hands and cupped them around her face, forcing her to look at him.

"Sara, I don't know how God soothes our deepest hurts. I don't understand how He comforts us and brings us out of the dark places," he whispered. "I only know He does. He will."

Gradually her sobs died away. When she finally lifted her head to look at him, he saw that the light that made her silver eyes glow was gone. His heart grieved that sweet Sara and her irrepressible positive outlook had been crushed.

"He will," he repeated.

"You're talking to me about God?" She tilted her head to one side. "I thought you were mad at God."

"I, um, was." He stammered to a halt, embarrassed now to realize how silly it was to think he understood God's plans. "I've been meeting with that new minister, trying to sort out some things."

"Oh, Kyle, I'm so glad that you're searching to restore your faith." She hugged him tightly. Kyle reveled in her embrace. Too soon she pulled away and straightened her apron. "Sometimes it's hard to accept God's ways, but you won't regret it. The most important thing is that you find Him again."

"That's what Rick keeps saying. Figure out the issues and work them through. The things he says have begun to strike home."

"Really? Do you mind telling me?" She waited until he was seated then sat across from him.

"No." Sharing with this woman seemed so right, so natural, that Kyle couldn't seem to help himself. "But the first thing I need to do is apologize. I hurt you and I never want to do that. I'm sorry."

"That doesn't matter. It's forgotten." She folded her hands in her lap. "Tell me the good stuff, the stuff you've learned about God."

"Okay. Well, Rick said my dad left me a legacy that it's my duty to pass on. I never thought of it that way but he's right."

Sara gave him one of her beautiful, warm smiles, encouraging him to continue.

"The things I loved about Churchill are the same things the boys need to learn," Kyle continued. "Learning how to deal with the hardships this land presents will help them find pride in themselves and realize they aren't weak, that they don't have to be patsies for some drug pusher or gang leader." He took a deep breath. "That's why I'm going to take them on an overnight survival trek next week. I've already okayed it with Laurel. It will be my Christmas gift to them."

"Before you go, you mean." Sara's face tightened but she kept a bead on him.

"Yes." But as he studied her face, Kyle knew he couldn't leave without trying to do something that would reunite her with the brother she so longed to see again. "Sara, would you mind if I talked to Samuel?"

"Oh, Kyle, that's such a lovely offer. But I don't think it will do any good," she said, frowning. "His letter is pretty adamant about not wanting anything to do with me. Maybe it's better to respect his wishes, but thank you, Kyle."

He nodded, still listening but mulling over the possibility of contacting her brother, anyway. Maybe he could get Samuel to at least talk to her. That would make a good Christmas gift and if it didn't work out, she wouldn't be disappointed.

"I've been talking to Rick, too," she told him.

Kyle didn't have to ask why. He knew the reason Sara had sought out Rick was to soothe her hurting heart over the family God seemed disinclined to give. If ever someone deserved that family, it was Sara. He knew she was also hurting over his rejection. She'd probably told the pastor about that. Again Kyle felt ashamed of his harsh words.

"I love working here. That day we were on the snowmobile I started to think that maybe God wanted me to stay, to keep working with the boys. But I don't think that anymore."

"Why?" He couldn't fathom Lives without Sara.

"Because God's ways aren't ours and just because I want something, doesn't mean He wants it for me." Her head dipped. "I have to leave."

"What's made you so sure?" Kyle sensed something else was going on.

"God doesn't want me here because I don't deserve the privilege of staying here," she whispered.

"Why do you think that, Sara?" His heart felt as if it was squeezed in a vise.

"Because I caused Maria's death." Sara shook her head, loosening a few tendrils of hair that slid down to caress her cheek. "That's why God wants me to leave. That's why I have to be alone. I don't deserve a family."

"Sara, no. God isn't like that." He tried to make her understand what he himself had only just begun to fathom. "God's love doesn't depend on us deserving it. God gives His love freely. Even if you did make a mistake, you asked for forgiveness, didn't you?" He waited until she'd nodded. "He looks at you and loves you as His precious child. He doesn't want you to suffer."

"Then why doesn't He answer my prayer for a family?" she demanded, eyes blazing. When he couldn't answer, she smiled the saddest smile he'd ever seen. "Don't worry, Kyle, I'll live on my own and continue to serve Him. It's just that I would have loved—"

With a small, tired sigh she rose and returned to the counter, where she continued rolling out the pastry she'd begun.

Kyle opened his mouth to argue, but what could he say? He couldn't tell her what was in his heart, that he wanted to be with her forever, to make her world happy and fulfilled. Because he couldn't do that. The doctors had been clear, the shrapnel had done its damage. There was little chance that he could father a child.

Sara wanted a family, children. Lots of them.

Kyle slowly turned and left the kitchen. He went to the family room and laid out the things he'd brought, ready to begin a survival class as soon as the boys returned from school.

But no matter how busy he kept himself, he couldn't shake the image of Sara in his arms, the light lemon fragrance of her hair filling his senses, sobbing as if her heart was breaking.

He thought again of the verse he'd read this morning in Psalms 66.

You let men ride over our heads, we went through fire and water, yet you brought us to a place of abundance.

"I'm trying to wait and let You bring me to that place of abundance," he prayed. "I'm trying to follow the directions You give."

Kyle stared out the window at the snow-covered land he loved.

"But oh, God, what am I supposed to do about Sara?"

* * *

"Two days until we go on our trek," Kyle told the boys gathered around him. "I've got a little quiz to see how ready you are."

Sara had spent the past few days listening in, pretending she wasn't paying attention as she knit a pair of mitts for Laurel. The truth was she reveled in every word Kyle said. She needed to hear the sound of his voice, to see his face come alive as he explained how to track, how to see wild animals without scaring them away, how to survive in the wilderness.

But after ten minutes Sara knew that today, for some reason, she couldn't listen anymore. It hurt too much. She had to get away. She waited until the boys huddled around the coffee table to work on their quiz.

"Can I borrow your snowmobile, Kyle?"

He frowned at her. "By yourself?" She nodded. "What for?"

"I need to get out." When he hesitated, Sara pleaded her case. "You've given me several lessons on it. I know my way around. I just want to be alone for a bit."

"Okay." He dug out his keys and handed them to her. "Don't go far," he ordered.

"Just toward town, I promise." She took his keys and hurried away.

"Sara. Can I talk to you for a minute?" Laurel watched her fasten her snow boots.

"Can it wait until I come back?"

"This won't take long." Laurel sat down across from her. "Honey, I know you said you only wanted to stay till Christmas, but are you sure? I don't have to bring the new cook out. You don't have to leave."

The choice dangled in front of her with tantalizing sweetness. Stay, see Kyle every day, see the boys change and grow.

"Laurel, I promised you I'd go before New Year's when I came here and I'm not changing my mind. Besides," she said very quietly, "this isn't where I belong."

"Then—"

"Where will I go?" Sara smiled. "I've been wondering that myself. I think I'll go back to Vancouver for a while. Maybe there's something there God would have me do."

"Honey, are you sure?" Laurel asked.

"No, I'm not sure at all," Sara muttered. "It's like there's a block between God and me, and no matter how hard I pray, I can't get through it. I was so sure He sent me here to find my family and reunite them. I thought that was His plan for me. But I was wrong."

"Sweetie." Laurel frowned but said nothing else, as if she didn't know what to say.

"It will be hard for me to leave here." She jumped up and hugged her best friend. "I've loved every moment of my time here at Lives."

Sara couldn't say any more. It was too hard. So she zipped up her coat, pulled on her mitts and grabbed Kyle's helmet.

"Take my cell phone, just in case," Laurel urged before she could get out the door.

"Thanks." Sara stuffed it in her pocket then hurried away, anxious not to weep in front of her friend.

But once she was on the snowmobile she couldn't stop her tears. She blinked furiously, trying to see the way before her. But the deep sense of loss, the feeling of being abandoned by God in Whom she'd placed so much trust, only added to the depression engulfing her. For once the softly falling snow did nothing to heighten her mood.

As Sara drove, she couldn't dislodge the images of the boys gathered around Kyle, his face intent as he taught them. He'd found his niche. He was a born instructor. Maybe he hadn't accepted it yet, but Sara knew in her heart that Kyle would be staying in Churchill. This was his home. He belonged here.

She didn't.

Why, God? I'm in love with Kyle. I could help him. I could help the kids. Why haven't You given me my dream?

Heartbroken, Sara soon realized she'd made the very mistake Kyle had warned her of over and over. She lost track of her surroundings. Where was she? Surely that lump of white over there was familiar? She slowed the sled to a stop then surveyed the area. Nothing seemed quite where it should be.

She was lost.

Using great care, Sara turned the sled around and tried to follow her tracks back. But the snow was falling more heavily now and it was difficult to find her tracks in the white-on-white landscape.

Fear rose as she recalled the many stories she'd heard about people getting lost in the wilderness. Without meaning to, she gunned the engine. The snowmobile spurted forward in a rush of motion, hit something then swayed sideways, throwing her off. Her head hit something hard. Everything went black.

"Sara should have been back before now." Kyle glanced from his watch to Laurel's face and knew that she was as worried as he was. "Has anyone seen her?"

Laurel shook her head, her face pale.

"I'll call Teddy, get him to drive out here and check along the way." He was grateful his friend was still in town. Teddy had talked of going to his son's for Christmas. "He's coming," he said, hanging up the phone.

"I gave her my cell phone, but she doesn't answer." Laurel's eyes met his. "Something's wrong." She wrung her hands. "I should have stopped her. She was so upset when she left."

"Upset?" Kyle's radar went on high alert. "What happened?"

"I don't know. I asked her if she was sure she wouldn't stay on after Christmas and she said no, she loved it here but she had to leave. She said she didn't belong here, but she does, Kyle. I should never have accepted her resignation."

Didn't belong?

The silliness of that statement stunned Kyle. Sara Kane belonged at Lives Under Construction as much as polar bears belonged in Churchill.

She belonged to him, she was in his heart, his very soul. She made his days worthwhile. And he couldn't give her up.

"What should we do?" Laurel asked him.

Kyle glanced outside. "Even if it wasn't storming, I can't track in the dark. By morning everything will be covered. I'd go out there right now if I thought it would do any good, but running off half-cocked won't help Sara."

"Then what?" Laurel asked.

"Pray." Rod stood in the doorway. It was obvious that he'd heard their concern. "It's what Sara would do. She prays about everything. That's why she has no fear. She doesn't depend on herself, she depends on God."

The words hit their target in Kyle's heart. Sara had

accused him of that before, of believing he had to rely on himself.

"Sara would tell us to trust God," Rod said.

"Out of the mouths of babes," Laurel murmured. She touched his shoulder. "I'm going to talk to the boys. I'll be back," she said, leading Rod out of the room.

Kyle looked out the window again, thinking of how he'd told Sara he was repairing his relationship with God. How far did that go? Far enough to trust God with Sara's life, no matter what? Trust God to face whatever problems might come?

That applied equally to the future. Kyle loved Sara, he knew that with every fiber of his being. If he told her, if he accepted the love she'd so freely offered, could he trust God to help him face whatever problems would come, problems he could never handle on his own?

"Yes."

"Yes, what?" Teddy asked, standing in the doorway.

"Yes, I love Sara. Yes, I am going to trust that God will work out our future, if she'll have me. And yes, we are going to find her." He looked at his friend. "Any problem with that?"

"Not one." Teddy grinned as he clapped Kyle on the back. "What's our next move?"

"We're going to organize a search party so that when this breaks, we'll be ready to go out and find her. But first, we're going to pray. Then I have an important phone call to make for Sara."

Teddy bowed his head and led them in a prayer for safety for Sara, for clear weather and for God's leading in finding her.

"Amen." Kyle said. "Now let's get to work."

Chapter Fourteen

Sara came to with the realization that she was freezing cold. She sat up, blinked away the flakes sticking to her lashes and found she was almost buried in the snow. Her fingers and toes tingled. She rose, moving gingerly to get her circulation flowing.

She glanced around hopefully, but everything was still covered in a downy blanket, obscuring whatever landmark might lie beneath. The knowledge hit like a sledgehammer.

She could die out here.

"God, I need help," she whispered, her heart like a block of ice in her chest.

Already the sky grew darker as evening crept in. Panicked, Sara felt in her pocket for Laurel's phone, praying she could get a signal.

But the phone wasn't in her pocket.

Though she looked for it, feeling around in the snow with her hands, she could not find it.

The first sign of hypothermia will creep up on you. You must be prepared to protect yourself. If you're lost, stay put. Dig a shelter in the snow, but make sure some-

thing is visible for searchers to see. Kyle's voice from this afternoon's survival lesson filled her mind.

Sara levered her hands under the snowmobile to right it. The machine was heavy and sitting awkwardly. At first it didn't budge, but she pushed back the ache in her head, amassed all her strength and shoved. Finally the machine flopped over onto its skis.

But when she attempted to start it, nothing happened. Over and over she tried the ignition but nothing happened. The last time she tried, the battery died.

Flurries whirled around her as the wind whipped the snow. Soon it would be completely dark.

Quickly Sara scraped snow together with her mittened hands and piled it high. The slightly damp snow packed easily. She pressed it around one side of the snowmobile, using the machine as a wall of her shelter. She swept the other side of the machine clear so the black seat and silvery skis were visible.

Satisfied she'd done her best, she slid inside her snow house as the remaining flickers of light faded. Before she packed the last bit of snow around her head, she glanced left. Her breath snagged in her throat.

Two lumbering white shapes plodded through the wilderness barely two hundred feet away.

Polar bears.

"Lord, please protect me," Sara prayed, her temples throbbing. Buried as she was, she could hear the whistle of the wind and nothing else.

It seemed she sat there for hours, on edge, waiting for the bears to find her. But they, too, must have sought shelter as the wind now screamed across the land.

"I always thought I was alone before," she whispered to the only one who could hear her. "But now I am truly alone. I thought I could make up for my mistake with Maria if I worked hard at Lives, helped in the community, made it better for other people. But I see now that it doesn't work. I guess that's why You haven't shown me the future and where You want me to go—because it doesn't matter."

A new gust of wind penetrated her frail shelter. She packed more snow to block the draft. Every so often she poked her head outside. Once she thought she saw the bears sitting together, watching her, before the whirling snow blurred everything.

She thought of Kyle. How she loved him. How she wanted the best for him, health and freedom from his pain, a solidifying of his faith to total trust in God. How she wished she could stay to watch him take a leadership role at Lives, be part of his world.

She suddenly knew with every fiber of her being that Kyle would come looking for her, and the thought of her mistake putting him at risk was more than she could bear.

Her head and her heart ached too much. Sara leaned back and let sleep overtake her.

Sara was cold, so cold.

Her lips felt cracked and frozen as she opened her eyes, with no idea of how much time had passed.

There was no sign any of her prayers had been heard. She had to let in fresh oxygen. She poked her head through the snow and immediately noticed the wind had died down. A hush enveloped the land. How light it seemed. Why?

Eyes widening, she blinked at the incredible beauty playing out in the night sky. Ribbons of misty green, turquoise, blue—oh, there were a hundred shades, and they spun and wove across the sky in the most amazing show. Because of them she could clearly see the polar bears, sitting in the same place, waiting and watching.

Then, as if a conductor had mounted the podium, the lights moved in sideways arcs so that Sara was almost encircled.

Praises rose from her heart.

In that moment truth dawned.

"I'm not alone. How could I be alone when You are all around me?" she whispered. "I am a part of Your family. You love me."

She had to be silent for a moment, to let it sink in. The lights grew more intense, more active, richer in color, mirroring the revelation bursting in her heart.

"You have loved me more than any family could have. You protected me, cared for me, brought me to a place where I could give to kids who need it so desperately. You're not asking me to leave. This is where You want me, here in Churchill, at Lives. This is where I belong." The wonder of it silenced her for a moment.

Then she thought of Kyle and her heart pinched with longing. She looked to the sky and felt heavenly reassurance. If Kyle couldn't love her, God would heal her heart. She had to trust Him to do that because Sara knew now with utmost certainty that she could not leave this place.

The lights swayed, deepening and changing color, beckoning her to full committal. Sara gazed at the heavens. *Trust,* they seemed to whisper.

Inhaling deeply, she nodded.

"I'm putting my future in Your hands, God. I love

Kyle, but I'm leaving him and my brother up to You. Your will be done."

The lights rippled and swelled as profound peace filled Sara. Her dream of a family, of Kyle—all of those hopes melted away. God was her Father. He would care for her. He knew best.

A song the boys had taught her rose to her lips. She sang it loudly, joyfully, uncaring of the bears that sat mere feet away. They, too, were God's creatures.

She had nothing to fear.

"Listen to me, Samuel. Your sister did everything she could to find you." Kyle grimaced when the other man interrupted. "Let me finish. You have no idea what Sara Kane is like, what she's gone through, why she's so desperate to see you again. I suggest you do some research online. When you read why she couldn't rescue you, perhaps you'll realize that Sara is the best sister you could ever hope to have." Kyle clicked off his phone.

"Are you sure that was wise?" Teddy asked.

"Probably not, but maybe it will help him get over his 'poor me' attitude." He frowned. "What is that racket?"

"Our volunteer force. Take a look." Teddy opened the computer room door.

Kyle gaped. Lives Under Construction bulged with people, spilling into the hallway, coming in the front door.

"Once they heard about Sara, they came. I think everyone in town is here. Everyone loves her." Teddy's face softened.

"I love her, too." Kyle checked the weather outside. It was as good as it was going to get. "Let's go talk to them," he told Teddy.

Rod got everyone's attention by whistling. Kyle smiled his thanks at the boy as silence fell.

"Folks, the storm is over for now, but weather reports say another one will start sometime later this afternoon. We have about three hours of daylight to search for Sara. I've laid out a grid pattern. We'll assign teams to each section. Have your cell phones with you and be sure they're fully charged. Now let's find Sara and bring her home. But first let's pray."

Oddly Kyle felt no hesitation about praying publicly. His certainty that he needed Sara is his life grew with every passing moment. If he had to, he would lay down his life for her. If she'd agree, he'd spend the rest of his days giving her everything he had.

He had to trust God that his everything would be enough for Sara.

At the end of Kyle's prayer, Pastor Rick added his own. Then the groups assembled and set out on their search. Teddy had set up a portable communications station in Laurel's kitchen. He quickly familiarized her with the system. The boys approached Kyle.

"We want to help search for Sara, too," Tony told him.

Kyle recognized how badly they wanted to help the woman who had so selflessly loved them. He called over one of the police officers.

"The boys want to help." He shot the officer a look that begged him to agree.

"We're going to do a search around town," the Mountie said. "We can use all the help we can get. Come with me, guys."

"Kyle?" Teddy beckoned him over. He pointed to a section on the map. "I didn't dare give this to anyone else. It's tricky to navigate and there are reports of a bear and her cub there. You're the one who knows this area the best."

"It's so far out. You think she would have gone that far?" Kyle asked, frowning as he studied the map.

Teddy's reasoning convinced him that it was possible Sara had mistaken a turn on the way into town. If she had taken the route he believed, it would take every ounce of Kyle's energy to get there and back with his leg aching as it was.

But he'd gladly do that and more to get Sara safe in his arms.

I can do all things through God, Who strengthens me. It was a promise his mom had clung to. Kyle tucked it deep inside, took a breath and nodded.

"Okay, let's go, Teddy." He grabbed his backpack, put the thermos of coffee Laurel gave him inside and zipped his snowsuit. "Pray," he begged her.

"Without ceasing," Laurel promised. She hugged him. "You bring her back."

"I intend to." Kyle set out on a borrowed machine with Teddy behind on his own. They'd need two sleds when they found Sara. Once in the open he revved the motor. Teddy followed. They raced across the land, taking a shortcut to get to the spot Teddy had marked on the map, ever aware that night was coming, fast.

After they'd gone ten miles without seeing anything unusual, Kyle stopped. He flipped the visor on his helmet to speak to Teddy.

"The marsh is ahead." He studied the ground but couldn't discern any tracks. "The machines will bog down in the weeds. I can't see anything to indicate she went in there. You?"

Teddy shook his head. "Nothing."

"The wind's picking up." Wind chill made the temperature dangerously frigid. Kyle checked his watch, grimaced. *Too long, God. It's taking too long.*

"It'll get colder now with the sky clearing," his friend noted. "Do you think Sara could read the night sky enough to navigate by it?"

"I doubt it." Kyle squeezed his eyes closed and summoned her lovely face to mind. *Dear Sara.* The image warmed him until he remembered the bear warning. "Sara's a city girl. I don't think she'd know much about survival out here." Panic reached down and squeezed his stomach into a knot. "What am I going to do if—"

"Don't give up." Teddy bowed his head. "God, we need help here."

Kyle silently added his pleas to the prayer but was interrupted when he lifted his head and suddenly gave a shout. Kyle strained to follow Teddy's pointing finger. Ahead of them, just to the right, the aurora borealis flashed an arc of incredible silver-green through the sky then undulated like an unfurling ribbon, lighting the ground ahead of them.

"Forward," Teddy murmured. He pulled down his visor.

Kyle said nothing, his focus on the land around them, his heart praying. The northern lights continued to shift, swelling and heaving, ever changing. Kyle had never seen them so bright.

But he saw no sign of Sara.

Dispirited, defeated and wondering if he'd run out of favors from God, Kyle stopped to stretch his leg. It ached abominably from being bent for so long. He knew he could not last much longer on the machine. Doggedly, he revved his engine and continued his search across the frozen taiga.

His thoughts went to his last meeting with Rick. They'd talked over a verse in Psalms 69, which Rick said David had written in the deepest hours of his distress.

For Jehovah hears the cries of his needy ones and does not look the other way.

"Please look my way, God. Please help," he kept repeating as he drove. *Where are you, Sara?*

Suddenly Kyle blinked. He took a second look then stopped his machine. Teddy followed suit.

Straight ahead, two polar bears sat as if transfixed.

Kyle couldn't understand why they stayed. All at once Sara's voice, cracked with strain but filled with determination, broke through the silence of the night as she belted out "Our God Reigns."

His heart bursting with joy, Kyle climbed off his machine and tramped through the snow, following Sara's voice, afraid to drive any closer lest he crush her refuge. Moments later he saw the black leather corner of the snowmobile seat jutting out of the snow and the tip of one ski.

"Sara! Where are you?"

Seconds later the hood of Sara's bright red jacket poked through the snow. "Kyle?"

He got down in front of her, digging madly, freeing her from the snow. With tender fingers he touched the blue spot on her temple then brushed his lips against it.

"Oh, Sara, you scared me to death. Are you all right? What happened?" He listened to her story, unable to stop touching her to assure she was unhurt.

"I'm fine." She smiled. Was there anything sweeter than Sara Kane's smile?

No longer able to stop himself, Kyle folded her into his arms.

"I love you, Sara," he whispered before he covered her lips with his.

For one stunned moment she didn't move. But the next second she had her arms around his neck. Her lips melted warm against his, returning his embrace, telling him everything he needed to know. She still loved him.

In the background, Kyle vaguely heard Teddy radioing that they'd found her, but he ignored it, awed that God had given him the desire of his heart. After a moment, Sara went very still.

"I'm pretty cold and my brain's not functioning perfectly," she murmured, tilting her head away, a frown on her face. "But did you say you love me, Kyle?"

"For ages, with all my heart, as deeply as a man can love a woman, yes," he said, kissing her between each phrase. "I love you, Sara."

"Then why did you push me away?" she demanded, her eyes showing her hurt.

"I'm sorry I did that. But I didn't think I had any other choice until God showed me a few things. We have a lot to talk about, sweetheart." He helped her up. "But it's going to have to wait until we get you home. Have a sip of Laurel's coffee. It will warm you for the ride home." He glanced at the bears that looked on with interest but hadn't moved. "Think they'll follow us?" he asked Teddy.

"Of course they won't." Sara grinned. "I can't carry a tune in a bucket. That's what kept them back there. They're well rid of me."

Teddy burst out laughing. Because her legs seemed wobbly, he and Kyle helped her onto Kyle's sled. Then Teddy pulled him aside.

"You're in pain. You don't have to drive back. We could get a chopper out here," he said.

"I am driving Sara home," Kyle told him, daring him to argue.

Teddy studied him for a moment then smiled. "So what are we waiting for?"

"Nothing. I have all I need." Kyle glanced at Sara then headed for Churchill. He was aware of the rising wind and the snowflakes that now fell in thick sheets, but felt no fear.

"They were so beautiful," Sara murmured when they arrived at Lives and she climbed off the sled.

"What were?" Kyle slung his arm around her waist, supporting her.

"The northern lights. God gave me my own private viewing." She laid her head on his shoulder. "I love you, Kyle. I don't have to search for my family anymore."

"No, you don't, my dearest Sara. We'll be each other's family." Kyle knew the others were waiting but he was loath to let her go, until she shivered. "Inside. We'll talk later."

"You'll be here?" she asked very softly.

"Whenever you want, for as long as you want, I will be here, Sara."

But as he watched her disappear into the throng of people waiting, Kyle wondered if she'd want him to stay when she learned the truth and realized he couldn't give her the family she craved.

Chapter Fifteen

Snuggled in a big, fluffy quilt, which Lucy insisted on, Sara turned so she was leaning against the sofa arm, facing Kyle. She looked into his eyes and knew he was struggling to tell her something.

"Did you mean what you said?" she asked, glad they were finally alone in the big family room.

"Which part?" He looked at her then smiled. "Of course I love you. Couldn't you tell?"

"No," she said simply. "As you said, I don't know anything about loving someone."

"Oh, Sara, don't repeat my stupidity. I was wrong and so are you. You know all about love. You've taught all of us—the boys, folks in town, me." He took her hands in his and brought them to his lips. "You've taught us all the true meaning of love. You go above and beyond for everyone. You refuse to take no for an answer. That's why I love you so much."

"But—" Sara struggled to put the pieces together in her mind. "If you loved me, why did you tell me you didn't? Would you have let me leave knowing that you loved me?"

"If God hadn't shaken me up?" He shook his head. "Truthfully, I don't know. I was so stubborn, so determined not to depend on anyone." He grimaced. "I was afraid."

Sara studied their entwined fingers and wondered. Was her love enough for him? Maybe he'd realize she couldn't be the kind of woman he wanted.

"Sara." He bent forward so she had to look at him. "Why do you think I've turned down three offers on the house? The last couple offered way more than my asking price but I made up an excuse not to sell because I couldn't leave you." A fierce look filled his face. "I promise I'll do my best not to lean on you too much and I will relearn how to do as much as God wants me to."

Her heart melted at his declaration. God had answered her deepest prayers. Sara flung her arms around his neck.

"My darling Kyle, we'll each have to lean on the other, and God." She kissed him then leaned back. "I come with a lot of baggage, Kyle. You're going to need patience."

"Not a hardship as long as you have patience with me." He hugged her. "Sara, I need to tell you something else."

"Okay." Worried by the grave tone of his voice, she drew back.

"Before this goes any further I have to say this." He inhaled then spoke. "One of the reasons I pushed you away is because I can't have kids. The doctors said my injuries make that almost impossible."

His words came out slowly. Sara sat frozen, absorbing everything he said. To never have her own child— no! She squeezed her eyes closed and prayed and once more the soft, sweet assurance rushed in. God was in charge and He would fill her life with joy.

"I know how much you want a family of your own," Kyle murmured. He tried to hide it but his face showed how much it cost him to tell her the truth. "I can't give you that. All I have to offer you is love."

Tears came to her eyes. *All he had to offer.* As if she was somehow getting second best with this loving, tender man who had risked his life for her.

"If you want to change your mind—"

She stopped his speech with the simple gesture of leaning over and covering his lips with hers. She kissed him as deeply, as passionately as she knew how, pouring her heart and soul into it. And wonder of wonders, Kyle kissed her back. When she finally pulled away she was breathless.

"I already have a family, Kyle. A huge one. Laurel, the boys, this town, Lucy and Hector. You. Especially you." She snuggled her head against his chest. "God has blessed me so richly."

"Are you still leaving, Sara? I'll live wherever you want to. We'll start over together." He blinked at the smile that lifted her lips. "What?"

"I'm not leaving Churchill, Kyle. I can't." She grasped both his hands in her small ones and explained. "Out in the snow I figured out what God wants for my future." She spread her hands wide. "Churchill is my home, Kyle. This is where God wants me, here at Lives, in town, in the church, helping out wherever I can. I couldn't help Maria. But I can help the boys who come here. That's what God wants."

"I'm certainly glad to hear that." Laurel stepped into the room. "Sorry to interrupt you two but I just discovered that our new cook isn't as accomplished as I'd expected. She's worried about taking on everything here and asked if someone would train her. As head cook, Sara, you could do that. We'll need help if my plan to expand goes ahead. Is that something you're interested in?"

"Head cook? Yes! Yes, yes, yes." Sara jumped up and hugged her boss. "I'd love to stay." She twirled around, her heart full of thanksgiving for the plans God had for her.

"Okay, then." Laurel smiled. "We'll talk in the morning. I'll leave you two alone now."

Sara flopped down on the couch, exhausted but so happy. "I'm so happy I can stay here. But knowing you're completely reconciled with God is the best thing of all."

"Yes, it is," he agreed, caressing her arm.

"What changed that for you?" she whispered, her fingers threading with his, loving the way he drew her close.

"Realizing that I couldn't keep you safe. It didn't matter what I did. I was powerless to get you home. I had to rely on someone else, on a whole lot of others. Finally I had to rely on God to show us where you were." He brushed his lips against her forehead then sighed. "That was so hard."

"Why?" she asked.

"Ever since I got hurt, I've had to depend on others in some way, shape or form. And I hated it. It made me feel like I was a loser. My doubts about my future magnified." He squeezed her shoulder. "But then there you were, pushing your way into my life and forcing me to care for you. How could I not love you?"

"I love you, too, Kyle. So much." Sara tipped her head up to receive his kiss. "God has answered so many of my prayers it's like Christmas has come early. What else could I possibly want?"

"Well." Kyle's eyes, blue whorls of uncertainty, rested on her. "I haven't got a job, Sara. I don't know if I can stay here or what I'd do. I was going to open a computer store in Winnipeg but—"

"I believe God has more important things for you to do, Kyle." Sara slid her arms around his waist and laid her head on his shoulder. "The boys that are here and the ones yet to come need you to teach them how to be men of integrity. God blessed you with wonderful parents so you can pass on the lessons they taught you. That's why He saved you in Afghanistan. That's why He led you back here. He'll work it out, Kyle. Just have some faith."

"You're going to be a wonderful partner, Sara Kane." Kyle drew his arms around her and showed her how much he needed her in his world. "So when should we get married?"

"But—" Marry him? Her heart stopped. She stared at him, thrilled by the thought of spending the rest of her life with this wonderful man.

"What? You don't want to marry me?" Kyle teased, playing with a tendril of her hair. But there was the tiniest doubt in his voice.

"Yes, I want to marry you. But you never asked me."

A moment later Kyle was kneeling in front of her, holding her hands and staring into her eyes.

"My dearest Sara, will you please marry me? I have no job, my house is on the market and I have no idea how I will support you. But I'm willing to trust God for what we need."

Trust Kyle to make sure he'd covered all the bases with his proposal. How she loved this man.

"Yes, Kyle. I will gladly marry you, because I love you."

She tilted her head to kiss him just as his phone rang, making them both laugh.

He spoke into it for a few moments, assured the caller that Sara was fine then handed the phone to her. "Someone wants to speak with you."

"Hello," she said.

"This is Samuel. Kyle called me. I was wondering if we might talk sometime."

Sara slumped into Kyle's tender embrace and closed her eyes.

"Sara?" the phone squeaked.

"Sorry," she apologized, staring into Kyle's loving eyes. "I just needed a minute to thank God."

"For what?" her brother asked.

"For giving me two wonderful men in my family." She laughed when Samuel said she might be making a mistake about him. "No. God brought you both into my life," she told him, staring into Kyle's rich, blue eyes. "And God doesn't make mistakes. Not ever."

Epilogue

On a warm July day the entire town of Churchill gathered on the windswept cliffs overlooking Hudson Bay for the wedding of Sara Kane to their own Kyle Loness. White tulle draped around an arch billowed in the breeze where Kyle, resplendent in his military uniform, waited for his bride with his friend Teddy and Pastor Rick.

Yellow wildflowers scattered blooms over the ground between rows of white chairs where guests waited. Then the jubilant tones of the wedding march brought Laurel down the aisle. Dressed in a pale blue dress, carrying a bundle of flowers the boys had picked an hour earlier, she led the way to Kyle then stepped aside.

Sara took a deep breath but before she could move, a deep voice asked, "May I give my sister away?"

She could only nod and cling to Samuel's strong arm as they walked slowly toward Kyle. Her groom grinned at her brother, obviously in on the surprise, but Kyle's gaze stayed locked on Sara. She handed the pale pink roses Rod had grown in Kyle's greenhouse to Laurel then took Kyle's outstretched hands. Together they faced

Rick, who gave a short homily on marriage before asking for their vows.

"Sara, I promise to love you with all my heart for as long as we live. You are my sun, my moon and my northern lights. I will love you forever." Kyle slid a solid gold band onto her finger, right next to the diamond he'd given her at Christmas.

"Kyle, you are a precious gift from God. I promise to love you. Always. Forever. As long as we live." Sara placed a hammered gold band on his ring finger.

"Kyle, you may kiss your bride."

As Kyle embraced his new wife, the boys whistled and the crowd clapped. The bride and groom walked back down the aisle. Amidst a shower of birdseed, they invited everyone to join them at Lives Under Construction for the reception.

"This probably isn't what Laurel had in mind for this place, is it?" Kyle asked Sara, smiling at the decorations their friends had strung everywhere.

"It's better." She kissed his cheek. "Congratulations on your new position as activities coordinator for Lives."

"There are going to be some changes," he told her. "New boys will be arriving."

"That can wait. You and I have a honeymoon." She threw her arms around his neck. "I'm going to love Hawaii."

"I'm going to love you, forever, always." Kyle embraced her, only pulling free when Laurel insisted they had to leave for the train. A procession followed them to the old depot and the entire community gave them a send-off.

As the train chugged away Sara sent a text message to Laurel.

"What's that about?" Kyle asked.

"I just told her North Country heroes make the best husbands." She grinned at him.

"Is Laurel looking for a husband?" he asked.

"Not yet. But I've turned it over to God." She chuckled at his droll look.

"Then Teddy doesn't stand a chance."

* * * * *

NORTH COUNTRY FAMILY

Trust in the Lord with all your heart and
lean not to your own understanding. In all your ways
acknowledge Him and He will direct your paths.
—*Proverbs* 3:5–6

This book is dedicated to my sister Darcy,
who sees a need and, quietly, in her own way, fills it.
Bless you, Darc.

Chapter One

"My dad's d-dead."

Rick Salinger ignored the December snowscape outside to study the face of the stuttering boy slouched on the train seat next to him. They'd been talking for the past half hour.

His heart ached for both Noah and his father, but at the moment he felt most saddened by the knowledge that Noah's father would never get to see his son grow and change. That sadness came from the knowledge that Rick would never get to see a son grow and change, either. He would never have a family. Because he didn't deserve one.

"My d-dad stole f-from our ch-church." Noah rubbed one eye then put his glasses back in place. "Th-then he k-killed himself. M-mom said he was t-too a-ashamed to t-tell us."

Rick wanted to hug the kid, but Noah's rigid expression said he wouldn't tolerate that.

"My f-father died r-running away. And now that's wh-what we're d-doing, too."

"Running away?" Rick stared at him, surprised by the disgust in the boy's voice.

"My m-mom calls it s-starting over," Noah muttered.

"That's way different than running away." Rick frowned when the boy shrugged. He tried a different approach. "You and your mom must miss your dad, Noah."

"M-my mom m-maybe. She c-cries when she th-thinks I c-can't hear her, but I d-don't cry for him." Noah's fingers tightened around his iPod.

"I'm really sorry," Rick told him sincerely. He suppressed a groan. What an inane remark. "That's not much help, is it? But you can pray about it."

"I don't p-pray," Noah said, an edge tingeing his voice. "N-not anymore."

"That's too bad because God hears the prayers of His kids," Rick said softly.

"Maybe He h-hears but He d-doesn't answer." Noah turned his head away.

"God always answers, Noah." A yearning to help this angry, fatherless boy swelled deep inside Rick. "You know, a lot of us make mistakes that we wish we could undo. But that doesn't mean God doesn't hear our prayers."

"Then wh-why doesn't He m-make things d-different?" Noah demanded.

Rick had asked himself that same question a thousand times, mostly whenever he was reminded of his last days as a stockbroker, right after he'd made that last, greedy, too-speculative gamble and lost his clients' money. Seniors, single parents, a fund to help the needy—they'd all put their trust in wonder broker Rick Salinger. And because he was so desperate to prove he was better than the no-account street kid he'd been, he'd skipped the due diligence and invested in a scheme that cost them everything.

With that memory came waves of guilt. For a moment he got sucked into it. Then he shook it off, forcing himself to focus on Noah.

"You want God to wave a magic wand and make it all better?" When Noah nodded, Rick smiled. "That would be nice, but I think God wants us to learn from our mistakes."

Noah didn't look convinced. "How do you kn-know for sure?"

"Because God is a loving Father who wants the best for His kids." Rick stifled a laugh at the look on Noah's face. Clearly the kid had no love for members of the clergy.

"My g-grandfather is a minister, t-too," he said after a long silence.

Rick waited for more information but Noah just added, "I wish m-my mom would w-wake up. I'm s-starving."

As if in answer, an anxious voice across the aisle, two rows back, called, "Noah?"

Rick watched Noah's shoulders tense. He waited for the boy to answer. When he didn't, Rick said, "He's here. With me." He half rose to identify himself and immediately got caught in the worry-filled stare of the loveliest brown eyes he'd ever seen.

A woman who looked too young to be the mother of this boy stood. She passed a hand over her jeans, straightened a sweater that accentuated the golden glints in her eyes then stepped into the aisle. Her blond hair caressed her cheeks in tumbled layers of tousled curls as she raked a hand through them.

He knew that face.

Rick scrambled to remember where he'd seen her before but came up blank. He was positive that he knew her, though Noah's mother didn't seem to know him. She barely glanced at him before she hunkered down beside her son.

"You were supposed to tell me if you were going somewhere, Noah."

Rick immediately understood that the harshness he heard in her voice came from the fear still lingering in her eyes. A mental image of her—younger, without the worry, carefree and happy—flashed through his head.

Where did that come from?

"S-sorry, Mom," Noah muttered. He didn't sound sorry.

"Noah didn't want to wake you so he moved over here. We've been chatting to pass the time." He thrust out a hand. "I'm Rick Salinger."

Instantly a barrier went up in her cocoa-toned eyes. After several moments' hesitation she slid her small hand into his for about half a second then immediately pulled it away.

"Cassie Crockett," she said with her chin thrust forward. "I'm sorry Noah bothered you."

"He didn't— Just the opposite, actually. Did you know your son is a cardshark?" Rick was certain he'd never met anyone named Cassie Crockett so he couldn't possibly know her, and yet that face…

Rick regrouped and grinned at Noah. "He beat me in six straight games of hearts."

"I've been there." A smile flickered at the corner of her lips. "Humbling, isn't it?"

"Very," Rick agreed, wanting to see what a real smile

looked like on Cassie Crockett. "But I was glad to have someone to talk to. Seventeen hours from Thompson to Churchill makes for a long ride, even if this part of northern Canada is the best of God's creation." He paused then asked, "Have we met before?"

"No." Short and succinct, her answer flew out almost before he'd finished asking the question.

"I don't mean to push it, but you seem very familiar to me," he said.

"I assure you, I have never seen you before." She held his gaze, dark brown sparks in her eyes defiant.

"I'm h-hungry, Mom." Noah looked at Rick, and seemed to sense an ally. "I b-bet Pastor Rick is hungry, t-too. We want b-breakfast."

"Pastor?" Cassie's voice squeaked. Her heart-shaped face paled as her eyes narrowed.

"H-he's a minister in C-Churchill." Noah seemed either unaware of or unconcerned about his mother's reaction.

"I am." Rick sensed that a change of subject would be helpful. "They serve a passable breakfast on board, Mrs. Crockett." He smiled again, hoping to allay whatever fears made her tense. "I could show you the way."

"That's okay," she said, her voice colder than before. "We're not ready yet."

"I'm r-ready, Mom," Noah contradicted.

"We have to clean up first." Cassie's brow furrowed as she studied her son. "Your hair needs combing."

"Then c-can we have breakfast with P-pastor Rick?"

Noah's blue eyes begged her, but Cassie seemed to be searching for an excuse not to join him, so Rick gave her an out.

"Maybe I'll see you there." He grinned at Noah. "It was nice meeting you. Thanks for the card game."

"It was n-nice m-meeting you, too," Noah responded. "T-thanks for telling m-me about Churchill. If we g-go to a r-restaurant, I'm g-going to order c-c-caribou."

"Good. But if anyone offers you *muktuk,* make sure it's fresh." Rick hid his smile and waited for the inevitable question.

"Wh-why?"

"Whale skin and blubber are best eaten fresh." Rick chuckled at Noah's dismayed look. "It's actually not bad when you get used to it." Then he nodded at Cassie. "Excuse me."

Apparently Cassie hadn't realized she was blocking his way. Her cheeks flamed bright pink as she stepped out of the way and beckoned to Noah to follow.

Rick tried not to hear their discussion as he waited for another passenger to move out of the aisle, but it was difficult not to eavesdrop.

"Why d-didn't we go with Pastor R-rick, Mom? I'm s-starving." Noah's stutter seemed to worsen with his temper. "I w-want to g-go n-now."

"Noah, behave." Cassie sounded irritated. "We'll go for breakfast soon, but not if you're going to make a fuss. That is not how a Crockett behaves," she said softly, almost too softly for Rick to hear.

"Mrs. P-Perkins said all C-crocketts behave b-badly," Noah muttered in a sullen tone.

"Mrs. Perkins was wrong." Cassie sounded desperate to shush her son.

"Th-that's what she said about y-you," Noah retorted. "Sh-she said you m-made the b-b-biggest mistake of your l-life."

Able to finally move forward to the dining car, Rick couldn't hear Cassie's response. Noah's words had raised a thousand questions in his mind—but first and foremost was this: Why, when she'd learned his profession, had she shrunk away from him as if he had the plague?

That question was quickly followed by another: Why did her offended look bother him so much?

In the dining car, Ned Blenkins stood waiting to take his order.

"Nice to see you again, Preacher. Same as usual?" Ned asked with his cheery smile.

"Yes, please." Rick accepted a cup of coffee.

"Won't take a minute," Ned promised.

Rick carried his steaming cup to the only empty table. Though most of the other passengers had finished their meals and now lingered over coffee, no one invited him to join them. He took a seat, reminding himself that eating alone didn't bother him. He deserved a lot worse than a solitary breakfast, he thought with a pang of fresh guilt.

Rick had seen most of the other people in the dining car around Churchill, though not in his church. He knew each member of his small congregation personally, and he suspected they all knew about his ugly past. In a small town like Churchill there were few secrets.

He'd been very honest in telling the hiring committee how he'd lost every dime of his own and that of every client who'd trusted him. He'd also told them how he'd found God, and of his vow to serve Him in an effort to rectify the wrongs he'd done. Though none of his parishioners had ever confronted him about it, Rick figured it was the reason why he hadn't attracted any new parishioners. Who wanted to attend the church of a man who'd caused such harm?

As he waited for his breakfast, Rick glanced at the paper his neighbor was reading. His heart took a nose-dive when he saw the headline of a small piece in the bottom right corner—"Local couple loses bid to sue publisher for risky book on investing."

"Not again," his soul cried.

He grabbed the paper off his own table and read the entire section. The leaden weight in his stomach grew as he read about a young couple desperate to have children. They needed money for fertility procedures. Now they were homeless because they'd mortgaged their house and sold everything they owned to invest their money after they'd read a book called *Untold Riches in the Stock Market.* Rick had written the book under the same pseudonym the publisher had used for six other how-to books in the same series. It was doubtful his authorship would ever be made public because Rick had signed a confidentiality agreement. But that didn't ease any of his guilt.

Almost five years later and there were still ramifications. Worse, he was powerless to stop it.

He read that the court ruled that though the book offered risky—perhaps even foolhardy—advice, the advice was not illegal and the lawsuit had been dismissed.

Oh Lord, he prayed silently. *How can I ever atone for all the pain my greed has caused?*

Overwhelmed by guilt, Rick had promised God that last day at the seminary that he'd give up his most precious dream—he'd clung to it all through the years he'd scrabbled to stay alive on the streets of Toronto—the dream of having a home and a family. Those two things were all he'd ever wanted—a place to call his own, and people who loved and cared for him.

It had cost Rick dearly to sacrifice that dream, but every time he learned of someone else who'd suffered because of him, he renewed his vow. It was his way of showing God he was worthy of His love.

But was he?

Defeat nagged at Rick as he thought about the eight months he'd been ministering in Churchill. By most measures, the lack of new members in his church probably meant he was a failure as a minister. But he'd promised God he'd serve where he was placed and for now, that place was Churchill. All he could do was his best until God sent him somewhere else.

"Eggs over easy with bacon." Ned set the loaded plate in front of him.

"Thanks, Ned." Rick palmed him a generous tip.

He'd barely lifted his head from saying grace when the door burst open and Noah stalked in, followed by Cassie. She quickly realized there was no empty table and frowned. Her brown eyes narrowed as she endured curious stares.

"Come and join me," Rick invited, rising. Noah didn't even glance at his mother for permission before he strode over. Cassie followed more slowly.

"We don't want to bother you," she said.

"You're not," he assured her. "You're welcome here."

Cassie hesitated.

"Come on, Mom. I'm s-starving."

Cassie ignored Noah, her gaze locked on Rick. She studied him for what seemed like ages before she inclined her head in an almost imperceptible nod.

"Thank you. We'd like to join you." She laid a hand

on Noah's shoulder. "On a scale of one to ten, how hungry are you?"

"F-fourteen." Noah slouched on the chair beside Rick as Cassie turned to place their order. His eyes widened at the sight of Rick's plate. "F-four eggs?"

"I guess I'm an eighteen on your scale." Rick laughed at Noah's surprise but his gaze was already back on Cassie as she made her way toward Ned. He could still smell her fragrance. Whatever it was, it suited her. Soft, very feminine with a hint of spice. Feisty.

You're thinking about this woman entirely too much. Do not get involved.

"W-won't you get f-fat?" the boy asked, his forehead pleated in a frown.

"I hope not." Rick hid his smile. After reading that article he was no longer hungry. He offered Noah the plate with the extra toast he'd ordered. Noah selected one half slice.

"Mrs. P-Perkins said my m-mom is f-fat," he muttered.

"No offense, but I think Mrs. Perkins, whoever she is, must need glasses." Rick smiled. "Your mom is beautiful," he added.

"I g-guess s-so." Silence reigned as Noah devoured his toast.

Cassie returned a few moments later with two glasses of juice and a cup of coffee. She raised one eyebrow at Noah when he reached for a second slice of Rick's toast but said nothing as she set the juice in front of him.

"Th-that's it?" Noah demanded. He looked at Rick sadly. "M-maybe *I'm* f-fat."

When Cassie chuckled, Rick focused on her face. Again he tried to recall where and when he'd seen her before, but, truthfully, it didn't matter. What mattered was that here was a kid who'd lost his dad and a woman who'd lost her husband, and there was something wrong between them. Maybe he could help. Maybe, if he could, he would find a measure of peace.

Churchill was his proving ground. If he couldn't do God's work here—if he couldn't help this community or kids like Noah—what good was he? And if his ministry failed, how could he ever earn forgiveness? Failure in Churchill meant it was doubtful another church would give him a chance.

God, I came here to make amends. Please help me do that for these hurting hearts.

But even if Rick could help this mother and son, he knew he'd never earn redemption.

"They have to cook your breakfast, Noah. It'll be here in a few minutes."

Cassie sat, her brow furrowing as she leaned near Noah's ear. "Please stop repeating things Mrs. Perkins said. I know she was angry. A lot of church members were. But most of what she said isn't true."

"Wh-which part *is* t-true?" Noah asked in a sour tone.

Cassie gave him a chiding look. She sipped her coffee and worked hard to look anywhere but at Rick. That green-eyed stare of his saw too much.

"Are you two visiting Churchill for long?" Rick smiled.

"We're n-not v-visiting." Noah eyed Rick's remaining slice of toast. Rick nodded. "M-my mom's going to work at l-luck."

Noah's struggle to get the word out pierced Cassie's

heart. The pain doubled when Noah noticed the other patrons' stares and ducked his head in shame.

"Luck?" Rick shook his head. "I don't think I know it."

"Lives Under Construction—LUC. It's a rehabilitation facility where troubled boys are sent to serve their time in the justice system. We shortened it," Cassie explained.

"Very clever. And I am very familiar with Lives— that's the shortened form we use here." He smiled at Noah's wide eyes when Ned set a loaded platter in front of him. "Here's your breakfast."

"N-not s-sure if I'm *th-that* hungry, Mom," the boy said.

"I thought we could share, especially since you ate Mr., uh, Pastor—*his* toast." Cassie felt her cheeks heat up. Why did this man fluster her? "I'm sorry but I don't know what to call you."

"Rick will do just fine."

"Rick it is." Cassie accepted an empty plate from Ned with a smile of thanks. She liberated an egg, a slice of toast and one strip of bacon from Noah's plate.

"Mrs. Crockett, are you the nurse Laurel's been expecting?" Rick's green eyes flared with surprise.

"Yes." Cassie added no other information. She figured his surprise now equaled hers, when she'd found out he was a minister. With his short, spiky dark hair, day-old chin stubble and that easy grin that embraced everyone, Rick looked nothing like the ministers she knew. "How did you know?"

"Laurel told me she'd hired someone." Rick must have understood the question on her face because he added, "Laurel Quinn and I are good friends. I go to Lives Under Construction a lot to work with the boys."

"Oh. Then you probably also know she has three clients with special needs arriving. The government insists she have a medical person on the premises to monitor their care." Cassie tasted her bacon and toast before continuing. "I'm also hoping to work a few shifts at the hospital while the boys are in school."

"That shouldn't be an issue. The health center can always use more help and the Inuit Transient Center will welcome you with open arms." Rick's attention slid to Noah who, having cleaned his plate leaned back in his chair. Rick smiled.

"Something about my job amuses you?" Hearing the belligerence in her voice, Cassie wished she'd controlled it. But she'd endured mockery once too often recently from people who claimed to be her friends and then doubted her.

"No, ma'am. Something about him amuses me."

Rick chuckled when Noah drained his juice glass and smacked his lips. "Feel better?"

"Much." Noah grinned.

Cassie's heart brimmed with adoration for this child of hers. Noah, twelve, had suffered deeply and dealt with so much since Eric's death. She'd made this move to Churchill hoping to restore the fun-loving kid he'd been before his father's death and the two years of misery that had followed.

Cassie suddenly noticed Rick studying Noah with an odd look. Was that longing in his forest-green eyes? As she wondered if he had any children of his own, a hundred questions about Rick Salinger suddenly swarmed her.

You can't trust him, she thought. *You trusted Eric*

and your father and they weren't there for you. Eric never even confided in you about losing those church funds. And then he was too proud to face his mistakes. You've paid for that a hundred times over and so has Noah. Now it's time to get on with your lives. Alone.

Cassie shut off the painful reminders. "Are there many churches in Churchill?" she asked.

Rick blinked and the shadows in his eyes dissipated.

"Four at the moment. Mine is the smallest."

"Because?" She chewed on a slice of toast while she waited for his answer.

"That's hard to say." He frowned. "It's either because I'm not very good at my job or because I'm not giving the kind of message people want to hear." He shrugged. "I'll leave it to you to decide, Cassie."

So different than her father. *He* would have insisted it wasn't his fault, that people were too hard-hearted to hear the truth. She liked that Rick took responsibility.

"I'm sure folks will come around in time," she murmured.

"I hope so, but that's God's job." He smiled, clearly comfortable in his skin. That also made a positive impression on Cassie. Too many people were out to impress and didn't care who they hurt in the process. That's why she'd stopped trusting.

That's why she'd come to Churchill.

"W-will we go to P-pastor Rick's c-church, Mom?" Noah asked.

"We'll see." The age-old parental response her father had always given seemed to fit. When she glanced up, she found Rick's attention on her again. From the speculative way he studied her, she thought he knew that he wouldn't be seeing them in his pews anytime soon.

"W-we haven't gone to ch-church for a long t-time," Noah mused, staring out the window. His forehead pleated in a frown of distaste as he glanced back at Rick. "My g-grandfather y-yells."

"Some preachers do," Rick agreed in a mild tone.

Cassie liked that Rick didn't prod Noah for more information. In fact, there was a lot about this man that she was beginning to like, and that made her nervous.

"My father is—was—a minister. He's retired now." She winced at her tone. A man like Rick, attuned to people's nuances, would realize she disliked mentioning him.

"I see." Rick grinned at Noah. "Don't worry, Noah. I don't yell in church. I mostly just talk. You're welcome to come anytime." He checked his watch then rose. "Will you excuse me? I've got some reading to do before we arrive."

Noah's blue eyes sparkled. "I c-can hardly w-wait to see Aunt L-Laurel."

"I didn't realize you were related." Rick's curious gaze turned on Cassie.

"Laurel and I met years ago in Toronto when I worked in pediatrics," Cassie explained. "She brought in clients from time to time and we became friends. Noah was very young then. He sort of adopted her. We've kept in touch over the years. I guess that's why she thought of me when she needed help with Lives."

"I'm sure you'll be a great asset, Cassie. We can use all the help we can get to reach Laurel's boys."

Cassie searched Rick's face. *We.* That meant they'd be working together. Would he judge her, too, when he found out about Eric? As she stood, she looked around at the Christmas decorations still hanging in the dining car. "It seems funny that there are only three days till New Year's Eve."

"Churchill's New Year's Eve is fantastic," Rick said.

"Wh-why?" Noah demanded.

"You'll have to go to find out. But I will tell you this—it's a town-wide party with amazing fireworks."

Rick gestured for them to precede him out of the dining car. Cassie felt stares as they walked toward their seats. She automatically smoothed a hand over her hip, then stopped herself. Her jeans were years out of date and her leather boots had seen far better days, but why should she care what Rick or anyone else thought about her?

She took a look around and saw that most of her fellow passengers, including Rick, looked as though they chose function over fashion.

They're not judging you, Cassie.

As she and Noah reached their seats, she glanced back and saw Rick joking with a woman nearby as he pulled a duffel bag from the overhead rack. He hadn't said anything about a wife or kids and he didn't wear a ring, but Cassie felt certain that a man with Rick's looks wasn't single unless he wanted it that way. He was too charming for it to be otherwise.

And nice, her brain prodded. Rick was definitely nice.

Cassie took a seat and closed her eyes. Pastor Rick Salinger was a mystery all right, but not one Cassie was going to explore. After the mess Eric had left her in and the condemnation of her church family, she just wanted to keep things as simple as possible. She would do her job and build a new life at Lives Under Construction. If she failed to get Noah straightened out here—well, she couldn't fail, that was all. Churchill was her last resort.

An ache tore through Cassie as she studied Noah. Since Eric's death Noah had been acting out. He'd been disciplined at school for his bad behavior and she'd tried to discipline him at home. Neither had worked. He'd progressively become more of an opponent than the son she adored.

She had to get him to change the path he was on, to let go of the brooding anger inside before he did something she couldn't fix.

Her gaze roamed the train until it rested on Rick. Rick said he helped the boys at Lives. Maybe he could—she didn't dare let herself think it.

Cassie Crockett had learned the hard way that you couldn't trust anyone.

It was a lesson she'd never forget.

Chapter Two

The weight of Cassie's decision hit when she opened her eyes an hour later and got her first view of Churchill.

She was alone, a single mom with a troubled kid to support in a cold, barren land where she had just one friend, Laurel. Had moving here been the right decision?

The train jerked. They were slowing down.

It didn't matter now if the decision was right or wrong. It had been made.

"We're here, M-Mom," Noah said. For the first time in many months a hint of excitement colored his voice.

The tired old train ground to a stop with much squeaking of brakes. Noah jumped to his feet. Cassie reached up to heft her overnight case from the storage compartment above. A hand slid over hers where it grasped the suitcase handle.

"Yes, Noah. I'm hurrying—"

The words died away when she turned and stared into Rick's dark green gaze.

"Let me help you with this."

Odd how his quiet offer made her feel as if she wasn't quite so alone.

Cassie nodded, swallowing when his warm fingers eased the handle from her hands, lifted the bag free and shifted it so it would roll forward. "Thank you."

"You're welcome." His low response, for her ears alone, made her feel cared for. She liked that.

You have no business liking anything about Rick, she scolded herself.

But the scolding didn't seem to stop her from appreciating the tall, lean man. A slanted smile played on his too-handsome face, warming her like a ray of sunshine. His easy manner made her drop her guard, feel comfortable. The pull of attraction toward him was like nothing she'd known before. She searched his eyes, trying to understand the connection she felt, ignoring the flutter in her stomach when he met her gaze.

"I appreciate your entertaining Noah during the ride," she said as they waited to disembark.

"He's a great kid." The pastor took her arm to help her as they stepped outside, grinning at Noah's astonished reaction to mountainous snowdrifts that dazzled in the brilliant morning sun. "Welcome to Churchill."

As they moved away from the crowd and down the platform, Rick stayed by her side, matching his strides to her shorter ones, rolling her case along as if it were a feather. He had the long, lean grace of a distance runner. Though Cassie noticed the many admiring stares he received, Rick didn't seem to. He smiled and greeted people, totally at ease.

By contrast, Noah stood aloof, surveying the area with a wariness Cassie wished she could help him shed. But how? Noah argued with her constantly over the least

little thing. Nothing Cassie had tried seemed to help re-
duce the stutter that had appeared several months earlier. Not even prayer.

"Noah could go inside to stay warm," Rick told her.
"But it's better if you wait here for the opening of the
container car to ensure all your stuff has arrived. If it
doesn't, you have to make a claim right away. You do
have more than this?" he asked, indicating her suitcase.

"Oh, yes." Cassie nodded. "We have more."

Laurel had explained to Cassie that she should bring
as much as she could and take advantage of the rail-
way's free transportation of patrons' goods because
shipping in everyday things could make living in the
North Country very expensive.

As Cassie looked around at the vast glistening beauty
of the isolated land, she decided the expense of living so
far north was worth it when she would be able to savor
this view every day. Maybe she hadn't made a mistake
coming here. Maybe life for her and Noah was finally
going to get better.

She shifted from one foot to the other, glad of her
coat's thick insulation, as endless pallets of bulky paper
items were off-loaded followed by boxes and trunks of
all descriptions. As Rick retrieved the items she pointed
out, Cassie became conscious of odd looks, the kind
that said the onlookers suspected they were a couple.
She stepped away from him to create some distance as
she counted her containers.

"Everything is here," she said.

"Good. And there are my snowshoes." Rick strode
forward and picked up a mesh bag.

"Do you like to snowshoe?" Cassie asked.

"I don't know. I haven't tried yet. I bought these at a

thrift store in Thompson." He chuckled at her dubious look. "My friend Kyle—he works at Lives, too—promised to teach me." He swung the bag over his shoulder only to set it down again when his cell phone rang. "Excuse me."

He looked at the caller ID, grinned at Cassie and put the phone on speaker.

"Rick? This is Laurel. I'm sorry to bother you but my van conked out." Though Laurel's frustration carried clearly in the crisp air, Cassie felt a measure of relief at hearing her friend's voice. "I'm at the garage and they say it has to stay overnight."

"But you're supposed to pick up your new nurse and her son," Rick guessed with a wink at Cassie. She couldn't help smiling back. There was something about his irrepressible good humor that drew her in.

"Yes, that's why I'm calling. I wondered if you might be able to give us all a ride back to Lives."

"I can because, fortunately for you, I left the block heater on my car engine plugged in while I was in Thompson," Rick said. "It should start without any trouble."

Cassie tracked his gaze to the thermometer on the side of the depot—minus twenty-eight degrees Celsius. No wonder she was shivering.

"I'll have to walk home to get it, though," Rick continued. "You're still at the garage, right? Why don't you stay put until I can pick you up?"

"I just collected one of the boys. How about if we meet you at the station? But before you leave could you find Cassie Crockett and her son and ask them to wait? She's blond, short curly hair—"

"I've already met her and Noah. In fact, Cassie's standing beside me."

"Hi, Laurel," Cassie called.

"Cassie! I can't wait to see you! We'll be there soon. Thanks, Rick."

"No worries, Laurel. See you in a bit." Rick tucked his phone back in his pocket. "You'd better wait inside until I get back." He blinked at the number of boxes and containers on the dock. "Where's the kitchen sink?" he teased.

"We—um, sold our house so we had to bring most of what was left," she explained.

Rick nodded, seeming to sense her discomfort. He hailed a man and introduced Cassie and Noah. "I was wondering if you'd be willing to use your truck to transport Mrs. Crockett's things to Lives Under Construction, George."

"Happy to, Pastor, but it might take a second trip. Lucy Clow's got me picking up a bunch of stuff she bought online."

"Again? Wonder what deals she found this time." Rick shared a grin of understanding with the other man then told Cassie, "Lucy's infamous for her online purchases, which she always donates to something in town. Will picking up your stuff later work for you, Cassie?"

"Later is perfect." Cassie noted the obvious affection between Rick and the older man. "Thank you, Mr. Stern."

"Cassie's going to be the new nurse at Lives Under Construction, George. She's also hoping for some part-time work at the health center." Rick gave her a small nod, as if to say, *Wait for it.*

"Well isn't that a blessing?" George beamed. "Our

health board has been trying to find another nurse for ages. You've got work whenever you want, Miss."

"Thank you very much, Mr. Stern." Breathless at the speed with which she'd found a second job, Cassie turned to Rick as George left. "Thank you for doing that."

"My pleasure." He checked his watch. "My place is about three blocks away. I'll have to let the car warm up so it'll be a while before I return. But Laurel should be here shortly. You and Noah can wait inside." Rick slid his hand under her elbow and steered her into the station. Noah followed without saying anything.

The peremptory way Rick directed her without waiting for her agreement triggered her dislike of being controlled. A host of memories of Eric's constant advice and bossy ways filled her head. Eric had seemed to believe she was unable to think for herself. He'd always tried to steer her, literally, and she'd always hated that.

Cassie jerked her arm free once they were inside the depot. "I could have arranged things for myself," she heard herself saying. "You didn't have to ask a stranger—"

"There aren't any strangers in Churchill, Mrs. Crockett," Rick interrupted in a gentle tone. "Up here we try to help each other because we might be the next in need."

"Of course," she whispered, contrite that she'd allowed her past to cause her to behave rudely. "I apologize. Thank you for everything. And please, Rick, call me Cassie." She forced herself to offer a tiny smile. "Noah and I will wait for you over there." She pointed to a bench in the corner.

Rick's good-natured grin returned. He pulled a pair

of knitted gloves from his pocket and put them on. "See you in a bit." Swinging his snowshoes onto his shoulder, Rick picked up his duffel and headed out of the station, toward the street that lay beyond the parking lot, obviously enjoying the brisk air.

Cassie glanced at Noah. Eyes closed, earbuds firmly in place, he swayed back and forth to his music, in his own world. She'd leave him alone, for now, but soon she'd have to find a way to get him to break free of his self-imposed isolation.

Her attention returned to the window and the minister who strode across the white-covered terrain. Rick Salinger unnerved her. Not only because of what he said or did but also because of who he was—a minister, like her father.

That was a very big hurdle in her book.

He's also straightforward, full of life and interesting.

All the same, Cassie was determined to keep her distance. No matter how much Rick piqued her interest.

As Rick sauntered back into the train station more than half an hour later, his brain was still struggling to put together a puzzle called Cassie Crockett. One minute she was standoffish and defensive, the next her barriers dropped away and she was warm and engaging. Was that only with him?

And why did he still feel as if he'd met her before?

Cassie sat in the corner where she'd said she'd be, but this was a totally different woman from the one who'd yanked her arm from his grip. She was laughing at something Laurel said, blond head thrown back, eyes dancing. For the first time since he'd met her, Rick thought she looked truly at ease.

"So you met Rick," he heard Laurel say.

"Yes." Cassie's low voice gave nothing away. Though her eyes widened when she saw him, her glance bounced off him, keeping his presence secret.

"He's a great guy and an even better pastor," Laurel said. Rick listened unabashedly while she spent several moments extolling his virtues. "You'll never make a better friend than Rick."

"Well, thank you, Laurel. I love you, too." Rick grinned when the older woman squealed in surprise, turned and then hugged him, ruffling his hair.

Rick basked in the feeling of being cared for. Since a wife and family were never going to be part of his future, he cherished every friendship God brought into his life.

"It's good to have you back, pal." Laurel patted his shoulder.

"Thanks. Who's this?" he asked, nodding at a boy who, like Noah, sat with earphones in his ears, swaying to music no one else could hear.

"This is Bryan." Laurel nudged the boy's shoulder.

In a desultory fashion, Bryan withdrew one headphone. "Yeah?"

"This is Rick, our pastor," Laurel said.

"Dude." Bryan slowly lifted his hand to shake Rick's. His grip was weak, his palms sweaty. Duty done, he immediately replaced his earphone and closed his eyes.

"I'm overwhelmed by my welcome," Rick joked.

"You got a better reception than I did," Cassie complained.

"If he ignored a beautiful woman like you, I don't feel so bad." Surprised he'd spoken his thoughts aloud, Rick glanced at Laurel. The smug smile on her face bothered him, but Rick ignored it. He leaned nearer Cassie. "We'll have to show him that we demand proper respect," he whispered with a conspiratorial wink. Then he turned to Laurel. "On my way in I noticed George has already picked up Cassie's things from the dock so I'm ready to leave here whenever you are."

Noah and Bryan picked up some of the luggage. Rick took the rest. Somehow everything fit inside his small car. Laurel insisted Cassie take the front seat beside him so she'd have a better view of her new home, but Rick noticed Cassie sat just about as far away from his as she could.

"We're off," he said as he fastened his seat belt. He left the parking lot and turned the corner to the highway, noticing Cassie's tight grip on her armrest when the tires slipped on a patch of ice before the treads caught.

"All this ice—" She made a quick glance over one shoulder at Noah.

"It's okay, Cassie." He smiled to reassure her. "Josephina will get us there safely. She isn't the prettiest vehicle around, but she almost always gets where she's going."

"Josephina?" she said. One perfect eyebrow arched. "Why not Joseph?"

"Joseph was a truck, my last vehicle." Rick made sad face. "He wasn't reliable at all."

"We won't go there, then," she said. The amusement on her face sent an unexpected quiver through him.

His brain instantly shot out warnings, reminding him to avoid entanglements. He was here to atone for his past, not get involved. That thought brought a tiny flicker of sadness that he fought to ignore.

"I promise you'll arrive in one piece," he said, noting her grip hadn't eased.

"But which piece?" Cassie teased in a tight voice. Once they were on the highway, she seemed to relax. "Just before Christmas I was in a fender bender in Toronto on very slick roads. I guess I'm still a bit skittish."

"We'll be there soon," he assured her.

Cassie glanced his way, her head tipped to one side. "Do you ever have doubts about anything, Rick?"

The question made him blink as memories from a host of very bad days from his past made him wince.

"You have no idea," he muttered as guilt rolled in.

Cassie studied him, a tiny frown marring her beauty. After that she remained silent until they reached Lives. Rick didn't mind. Her question had sobered him.

"We're home," he said as he turned off the motor.

"Finally." Bryan quickly unfolded himself from the backseat.

"A tall guy like you, you'll be glad Laurel has a van." Rick watched him stretch. Something about the kid didn't seem right. When Bryan headed for the house, Rick called him back.

"Your bag?" he reminded.

"What, no bell boys?" Bryan attempted a laugh but it fell short. He swiped a hand across his face to remove a sheen of sweat, which was odd given the frosty temperature.

Rick also noticed that Bryan's hand shook when he reached for the suitcase handle. The boy seemed confused as he struggled to maneuver his way to the door. Several times he veered off the pathway into the snow. Concerned by Bryan's unsteadiness, Rick moved to assist him. He arrived just in time to catch Bryan as he slumped.

"Cassie!" Rick yelled. She was there in a second with Laurel.

"Bryan's just been diagnosed with diabetes," Laurel said.

"Get him inside and lay him on the floor," Cassie ordered after a quick look. "Laurel, we'll need some orange juice or something sweet."

Totally out of his depth, Rick appreciated Cassie's orders. He carried Bryan inside then propped up the boy's head as Cassie dribbled some orange juice in his mouth.

"What's wrong with him?" he asked.

"I'm guessing his blood sugar's too low." Concern darkened Cassie's eyes as she monitored the boy's pulse and checked his pupils. "Bryan, when did you last test?" she asked loudly when his eyelids fluttered.

"Didn't." His head lolled into unconsciousness.

Cassie hissed out a sigh of frustration. She looked at Rick. "Can you go through his suitcase and find a small case? It would have test strips, syringes and a vial in it."

Rick did as she asked. When he found the container, he unzipped it and held it open in his palm so she could easily get what she needed.

"Thanks." With precise movements Cassie pricked Bryan's finger and swiped it over a test strip, which she then stuck into the small monitor. She grimaced at the reading, measured out the correct dose from the vial and injected it into Bryan's stomach. After a quick glance at Noah who stood watching, she offered him a smile then returned to monitoring her patient.

Rick noted the tender hand Cassie swept across Bryan's forehead and the kindhearted words she spoke. To anyone watching, Bryan might have been her own child.

"Why didn't he inject himself?" he asked, keeping his voice hushed.

"The doctor's report says he's struggling to accept his illness." Laurel stood beside Noah, watching.

"A lot of kids do," Cassie explained. "They think that if they ignore it, it will go away." She looked at Rick, grim certainty in her eyes. "It won't go away. Bryan's got to learn to handle his diabetes or it will kill him."

"Then we'll help him do that," Rick assured her.

Cassie gave him a funny look before she turned her attention to Bryan once more.

"Okay, he's coming around. Laurel, could you bring a wet cloth? Can you help him sit, Rick?"

"Sure." He slid his arm around Bryan's back and eased him upright. "Take it easy, big guy." When Bryan's bleary gaze met his, he teased, "Is this any way to begin your first day here? Forgetting to take your medication?"

"I didn't forget," Bryan said, slurring his words a bit, but fully aware.

"You must have forgotten," Rick told him in a serious tone. "Because deliberately not taking it sounds dumb, and I don't think you're dumb." He sounded more confident than he felt, and he prayed that God would use his words to help Bryan. "Diabetes is not a death sentence."

"It feels like one to me." Bryan accepted Rick's hand to pull himself upright. He wavered a bit before plopping on a kitchen chair.

"Diabetes isn't the end of your life, Bryan." Rick sat across from him. "In fact, it could be the start of a new life for you, a new beginning here at Lives Under Construction."

Bryan glanced at Laurel and Cassie as if to ask if Rick was serious. But after a moment his gaze returned to Rick, who caught a flicker of curiosity under the boy's tough attitude.

"New start?" the boy demanded. "How?"

"Well, think about it. Nobody here knows you or what you did before you came here. You've got a chance to begin a new year with a clean slate." One glance at Cassie's serious face told Rick he had to make his words count. "Managing your diabetes can be your first step to making your future into whatever you want."

"You make it sound easy," Bryan muttered.

"Oh, no, I didn't say that. But nobody but you can decide your future, Bryan." Rick paused to let that sink in. "You have to choose if you'll waste the opportunity you've been given at a new life, or accept the challenge and use this time to figure out how to build yourself a better world."

Bryan snorted. "I never heard anyone claim going to juvie was getting a break."

"Well, then, let me be the first to offer you a new perspective. Besides, this is not juvenile detention. It's where lives are under construction, on the way to being changed." Rick held his breath, waiting for the boy to decide.

Bryan studied him for a long time, his eyes searching. Rick could tell that he was at least thinking about what he'd heard.

"You should rest for a while, Bryan," Cassie said.

"Yeah. I feel tired. The plane was bumpy. The guy

guarding me got sick." He pushed to his feet and followed Laurel to the room he'd been assigned.

Rick rubbed a hand across his face, silently praising God for His help.

"How did you know to do that?"

Rick blinked. Cassie stood in front of him, a puzzled expression on her face. "Do what?"

"Talk to him like that, get him to face his issues and see them from a new perspective." She frowned. "You convinced Bryan he could start over. I think maybe you got through to him. How?"

Shifting under her intense stare, Rick knew there was more to her question than simple curiosity. He glanced around, saw Noah seated in a corner with the luggage, earbuds back in place.

"I prayed for the right words, Cassie. If they hit home it was because God used them, as He used you," he added.

"Me?" she said, almost rearing back in surprise.

"You treated Bryan as if he were Noah," he said softly. "You cared for him with love and tenderness. He felt that. All I did was try to help him see that not everything in his life is bad. There is good in the world if he'll only drop his defenses and accept it."

"But the words you used—" Her voice trailed away.

"Lives Under Construction *is* a new beginning for Bryan," Rick reminded her. "He's away from whatever circumstances got him into this situation. He *can* start over, if he wants to. It's the same for you and Noah, isn't it? It doesn't really matter what brought you here. What matters is what you do with this opportunity."

She studied him until they heard the sound of footsteps in the hall.

"Rick, you're home," a warm voice said. A slim, obviously pregnant woman embraced him, then turned to Cassie. "I'm Sara Loness," she said stretching out a hand. "I'm the head cook. Welcome to Lives."

"Thank you. I'm Cassie Crockett." Cassie shook Sara's hand then nudged Noah who finally rose. "This is my son, Noah."

After Sara greeted Noah, Rick explained what had just happened.

"Poor Bryan. I'll make sure supper doesn't have a lot of sugar," Sara assured him.

"And you should probably keep those away from him," Rick said, eyeing the platter of cinnamon buns on the counter. "But not from me."

"Why is it some people can eat whatever they want and never gain an ounce?" Sara smiled at Cassie. "I made extras," she said to Rick as she set plates and forks on the table.

"Thanks." Rick nudged Noah to the table then held Cassie's chair. Rick took note of the fact that Cassie startled a bit when his hand accidentally brushed her shoulder.

"I thought I saw a skating rink outside," Cassie said, her voice betraying nothing.

"Sara's husband, Kyle, made it. He's just coming in." Rick waited until his friend entered the kitchen. Then he introduced Cassie and her son. "Kyle's the activities director at Lives. He and I are teaching the kids hockey. It fosters cooperation, patience, a whole host of things." Rick suddenly felt restless under Cassie's scrutiny, as if he was being assessed for something, though he couldn't imagine what.

"Want to join us?" Kyle asked Noah.

"I n-never p-played hockey," Noah muttered.

"Between Rick and Kyle, who are the biggest hockey addicts in the world, you'll soon learn," Sara teased. "Do you like milk with your cinnamon buns?" Noah's eager nod made her laugh. "So does Kyle. What about your mom?"

"Sh-she's on a d-diet so s-she won't g-get f-fat." Noah actually grinned when the others burst into laughter.

"Noah Crockett! I am not." Cassie flushed a rich red.

"Bad mistake, Noah, my man," Rick told him, laying a hand on his shoulder. "Let me give you some advice. Never mention the words *fat* or *diet* in the presence of a woman." He leaned over and whispered very loudly, "It makes them grumpy."

Cassie and Sara shared a look.

"Here come the rest of the boys," Sara said. "They were at a sledding party."

When the current residents trooped into the kitchen, Sara introduced Cassie and Noah. "These fine fellows are Barry, Rod and Peter," she said. "Michael and Daniel won't arrive until tomorrow and Bryan is upstairs with Laurel," she explained to the boys. "He's not feeling well. I suppose you're not hungry in the slightest after the sledding party."

As one they began to protest.

Sara grinned. "Yeah, dumb question. After you wash you can join us."

As they rushed to comply, Kyle left to answer the phone. Rick noted Noah hadn't engaged any of the other boys, simply nodding at the introduction and returning to his music.

Rick knew why. That stutter was going to cause problems.

The first time he'd spoken to Noah he'd felt a familiar nudge in his heart. Experience told him that was God's prodding and it meant he was to help Noah. But how?

A moment later he had his answer.

When Sara disappeared inside the walk-in cooler leaving them alone, Rick decided to sound out Cassie while her son was still involved in his music, before the others returned.

"Noah told me his dad killed himself," he murmured. "That must have been very hard for you."

Her whole body dropped as if he'd settled a weight on her shoulders. Silence stretched between them. Finally Cassie spoke.

"Very hard, but harder on Noah, I think."

"If there's anything I can do to help," he offered.

It was obvious Cassie struggled to accept his offer. But after a long moment, she nodded.

"There might be."

"Just name it," he said.

"Would you be able to talk to Noah the same way you talked to Bryan?" Cassie asked in a hushed voice. "He's been hurting, trying to understand why his father would do that. I can't seem to reach him. But you might, the way you did with Bryan."

Rick's heart swelled with compassion for this mother's hurting heart.

"Please?" she whispered.

"I don't know that it will make any difference, Cassie, but I promise I'll do whatever I can to help Noah," Rick said, just before the other boys burst into the kitchen. He leaned closer. "The offer is open to you, too, if you want."

She shut down—there was no other way to express

it. "Thank you, but I don't talk about the past. I appreciate whatever you can do for Noah, though."

It was a warning. *Back off.* And yet as he sipped the coffee Sara had served him, Rick knew he was going to have a hard time doing that. Her husband's suicide had affected her whether she admitted it or not. He had a hunch that refusing to discuss it was doing just as much damage to her spirit as it was to Noah's.

Don't get involved, his brain chided again.

She's hurting, his soul answered. *Am I not here to help others? How else can I make amends for my past?*

His brain was ready with a retort.

Is it only amends you want to make? Aren't you also trying to impress her?

His conscience reminded him that he needed to keep his motives clear, to focus on his mission.

He lifted his head and found a pair of beautiful brown eyes watching him.

Staying focused on his goal definitely wasn't going to be easy.

Chapter Three

"What's wrong, Rick?" Lucy Clow demanded on Saturday morning.

The diminutive septuagenarian, retired missionary and acting church secretary laid a model airplane kit on his desk.

"What's that?" he asked instead of answering.

"Vacation Bible School crafts for next summer, if you approve. I bought a ton of airplane kits online." Wispy tendrils of Lucy's snow-white hair straggled across her furrowed brow.

"Cool. Thanks for thinking ahead." Rick loved this woman's heart for God's work. "You've been poking at your hair again,"

"Forget my hair." The way Lucy clapped her hands on her hips made it clear he wouldn't escape her question. "Tell me what's eating you."

"Noah Crockett." Rick leaned back in his chair. "He's closed himself off. I promised his mother I'd help him, but I'm not making much progress."

"With his mother?" Lucy laughed at his expression

and sat on a nearby chair. "There's nothing wrong with being attracted to someone, Rick."

"You know I can't get involved that way with a woman, Lucy. I've told you about my vow to God."

"I know what you promised God. I'm just not sure He asked for or even wanted your promise." Lucy frowned at him. "You keep beating yourself up over the past when God's already forgiven you. How is that any different from Noah acting out and staying aloof?"

"Noah hasn't hurt hundreds of people with his greed. I have. I thought I was too smart to get caught in a Ponzi scheme. That guy took all the money I handed over and instead of investing it, he used it to pay off his old clients." He groaned at his colossal ego. "Who else but an arrogant, materialistic creep would write a know-it-all book on how to beat the system and then lose his clients' money as well as his own to a slick-talking salesman?"

"God forgave you, Rick," Lucy murmured. "Forgive yourself."

"I can't." He sipped his now-cold coffee. "Not when that stupid book keeps selling and there's not a thing I can do to stop it."

"I noticed the royalty check when I deposited the offering last week," Lucy murmured. "I suppose that's what brought your guilt rushing back."

"It's never left," he muttered. "If only they'd stop selling that book." His hands fisted at his helplessness. "I feel that there are still people who are losing everything because of me."

"I guess you could always write another book against those practices."

"I can't." He shook his head then raked his fingers through his hair. "The agreement I signed doesn't allow me to contradict anything I wrote or reveal myself as the author."

"It's in God's hands, Rick." Lucy's quiet voice brimmed with comfort. "Leave it there."

"I'm trying. Anyway, it's not me we're talking about. It's Noah." He sighed. "Under that 'Who cares' attitude is a simmering cauldron of anger. I promised Cassie I'd help him, but he won't confide in me. He keeps burying himself in his music."

"I was practicing the piano for Sunday service while he was waiting for you yesterday," Lucy said thoughtfully. "He sat in the back and pretended to ignore me, but I heard him hum along. A couple of times he even sang a line. The kid has a pretty good voice."

Rick froze as an idea bloomed.

"You look funny." Lucy reached into her pocket. "I've got some pills for indigestion—"

"Lucy!" Rick hooted with laughter. "You, my dear secretary, are a genius."

"I tell Hector that all the time." She frowned at him. "But why am I a genius today?"

"Music." He kissed her cheek. "I'm going to start a kids' choir, Lucy, and I'm going to ask Noah to join. Will you play for us?"

"Me?" Lucy wrinkled her nose. She held out her fingers, bent with the ravages of arthritis. "I can't play that fast kids' stuff very well, Rick, but I guess I could help until you find someone else."

"Bless you." Rick grabbed his coat and gloves. "I'm going out to Lives to ask Laurel and Cassie if the boys can join. Then we'll put out the word all over town." He pulled open the door of his office then turned back and hugged the tiny woman. "You're a peach, Luce."

He was almost out the door when Lucy muttered, "I'd rather be a genius."

"You're both," he called.

As he gunned his snowmobile and headed out of town toward Lives, his heart raced with excitement. As he went, he prayed, *Let this choir be a blessing, Lord. Let Your word through music touch the kids' hearts and souls with healing. Especially Noah's. And Cassie's, too.*

Invigorated, he began formulating a list of songs that might help Noah face his anger. Once at Lives, Rick jumped off his machine and rapped on the door. When no one answered immediately he rapped harder. Finally the door opened a crack, revealing Cassie's tousled head and bleary-eyed face.

It wasn't lost on him that his heart beat a bit faster at the sight of her. But he ignored that fact as best he could.

"Hi." Rick blinked, checked his watch and winced. "I'm guessing you weren't up yet?"

"It's Saturday, Rick. Barely past nine. And it's New Year's Eve. We're all sleeping in." She smothered a yawn and opened the door wide. "But I'm up now. Come in."

"Sorry. I didn't think of the time," he apologized, his brain busy admiring the robe she wore. Delicately crocheted, it began in pale aqua at the bottom and grew progressively darker, drawing the eye up to where it turned a rich emerald tone in the lacy collar framing her face. "You look lovely."

"Nice of you to say, Rick, but I had my first shift at the hospital and worked till four this morning. I don't think 'lovely' applies." Cassie turned to get the coffee container out of the fridge.

"I do." He saw her pause a moment before she continued setting the perc. She flicked a switch and a moment later the rich fragrant aroma filled the room. "I'm really sorry I woke you."

"It must be important." She perched on a stool in the corner. "Do you want me to get Laurel?"

"Not yet. Though I do want to get her permission, and yours," he added.

"For what?" she asked around another yawn.

"For Noah and the boys to join a choir, a *kids'* choir," he emphasized.

Cassie tilted her head to one side. "Noah used to sing in a choir at home—" She stopped. "If he's interested I'm all for it."

"Hi, Rick." Laurel leaned against the door frame, glancing from him to Cassie. "All for what?"

"My kids' choir," he told her, noticing how tired she looked. "I wanted to ask your permission for the Lives boys to join, but we can talk later."

"Good because at the moment my brain is mush. I stayed up too late working on my taxes. Teddy Stonechild has me convinced I'm doing something wrong." She blinked sleepily. "If you'll excuse me I'm going to return to my dream life on a tropical beach. Good night—I mean morning." She waved a hand and left.

"Teddy was here?" Rick asked as Cassie poured coffee for both of them.

"Last night. Cream?" She held up the jug.

"Thanks." Rick nodded when she'd added the right amount. "I didn't realize he was back."

"Back? He doesn't live in Churchill?" This time Cassie sat directly across from him.

"His real home is in Vancouver. But he visits Churchill a lot." Rick savored the delicious brew. "Your coffee is fantastic. Much better than the slough water I had at the church."

"Do you live there?"

"Almost." He chuckled. "The church has a small manse. It's cozy." He refocused.

"Teddy's an interesting character. What else do you know?" she said.

"Kyle told me Teddy came as a client for his dad's tour business years ago and has kept coming ever since. I believe Teddy owns a hotel business that his son now runs."

Cassie nodded, then tilted her head to one side. "So what's the inspiration behind this choir of yours?"

Rick hesitated to broach the subject on his mind. "I've talked to Noah a couple of times."

Cassie perked up. "And?"

"I think he wants to open up but doesn't know where to start," he said. "Is there anything you can share with me that would help me understand what he's going through?"

"Like what?" Rick could see Cassie's barriers go up again, and he knew he had to tread very lightly.

"Maybe if I knew some details about what happened, I could make him feel that he could confide in me."

"I don't discuss my past, Rick." Her lips pinched firmly together. "I just want to forget."

"I understand." Rick could almost feel the pain emanating from Cassie, and he was caught off guard by how much he wanted to ease it. "Losing your husband must have been very difficult. I'm not trying to pry. But can't you tell me something? For Noah's sake?"

Cassie sat silent for several minutes, motionless, her gaze locked on something Rick couldn't see. Finally she took a sip of her coffee. Cradling the mug between her palms she gave a huge sigh.

"What do you want to know?"

"Anything you think will help Noah." Rick waited, silently praying until finally she spoke again in a cool, matter-of-fact voice.

"My husband's name was Eric. I married him thirteen years ago, when I was eighteen. He was twenty-seven. He died two years ago. He drove on an icy street at high speed. Deliberately. He hit a tree and died."

Rick fought to keep his reaction to Cassie's horrific story as neutral as possible, for her sake. Now he understood her discomfort on the icy ride to Lives from the train.

"Do you mind telling me why Eric did it?" he asked gently.

"He was an accountant. He served on our church board and agreed to be board treasurer, to oversee a fund-raising campaign to build a new church." Cassie looked at him, her brown eyes guarded. "Eric was supposed to invest the building fund in something the board had chosen."

Cassie's voice broke and she paused to regain her composure. When she did, she said, "But Eric had other plans for the money. Plans I never knew much about." She frowned. "The congregation was excited about getting a facility that would give them room to expand their programs. Eric received a lot of phone calls from people wanting to know when there would be enough money to start building."

Compassion filled Rick. The way she avoided looking at him told him he was causing her pain by asking her about the past. Yet he needed information in order to help.

"Was that when Noah's stutter began?" he asked. "After his father died?"

Cassie shook her head, her eyes pleading with him not to make her say any more.

"I only want to help him, Cassie. Whatever you tell me is in strictest confidence, but I need to know," he said. Without thinking, he slid his hand across the table, over hers.

For a few moments Rick was certain she would tell him to forget it, that she didn't want to talk anymore. But she looked at him for a long time, and Rick held her gaze. Gradually her shoulders relaxed and her brown eyes lost their dark anger. She slowly pulled her hand away and exhaled.

"Tell me," he murmured.

"Noah's stutter started quite a while after his dad died, after everyone in the church turned on us when they discovered the money was gone," she said tiredly. "I became their scapegoat and Noah, too. The kids at school tormented him, called him the son of a thief." Tears formed on her thick golden lashes. "Noah was a total innocent. We both were. But when I tried to explain, no one would listen. To them we were as guilty as Eric. Noah's friends dumped him, parroting the nasty ugliness of what their parents said. That's when he began to stutter."

"Cassie, I'm so sorry." Rick hated the tears streaming down her lovely face. Holding her was folly, but how could he not offer her comfort?

He stood and moved to sit next to her, taking her in his arms slowly, gently, in case it wasn't what she wanted. He felt the tension break in her as she wept against his shoulder.

"They were Christians, Rick. They were supposed to love us."

"Yes, they were." How he wished he could ease this load from her. It broke his heart that her husband had caused so much grief and then abandoned her to face the consequences, that God's children had wreaked so much havoc on her son. "I'm sorry they didn't love you as Christ taught, Cassie. People are more important than lost money."

"Oh, they got their money." Cassie pulled out of his arms, dashing away her tears. Her voice grew harsh. "I sold the house and gave the money to the church to cover the loss."

She'd sold her home? Rick couldn't imagine what that decision had cost her, a single mom responsible for housing her child.

"I didn't do it because I felt guilty," Cassie said, her tone short. "I did it because I wanted them to stop torturing my son. But they didn't. They thought it wasn't enough, that I should cover the two years of interest they'd lost."

"But surely when you explained—"

"I stopped explaining," Cassie said, her voice passionless. "They displayed nothing but hatred for us. Before he ended it all, Eric tried to make it right. He sank every bit of our savings into trying to rebuild their fund. But he couldn't do it. So when he was gone, I found out there was no cushion for Noah and me, no life insurance, nothing but my part-time nursing salary to support us."

"Your parents couldn't help?"

"My mother died when I was nine. Ever since then my father has been…busy." Cassie's voice dropped. "He blamed me, too, for not knowing what Eric was doing. So I stopped trying to defend myself."

Rick could see how much it cost Cassie to say this. He longed to pull her back into his arms, but for a moment, he questioned his motives. Did he want to offer her more comfort or did he simply love the feel of her in his arms? He wasn't sure he wanted the answer to that question.

"The day Noah got beaten up by his former friends was the day I knew getting him more counseling wouldn't help. We had to leave." Her eyes were dark beneath her damp eyelashes. "But leaving hasn't helped. I can't get him to let go of his anger."

"We'll figure out a way," Rick assured her. "Don't worry, Cassie. Once the two of you are involved in our church groups—"

"I won't be involved in them." She looked at him with an iciness that dared him to argue. "I can't be in a church, near people who call themselves Christians, without having it all come rushing back."

"These are not the same people, Cassie."

"But it's the same God. Where was He when my son—my *innocent* son—was being bullied? Why didn't He help us?" She glared at him, demanding answers.

"He did help you. He led you here," Rick murmured. "To a new life and a chance to start over."

"I will start over," she said with a nod. "But I don't intend to make the same mistake twice. I will not trust God again. It's too hard when He fails to come through."

"Cassie—"

"Don't." She shook her head. "I know what you're going to say. It's the same thing my father said to me. *Jesus never fails.*"

"It's true."

"In my case it isn't." Cassie held up a hand. "Don't

trot out any more verses, Rick. I'm a preacher's kid. I've heard them all. But I don't believe in them. Not anymore."

So much pain. Rick knew he had pushed Cassie to her limit, and now it was time to back off.

"I'm sorry."

"So am I." She emptied her cup in the sink then turned to face him, her voice hard. "I hope you've heard enough to figure out how to help Noah because I don't intend to talk about this ever again."

"I appreciate your confiding in me," he told her quietly.

"If Noah wants to sing in your choir, I have no objection. If he wants to attend your church, that's also fine." The gold in Cassie's brown eyes flashed. "But don't expect me to do the same. Despite my father's admonitions about fleeing the fold, and any rebuke you might want to add, I will not be part of your congregation, Rick. Now, excuse me. I need to change."

Cassie swept out of the room and in that instant Rick's heart rate ripped into skyrocketing overdrive.

He suddenly realized why her face seemed so familiar.

Rick had seen a photo of a young Cassie every time he'd visited John Foster, the minister who'd saved him countless times while he was living on the streets, and who'd mentored him on his path to salvation and helped him get into seminary.

John carried a picture of Cassie in his wallet, and had a larger one on his desk. Sometimes Rick had come upon him staring at her photo, murmuring a prayer for her.

If he was honest, Rick had to admit he'd also been a little resentful of Cassie. She had a real home, a fantastic father who loved her, people who took care of her and made sure she was safe.

It had seemed to Rick that Cassie had everything and he had nothing. No family, no permanent address, no one who cared if he came or went. Even worse, there was no one to soothe his hurts. Oh, how he'd longed for that.

Rick wasn't sure how it had happened but the more he saw Cassie's photo, the more he'd stared at it, until he'd begun imagining a future in which he had all the things she did—a home, a family and love.

Funny thing was, as he and John deepened their friendship, Rick began to understand how deeply the caring father mourned the fact that he wasn't able to be with his daughter as much as he wanted. And why hadn't he?

Because John had been spending his time with Rick trying to help him find a way out of his life on the streets.

One more thing Rick had to feel guilty about.

His soul groaned under the weight of it.

When Cassie finally returned downstairs, the house was bustling and Rick was gone.

"L-look, Mom," Noah said, excitement glowing in his blue eyes. "It's s-snowing like c-crazy."

"Sure is," she agreed after a glance out the window. "Does this mean the fireworks for tonight are canceled?" she asked Laurel.

"Rick said he thought they would be. He's gone to set up a post at the church in case anyone gets caught in the storm and needs refuge." She smiled. "He's always thinking of others."

"P-pastor R-Rick is going to s-start a choir," Noah told her. "He a-asked me to j-join."

"That sounds like fun." Cassie held her breath, unwilling to show any hope that he would get involved in something with his peers. "Do you think you will?"

"M-maybe. I l-like singing."

"Good." Cassie exchanged a nonchalant glance at Laurel, knowing she'd understand. "So what will we do for New Year's Eve?"

"I'm glad you asked," said Cassie's friend.

Laurel already had a list of things she needed to prepare so the boys would enjoy their evening despite the fireworks cancellation. Cassie was glad to keep busy, hoping it would keep her mind off her conversation with Rick, when she'd dumped her past all over him, wept on his shoulder and then told him she'd never darken the door of his church.

She felt stupid, weak and ashamed that he'd seen her so needy, but being in his arms had felt wonderful.

Though Sara and Kyle were away for the holiday, Sara had left the freezer and cooler well stocked. Cassie and Laurel chose two casseroles and set them to bake for dinner, then prepared snack foods for later in the evening. They were putting the finishing touches on a series of sweet treats when the power went off.

"I was afraid this would happen with that high wind," Laurel said when it hadn't come back on after twenty minutes. "I need to go out to the shed and start the generator so the furnace will keep us warm."

Cassie watched her bundle up, unable to stem her worry. She stood at the window in the front hall and tracked Laurel through the whirling snow to make sure she arrived safely. But when minutes turned into half an hour and Laurel hadn't come back, worry burgeoned into fear. She'd just put on her coat to follow her friend when she saw Laurel pushing her way back through the drifts.

Cassie glanced at the light in the hall. The bulb remained unlit.

Apprehension filled her, but she tried to hide it as she met Laurel at the door. Once her friend was safely inside she quickly shut out the wind and snow.

"What's wrong?" Cassie asked quietly.

"I can't get it to start, though I tried about a hundred times." Laurel shivered as she rubbed her hands together. "Kyle tested it last week. It should be fine."

"So what do we do now?" Cassie whispered.

"I don't know," Laurel admitted. "We have to have heat so I'm going to read the manual again. Maybe I missed something." She hurried to her office.

Cassie stood in the hall. She wrapped her arms around her waist and shivered, trying to fight off her fear.

"M-mom, Laurel's c-cell phone is r-ringing," Noah bellowed from the kitchen.

Cassie answered. Her heart jumped a beat when she heard Rick's voice.

"Hey, Cassie. I tried the landline but I couldn't get through," he told her. "Is everything okay?"

"The power's out," Cassie murmured, keeping her voice low so the boys wouldn't guess from her tone how vulnerable she felt. "I guess that took out the phones."

"You haven't started the generator yet?" Rick sounded puzzled.

"Laurel tried. It won't start." Cassie went to Laurel's office but didn't find her there. "Laurel's not available right now. I'll have her call you." She didn't want to keep him when he must have things to do, but the sound of his voice was so reassuring.

"I contacted the power utility. A line is down. Apparently it will be a while before power will be restored."

Rick paused for a moment. "But you guys need heat and that means the generator. I'm coming out there."

"In this storm?" Cassie glanced outside. Fear tiptoed along her spine. "It's too big a risk."

"Not at all. I know the landmarks along the way. I won't get lost," he assured her. "Besides, Kyle's taught me all the wilderness survival techniques he knows." He paused a moment. "I can't just leave you there, knowing you're in trouble."

"But it's so dangerous to travel in a storm."

"It's nice of you to worry about me, Cassie, but I'll be fine." His warm voice eased some of her concern. "See you in a bit."

"Please be careful," she whispered.

"Always."

Cassie hung up, unable to stem her worry. So many things could happen to Rick.

To keep herself busy, she set the table and mixed up a salad, trying to maintain her facade that nothing was wrong until Laurel decided how she wanted to explain the situation to the boys. A few moments later Laurel returned, having taken a second shot at fixing the generator. Cassie filled her in on Rick's call.

"I tried to talk him out of it but he insisted," she told Laurel helplessly.

"He would. That's the kind of man he is. Always giving for others." Worry showed clearly in Laurel's frown. "Can you keep the boys busy? I'm going to pray for Rick."

"I hope it works," Cassie told her.

"Prayer always works, Cassie. God always hears us. Romans says, 'Anyone who calls upon the name of the

Lord will be saved.'" Laurel gave Cassie a quick smile before she left the room.

Cassie wasn't as certain as Laurel about God's protection, but she'd had enough conversation about God for one day.

Lives got chillier as the day went on. Laurel explained their predicament to the boys, who grew increasingly more solemn as they waited for Rick. Though it was barely mid-afternoon, the light was fading fast. Cassie knew that Rick's chances of arriving safely during the storm dropped considerably with every minute that passed.

When the last of the day's light faded, Cassie and Laurel raided Kyle's cupboard for emergency lanterns, which the boys began cranking. Then Cassie asked them to cut used milk jugs into candleholders.

"Wh-what are they f-for?" Noah asked.

"We'll put them in the windows so Rick can find us in the storm." It was silly, but Cassie couldn't suppress her desperation to do something, anything, to help Rick reach them. Surely God wouldn't let anything happen to His emissary, would He?

He let other things happen.

Her heart squeezed tight at the foreboding that filled her. Cassie began to wish she could pray. But she couldn't get the words past the distrustful block in her throat. God had let her down before. How could she trust Him now, with something as important at Rick's life?

Then, above the whine of the raging wind, she heard the roar of a snowmobile. Her heart surging with relief, Cassie followed Laurel and the boys to the front door where they all urged Rick inside.

"What is this, an honor guard?" he joked, dragging off his helmet.

Everyone laughed, shattering the tension. Laurel urged the boys to go back to their warm quilts in the family room while Cassie helped Rick slide off his snow-covered coat. When his green eyes met hers, her heart beat so fast all she could manage was, "Welcome."

Cassie didn't think she'd ever been so glad to see someone in her entire life.

"Awful night to host a party." Rick tossed her a brash grin then kicked off his boots. Cassie and Laurel followed him as he hobbled to a kitchen chair and rubbed his toes. "Sorry it took so long. I made a wrong turn. Kyle will ream me out when I tell him," he said, looking slightly abashed. "Thanks for lighting those candles. Believe it or not, they helped."

"That was Cassie's idea." Laurel turned to wink at her.

"Thank you, Cassie. I appreciate it." Rick's gaze clung to hers a bit too long before he turned back to Laurel. "Give me a few minutes to get the ice off my feet and I'll go check on the generator. I brought some extra gas for it in case you're low."

"We have lots of gas. I just can't get the thing to start," Laurel complained.

Cassie smiled as the boys returned and gathered around Rick, drawn in by his charisma. Wrapped in their warm blankets, they sat on the floor at his feet, asking a thousand questions, barely waiting for answers.

Rod had been at Lives the longest and had beaten Rick at checkers many times. Bryan had begun to adapt to his diabetes, thanks to Rick's encouragement. Barry was the quiet one, but his adoration of the young pastor was clear. Michael suffered from depression and Daniel dealt with the aftereffects of drug use. The newest arrivals were still finding their way at Lives, but as Rick laughed and joked with them, each boy joined in.

Every so often Rick's eyes lifted in search of hers. Each time Cassie pretended to be busy, too aware of her heightened response to him, too embarrassed by the surge of relief that had filled her when he'd walked through the door.

"Okay, I'm ready," Rick said to Laurel as he rose. "Got a couple of flashlights?"

She handed them to him. "I'm coming, too," she said. "I need to see what's wrong."

"Okay. See you guys in a bit," he said cheerfully. With a smile that seemed to be just for Cassie, he and Laurel left.

Cassie wasted the next ten minutes telling herself she would have worried about anyone who had been out in a storm like this. By the time the power flickered on, she'd almost convinced herself it was true. But when Rick returned and accepted the hot chocolate she handed him, her heart was still thudding and she couldn't catch her breath.

With the furnace blasting out heat, Lives quickly warmed up. Cassie and Laurel finished preparing supper using candlelight to save the generator because no one knew when power would be restored. Then they all gathered around the big table to eat.

Cassie was not surprised in the slightest that Rick made the meal joyful, from his grace of thanksgiving to the jokes he shared.

"He's got the boys so busy laughing there's no time for them to miss their families," Laurel said as they cleaned up the kitchen. "Just another reason I adore that man."

Laurel coaxed Rick into leading the games she'd

planned, and Cassie couldn't help but laugh when he refused to let either of them sit out, despite their protests. Cassie didn't mind. The room resounded with loud and happy laughter and she couldn't remember when she'd had so much fun. Even Noah seemed to lose his reticence, begging her to join in a game of Twister that left Cassie feeling like a pretzel.

"You're good at this," Rick told her, offering a helping hand up. When she took it, she felt the warmth of his hand against hers.

"I have to be—it's Noah's favorite." Once on her feet, she let go of his hand, anxious to break the connection between them.

What was wrong with her tonight? Were her responses so strong because she'd been afraid for Rick?

"It's getting close to midnight," Rick said. "Maybe we should fill the punch glasses so we'll be ready for a toast."

Since the others were busily arranging the white domino tiles for a game, Cassie agreed. She and Rick worked together. After their hands touched for the third time, Cassie couldn't remain silent.

"I was so scared for you," she said in a half whisper so the boys wouldn't hear.

"Really?" His eyes widened. A smile stretched across his face. "That was nice of you. I don't think I've ever had anyone worry about me before."

A pleased look stayed with him even after they'd finished filling the glasses. Such a small thing, yet he seemed delighted by it. Cassie couldn't help wondering why this handsome and very nice man didn't have anybody who cared about him.

Soon they were finished and all was ready for the midnight hour.

"One more minute," Rick said, smiling. "Then we start a new chapter in our lives." He tapped a spoon against a glass. "Hey," he called. "Are you guys ready for our New Year's toast?"

The boys grabbed their glasses, laughing as they counted down the seconds. Her mind working furiously, Cassie moved as far as possible from Rick. She could not, would not get caught next to him at the stroke of midnight. Her cheeks warmed at the thought of his lips touching hers and she scolded herself for her imagination. But when she caught his gaze she knew that he'd been thinking along the same lines, and that flustered her even more.

"Ready?" she asked Noah, tearing her gaze from Rick's.

"Y-yeah." He blinked as Laurel's big wall clock chimed the midnight hour.

"Happy New Year!" Cassie clinked her glass with her son's. "May it be your best year ever, Noah."

"Happy N-New Year," he repeated.

The boys moved around, eager to tap their glasses against everyone else's. That was how Cassie ended up next to Rick, despite her best efforts.

"Happy New Year, Cassie," he said softly.

It was only their glasses that made contact, but the effect was the same as if his lips had touched hers. She spilled a few drops of punch on her fingers as she tried to find her voice.

"Happy New Year," she whispered.

His eyes held hers for a long timeless moment. Finally he turned toward the boys and led them in singing

"Auld Lang Syne." Cassie forced herself to breathe in and out slowly, causing her heart rate to eventually return to normal by the end of his short but fervent prayer asking God to bless each of them in the year ahead.

"Let's share our resolutions," Rick said.

"What's a resolution?" Rod asked.

"Grab your snacks. We'll sit in the family room," Laurel said. "Rick can explain."

Cassie sat on the arm of the sofa beside Noah and waited until everyone had settled, curious to hear what Rick would say.

"Resolutions are plans we make to accomplish specific things in the coming year," he explained in a solemn tone. "It's a goal to focus on. For example, my resolution this year is to serve God with all my heart, even when it means sacrificing my own plans."

Cassie frowned. The way Rick said it made it sound as if he was trying to make up for something. What was her resolution?

"What about you guys? Any idea what you'd like to accomplish in the new year?"

Rod grimaced. "My resolution is to figure out math."

"That's a good one," Rick encouraged. "Hard, but good. Anyone else?"

"Mine is to get another saxophone," Michael said, his blond curly head tilted to one side.

"You play sax? You and I could brainstorm on that maybe," Rick offered.

"I'd like that," he said shyly.

Cassie was surprised Michael had answered at all. According to the file she had on him, he was suffering from depression. He certainly hadn't volunteered any information previously. It must be Rick who was helping him find his place.

"I'm going to get along better with others this year," Laurel said.

Soon Rick had coaxed each boy to talk about some plan for the future—everyone except Noah, who'd said only that he'd think about it. Cassie's heart was still aching from Noah's withdrawal, so she was not prepared when Rick called her name.

"What's yours, Cassie?" Rick's gaze pinned her.

"My resolution?" She blinked in surprise, though she knew she should have expected the question. But what to say?

Like a giant wave, the hurt rolled over her, lending a sharp edge to her voice when she said, "I'm going to rebuild my life this year."

Rick studied her for several moments. Was that pity in his eyes? Cassie did not want pity from this man. She shifted uncomfortably, aware that the boys were now staring, too.

"Well, you're in the right place, Cassie, because that's what we do at Lives Under Construction, right, boys?" Laurel said, kindly drawing the attention away from her.

"Thank you all for sharing," Rick added. "I'll pray God will help each of you fulfill the desires of your hearts."

In the clamor of the next hour of games, Cassie often felt Rick's eyes on her. She studiously avoided looking at him, forcing herself to join the fun, suppressing all that she was feeling. But when her eyes accidentally met his, she knew she wasn't fooling him.

When the boys could no longer hide their yawns, Laurel said it was time for bed. She convinced Rick to sleep in the family room because of the storm, and then Cassie persuaded Laurel to leave the cleaning-up to her.

She'd just snapped off the kitchen light and was about to go to her room when Rick's touch on her arm stopped her. She shifted so his hand dropped away. "Yes, Rick?"

"I wanted to wish you the very best with your resolution, Cassie." His green eyes swirled with something she couldn't define, something that made her knees weak against her will. "I hope God will bless you and Noah as you start a new life here. I'll pray you find what you need in Churchill and at Lives."

"Thank you. Happy New Year to you, too, Rick," she said quietly. "Thanks for coming to our rescue."

She wanted to say good-night and go, and yet somehow she couldn't leave. Time stood still, holding her immobile for several long moments, unable to leave. Finally he spoke.

"Good night, Cassie. God bless."

Cassie turned and left the room, almost running in her haste to escape the rush of emotions that filled her. She sat on her bed, staring out the window at the storm that was no match for the private storm raging inside her, thanks to the way Rick had looked at her.

What was that she'd seen in his eyes? Was it pity? Sorrow? Need?

What did the handsome pastor want from her?

Perhaps that was the wrong question. Perhaps instead, she should be asking what did *she* want from him?

Chapter Four

A week later Rick accepted a refill of coffee from the waitress at Common Ground, the town's favorite coffee shop, suddenly aware that he'd been admiring the way Cassie's gold sweater accented her eyes for way too long. Those brown eyes had captivated him from the first time he'd seen that childhood picture in her dad's office. He should have told her up front that he knew her father, but guilt held him back. He was part of the reason she didn't get to spend time with her father.

Not only that, but imagining Cassie's disgust if she knew about his past, the whole ugly story, made him hold his tongue.

"I'm glad I spotted you in here, Cassie. Doubly glad you invited me to share coffee with you. I've been wondering how Bryan's doing keeping track of his blood sugar levels."

That wasn't what he'd wanted to talk about at all, but he couldn't just blurt things out.

"There hasn't been an overnight change. I still have to remind him periodically to check. But he's getting better at taking responsibility," she said quietly. "We haven't had any more incidents like the day he arrived."

"Great. That's progress." Rick paused. "And Noah?"

"He's had two days of school and it seems like he's wound tighter than ever," Cassie said. "I'm running out of ideas."

"I've been trying to reach Noah without being too obvious. So far, he's polite but closed up like a clam." Rick smiled, hoping to ease the furrow that marred her forehead. "But don't worry. I'm not giving up."

If only Rick could only find a way to help Cassie's son as her father had helped him, maybe he could make it up to Cassie for taking so much of her father's time.

"I know it's not easy. You're busy with your congregation." Cassie's eyes brimmed with hidden emotions, emotions that were just out of his reach. "I appreciate your taking time with him, Rick."

"He's a good kid. I enjoy talking to him. We've discovered we have a common interest in astronomy." Rick studied her. "How are you doing? Is the job at Lives what you expected?"

"It's much different than working in a hospital." She fiddled with her coffee cup. "Mostly working at Lives is a breeze."

"Mostly?" Rick leaned forward.

She smiled ruefully. "I've been trying to figure out how to help Michael. He struggles with seizures, you know. He needs an outlet to help him relax."

"Your mother's heart overtakes the nurse in you, doesn't it?" A rush of admiration swelled inside him.

Her cheeks pinked and she looked down, avoiding his scrutiny.

"All Michael talks about is his saxophone."

"Which is where?" Rick found himself admiring the way tendrils of her golden curls caressed the nape of her neck, and forced his eyes back to her face.

Cassie met his eyes. "I don't know."

"If you can find out when and where he last had it, maybe we could try to get it back. What do you think?"

"I think you're a good person to work with," Cassie murmured. "I'll ask him. Thank you for the suggestion."

"My pleasure." He swallowed the last of his coffee. "I've got to get going. Lucy promised she'd practice playing the choir music with me this afternoon. We plan to start up next week." He slid his arms into his jacket. "You are coming with the boys to the fireworks tonight, aren't you?"

"After all the buildup you've given it?" Cassie chuckled. "I wouldn't miss it."

Rick was trying to ignore the fact that she had the most wonderful smile, which was probably why he spoke without thinking.

"Mind if I join you to watch them?"

When she didn't answer, he wondered if her silence meant she wanted to refuse. "You and the boys," he amended.

"The more the merrier." Cassie nodded slowly, as if she'd hunted for a way to get out of spending the evening with him and couldn't think of one. "But if as many people show up as you claim, it might be difficult to find us."

"With those rowdy boys in tow?" He shook his head and grinned. "Finding you will be a cinch." Rick decided he needed to have another chat with God, especially with regard to Cassie Crockett. He was getting too interested in her and that did not bode well for keeping his distance. "Can I ask you a question completely unrelated to Bryan?"

"I guess." She blinked, her confusion evident.

"You wear the most unusual sweaters. I've never seen anything like them. I wondered where you get them."

"This?" She plucked her sweater away from her midriff. "I made it."

"Really?" Surprise rendered him speechless as he imagined Cassie bent over knitting needles. His mental picture of a nurse was a steady, hardworking, earnest soul. Somehow he'd never thought of a nurse as artistic, yet the creativity displayed in her sweater showed a mind that loved beauty. It revealed yet another aspect of her that intrigued him.

"Why did you ask?" Cassie studied him with a certain probing look. Her "nurse" look, he'd dubbed it.

"There's a woman, Alicia Featherstone. She teaches native culture at Lives. She also has a store in town where she sells unique things to tourists and residents alike. Many native artists sell their work there." Rick noted the way her eyes flared in interest as she leaned forward.

"I'd like to see it. How do I get there?"

He described the location, then hesitated.

"What aren't you saying?" Cassie asked.

"I don't want you to think I'm nosy, but Alicia and I were both at Lives when you were at the hospital the other day. She admired a sweater much like the one you're wearing. Alicia's always looking for artists to stock her store so I thought you might want to sell some of your work. You did say you were hoping to earn some extra money," he added. "Alicia's great about taking things to sell on consignment, or so I've been told."

"She liked my sweater enough to want to sell it?"

Cassie blinked. "Then I will definitely talk to her. Thank you." Her glance was turning into a stare. She flushed and dragged her gaze away. Feeling self-conscious, she grabbed her satchel off a nearby chair and withdrew the contents.

"What's that?"

"This is my current project. I took it to the hospital to work on during my break today."

It was going to be a sweater. Rick could discern that much. But it seemed far too big for her. And in his opinion the taupe and beige tones were the wrong colors for her fair complexion.

"It looks complicated," he finally managed, unable to think of anything else.

"It is. It will look like this." She pulled a sketch from her bag and placed it on the table for him to see. Her fingers trembled a little as she smoothed it out. "I started it a while ago. It was going to be a Christmas gift for Eric."

Rick suddenly understood.

Cassie swallowed and visibly gathered herself. "But the yarn was very expensive and it seemed wrong to waste it. It's way too big for Noah, but I can always give it away."

"It's very fine work." His fingers seemed to reach out of their own volition to touch the length she'd already created. "It's nothing like the ones you make for yourself."

"No. I hand-dye my sweaters because I can never find anything bright enough." She laughed and the tension disappeared. "I'm afraid I'm addicted to color. Eric wasn't."

Her voice died away. She stared at the yarn she held, her face a misery. Rick couldn't stand to see it.

"You can talk about him, Cassie," he murmured. "You can tell me anything you want to."

"What do you mean?" She frowned at him, a wary glint in her eyes.

"I don't suppose it's easy to talk to Noah about his father. Moms always want to help their kids think the best of their parents, even when it isn't always true."

Rick wasn't sure why he added that last part. It was something in Cassie's manner that made him wonder if there might have been something bad going on with Eric.

Or was he simply envying her because she'd found someone to share her life and he couldn't?

"I don't want to talk about Eric," she said firmly. Cassie stuffed her work back in her bag. "This is just a hobby."

"A hobby is a good thing to have up here when the days are short and the nights long and dark." The jewel tones she wore enhanced her natural beauty, but Rick didn't say that. Instead, he said, "Go talk to Alicia, Cassie. If nothing else, you'll find a friend."

"Maybe I'll go see her before I head back to Lives." When Cassie smiled—truly smiled—it dissolved the tension lines around her eyes and revealed the full extent of her beauty.

Rick cleared his throat. "I'd better get going. See you tonight."

As Rick left the restaurant, his head rang with a question—how could he escape the magnetizing lure of Cassie Crockett?

Did he really want to? His entire life he'd longed for someone special to help create the family he wanted. But he'd made that vow.

Until now, it hadn't been a problem. This was the first time Rick had feelings for someone since then. The agonizing thing was, he could never act on them.

Cassie studied Rick's disappearing figure. The big picture windows allowed her to watch him saunter down the street, talking to everyone he met. A small, silver-haired woman met him at the church steps. Rick's face broke into a smile at something she said. Then he held out his arm and escorted her into the church.

Cassie finished her coffee and prepared to leave as her mind swirled with questions about Churchill's youngest minister. Rick had an amazing ability with people. *Please God, let him find a way to help Noah.*

As quickly as the prayer filled her brain, she pushed it away. God didn't answer. There was no point in asking.

Cassie was about to leave the coffee shop when someone said, "I've been wanting to talk to you. You're Cassie Crockett, the new nurse at Lives Under Construction. I'm Alicia Featherstone."

"It's nice to meet you."

"Let me pay for my coffee and then we can talk at my store. It's called Tansi—that's Cree for 'Hi, how are you?'"

"Oh." Startled that this woman knew her, Cassie found herself escorted down the street and into a small shop. There she became entranced by the assortment of crafts. "This is a wonderful place," she murmured in awe.

"Thank you." Laughter rang in Alicia's voice.

"Rick Salinger told me you were interested in my sweater."

"Oh, Rick—he's such a sweetie. I've never met anyone with a bigger heart." Alicia leaned forward. "I loved your sweater. I have a hunch you wear the one I saw at Lives, but I'd love to see what else you have."

"Right now, just this." Cassie set her bag on the counter and undid her coat before she lifted her work out of her bag.

"I love this scarf of yours." Alicia examined it more closely. "Anything else?"

"So far, just this." Cassie withdrew the sweater she'd planned for Eric. "It isn't finished yet, but this is what it will look like." She set the sketch on the counter beside her sweater.

After examining the sweater, Alicia slid it back into the bag. "Bring it in when it's done." Then she reached out to finger Cassie's scarf. "This is so beautiful. I love the color. Could you make six of these for me?"

"Yes, but the color won't be an exact match." Slightly dazed by the request, Cassie explained about her dying process and the need for hand-washing.

"We'll make a tag with those instructions." In a brisk tone, Alicia explained how she operated. "All your supplies are your responsibility. You tell me how much you need and we'll set a price, but you won't get paid until the item sells. Is that suitable?"

"It sounds fine." Bemused by the speed at which she'd found another job, Cassie nodded.

"Great!" Alicia grinned. "I'm glad Rick told me about you, Cassie. I'm going to love selling your work. Isn't he a great guy? We're lucky to have him in Churchill."

As Cassie listened to the other woman sing Rick's praises she wondered for a moment if there was something other than friendship between the two.

Then she reminded herself that it shouldn't matter to her. A wiggle of dismay filled her. She'd always suspected Rick must have someone who cared for him. He was too nice for it to be otherwise.

"Sometimes I think Rick and I are the only two single people in Churchill," Alicia joked. "We're both determinedly single so it's nice when more singles move to town. Welcome."

"Thanks." So Rick and Alicia weren't a couple. Why did she feel relief? "I'd better go get started on those scarves," Cassie said.

"You have wool already?"

"Several boxes of it." Cassie chuckled at Alicia's surprised face. "I brought it with me when we moved."

"Good. Come and have coffee with me sometime," Alicia offered.

"That would be fun. Thank you, Alicia. Bye." As Cassie left, her heart sang at the chance to earn money to put in her meager savings account. Thanks to Rick—again. He was turning out to be a lifesaver in a lot of ways.

Her heart gave that funny bump of joy that warmed her inside whenever she thought of Churchill's young pastor.

Perhaps she should add her heart to the list of things she could no longer trust.

When Rick stopped by Lives just before the boys returned from school that afternoon, Cassie hid her smile. Judging by how often he'd arrived in time for meals, she thought it was pretty obvious the gregarious Rick hated eating alone. And, of course, this afternoon *was* hockey practice.

Rick was unbuttoning his coat as the boys trooped in, sniffing the air still redolent with Sara's freshly baked cookies. Cassie waited for Noah, hoping today had been a better day. When he finally strolled into the kitchen, her hopes took a nosedive. The right side of his face was red and swollen, particularly around his eye.

"What happened?" Cassie rose, wanting to enfold him in her protective arms but suppressing the urge, mindful of his glare of warning.

"I g-got h-hit b-by a b-ball." Noah clenched and unclenched his jaw. "H-here." He thrust an envelope toward her.

"You were playing ball in the snow? I see." Cassie read the explanation from the principal. *Your son was involved in an altercation. Neither child was seriously injured but we will be requiring him to do detention.* It was signed by the principal. She glanced around. None of the other boys said a word and they looked everywhere but at her.

"The best thing for an eye like that is cold. Is there a bag of peas in the freezer?" Rick's apparent nonchalance reinforced her instinct that now was not the time to make a motherly scene.

"I'll check." Cassie took one more look at her son, then opened the freezer door while Rick carried carafes of hot chocolate and a platter of cookies to the table.

As her pregnancy progressed, Sara now frequently rested in the afternoon. Cassie chipped in to help as often as she could. Lucy Clow also appeared almost every day to help, as well as some other local women. Now Rick was pouring mugs of cocoa for the boys. He made no bones about helping out anywhere he was needed, Cassie noted. Including with her son.

"Mind if I share your snack, guys?" Rick asked. "I'm hungry."

"You're always hungry when you come here." Rod gave him a cheeky grin. "Don't ministers get paid? Can't they afford their own groceries? Or can't you cook?"

"The answers to your questions, in order, are yes, yes and a resounding yes. In fact, I am an expert cook. As you should know, since you've chowed down my fried chicken," Rick said in his own defense. "But it's no fun cooking for yourself. Besides, I'm not as good a baker as Sara is."

"Keep that in place for a few minutes," Cassie told Noah, pressing the bag of peas against his face as she regained her composure. "It should take down the swelling a little."

"S-stop f-fussing," Noah said in a harsh tone, exactly as Eric used to.

Cassie opened her mouth, caught Rick's warning glance and swallowed her response. She turned to refill her coffee cup while surreptitiously rubbing away the tear that had squeezed out the corner of her eye.

"She's not fussing, Noah. She's doing her job as a nurse and a mom," Rick gently corrected.

Cassie was grateful for his support. When she returned to her seat, Rick's eyes met hers with an intensity she couldn't avoid. A moment later Rick leaned over and whispered something in Noah's ear. Noah frowned, muttered "Thanks" to Cassie, then returned to his hot chocolate.

Cassie wondered what Rick had said.

"So, you guys have lots of homework?" Rick asked the group, lightening the tense atmosphere. "Probably won't have much time left to play hockey, will you?"

"You wish." Again Rod's sly grin appeared. "We got

together at lunch hour and did most of it. Ten minutes or so and I'll be ready. You guys?"

The other kids nodded their agreement.

"And you, Noah? Are you going to be able to play?" Rick asked. "Did you do your homework during lunch, too?"

The boy's quick flinch told Cassie all she needed to know but she said nothing, content to let Rick handle her recalcitrant son.

"No." Noah's sullen glare said it all.

"Oh. Right. You were hit by a ball. At lunch, huh?" Rick nodded then rose. "Too bad you have to miss practice today."

Noah made a face at Rick but there was no malice in it. Cassie felt a twitch of hope that maybe finally someone was finally reaching her son.

She would have liked to hug Rick for that, but that would be foolish. He was just being a nice guy. Still, she couldn't get used to it.

"Well, guys, I'll get my skates on and dig the equipment out." Rick put his used cup and plate in the dishwasher. "The Lord's given us a nice warm day."

"It's not what I'd call warm," Michael hooted in derision. "But at least it won't be too cold for the fireworks tonight."

"Good thing it's a Friday and you can stay up late," Rick said.

"Does that make a difference?" Cassie asked with a small smile. "It will be dark in half an hour. They could shoot the fireworks off before supper."

"Now what fun would that be?" Rick joked.

His teasing wink stopped her breath and any rebuttal

she might have made. For one brief moment, she let herself imagine that she could relax her guard and trust Rick.

Rick smiled, his eyes focused and intently unnerving, as if he could see into her soul and read the questions and doubts that hammered at her. "I'll be ready whenever you are, guys," he said to the boys, then walked out of the kitchen.

It was several minutes before Cassie started breathing normally again.

"Don't you love fireworks?" Rick grinned at Cassie as the first boom resounded across Hudson Bay.

"Yes, I do. I wasn't allowed to see them when I was a kid. My father figured I'd be too tired the next day, though why he'd care I don't know. He was never home much to notice me."

Her memories about her father created a lump in his throat. Why hadn't he told her the truth days ago?

Cassie raised an eyebrow. "What's your excuse?"

"I need an excuse to enjoy this?" Rick gazed up at the light display to avoid looking into Cassie's eyes. "I don't have one, other than I get caught up in the dazzle of it all. When that powder goes off, all eyes get lifted up to the heavens and everything stops to admire its beauty." He murmured, "'The heavens are telling the glory of God; they are a marvelous display of His craftsmanship.'"

"Psalms 19." Cassie tilted her head upward. "I memorized that in girls' club years ago. So how did you get permission to stay up and watch them when you were young?"

Rick hesitated. He hadn't told her anything about his past yet. Maybe now was the time to start. "I was a street kid, so there wasn't anyone to tell me when to go to bed. Sometimes there wasn't a bed, actually," he said, attempting to joke. His voice sounded funny, even to his own ears.

He had to tell her he knew her father. How could he expect her trust if he wasn't honest? The absence of truth meant he'd essentially been lying to her and he didn't want to do that anymore.

"I didn't know that." Her voice brimmed with sympathy. "I always think the hardest thing in the world is for a kid to grow up without a family. What happened to yours? If you don't mind telling me," she added after a slight pause.

"It's not that I mind telling you, it's that I can't. I don't know what happened to them. I have no family." Saying it still hurt—he couldn't deny that. "At least none I know of. The only thing I remember is living on the street. Maybe I wiped it out, maybe it will come back someday, but all I know is that I grew up in Toronto."

"What's your first memory?" Rick noticed her gaze slide from the sky to Noah, then to him.

"It's not the first but it's my best one from those days. I was starving, panhandling to buy something to eat. A man handed me a couple of bucks then told me about his church. He said they had what you'd call a soup kitchen. The next day I went and I loved it." Rick smiled at the memories. "The man was there. He welcomed me, acted as if I was the best thing since sliced bread. He made me feel worthwhile, important. Loved." He choked up at the word. It took a few moments for him to regain control. "He was the reason I kept going back."

"I'm glad you found him." Cassie peeked at him through her thick lashes. Rick knew this was the moment when he should tell her the truth, but somehow he couldn't seem to do it. He didn't want to see the hurt fill her eyes, eyes that he had come to know so well in such a short time.

"Me, too. Anyway, that church basement is my first really good memory." He touched her arm to draw her attention to the balls of blue sparks now exploding across the sky. "I don't remember how I knew I was Rick Salinger. I just knew."

"It must be hard not to know your history." The sympathy exuding from her warmed his soul like a healing balm.

"I can't say. I've only ever known that I was alone." He pretended it didn't matter, but he couldn't fool himself that the age-old ache to have a home of his own and a family who loved him wasn't still alive deep inside, despite his vow to sacrifice both.

In a flash Rick relived moments of sheer terror from his past: hiding from a gang, trying to stay awake so he wouldn't get mugged or beaten, or worse, friends dying from drug overdoses. A shiver ran through him at how close he'd come to losing his life. If not for God and Cassie's father—

"I'm sorry no one was there for you, Rick." Cassie must have seen through his pretense because her brown eyes grew soft. She touched his shoulder. "To be on your own at such a young age must have been terrifying. I wish I could erase the pain for you."

"Thank you. But after that first day at the church, I wasn't totally alone any longer. That man became a good friend."

Cassie's tenderness was almost Rick's undoing. No one except her father had ever expressed such compassion toward him and it overwhelmed him. As the light show continued to explode around them Rick gulped down the lump in his throat, grasping for composure. He couldn't tell her he knew her father now. Not when he was wasn't sure he could remain in control.

"How's Noah doing?" he asked, changing the subject.

"Okay, I guess." Cassie sighed. "He wouldn't say anything else about what happened with his eye but I don't think he got hit by a ball."

"No." Rick had suspicions, but for now that's all they were. He wouldn't say more until he was sure. He waited for her to continue, watching her stare across the snow-covered beach to where her son stood alone, apart from the other Lives' boys.

"His stuttering was worse today. That's usually a sign that he's bothered by something. He didn't say anything to you?" She peered at him through the flickering light shed by a bonfire behind them, higher up the beach.

Rick shook his head. Colored sparks flared in a river-fall of light across the ice. "Tell me about your child-hood, Cassie."

"Not much to tell." She avoided Rick's stare, but he could sense that she had more to say.

Whether it was their isolation from everyone else that led her to confide in him or the intimacy that the semi-darkness seemed to offer, Rick wasn't certain. All he knew was that her next words seemed torn from her.

"After my mom died, my father was too busy with his ministry to bother much with me. I always suspected he wanted a son to follow in his footsteps, so I was prob-ably a disappointment to him." Her words revealed a depth of hurt he guessed she usually kept hidden.

"I'm sure he loved you very much," Rick said, want-ing to say more.

"Then how come he never came to my awards days or the father-daughter events?" she shot back. "How come he was always too busy to see me in the school play? How come he missed my school graduation?"

The ache underlying those words made Rick want to comfort her, to pull her into his arms again the way he had the night she'd told him about Eric. If he didn't feel so guilty, he probably would have.

"Forget it." Cassie inhaled a shaky breath, then exhaled in a short sharp laugh. "I don't know why I told you that."

"Because you needed to say it." Rick settled for touching her shoulder as a means of trying to offer comfort.

"He'd apologize, say how terribly sorry he was that he'd been detained. That's what he always called it—detained. He always said he'd make it up to me, but how do you make up for lost special moments?" She shook her head. "I never understood how he could preach about responsibility to other people and yet abandon me."

"He didn't do it purposely." Cassie gave him a sharp glance, and Rick took a breath. This had gone on long enough. "Cassie, is your father John Foster?"

A blast of brilliant fireworks went off above their heads as Cassie gasped, "How did you know that?"

"I knew your dad," Rick finally admitted. "It was his church where I found solace. Your father is the one who welcomed me, fed me and got me out of scrapes more times than I can remember."

Cassie stared at him as if she couldn't comprehend what he was saying. "Well, at least he helped someone." Her raspy laugh wasn't covered by the racket from the explosives.

"Purposefully or inadvertently," Rick continued, trying to figure out the best way to salvage the situation, "we all hurt the ones we love, Cassie. But one thing I always knew about your dad—the thing all us kids knew—was how much John loved you." What was going on behind those stunned brown eyes of hers? "Remember I said you seemed familiar?"

"I thought it was a come-on," she rasped.

"No. I recognized you. I just couldn't remember why." Rick put both his hands on her shoulders. "Then I remembered. He carried your picture in his pocket and he showed it to everyone. He also had a photo of you in his office. He bragged about you all the time."

Cassie took a few steps away from Rick as if to process his words. Rick decided to just stop speaking for a moment, to let her get a grasp on what he was telling her.

"I can brag about Noah, but unless I'm there for him, it doesn't matter," she finally said.

"Cassie." Rick grasped her arm and turned her toward him. He pointed to his chest. "I'm one of the reasons he wasn't there for you."

When she spoke, her tone was scathing. "You don't have to make excuses for him."

"I'm not. Your dad was the man who welcomed me every time I went to his church. He's the one who made us street kids feel safe, wanted, even if it was just for as long as we were with him." He squeezed his eyes closed and whispered a prayer of thanks for the reprieve he'd been granted.

When he opened his eyes, Cassie had a hard look on her face.

"Your father made sure I had something to eat when I was so hungry my ribs touched my backbone and I didn't have money to buy anything to shoot up and take the pain away. He was the one who got me to talk about goals and dreams for the future and helped me see I could reach them. He helped me find a way to go to college." Rick inhaled and laid out the bare truth. "I'd be dead now if your dad hadn't come looking for me when I was teetering on the edge. He dragged me, kicking and screaming, into drug rehab. He refused to let me escape his love."

"My father isn't like that." Cassie's brows drew together.

"He was exactly like that, Cassie. He was the closest thing to a father I ever knew. Tough, demanding, but also fair-minded and loving," Rick insisted. "John made sure we had coats and gloves for the winter. He made sure we always had Christmas dinner and a gift of some kind, and then he'd tell us about God's gift to us." Guilt suffused Rick. "If he wasn't there when you wanted him, Cassie, it was because of me, because your dad was taking care of me."

"I can't believe this." She wrinkled her nose in disbelief, but her voice held an edge. "He never told me anything about this. Nor did his church staff, and I spent a lot of time with them."

"But that was John," Rick argued. "He wasn't into bragging. He just did what he thought was right." The anger on Cassie's face convinced him that he wasn't explaining things correctly. "When I was struggling to stay straight, I went to see your dad. He told me off, said there are no guarantees in life. You make a choice and you live with it. He picked up your picture and looked at it for a long time."

When Cassie glanced up at him, Rick couldn't help himself—he reached out and touched her hair as tears filled her eyes. "He said he loved you more than life it-self, but he was afraid his choices had hurt you. I never knew what he meant until now."

Cassie stepped away from him again, needing space. "John loves you, Cassie. Deeply. We all knew it and envied you for that love." Rick saw her flinch. "Maybe he spent too much time with us and his other church work, but that doesn't mean he didn't love you dearly."

"Really?" Cassie's eyes were ablaze with anger now. "Then why, after Eric's death, when I needed support against all the blame and accusations of my church, did my *loving* father tell me I needed to ask God's forgive-ness? Why did he imply I was to blame for Eric's ac-tions? Why didn't he at least offer to help us financially?"

"I don't have the answers," Rick said, helpless against her tide of anger. He wanted so badly to help her see John as he did—a loving, caring parent. And yet Rick knew there were no perfect parents. "Maybe you mis-understood what he was saying."

"Believe me, I got his message loud and clear." Cassie stood rigid, apart, alone. "I got in the way of his 'calling.'"

Rick prayed for words to help her rebuild her rela-tionship with her father. But all he could think about was the part he'd played in creating a barrier between the two of them.

"All I know for sure is that your father loves you, Cassie," he said in the stillness of the moment between bursts of fireworks. "And that kind of love doesn't change or die. Your dad loves you very much. But the time he should have spent with you, he spent talking to, helping me. It's my fault he wasn't there for you."

"If my father did something that helped you when you were a kid, I'm glad." Cassie's words were sharp, like ice crackling in the bay. "But nothing he did for you will make me forgive the pain and suffering he put me through then, or wipe out the way he, of all people, judged me for Eric's mistake."

"You might think you don't need your father in your life, but what about Noah?" Rick murmured.

"There is nothing my father could give Noah that I can't. Nothing." Her eyes held his. "What gives you the right to say I should allow my father in my son's life? I confided in you, Rick. You're a pastor, you owed it to me to tell me you knew my dad. Yet you waited. Why? Because you thought you could soften me up?" Head lifted high, Cassie glared at him. "Do you know how betrayed I feel? You've just confirmed that people, especially ministers, are not trustworthy." She walked away to join Laurel by the fire.

Rick stayed where he was. His heart ached as he replayed Cassie's words. She was right to feel betrayed.

It's my fault Cassie and her father are estranged. How can I make it up to her? To John?

Make it up to Cassie? How ridiculous. Rick was still withholding the truth. Not that John's finances were any of his business, except that it was his fault and he knew nothing he did could compensate for the damage he'd done.

Still. Cassie needed to shed the sorrow surrounding her past. She said she wanted to forget, but that wasn't possible with the soul-deep anger festering inside her. Like Noah, she needed to purge her resentment before she could move on. "Lord, please help her. Help me to help her." Rick offered the same prayer as he drove home. But questions had lodged in his heart, questions that demanded total honesty.

Am I so desperate to help Cassie so she'll regain her place in God's family, or because I feel guilty that her father neglected her for me? Or is something more at stake?

Cassie was like a bright light in his life. She gave him strength and support and the feeling that someone cared. And now he was addicted. He wanted to be her support, her bulwark, the one she could count on.

Okay, maybe he'd ruined what they'd begun building, but he couldn't believe that. Because if he did, then he'd have nothing.

But his vow wasn't going away. He'd made it, he had a duty to be a man of his word, to honor his commitment. Rick struggled through the night. By morning he knew only one thing. He had to resist his personal feelings and step back from Cassie Crockett.

She was off-limits. But he couldn't just walk away from her needy heart.

The knot was too big for him to unravel. All Rick knew for sure was that God put him here to minister. For now he'd focus on his ministry to the Lives' boys, and Noah. Eventually, God would show him how to help Cassie.

Maybe He'd also show Rick how to ignore the feelings for her that were now rooted deep within his heart.

Chapter Five

In the three days that followed, Cassie spent every spare moment knitting scarves for Alicia, desperate to enrich her depleted savings. Then she'd start building an education fund for Noah.

As she sat at the kitchen counter, working on Alicia's scarf order, Rick's words tormented her. She couldn't wrap her mind around the fact that all those years when she'd thought her father had been avoiding her, he'd been helping homeless, parentless kids like Rick. She'd misjudged her father back then.

A tiny voice inside kept asking if she'd also misunderstood his words after Eric's death.

During her past two night shifts, Cassie had replayed her father's words over and over, desperate to understand their meaning.

You blame Eric. You blame God and the people who worship Him. You even blame me. Is it really us you can't forgive, Cassie? Or is it yourself?

Back then she'd been seething with resentment, certain he'd been hinting that she was at fault for Eric's mistake. Now, as she reexamined every memory, every event and every thought, Cassie was no longer so sure her interpretation had been right.

She had Rick to blame for her doubts, for putting the idea in her mind that she might have misjudged her father. She'd suffered the injustice of being wrongly judged. She could not tolerate the thought that she'd done the same thing to someone else, even her father.

She resented that Rick hadn't told her the truth earlier, but at least he had told her. Maybe she owed him an apology.

"Hi." Rick stood in the doorway to the kitchen, holding two stacked plastic containers in his hand.

"Hi." Cassie's heart gave its usual bump of excitement, betraying her as always. "What's up?" she asked, trying to quell it as she clicked her knitting needles together.

"Kyle told me Sara's doctor insists she gets off her feet more often so she has to cut back on baking." Rick's green-eyed gaze looked wary, as if she might lash out at him again. "I made a treat for the kids."

"That was nice of you." She strove to maintain perspective, desperate to keep this conversation from becoming personal, as so many others had. Rick Salinger already knew way too much about her. A little distance between them would be a good thing. "What did you make?"

"Devil's food chocolate cake." A smug look flickered across his handsome face.

"Is a minister supposed to be making devil's food?" she asked, tongue-in-cheek.

"I don't know if there are rules about cake. I didn't check." He set a large container on the table and revealed his masterpiece. "Four layers with double fudge frosting."

"Show-off." She chuckled at his obvious pride. "We'll be lucky if we don't *all* end up with diabetes after all that icing."

She recognized that he was hovering, trying to gauge her mood, so she nodded toward the coffeepot.

"Help yourself and have a seat."

"Thanks. Speaking of diabetes—how's Bryan?" Rick poured himself a cup of coffee, then sat across the table from her and thrust out his long legs. "Or do you and I need to initiate phase two?"

"What's phase two?" Cassie tilted her head to one side, curious even though she'd promised herself she would not be enticed by Rick's charisma.

"I don't know yet. I was waiting to see if we needed it before I came up with a plan." His wink and the smile slashing across his rugged face lent him a rakish look that crushed Cassie's resolve to keep her distance from Rick Salinger. "Maybe some kind of one-on-one intervention at my place that involves my lip-smacking elk burgers and sweet potato fries?"

"I had no idea you could get sweet potato fries up here."

"Churchill isn't exactly the end of the earth, you know." He chuckled at her raised eyebrow. "If you have the moolah, you can get anything. I don't have money, but I do have friends. One of them gave me some elk meat, and I brought a bag of sweet potatoes with me from Thompson a couple of trips ago."

"I thought people usually brought back clothes or books," Cassie teased. "You bring sweet potatoes?"

"Each of us has a secret vice. Mine is sweet potato

fries." As he smiled at her, a silence fell between them, and Cassie wondered if he, too, was thinking about what had happened at the fireworks.

Rick leaned forward to peer into her eyes. "You're quiet. Are you worried about something?" He crossed his arms over his broad chest and waited. Cassie liked that he didn't try to rush her.

"Not exactly worried," she corrected. "More like confused."

"About?"

"My father." Cassie felt as if she was tiptoeing through a minefield as she tried to explain. "The other day you suggested I might have misunderstood what he said to me. I don't think I did, but—"

"But on the off chance you did—" He smiled. "You want to be sure, is that it?"

Cassie nodded. "I'm not exactly sure how to find out."

"I usually depend on God's leading," he said in a serious tone. "A little nudge of conviction deep inside often tells me when I need to right a wrong."

"I don't have any nudge of conviction. Certainly not from God," Cassie muttered almost, but not quite, beneath her breath.

"Don't you?" Rick's smile flashed again. "Isn't that exactly what your doubts are? When we begin to question something we thought was true, it's usually a sign that we need to seek God's guidance. Why don't you try doing that?" Steel-strong assurance laced his voice. She envied him that. "God doesn't let people down, Cassie. Not ever."

He let me down, she thought.

"Refusing to forgive is an acid that eats at you," he

added very softly. "It hurts *you* most of all. If you can find a way to forgive, it allows your heart to heal." He paused, his gaze holding hers. "I'm sorry for not being honest, Cassie. I should have told you as soon as I remembered. I didn't because I wasn't sure how you'd take it and I was afraid you wouldn't want to be friends anymore."

Cassie didn't get a chance to respond. The boys burst into the house and ran into the kitchen, thrilled to find Rick sitting there. Cassie caught her breath at the pure delight that filled Rick's face when he saw them. How was it that this man who obviously loved kids didn't have any of his own?

Stop thinking about him. You can't trust him, remember? Or maybe you can, but you shouldn't. You're not getting involved.

"Hey, guys." Rick grinned when, as one, the boys froze, almost drooling as they gaped at his chocolate confection sitting on the table.

Cassie laughed when Michael whispered, "Is that edible?"

Rick faked an indignant frown. "I'll have you know I baked that baby from scratch. With these hands." He extended his arms, as if to prove it.

Cassie sat back as he cut and proudly served his cake. Her awe at his thoughtfulness grew when he handed Bryan a plate with an individual chocolate cake.

"This is sugarless, Bryan," he murmured. "You can eat as much as you want."

"Hey, thanks, man." Bryan's face lit up. While the other boys bickered good-naturedly about who got the biggest slice, Bryan sat happily devouring his own private cake.

Cassie glanced at Rick and caught him studying her. She inclined her head toward Bryan and smiled. Rick nodded, but his gaze remained on her. Uncomfortable under that unblinking stare, Cassie grabbed the scarf she'd been making and worked while the kids bantered back and forth.

"Homework?" she asked when a pause in the conversation allowed.

"None. We had an assembly this afternoon," Rod answered. "We can play hockey until suppertime. Come on. Let's go, guys."

With a great deal of noise and shuffling, they cleared and loaded their dishes in the dishwasher, thanked Rick then hurried away. Noah left with them, but she noticed he hadn't said a word. That didn't bother her as much as the fact that he'd eaten only half his cake. She couldn't be sure, but she thought she saw him wince when Rod jostled his shoulder.

"Cassie, did you notice Noah?" Rick's green eyes grew dark with concern. "His shoulder?"

"I noticed." Seeing a mistake in the knitted row she'd just completed, she began tearing it out.

Rick sat down beside her. "What would you like to do?"

"I don't know." Cassie realized she was making a mess of her work so she set it aside. "Normally, Noah grumbles about every ache and pain, but he didn't say a word today."

"I'll try to sound out the other boys. Maybe they know what's up with him." He squeezed her shoulder. "Are you okay? Or maybe I should ask if *we're* okay."

Cassie looked up into his eyes, her stomach doing somersaults at his use of the word *we*. She nodded, knowing what he meant. "We are. It's all just confusing and complicated, and I'm not sure how to straighten everything out."

Rick rose. "Well, I'm sorry if I contributed to that confusion." Then, he gave her a heart-stopping smile and said, "Have some faith, Cassie."

Faith? she thought as he left. *Faith in what?*

She didn't trust God anymore. Faith in Rick? She wanted to trust him so badly. But she'd learned the hard way not to make herself vulnerable. So the only person she could have faith in was herself. And she had no answers.

With a heavy sigh, Cassie picked up the scarf-in-progress. As she began to work her needles, she realized that while Noah had left with the others, he hadn't gone outside with them—he was standing by the back door. She decided she'd try to have a private talk with him.

But when she went to him, he wouldn't let her get near. His face was ashen.

"Noah, what's wrong?"

"N-nothing." He stepped back, wincing when she touched him as if he were in pain.

"Honey, what's wrong with you?" she asked as her fears multiplied. "Talk to me."

"I t-think I have t-the flu. I'm going to m-my room." Without another word, Noah went inside his bedroom and closed the door.

He refused to talk to her the rest of that evening. Cassie had never felt more alone. Laurel was buried in government forms. Sara and Kyle had their own issues with the coming of their baby. The only person left to confide in was Rick. Her reactions to him disturbed her, but she had to ignore that because she had to do something about Noah. Someone had hurt, was hurting Noah and she had to put a stop to it.

Cassie inhaled deeply then picked up the phone. "Rick? I need help."

Ten minutes later she hung up with a sigh of relief. Surely Rick's offer of a meal of elk and sweet potato fries would make Noah open up.

Thank heaven for Rick.

"Come on in. Welcome."

The next evening Rick threw wide the door of his tiny cottage, shoved a box of old newspapers out of the way and stood back so Cassie and Noah could enter. "Sorry about that. I love reading the papers but I'm not faithful about getting them to the recycling center. You can lay your coats over that chair if you like. I don't have the luxury of a front hall closet."

"You certainly have the luxury of a fantastic view," Cassie said with a burst of enthusiasm. She quickly shed her outerwear, walked straight to the picture window overlooking the bay and peered out. "What are those things on the water?"

"Ice f-fishing h-huts," Noah stammered.

"He's right," Rick said with a smile. "They pull a hut onto the ice, cut a hole in the ice, drop a fishing line and then wait for a fish to bite."

"Really?" Cassie glanced at her son, surprised by his knowledge.

"The hut protects the fishermen from the wind. Some of them have heaters, too. There was a guy who even had a recliner in his. I call that fishing at a luxury level."

Rick could tell just by looking at Noah that he was probably going to have to carry the conversation this evening. That was fine—he was prepared for that. He'd prayed for the chance to reach Noah. This was that chance and he was grateful for it.

"Have a seat," he invited. "It will be a few minutes until dinner's ready."

"It smells wonderful." Cassie sat.

"Let's hope it tastes as good as you think it smells." Rick sat down next to Cassie, waiting to see what Noah would do. Noah then sprawled in Rick's favorite reading chair, no doubt attempting to create some distance. "So, how's it going, Noah? Managing to make friends at school?"

"I g-guess." Noah wouldn't look at them.

"I was talking to a friend of mine who teaches and he says the school is starting some self-defense lessons. Do you think you might be interested in that?" Rick asked, hoping to keep the evening light so the boy would relax and maybe open up.

Noah lifted his gaze. "I d-don't know," he muttered after a sideways glance at his mother.

"I studied it a few years ago. It's a good way to learn self-discipline."

Cassie was frowning, "I don't think—"

Rick saw Noah glare at her and nudged her.

"What do you think, Noah?" he asked.

"I might be interested," Noah said after a quick glance at Cassie.

"I'll let you know when the first meeting is and you can check it out for yourself, okay?" Rick waited for his nod. "I hear you guys are taking an evening field trip next week to see the Northern Lights from the viewing dome."

"Uh-huh." Noah's blue eyes shifted away.

"I might ask to tag along for that," Cassie said with a chuckle. "I've seen the lights at Lives, of course, but to watch from a viewing dome with someone explaining the flares would be really interesting."

"You're lucky you're here now." Rick leaned back.

"L-Lucky? Why?" Was that a flash of interest in Noah's eyes?

"January is the best month to see the Northern Lights. Fortunately, we've had unbelievably clear skies, thanks to that cold snap." Rick chuckled. "There's a blessing to everything."

Cassie's eyebrows lifted and she gave him a droll look just as the oven timer went off, breaking the silence.

"Dinner's ready." Rick led the way to the kitchen and seated Cassie and Noah. "I hope you enjoy it." He set a platter of his sweet potato fries on one trivet and the elk burgers on another, then pulled a plate of burger fixings from the fridge. "Shall we say grace?"

Both Cassie and Noah bowed their heads.

"Thank you, Father, for this food and these friends. Bless us now with Your presence, we ask in Jesus' name. Amen." Rick lifted his head and smiled. "Cassie, why don't you start the potatoes and Noah can start the meat."

As they ate, Rick kept the conversation light by asking Noah questions and inserting amusing anecdotes about his own youth on the street.

"It m-must have been n-nice to be your own b-boss." Noah tossed Cassie a glare.

"It might seem that way, but it was actually pretty difficult, Noah."

"Wh-what was s-so bad ab-bout it?" Noah demanded.

Rick chose his words carefully. "Maybe it was having to go through the garbage to find something to eat. Or trying to stay warm without getting arrested, or not being able to shower." He wanted Noah to realize what not having a home or a loving parent meant. "No, actually, I think not having anyone who cared about me was the worst of all. It's not a life I would ever want you to go through, Noah."

"How d-did you s-survive?" Noah leaned forward, his food forgotten. Rick could see that he'd gotten the boy's attention. He sensed that Cassie was sitting very still, practically holding her breath.

"People's generosity, church soup kitchens, shelters if they weren't too full." Rick shrugged. "I believe God protected me. I got into several situations where I could easily have died and didn't. I give thanks for His love every day."

Rick could feel Cassie's eyes on him but he focused on connecting with her son.

"Did you have gangs where you lived, Noah?" Rick studied the sullen boy.

"S-sure." Noah clearly didn't want to talk about it. "Can I h-have another b-burger? I n-never had elk b-before but it t-tastes really g-good."

"The secret is to cook it very slowly. Otherwise, it comes out tough as boots."

"I n-never ate th-that, either," Noah joked.

Rick chuckled as he shared an amused glance with Cassie. When was the last time they'd heard the boy make a joke?

When Noah scooped the rest of the fries onto his plate, Rick smiled and warned, "Leave some room for dessert."

"Wh-what is it?" Noah asked.

"Rice pudding." Rick almost laughed as disdain filled the boy's face.

"O-old p-people's f-food," he scoffed.

"Not the way I make it." Rick intercepted Cassie's reprimand by offering her the last burger. The last thing he wanted was for Noah to retreat back into his shell.

"It was all delicious, but I've had enough, thank you." She leaned back. "Where did you learn to cook, Rick?"

"I took lessons." He was used to the surprised stares.

"Man, c-cooking lessons?" Noah's face said it all—*wuss.*

"Remember, I never had a parent to teach me and I like to eat," Rick said, meeting Noah's stare head-on. "Besides, women love a guy who can cook."

"D-doesn't look l-like it w-worked for y-you," Noah shot back after a quick survey of the house.

Cassie's face turned a deep shade of crimson, but she didn't say anything to Noah. Rick shrugged off the boy's comment, though the words hit a nerve deep inside.

"I don't think God has plans for me to marry," he said, finding himself avoiding Cassie's gaze. "Did your dad cook?"

"N-no. That was M-Mom's j-job." Belligerence glowed in Noah's blue eyes as he watched Rick remove their dinner plates.

"Lots of men think that way. But everyone should learn how to take care of himself, Noah," Rick said quietly. "That's the meaning of becoming an adult."

Noah's mouth pinched tight.

Lord, help me help them.

"What about when your mom was at work?" Rick asked.

Cassie opened her mouth to speak, but Rick gave the tiniest shake of his head. After a moment of indecision she gave in, but her expression warned that she would not allow Rick to continue to probe into their past.

"M-Mom had it r-ready for us." Noah glared at him.

Rick nodded, his suspicions about Cassie and Noah's past confirmed. Her husband hadn't been willing to do his share while she worked, and he'd taught Noah by example. As Rick set the bowls and spoons on the table, he noticed Noah absently rubbing his shoulder, as if it were still bothering him.

"Did you mind your mom going to work?" Rick asked.

"I d-dunno." Noah lifted his head just enough to shoot Cassie a dark look. "S-she worked a l-lot m-more after D-dad died."

"I had to, Noah," Cassie exclaimed. "We needed my salary to live on."

"It couldn't have been easy for either one of you." Rick set the steaming pudding beside his place. He served Cassie first, then a frowning Noah. "I'm sure your mom would have preferred to be home with you. Sometimes parents have to make hard choices."

Noah muttered something unintelligible as he accepted his dish with a turned-up nose. When he tentatively tasted his pudding, his eyes expanded. "Hey, it's g-good."

Rick burst out laughing. "You were expecting gruel?" he asked.

For the first time that evening, Noah smiled. "S-sort of," he admitted.

"It *is* delicious, Rick." Cassie smiled, but Rick noticed that the smile didn't reach her eyes.

"Thanks." He laughed when Noah scooped the last spoonful from his dish with gusto, then held out his bowl for a second helping. "Maybe Noah and I could make it at Lives one night." Noah shot him a dubious look. "It would save Sara from making dessert."

"Isn't th-that what she's p-paid for?" Noah asked.

"Noah!" Cassie's cheeks burned.

"Is that why you think Sara works at Lives?" Rick asked. "For the money?" He shook his head, deliberately keeping his voice light. "I'm pretty sure she could get two or three times her salary at a fancy hotel in Vancouver."

"Then wh-why doesn't s-she?"

"Because she loves the boys," Rick told him quietly. "Sara never had anyone to love or care about her when she was young. She doesn't want another kid to go through what she experienced. She wants everyone who comes to Lives to feel loved. That's why she spends so many hours coming up with delicious meals. Not because she *has* to," he emphasized. "Because she *wants* to."

Noah said nothing, but as the boy stared at the table, his second dish of pudding half-eaten, Rick could tell that what he'd said had made an impact. He shifted his gaze to Cassie and she nodded her approval.

"Well, if you're both finished, I guess it's time for cleanup." Rick winked at Cassie. "I have a rule in my house that women don't do dishes. So I guess it's up to you and me."

Noah jerked upright, his face full of dismay.

"Come on," Rick urged him. "Let's get started."

"Wh-where's the d-dishwasher?" Noah looked around the kitchen.

"Don't have one." Rick stacked their plates nonchalantly. "I do dishes by hand. Come on, dude. I've got a game ready, but we have to clean up this mess so we can use the table."

Noah stayed put until Cassie raised her eyebrows. He rose slowly, using his fingertips to carry the dirty dishes to the counter. Rick had to grin as Cassie turned away to hide her amusement.

"Don't worry about getting your hands dirty, son," he said in an avuncular tone. "They'll get really clean when you start washing."

He gibed, cajoled and teased Noah mercilessly, waiting for the boy to explode. But Noah didn't. He was angry, no doubt about that. But he stuffed down his emotions and soldiered on, which was the way he dealt with everything.

"Good job, Noah," he said as he removed the waterproof apron he'd tied around the boy's waist when they'd finished. "When Sara and Kyle come for a meal, Kyle refuses to wash dishes. He *claims* he has an allergy to dish soap."

"I th-think I d-do, too," Noah sputtered. He held out his reddened hands as proof.

"Nah," Rick said after a quick inspection. "That's just hot water. Really, thanks for your help, Noah. I hate doing dishes alone. Come on, let's play."

Noah didn't say anything, but he didn't look quite as miserable as he had. They played several rousing games and with each one Rick noticed that Noah seemed to shed more of the negativity that had clung to him since he'd first arrived.

"How about a drink before the next round?" Rick

asked. "I could make some cocoa. I promise not to make you wash the cup, Noah."

Noah actually smiled, but his attention was on something else.

"N-no, thanks," Noah said. "C-could I l-look at those old b-books?" He motioned to a stack on the bookshelf in the farthest corner of the living room.

"You like old books?" Rick couldn't hide his surprise. He hadn't taken Noah-of-the-earbuds for the bookish type.

"I l-like h-history," Noah stuttered.

"Help yourself, then. Your mom and I will stay here and talk." Rick turned on the kettle then switched on his stereo. Soft hymns of praise filled the room. "Cocoa or coffee?" Rick asked Cassie.

"Cocoa's great." She had her knitting out. The needles clicked furiously.

By the time Rick set a big mug of cocoa in front of Cassie, Noah was sitting on the floor, swaying to the music, totally engrossed in the book he was reading.

"Thank you for doing this," Cassie murmured.

"I don't know if tonight has helped him much, but I've learned a few things." Cassie raised a questioning eyebrow so Rick continued, keeping his voice very soft. "He's suppressing a lot of anger—more than I had realized."

"I'm not sure I know what to do about it, though. He's still not ready to talk." Cassie's brown-eyed stare brimmed with doubt.

Trust, Rick wanted to urge her. *Trust God to help.* "As long as you keep talking to him, that should help." He sipped his cocoa, then decided to say what was in his heart. "It won't be an easy path, but God will be with you if you ask Him, Cassie. God's love isn't conditional. It's everlasting. No matter where you go, what you do, He will always love you. You can never escape God's love."

"You sound like my father." It was clear by her tone that she didn't mean this as a compliment.

"Have you figured out what to do about that yet?"

He could see that she hadn't in the tense rigidity of her shoulders He felt a little tense, too, knowing that he still hadn't told her the complete truth about his relationship with John.

"You keep saying God's love endures," she finally said, sounding very much like her angry son. "That we can't lose it."

"You can't." Rick couldn't stop himself from reaching out and brushing a wispy curl from her cheek with his forefinger. "Is that what you think, that you've lost God's love? Because you're wrong. God loves you, always has."

"Then why doesn't He show it?"

"Why do you think He hasn't, Cassie?" Rick's heart ached for the pain she kept built up inside. "He brought you away from your troubles, gave you several jobs here in Churchill. He gave you a wonderful friend in Laurel, and the chance to make more friends. God didn't abandon you, Cassie. He's right beside you."

Rick wanted to say more, to make her see how deep God's love for her was. But Noah stood at the end of the table, his face red and angry.

"What's wrong, Noah?" Cassie frowned.

"Wh-why do these b-books have my g-grandfather's name in th-them?" he demanded, thrusting out his hand with an old volume clutched in it.

Cassie looked at Rick in surprise.

"When I was living on the streets, your grandfather helped me, Noah. A lot." Rick said it evenly, meeting the boy's glare head-on. "Because of him I was able to finish school and college. Later he helped me get into seminary. Those books were his gift to me when I was ordained."

Rick knew he was in trouble before Cassie shot him a warning glance.

"You kn-new." Noah glared at Rick. "Y-you knew and y-you didn't t-tell us. Didn't you think you should tell us you knew my grandfather?"

"Noah, honey—" Cassie's voice died away as the truth dawned on Noah.

"I see." His gaze narrowed, his mouth tightened. "He already told you. I'm the only one who didn't know." His voice grew icy. "P-protecting m-me again, M-mom?" The scathing way he said it brought tears to Cassie's eyes.

"She didn't know about the books, Noah. *I'd* even forgotten how my collection of old books got started." Rick felt as if every inch of ground he'd gained with Noah was sliding out from under his feet. Worse than that, Cassie was now in trouble with her son, too.

"I w-want to l-leave." Noah dropped the offending book on the table, walked toward the door and grabbed his coat.

Cassie rose to her feet slowly. Her eyes met his and he knew exactly what her silent stare was asking.

Where's God now, Rick?

Chapter Six

For an entire week Cassie fretted over Noah. No matter how she examined her situation, she could not align it with Rick's assurance of God's love.

If God loved her so much, why didn't He help Noah?

But actually, maybe it wasn't God's fault. She probably should have told Noah that Rick had known his grandfather, especially because she knew how much Noah resented being kept out of the loop. He felt she treated him like a child.

She watched as Rick led the kids through their songs, savoring the familiar tunes. But she lost all sense of space and time when Noah began to sing in a pure, clear tenor tone.

He had his grandfather's sense of music. Her dad had always loved singing and for a moment she desperately wanted to hear his voice again.

"Still brooding over Noah?" Rick slid into the pew where she'd sat to wait while the choir members cleaned up after practice.

"I'm not brooding," Cassie said defiantly, then sighed. "Maybe I am."

"I'm sorry." Rick touched her hand and Cassie felt that electricity she'd been working so hard to ignore. "What does Noah say?"

"He won't talk to me. He hardly speaks at all anymore because his stuttering is so bad. And this morning I noticed two new bruises." She swallowed the tears that threatened, hating that she'd become so desperate to confide her worries in Rick. "I think he's fighting. He did in Toronto. That's one of the reasons I decided to move."

"I wanted to talk to you about that." Rick's green pupils bored into her. "One of the choir kids hinted that Noah's being bullied."

"That's what I was afraid of. I'm sorry you're so deep in this with us, Rick," Cassie said and meant it. "Ordinarily I'd sound out Laurel, but she's busy trying to get another grant and I don't want to bother her with my problems."

"You can talk to me anytime, Cassie. You know that."

"Thanks." Cassie told herself not to feel special, that Rick gave that smile to everyone. But that did nothing to douse the warm glow inside. "I've had three conferences with Noah's teachers this week. Each of them expressed worry about his negative attitude. I don't know what to do anymore."

"Pray. Trust God to help you." Rick gave her a sad smile. "I know what you're going to say, Cassie. You don't feel you can trust Him."

"No, I don't," she said.

"You're taking the view that bad things are God's fault because He doesn't stop them." Rick leaned forward to thank Bryan for gathering the choir's music.

Cassie couldn't help noting how unfailingly polite Rick was to everyone. He had an amazing rapport with a lot of Churchillians. Rick showed compassion and understanding, which made her feel terrible about being suspicious of his motives. And yet, she'd seen her father use his charm to coerce his board into doing as he requested. And Eric had flaunted his early triumphs with the church's investments in order to get more from the congregation.

So, even though Cassie was impressed by Rick's interactions with the boys at Lives, she couldn't help suspecting that somehow, some way, he would use those triumphs to his own advantage. That's what the charismatic men she'd known had done. Guilt over her suspicions nagged her, but past experience was hard to shake.

She heard Rod call, "Snowball fight," and the rush of feet hurtling toward the door. Then all was quiet inside the church.

"Cassie?" Rick's hand pressed hers, drawing her attention back to the present, to the gentleness of his touch and his voice.

Somehow Rick only had to touch her, to reassure her, and her reservations about him flew from her mind. She had to be careful.

"Where did you go to just now?" He leaned forward, his focus totally on her.

"I was thinking about my father and Eric." And, because honesty was the best policy, she felt compelled to add, "and you."

"Me?" Confusion filled his expressive eyes. "Are you likening me to these men you don't seem to hold in very high esteem?" There was no amusement in the question.

"Not exactly. It's more that I see their actions more clearly now in hindsight," she said.

"And you think I'm like them." There was no anger evident in Rick's voice or his expression. He simply leaned back and waited for her explanation.

And that, Cassie decided, was the difference.

"I don't think you're like them at all. You don't work people."

"You mean I don't use them?" He raised one eyebrow, then smiled when she nodded. "Everyone has problems they're working through, everyone has reasons for their behavior that I can't possibly fathom. Everyone is doing the best they can to get through their lives." He shrugged. "It's my job as a pastor to help them on that journey, not to judge them."

"Does that apply to those who wrong you?" Cassie asked. As she waited for his answer, she was distracted by his good looks. His dark hair was a tousled mess. On someone else it would have looked unkempt but on Rick it added a mischievous quality and rendered him younger-looking than his thirty-one years.

"It applies to everyone, Cassie." Rick's dark eyes glowed as he spoke. "Yes, I get frustrated when people don't see my vision or accept my ideas. I'm human. But getting frustrated doesn't mean I expect them to give up their principles or objections."

"Why not?" His statement roused her curiosity.

"Because God shows Himself in different ways to different people. I have to keep my focus on showing God's love to people and leave the rest up to Him." Rick smiled. "And He does love us, Cassie. In Psalms it says He keeps an eye on us all the time. He remembers our prayers and He gathers our tears in a bottle. Those are the actions of someone who loves us dearly."

She mulled that over. But before she could pursue it, Michael burst into the sanctuary.

"Cassie, you have to come. Noah fell and hurt his arm."

Oh, God, her heart cried.

"He's sitting in the snow," Michael added as he raced beside her through the foyer. "When we try to help him up, he screams."

"He'll be okay, Cassie," Rick said, his quiet assurance filling her ear.

"Because God will help?" she demanded as she shoved open the door. "I should never have brought him to Churchill." Rick followed close behind. She saw Noah on the ground and her heart stopped. "It was a mistake."

"Or maybe God will turn this into a blessing," Rick murmured. Cassie ignored him and raced to her son.

"Where does it hurt?" she asked Noah, brushing a tender hand across his tousled hair.

"My arm. I think it's broken."

"I think so, too," Cassie murmured. "We have to get you to the hospital so they can set it. We'll help you stand, honey." She felt Rick move silently to help Noah stand and was overly conscious of his strong, supporting hand under her elbow, helping her into his car after they'd settled Noah. It would be so easy to lean on Rick. But his comment about Noah's injury being a blessing infuriated her. How could getting hurt be a blessing? She remained silent while Rick drove them to the medical center. Rick sat only inches away, but she couldn't speak to him.

To think that she'd been teetering on the edge of trusting.

Rick was wrong. God should have protected her boy. God's love had failed Noah.

But so had she.

"Noah?"

Rick watched as Cassie tentatively stepped into the treatment room after talking to the doctor, her face ashen. He followed her not because he had a right to be there, but because he very much wanted to help, to erase the vestiges of terror that he could still see in her eyes.

"I'm f-fine, M-mom. The d-doctor says I b-broke my a-arm." Noah moved his head when she reached out to smooth his hair.

"He also said you have a lot of bruises that have nothing to do with your broken arm. How did they happen, Noah?" Cassie sat on a chair next to the bed where he was perched.

"I keep slipping on the ice."

Cassie kept her intense gaze on his face. "You've become quite clumsy lately. Is that what you want me to believe?"

"Y-yes." He turned his head, shifting to gaze out the window.

"Look at me, Noah." Cassie waited for her son's attention.

Rick longed to beg her not to push the boy right now, but he saw her desperation and knew she needed answers. After hearing the doctor's concern about her son's bruised body, she had to be scared.

The boy turned his head and stared at his mother, but his blue eyes were devoid of emotion.

"Someone told Rick you're being bullied," she said in a quiet but anxious tone. "Is that true?"

"No." Noah didn't flinch, didn't move away, but neither did he embrace his mother when she sat beside him and slid an arm across his shoulders.

"You can tell me the truth," she murmured. "I just want to help you."

Cassie studied him for an interminable moment. She finally drew her arm away when Noah refused to answer. Rick's heart hurt for her, knowing that she was reeling from the way her beloved son was shutting her out.

"Aunt Laurel is in the waiting room. She came as soon as she heard. Once your arm is set, we'll take you home." Cassie moved away and looked out the window. Rick could see the tears on her cheeks from where he stood.

The medical staff arrived and began to construct the cast that would immobilize Noah's arm.

"It's a fairly clean fracture," the doctor told Cassie. "Six weeks should do it." He turned to Noah. "This needs to heal so no roughhousing and no hockey. See me in a week to check on things. Got it?"

Noah nodded. The doctor asked Cassie to step outside again, and Rick grabbed his chance to be alone with the boy.

"You want to tell me what's really happening?" He stared into the pain-filled blue eyes. Noah shook his head once, firmly. "I might be able to help you."

Nothing.

"There are ways to handle bullying, Noah," he assured the boy quietly. "Ways that won't leave you vulnerable as the scapegoat for someone else. But the first step is to talk about it, to figure out what we're dealing with."

Noah's implacable stare told Rick he was wasting his time.

"Okay. But if you ever want help, you call and I'll be there. Deal?" He held out his hand.

Noah didn't shake Rick's hand. As his mother returned, he climbed off the table.

"S-see you l-later," he said. Then he walked through the door and headed toward the waiting room.

Laurel rushed over to them. "He's going back to school?"

"For now." Cassie sank onto a chair. "His whole body is a mess of bruises. The doctor says there are visible signs that Noah is being bullied." Cassie blinked furiously. "I have no idea what to do," she admitted, her voice broken.

"Pray," Laurel advised. "Sooner or later he'll open up."

Rick agreed about the praying part. Anger festered inside the boy and it was getting worse with every day that passed. But he couldn't say that to Cassie, wouldn't add to her anguish.

"I'll pray for him," he said, "and I'll try to get him to talk to me. Don't worry, we'll figure it out. Maybe you could arrange a phone call between Noah and his grandfather, Cassie."

"Why?" She glared at him.

"Because I believe he needs to talk to someone. He's mad at me for not telling him I knew your dad, and he doesn't seem to want to open up to you." Rick noted Cassie's wince and wished he'd phrased that better, but he pressed on. "Maybe if you spoke to your father, told him what's happening, maybe he'd get Noah to talk."

"I'll think about it," she murmured, her face troubled.

Rick wanted so badly to smooth away the worry. That's when he knew he was getting too involved with this little family—and for the wrong reasons. Was it God's love he wanted to demonstrate, or was it the need to take care of Cassie because of the feelings that continued to flourish inside his heart, despite his efforts to rout them?

Both. It was both.

It was time for him to distance himself from this impossible attraction for Cassie while figuring out a way to help her. He just wasn't sure his heart would survive the process.

"Noah could you stay after practice?" Rick asked.

Noah's lips tightened but he nodded. When they'd finished and the others were outside playing in the snow, Rick began his apology.

"I really am sorry I didn't tell you I knew your grandfather. I should have. He was a very important man in my young life. I honestly did forget about the books, though."

Noah studied him for a long time then finally shrugged. "Doesn't matter."

"Sure it does. Your grandfather is obviously an important person to you. I should have said something." Rick waited, praying. *Please let him talk. Please.*

"He's the only one who's honest with me," Noah muttered.

Aghast, Rick couldn't hide his astonishment.

"You don't think your mom's been honest with you?" he asked.

Noah held his gaze for several moments. Then he looked away.

"I didn't say that," he said. He rose. "I need to go. They're waiting for me."

Rick placed his hand on the boy's good arm and waited until he had his entire attention.

"Just for the record, Noah. I will always be honest with you."

"Sure." Noah left.

Rick sat on a pew and tried to figure out the meaning of what he'd just heard. He'd keep working on Noah, find out more. Then he'd talk to Cassie.

Rick paused on the threshold of the family room at Lives, watching as Cassie knelt beside one of the boys in the throes of an epileptic seizure.

"Relax, Michael," she murmured in a reassuring tone.

"Anything I can do?" Rick asked.

She looked up, startled, glanced at him and shook her head.

In the week since Noah's incident Rick had been visiting Lives Under Construction a lot. He'd specifically chosen times when he knew Cassie had a shift at the hospital so he could meet up with Noah. But now, seeing her pretty face, his heart took up the familiar double-time rhythm in his chest, forcing him to realize he'd had little success in quelling his responses to her, but at least he'd found a tiny crack in Noah's armor.

"He's coming out of it now." After checking her watch, Cassie noted the time in a little booklet she had in her pocket. Worry clouded her eyes, but the loving touch of her ministering hands continued.

Rick knelt opposite Cassie to clasp Michael's hand in his. She tossed him a brief smile.

"Lie still for a moment and get your bearings," she urged as Michael's eyelids fluttered.

Michael's amber eyes slowly opened. He stared at her, misery and shame swirling in his gaze.

"It was worse this time, wasn't it?" he asked in a slightly slurred tone.

"A little longer," she agreed.

"I wish it would just kill me." Grimacing, he accepted Rick's hand to help sit up.

"Don't say that, Michael," Cassie said. "These attacks will diminish eventually. The doctors told you that."

"Yeah, but when?" He touched his temple gingerly. "I think I hit myself."

"You knocked against the table before I could catch you," Cassie explained. "I'm sorry."

"It's not your fault." Michael's voice carried a return of the depression Rick had heard in several previous visits.

"Do you feel like getting up, maybe moving to the sofa? It might be more comfortable." Cassie smiled her thanks at Rick when he helped the boy stand upright.

Michael's feeble grip fell away as he lowered himself onto the couch. "Is it a sin to want to die, Rick?"

"Well, I don't think God appreciates us rejecting His gift of life," Rick temporized, his radar going into full alert at the question.

"I think dying is the only way I'll ever be free of these seizures," Michael murmured.

"That's not true," Cassie countered.

But Rick heard the reservation in her tone. He watched as she draped a damp cloth on Michael's brow and smoothed his hair. He'd seen Cassie's devotion to her patients before, but this was more than a nurse doing her job. This was Cassie's motherly heart enfolding a troubled kid.

"Can I tell you something, Michael?" Rick sat down across from the prone boy, shifting so Michael could see his face without altering his position.

Cassie sat down near Michael, as well, intently observing him. Rick inhaled then spoke the words God had laid on his heart.

"You're not here by accident, Michael. You're here because God has plans for you. Good plans."

"How do you know?" Michael shifted a little higher on his pillows, his interest clear.

"It's in the Bible. There's a verse where God says He knows the plans He has for you, plans for good and not for evil, plans to give you a future and a hope." Rick smiled.

Michael visibly struggled to adjust his thinking.

"Maybe it's hard to see now, but God has good things in store for you," he said, feeling the intensity of Cassie's stare. "What you have to do is be ready for them."

"How? I can't stop the seizures." The hope that had flickered in Michael's eyes sputtered out. "None of the doctors can tell me if they'll stop for sure. What hope is there in that?"

"The hope isn't in the situation, Michael. The hope is in God. You trust Him to keep His promise to help you." When Cassie checked Michael's pulse again, Rick rose. "We can talk again whenever you want. But I think Cassie would like you to rest now."

"Yes, I would." She took the damp cloth from Michael's forehead. "Rest for a while. Think about something nice."

"Like my saxophone," he murmured in a drowsy tone.

Cassie beckoned to Rick to follow her out of the room, closing the door gently. Once they were in the hall, she said, "I did ask him if he knew where his saxophone was, after you suggested it. He told me his parents sold it to punish him."

Rick shook his head in dismay as they walked toward the kitchen.

"Thanks for your help. Michael seemed to relax after you quoted that passage from Jeremiah. It used to be a favorite of mine, too."

"Not anymore?" He noted the yawn she couldn't quite smother.

"Oh, I still think it's a great verse." She poured herself a second cup of coffee.

"Just not for you. Right?"

"Something like that." She lifted a hand to rub the back of her neck.

"You're tired."

"I was up with Daniel last night." She sighed. "He's still struggling with withdrawal so he has nightmares. I try to be there when they get too intense."

"You care a lot about these boys, don't you?" Rick didn't have to ask. He already knew the truth, saw it in the tenderness of her gaze whenever it rested on one of the boys. He also saw that the burden of caring for them was wearing her down. "You need a break. Get on some warm clothes."

"Why?" She blinked at him in surprise.

"We're going snowshoeing."

"I don't know how to snowshoe," Cassie sputtered. "Besides, I have to keep an eye on Michael."

"I'm sure Laurel will be happy to check on him while you're out. Any other excuses?" He grinned when her mouth opened and closed several times. "I didn't think so. All work and no play makes Jack a dull boy, but it does the same thing for Jill."

"Something you learned in medical school?" Cassie gibed.

"Seminary." He chuckled when she rolled her eyes. "Well?"

"Truthfully? I'd love to get some fresh air. I'll check with Laurel and see if it's okay with her. I'll change and be right back." She hurried to the door, paused then turned. "You're sure you have time?"

"Positive," Rick said, ignoring his better judgment, which told him that this wasn't the way to create distance. "I'll get my gear out of the car."

Kyle was waiting for him when he returned. "I didn't realize you were here. Were you looking for me?"

"Actually, yes." Rick felt his face heat up when Cassie appeared and Kyle took a moment to look back and forth between them. "Michael had another seizure. He's resting now so I suggested Cassie take a break and go snowshoeing with me. Can she borrow your snowshoes?"

Kyle raised an eyebrow but all he said was, "Sure. They're inside the shed. Have fun."

"Thanks." Rick zipped up his suit and grabbed his

gloves, grateful that his friend hadn't demanded an explanation right then and there—because he didn't have one.

He checked that Cassie was ready to go. "Okay?"

She nodded.

The early afternoon sun blazed on the white snow, almost blinding in its intensity. Rick helped Cassie strap on Kyle's snowshoes then donned his own. Cassie caught on quickly and soon they were tramping over the tundra, their breath forming white clouds around them.

"You're good at this," he complimented.

"It's actually a lot of fun," she puffed, pausing to gaze around. "I've wanted to get out and explore but haven't had much time. Oh, look." A rabbit scurried across the snow, barely visible as he blended into his surroundings.

"There's a small creek over there," Rick told her. "Not that it will be running in this weather, but that thicket makes a good hiding place for animals. Want to take a look?"

Cassie nodded and set off at a quick clip. Rick followed, admiring the way her blond curls framed her face. Cassie was truly beautiful. There was no denying it.

Rick quickly checked the direction of those thoughts. This was an outing to have fun. That's all.

Something cold and wet smacked him on the side of his head.

"Hey!"

"I thought maybe you'd fallen asleep," Cassie teased, her laughter echoing across the barren land. "How come you slowed down?"

"I got caught admiring the view," he muttered as he scraped snow from his collar.

"What did you say?" She tipped her head to one side like a curious bird, the pure angles of her face lit by the sun.

"Nothing." Rick forced his mind to clear. In several quick strides he was beside her. "You want a snowball fight? I can give you a snowball fight." He bent to scoop up a handful of snow and rolled it menacingly between his hands.

"No, no!" she yelped, turning awkwardly to race across the snowpack as quickly as she could. "I was just teasing!"

Rick followed, took aim and threw. The snowball landed on the top of her green hood. Without pause he made a second missile and hit her in the back. Cassie's laughter echoed through the afternoon but soon her speed tripped her up and she landed with a whoosh in the snow.

Rick plowed toward her, forming another snowball as he moved. When he reached her, he loomed over her. "Prepare to have your face washed."

"I'll freeze," she protested, still chuckling. When he leaned down, she squealed, but in an about-face of courage, tipped her head so she was looking directly at him. "Okay, I'll take my punishment."

Rick was instantly caught up in her brown eyes, in the way her curls kissed her cheeks and the proud thrust of her chin, daring him. Finally he tossed the snowball over her head then held out a hand.

"Come on. If your racket hasn't chased away every animal within ten miles, we might still see something."

Cassie's laughter died as she studied him. Then she

held out her mittened hand and let him pull her up-right. Cassie's snowshoes got tangled in his and she lost her balance, tumbling against him, her hands pressed against his chest.

Her brown eyes, huge now, met and held his. "Sorry."

Rick's arms automatically went around her. He couldn't speak, couldn't move, couldn't tear his gaze from her. His heart threatened to pound through his chest. He felt certain Cassie could hear it, but all he could do was stand there, stunned by the strength of his urge to kiss her, to touch his lips to her soft mouth. He leaned forward just the tiniest bit.

"R-rick?" Her voice emerged in a breathy gasp. Seconds passed and he didn't release her. At last, she dropped her hands from his chest and stepped back, un-tangling her snowshoes from his. "I thought we were going to see some animals," she murmured.

"We are." Rick exhaled. "Race you."

He wheeled away and marched across the snow in giant strides, surging toward the thicket, inhaling deeply as he moved, trying to cleanse his heart and mind of Cassie. He glanced back once. She was standing where he'd left her, studying him.

Determined to regain control, Rick faced forward and kept going until he reached the tree stump where he often sat and watched the animals. He filled his lungs and forced his heart to slow down. By the time Cassie arrived, he had regained his composure. He even man-aged to give her a friendly smile, as if he'd totally dis-missed the intimate moment they'd shared.

"Have a seat." He swiped the snow off another stump and patted it. "It's not the most comfortable, but it's the best view."

"It's pretty here. It looks like a Christmas wonderland." Cassie, too, seemed determined to ignore those few awkward minutes. She sat down next to him, her shoulder brushing his.

A short while later a white-coated Arctic fox appeared not thirty feet away. Cassie made no sound, though when the fox came within several feet of them, her hand slid into his.

"It's okay," Rick reassured her in a low murmur. "She's checking us out. She probably has a den with kits in it nearby. Try not to move."

He sat beside Cassie, too aware of her so close to him. He felt every motion she made, heard her swift intake of breath when the mother fox carried one of her babies into the snow for a quick wash, then hurried it back inside when a dark shadow circled overhead.

"She won't come out for a while now," he explained. "She knows there's danger."

Several moments passed before Cassie's hand slid out of his. "We've been gone awhile," she said checking her watch. "I should get back and check on Michael."

"Okay." Rick rose, sad that their few moments alone together were over but also somehow relieved that they'd soon be with other people. He needed to get his thoughts in order, to remember the vows he'd made to God and to focus on God's priorities.

He pushed through the snow in silence, following the trail their earlier tracks had made. He focused on what he saw. Frosted crests of snow peaked among wild grasses that had pushed through wind-polished hillocks of white.

"It's very serene, isn't it?" she said in a hushed voice.

"Yes." Rick wished he felt that serenity inside. Instead, he felt off-kilter and confused. He waited until they were almost back to Lives, then he turned to face Cassie.

"Is something wrong?" Cassie asked, a question on her face.

Rick had been going to say something about the two of them, but suddenly he couldn't find the words. Anyway, he didn't want to break the connection he'd felt. Not yet.

"I wanted to ask about Noah," he said instead. "I'm guessing you haven't made much progress?" He waited for the shake of her head. "He's been very quiet at choir, too. I thought he might stop coming, but he hasn't."

"I'm glad."

"Me, too. He seems to enjoy singing," Rick murmured. "I wish I could give him more attention, but I have my hands full with directing the boys and accompanying them on guitar."

"I thought Lucy was playing piano." Cassie undid her snowshoes.

"The arthritis in her hands makes it too difficult for her. Playing on Sundays is the most she can manage." Rick met her gaze when she looked up at him, but he had to look away. Those few moments in the snow kept intruding.

"I suppose I could help, if I'm not called in for a shift," Cassie offered hesitantly.

"We'll gladly take any and all help," he said. "What would you like to do?"

Cassie looked at him as if he'd grown two heads.

"Play," she said. "I thought you wanted a pianist."

"You play the piano?" He grinned. "I wish I'd known that a couple of weeks ago."

"The only thing is, I wonder how Noah will react," she said. "What if my being there makes his stuttering worse?"

"That won't be an issue," Rick assured her as he stepped out of his snowshoes. "Noah doesn't stutter when he sings."

"At all? I mean he didn't the day I was there, but I thought that was an exception." Cassie's face lit up.

"His voice doesn't falter on a single note."

"Maybe this is one area where he could shine," Cassie said.

"That's what I'm thinking." Rick walked with her toward the house.

"Can I ask you something?" Cassie pulled her hands from her mitts and blew on them to warm them.

"Anything. My life is an open book." Curious to hear her question, he waited.

"Why do you spend so much time at Lives? Are you hoping your work here will help you get a promotion to a better church?"

Rick bristled at the insinuation he thought he heard in Cassie's words, then decided her question was legitimate, given her past history with those who'd called themselves Christians. He looked into her eyes and spoke from his heart.

"I'm not interested in padding my bio, Cassie. I try to help wherever I can because that's what I promised God I'd do." He shook his head at the cascading memories. "I've made a lot of mistakes, hurt a lot of people. If one kid avoids the same mistakes and the repercussions because of me, then maybe I'll have repaid a bit of the debt I owe God."

She studied him for a long time, her gaze searching, questioning. Finally, she nodded and led the way inside.

As Rick followed, an inner voice reminded him he'd also promised God that he would give up his yearning for love and a family of his own. And yet, every day he was getting more entangled with lovely Cassie Crockett and her son.

Worse than that, Rick still hadn't been completely honest about his past with her father. He hadn't told her that he was the reason her father hadn't been in a position to offer her any financial help when Eric died.

For a moment, the thought of everything Rick had cost Cassie and Noah was almost more than he could bear.

Chapter Seven

The whirling snowstorm outdoors matched the blizzard of confusion inside Cassie's soul. This crazy attraction to Rick Salinger muddled her thinking. One moment she could hardly wait to see him, the next she was desperate to avoid him.

"Mom? C-can we h-have some m-more p-popcorn, p-please?" Noah held out the massive bowl she'd filled only a few moments ago. At least, that's what it seemed like.

"Sure. Why don't you make it?" She watched as he measured oil and popcorn kernels, then slid the pot back and forth over the stove. The mouthwatering aroma of warm popcorn quickly filled the room. "Are you okay?" she asked, wishing he'd talk to her.

"I'm s-sick of this s-stupid cast." Noah flicked off the switch on the stove, but couldn't lift the pot to empty it. He stood back while Cassie did that. "I wonder if Rick will cancel."

"Cancel?" She frowned. "Cancel what?" After two consecutive night shifts at the hospital, her mind felt jumbled as her body took its time readjusting to regular hours.

"He s-said he was g-going to come t-tonight, with h-his guitar, so we c-could have a s-sing-along." Noah peered out the window. "Maybe h-he won't make i-it in this."

"Do you like singing?" She pretended nonchalance, nibbling on a handful of popcorn while Noah melted butter.

"Yeah. The c-choir is g-great." Noah's face beamed with enthusiasm. Cassie was astounded. She couldn't remember the last time she'd seen him look so happy.

"Rick asked me to accompany the choir because Lucy's struggling with the music. Will that bother you?" Cassie asked.

"Nah. Mrs. Clow m-makes lots of m-mistakes." In the midst of pouring melted butter over the popcorn, Noah's head lifted. "What's th-that?" He dropped the butter dish and raced toward a window. "It's R-Rick and s-someone else," he said. "Mr. S-Stonechild, I th-think. They're r-riding a s-snowmobile."

Cassie heard Laurel going to the door and hid a smile as she imagined her friend's reaction to seeing Teddy Stonechild again. The couple never seemed to hit it off, though they snuck looks at each other whenever they were in the same room. Cassie wondered if, in spite of their bickering, they were secretly attracted to each other.

Rick's voice echoed down the hallway.

There it went again, her silly thumping heart almost pounding out of her chest. Cassie was tempted to rush upstairs in an attempt to avoid him, but that would be childish.

Besides, she wanted to see him again.

"You keeping this popcorn for yourself?" Rick asked from behind her, laughter in his deep rich tone.

"That's Noah's. You'll have to ask him." Her skin prickled at his nearness but she turned and faced him, anyway, hoping her face didn't give her away.

"Can I share your popcorn, Noah?" Rick grinned.

"S-sure." Noah's face lost its bored expression as he handed Rick a bowl.

"Thanks." Rick served himself fully one-third of the popcorn they'd just made. He winked at Cassie over his shoulder. "I like the buttered stuff best."

"So do I." Noah stared at the mostly unbuttered remains.

"I'll melt more," Cassie told him, going to the stove. "Rick, I'm surprised you got here in this storm."

"This isn't a storm. This is a little dustup." He laughed out loud. "At least that's Teddy's take. The man is fearless."

"W-was it f-fun, coming h-here?" Noah asked.

Cassie glanced at Rick. She didn't want Rick to encourage her son to take risks.

Noah, she suddenly realized, was beginning to look up to Rick. Too much?

Rick's green eyes locked with hers in understanding. Then he turned to Noah.

"Not exactly fun, Noah," he said in a sober tone. "But we're both fairly experienced on this terrain and we always note our landmarks. I'm not sure we'll be able to go back tonight, though. The wind has kicked up a lot since we left."

"You could have canceled," she said.

"I promised the kids I'd be here and I keep my

promises." Time seemed to freeze as Rick's gaze clung to hers.

In a flash Cassie recalled every instant of those moments in the snow when his arms had wrapped around her and she'd felt his heart race. His green-eyed stare told her he'd been as affected by the encounter as she had. While that flattered her ego, it also terrified her. She didn't want to be under the influence of attraction. Not ever again.

"Mom, you're g-going to burn the b-butter."

She blinked and found Noah staring at her. "Sorry. Here," she said, pouring it on his popcorn.

"Your mom is probably tired from her hospital shifts," Rick said. "Why don't we invite her to join us in singing."

"N-no w-way." Noah shook his head vehemently.

"Why not?" Rick frowned, clearly bothered by his abrupt refusal. "Your mom deserves to have some fun. She works hard and—"

"She c-can't s-sing," Noah told him. "Th-they even k-kicked her off the ch-church choir."

"Noah!" Cassie's cheeks burned. She was totally embarrassed by Rick's laughter. "Let's hear if you do better," she snapped before scooping up the bowl of popcorn and going into the big family room.

"Noah, my man, you have to be more careful about the lady's feelings," Rick whispered just loud enough for her to hear.

Cassie ignored their smothered laughter and handed the bowl to Michael. "Help yourself," she ordered, "and pass it to the others. Rick's already eaten his share and Noah doesn't want anymore."

"Hey!" Noah protested. "N-not t-true."

Cassie was glad for the clamor that followed Rick's entrance. While the boys high-fived him, she sat in a corner chair and waited for her face to cool off. But she couldn't keep her eyes off the handsome preacher, especially when he pulled out the ukulele he'd brought in his backpack and began coaxing music from it.

How could one man be so blessed? Rick had good looks, the most gentle, giving spirit she'd ever known and an unbelievable ability to play and sing.

Sometimes, Cassie decided, life was not fair. How was she supposed to stay away from a man like Rick?

As the boys sat in a circle around Rick, Cassie could only watch, astounded by the way he used his musical gift to reach each boy. Most of them hadn't sung before but Laurel had coaxed them to join the choir. Now they didn't even suspect Rick was teaching them harmony as he guided them through a series of choruses, encouraging one boy to take the lead line here and another there. Even the most reluctant couldn't help joining in on the fun.

Now, for the first time, Cassie was truly grateful her parents had insisted she take piano lessons. Those years of lessons gave her the ability to realize the extent of Rick's talent. This was a man whose music poured from his heart and his soul.

Rick even managed to draw Laurel and Teddy into the singing. Without pause he adapted and arranged songs to suit everyone. Watching him, understanding flooded her. Rick's ability to engage everyone around him lay in his openness with them. He accepted everyone as they were—warts and all. Despite opposition, he kept right on doing what he thought was right.

Cassie envied him that quality—especially because she didn't have it.

Was that why Noah admired him so much? Because Rick was strong and focused? Was that why she admired Rick? Because his faith didn't wobble as hers did? Because he knew what he believed and he trusted God no matter what?

It wasn't that she didn't want to trust God. But— there was always that "but" of fear that He'd abandon her. That's what she couldn't shake.

"It's getting late, guys. I think Laurel would like us to conclude our sing-along." Rick strummed a slower, quieter tune. "How about if we sing this one like a prayer of thanks to God for giving us His son as a token of His great love for us."

He played the first chord. As one, the boys' voices rose in a sweet offering of praise. Cassie's heart cracked as the young voices soared and filled the room. She'd once been like that, devoted to God, determined to serve Him no matter what.

Rick caught her eye and smiled. His face shone as his voice blended with the boys' in a mellow tenor. Sometimes he dipped into harmony. At others his voice spiraled with the melody, worshipping. His eyes closed as the last voice died away into hushed silence until nothing but the whine of the wind outside was audible.

"Thank You, God, for these boys, for Lives Under Construction and for Your love. We ask you for a restful sleep and bright hope for tomorrow. In Jesus' name. Amen." Rick opened his eyes and smiled at each boy. "Good night, guys."

The reverence of the evening seemed to linger as the boys expressed their thanks then filed out. Laurel hurried to find quilts for Teddy and Rick, claiming there was no way they could get back to town with the almost whiteout conditions that now whirled outside. Teddy left to check that everything was okay outside, leaving Cassie alone with Rick.

"I never fully appreciated what an amazing talent you have," she said sincerely.

"It's a sweet time with God when hearts are in harmony." He put away his ukulele then sat down beside her and studied her. "You look pensive."

Cassie studied the lean lines of his face, the heart-stopping splendor of his emerald eyes and the way his smile revealed his inner joy. She decided this wasn't the moment.

"Come on, Cassie. You can tell me anything. I'm a minister, remember? I've heard it all." His hand closed around hers and gave it a squeeze. "What's wrong?"

"I'm concerned about Noah," she said, easing her hand from his as she tried to quell the tremors his touch aroused.

"We all are," he agreed.

"This is something different. Something to do with you." With Rick studying her so intently, Cassie hated saying the words, but the facts hadn't changed. "Noah's getting very attached to you. His face when he realized you'd arrived—" She gulped, shook her head. "I don't want him hurt, Rick."

"I'm not going to hurt Noah, Cassie." Rick looked stunned as he said the words, as if what she was concerned about was a complete impossibility.

"You won't be able to help it," she shot back, angry that her tears were so near the surface. "You'll leave, move on to something better, as you should. You have your life to live. But Noah." She stopped, swallowed, then continued. "I believe Noah will be devastated when you go."

"I'm not leaving, Cassie," Rick insisted.

"Not yet," she responded.

"Well, I won't say not ever because none of us knows the future. But as far as I know, I am staying here in Churchill." He ducked his head so he could peer into her eyes. "Is this wishful thinking on your part?"

There was a hint of humor in his question but Cassie ignored it. She was deadly serious. "Noah's beginning to look up to you, Rick. He talks about what you say all the time. I can hear in his voice that he's starting to admire you as he hasn't admired anyone since—"

"Eric. Who left him. I get it, Cassie. But I am not his father and I don't abandon people." Rick's forehead furrowed suddenly. "Is this your way of asking me to back off from trying to help Noah?"

"No!" She shook her head, surprised by how little she wanted Rick to leave them alone. "Noah needs you in his life."

She needed to make him understand. "It's just that working here, seeing the problems these boys have as a result of dysfunctional homes, has made me even more aware of my responsibility to Noah and of how quickly he could become attached to you."

Rick's hand covered hers, warm and protective. "You're a great mother, Cassie. I promise I'm not just going to disappear on Noah. You have my word."

"Thank you." Cassie swallowed. She wanted to trust him, wanted to believe in him so badly. But vestiges of the past held her like chains.

"You have to trust someone sometime, Cassie. Trust me. I won't let you down."

She opened her mouth to respond but a loud wail, followed by Noah's bellow, interrupted.

"M-mom! It's M-Michael!"

Cassie rose and raced out of the room. Michael was on the floor of the room he shared with Noah, his body contorted in a grand mal seizure. Her heart sank at the realization that this seizure was far stronger than any Michael had suffered before. She grabbed a washcloth off a nearby chair, rolled it up and placed it between his teeth to protect his tongue, then turned his head to one side. When she realized Rick was behind her, she motioned him to kneel by the boy's head.

"Stay here and keep him from hurting himself. I have to get his anticonvulsant." She ran down the hall to her medicine cabinet, loaded a syringe and hurried back. Kneeling, she plunged the needle in, but Michael didn't seem to respond. "Rick, get Laurel."

"I'm here," her friend said. "What do you need?"

"Alert the air ambulance. I want Michael airlifted out to Winnipeg." Cassie grabbed a blanket from the bed and draped it over him to keep him warm. "He needs to see a specialist as soon as possible. Make sure they know they need a nurse on board. If they can't get anyone, I'll go with him."

Laurel nodded and hurried away. Cassie looked at Rick.

"Tell me what you need," he said. His eyes met hers.

"Will you take Noah out of here and get him set up in a different room for tonight?"

Rick touched her shoulder. "Don't worry about anything else, Cassie. Just help Michael."

"I don't think I can do any more for him," she murmured sadly.

"God can. Trust Him, Cassie. I'll be right back." Rick squeezed her hand then left, closing the door behind him.

Trust God. Dare she? What if He failed her?

Cassie wavered, but in the end she was too afraid to trust Him so she concentrated on Michael, noting every change as he began to regain consciousness. Over and over she uttered words of encouragement, assuring him that he was safe in his room at Lives, willing him to come out of it.

"You had a seizure, Michael. But it's okay. You're okay." The seizure slackened so she removed the cloth from his mouth. "I'm here, Michael."

Finally he began to rouse, eyelids flickering until at last, he opened his eyes and peered up at her. Cassie checked his pupils and his pulse before she heaved a sigh of relief. He was okay for now. But what about in the future? The seizures were getting longer and more intense. Where was God's love for this poor boy?

"Relax now. Sleep if you want. You're okay," she repeated over and over.

A few moments later Michael drifted to sleep. Cassie took his vitals several times more, watching as slowly— too slowly—they returned to normal.

"Everything okay?" Rick whispered.

"For now. Can you stay with him for a few minutes? I have to call his doctor."

"Sure. Should I move him to the bed?"

"No. Leave him here for now. I don't want to disturb him."

When Rick held out his hand to help her up she took

it, glad to rely on his strength. She didn't expect it when he pulled her into his arms and drew her close.

"Cassie. Take a breath. Lean on me."

Lean on him? Dare she allow herself that luxury? But it felt right to lean her head on his shoulder, to let him smooth his hands over her shoulders and ease the stress there.

"Michael's going to be fine." Rick's voice held such confidence, such peace that Cassie couldn't argue. It was enough to smell the musky spice of his aftershave, to relax her guard, if only for a minute, and let someone else take over. "God's in control."

"How can you be so sure?" she whispered. It felt so right to rest in Rick's arms.

"Because I trust Him and because I know He cares for Michael far more than any human ever could." Rick stroked her back and shoulders as he spoke, soothing her.

Suddenly Cassie realized that she was too close to this man, too needy, too dependent. When she was in his arms, she wanted things she couldn't have. She was afraid to trust him. She eased out of his embrace, the loss of his arms around her like a physical pain. "I need to go."

"I know." Before he let his arms drop away, Rick pressed a kiss against her forehead. "You're an amazing woman, Cassie Crockett. God has blessed you with a wonderful talent for caring for those who hurt."

"God has?" she asked, irritated by the comment.

"Yes, God." Rick stepped back, smiled and touched his forefinger to her cheek. "That sense of compassion that's embedded so deeply inside you is straight from God. He's gifted you with the empathy to see a needy heart or a hurting body and help. Let go and let Him work through you."

Cassie left the room to make her phone call with Rick's words ringing in her ears. Let God work through her? It was a prayer she'd prayed throughout her teen years—to be used by God. Instead, she felt used by her husband and her father. Was she now finally where God intended her to be—alone and broke, with a son in emotional trouble?

And falling for a man who deserved to be trusted and loved—two things she was no longer sure she could do?

Rick lay sleepless on Noah's bed, thinking of Cassie and all she'd done tonight. She was a woman beyond compare.

Michael's rhythmic breathing filled the room.

Thank you, Lord, for being with this boy. Please help me help him overcome the depression that is upon him.

There were so many needs in this building, so many hearts that needed the Master's mending. Rick spent the next hour praying for each one.

When he was finished, he thought about jobs he needed to do at the church, office work that had waited too long, visits he'd been meaning to pay.

But no matter how he tried to avoid it, his thoughts always returned to those precious few moments when he'd held Cassie in his arms.

The sweetness of her, the love she showered on kids society wanted punished—that stuck with him. She really loved these troubled kids. She was an awesome mother.

Rick replayed the years he'd struggled to live on the streets and imagined how different it would have been had Cassie been there. What would it be like to have her to lean on when his job overwhelmed him and he felt unable to comfort another soul? What would it be like to let her comfort him?

He felt dazed by his thoughts. He was beginning to care for her. He wanted to help her through the tough times and the good. He wanted to be able to run to her when life overwhelmed.

But that couldn't be.

He couldn't care for Cassie Crockett. Not if he was going to keep his vow to God.

The joy he'd known leeched away. Love, companionship, a family—that wasn't for him. God didn't want that for him.

Then he remembered her earlier question about leaving. Was that what God was telling him, that he should leave here if that was the only way he could keep his vow?

The thought of leaving this place he loved, of walking away from the woman who made him yearn to fulfill his dreams, filled Rick with pain.

"Please don't make me," he whispered.

But what choice did he have? If he couldn't control these feelings for Cassie, if he couldn't figure out how to keep his vow without losing her, then leaving might be his only choice.

The rest of the night passed in a tug-of-war as Rick fought to suppress his feelings. He begged God to take away his tender feelings for her. Just before dawn he finally gave in and asked God for a new mission, a place to go where he would not be tempted to break his vow to serve God alone.

He'd promised Cassie he wasn't leaving. He'd repeated that promise to her and he'd meant it. The thought of breaking that promise filled him with pain. But what choice did he have?

I'm not going to renege on You, he promised as night turned to day and the inhabitants of Lives began to stir. *I won't let my feelings for Cassie come between us. But please, help me.*

But for the first time in a very long time, Rick couldn't reach Heaven. An impenetrable barrier seemed to lie between him and God.

And that only added to his guilt. He was a failure.

Chapter Eight

Cassie woke, nose twitching as the aroma of coffee assailed her. Michael lay in the same position on the floor, sound asleep. His slightly improved color did nothing to curb her worry. If she had to, she could summon local help, but Cassie knew they wouldn't have the equipment needed to thoroughly evaluate and treat her patient. He needed a specialist.

She showered and dressed. On her way to the kitchen she noticed that the winter storm had almost spent itself. Hopefully it wouldn't be long before the air ambulance arrived.

"Good morning." Rick sat at the dining table, rumpled-looking, his lined face giving away his restless night. And yet, he still looked as handsome to her as he always had.

"Morning." Cassie tore her gaze away and poured a cup of coffee. When she sat down across from him, he leaned forward to peer into her face. "How are you?"

"I'm fine." She sipped her coffee, waiting for the caffeine to take effect. "Is Laurel up?"

"Yes." Rick nodded. "She's been on the phone. Apparently there was a disaster at a mine north of here and all the air ambulances have been directed there to handle the victims. Since Michael isn't in immediate danger, they've put him on a wait list."

"He can't wait," Cassie said, frustrated by the delay. "He needs to be assessed immediately, before he seizes again."

"That's what Laurel thought. That's why she's doing her best to persuade the correctional service to send a plane to take him to Winnipeg. Don't worry, Cassie." He reached across the table to cover her hand with his. A second later he pulled his hand away with a strange look on his face.

"Are you sure you're okay?" Cassie asked, confused by his actions. His expressive green eyes looked troubled.

"I'm fine." There was an edge to his voice she'd never heard before.

Why was he acting so strangely? "I guess I'd better pack a bag."

"In case you have to go with Michael?"

"I'm afraid he'll have another seizure on the way. The air ambulance would have medical staff on board, but if Laurel gets a plane and there's only a pilot…" Her voice trailed away.

Rick nodded his understanding then drew away at the sound of voices in the hall. He probably didn't want the boys to see them huddled together. For a moment Rod teased him about not helping Teddy shovel the newly fallen snow outside, but he quickly noted Rick's serious expression. A hush fell as the boys quietly took their places at the table.

"Is M-Michael o-o-kay?" Noah asked in a sober tone.

"Yes." Cassie explained that he needed to go to Winnipeg, and that she might go with him.

"Michael gets his own plane? Man." Daniel's grin flashed. "Like a rich man."

"That's me." Michael's bitter tone resounded as he strode into the room and sat down. "The guy who gets all the breaks. Brain injuries, seizures—wow, am I lucky."

"He was just teasing, man." Rod did his best to make peace.

"I hope the plane crashes," Michael snarled. He jumped out of his chair, knocking it to the floor. The sharp crack startled everyone, including Michael. He wheeled and left the room in a rush.

"We didn't mean to bug him," Rod apologized.

"It's okay." Rick explained that Michael needed their support and prayers. He soon had the other boys agreeing to pray for Michael.

"I don't know how you do that," Cassie marveled after the boys had finished their breakfasts and left. "The way you get the boys on board with befriending Michael even though he always pushes them away— it's amazing."

"It's a matter of making them realize that they could be in Michael's shoes and need someone to rely on." He shrugged. "Everybody needs a friend."

Cassie thought about how Laurel had been her only friend for so long—until Rick. Rick seemed like the best friend she'd ever had.

Did that mean she could trust him?

"Why don't you go get ready? I'll talk to Michael," he offered.

"Thank you." Her eyes met his.

"That's what friends are for," Rick murmured.

Cassie paused in the doorway and turned to look directly at him, searching his eyes. "Is that what we are?" she asked before she could stop herself.

Rick stopped chewing. He set down the remainder of his toast, then said, "What else could we be, Cassie?"

It wasn't so much his question that bothered Cassie. It was the tone underlying his words—it sounded almost like a warning. Did he think she expected more than friendship from him? Would he reject more? Confused, she left the room.

As she was packing, she puzzled over her reaction to his question. She felt dismayed, even disappointed. Why?

Because in her heart of hearts, she thought of Rick as more than a friend.

The knowledge startled Cassie so much that she stayed in her room until she heard Laurel calling her. By then she was eager to leave, eager to escape the miasma of questions Rick had caused.

"A plane for Michael will be here within the hour," Laurel told her.

"I'm ready," she said. She sought out Rick, who was now alone in the family room.

"I want to ask you a favor. Would you please watch out for Noah?" she asked, even as she wondered if it was a mistake, if that comment earlier about being friends was his way of trying to communicate to her that he wanted distance. "I'm worried he'll get in a fight—"

"Cassie." Rick rested his hand on her shoulder. "You don't have to be afraid. God has His hand on that boy. I'll be here if Noah needs me. Trust me."

Trust me.

"Thank you," she said with heartfelt gratitude.

Part of her hated to leave. Questions about Rick plagued her. But another part of her was afraid he didn't want anything more to do with her. The very idea filled her with sadness and she realized that Rick had become a large part of her world.

Cassie felt Rick's gaze follow her as she grabbed her bag. His hand covered hers as he took it from her and they headed out to the car with Michael and Laurel. Rick helped Michael into his seat and offered his iPod with music for the boy to listen to. Before he got into the driver's seat, he leaned in to check on Cassie in the passenger's seat. His face came so near to hers, Cassie had to force herself not to reach out and cup his cheek in her palm.

Trust me.

At the last second, Cassie touched his hand and leaned forward.

"I do trust you, Rick."

His eyes blazed a brilliant jade-green. A smile stretched across his face. For a brief second, Cassie thought she saw sadness in his smile. Then he took her hand in his. "You won't be sorry you did, Cassie."

She hoped not.

"We've had two storms in the two days since you left. Somehow you've managed to return before the next one hits," Laurel informed her as she drove Cassie to Lives from the airport. "Michael comes back when?"

"A week, maybe." Cassie gazed at the beauty of the white landscape blazing in the winter sun. Funny how good it felt to leave Winnipeg. Funny how it felt as if she was coming home.

Funny how much she wanted to see Rick.

"That is, a week if he does okay on his new medication."

Cassie didn't hear much of the rest of Laurel's comments. She was too anxious to see Noah again, to make sure he was safe. To make sure Rick had kept his promise. So when they pulled into the yard she jumped out, grabbed her case and hurried inside Lives.

As she set the bag in the foyer, she heard Rick's voice in the family room. Her silly heart bounced with joy when she found him and Noah together, focused on a chessboard.

"Hi, Mom," Noah said. His smile flashed at her.

"Hi, yourself." She bent and hugged him, surprised that he not only allowed it but he returned it. Stunned, she stood back to survey him. Her son seemed calmer. Her eyes met Rick's. Whatever wariness she'd seen in him before she left was gone now. "How are you, Rick?"

"Getting beaten to a pulp by this guy," he said with a growl at Noah. "Otherwise I'm fine. Michael?"

"He's on some new medication. Once he's settled into it, he should start feeling better." Cassie sat down. "And everyone else?"

"Fine as frog's hair, as an old friend used to say." Rick kept staring at her, as if he couldn't get enough of watching her. Cassie felt the same. Finally he broke the connection between them when Noah reminded him it was his turn. He moved his piece too quickly and Noah seized it, checkmating him. "See what I mean?" he groaned.

"I keep t-telling you, y-you have to concentrate." Noah rolled his eyes. "You always f-forget."

"Yes, I do," Rick agreed, his gaze returning to Cassie.

"Do you have homework, son?" Cassie asked. When Noah nodded she raised one eyebrow. Without a single argument, Noah rose, thanked Rick for the game then left. Cassie looked at Rick. "What have you done with the real Noah?"

Rick shrugged.

"I'm serious. It sounds like he's stuttering less and he's certainly less belligerent. No problems?"

"Nary a one. We've been talking a lot. I think he's begun to heal, maybe." Rick smiled, then tilted his head to study her. "You look rested."

"I feel rested. Once I got Michael to the hospital, the staff took over. There were some long consultations with his doctors but other than that, I was free until the plane left today. I managed a little wool shopping." Cassie chuckled when he rolled his eyes. "Because the two boxes I have in my room aren't enough."

"Alicia will be glad. She's sold out of everything you made. I guess that means you'll be busy for a while." Rick's smile flashed again. "As if that's anything new."

"Anything interesting happen while I was gone?" she asked.

"Some of the kids who don't want to sing in the choir asked if they can form a band. Kyle's been encouraging it by pounding on a set of drums." Rick rolled his eyes. "Lucy's gotten on board, too, with her latest on-line purchase—used instruments from a school band."

"A saxophone?" she asked hopefully.

"Not yet, but soon I hope. I've now got half the town's adolescents nagging me to get the band started."

"You wanted youth participation, right?" she teased.

His smile warmed her. It felt as if the part inside her that had frozen hard against letting anyone get too close had begun to thaw. Cassie could hardly believe it.

"I have to make some calls. I'd better get going." Rick led the way to the front door, and Cassie caught the scent of his aftershave. She found herself inhaling deeply.

"I'll be glad when Michael returns," Rick said. "We've missed him. I don't think the boys like the change. I guess most people don't. They find it threatening."

Cassie frowned. Was Rick hinting at something?

"I appreciate your help with the choir, Cassie. A lot." He slipped his fingers into his leather gloves as if delaying looking at her.

"And I appreciate yours with Noah. Did he tell you anything I should know?"

"We mostly just talked." Rick's gaze slid away.

"Well, thank you for doing that." She kept her tone even, though something inside her went on alert.

"You're welcome." Rick seemed mesmerized by the collage of Northern Lights photos hanging on the wall above her head.

"Noah admires you," Cassie murmured. "I think he'll consider whatever advice you give him."

"I should go," Rick said somewhat suddenly.

"Wait." Cassie's bag sat in one corner, reminding her. "I brought you a present." He raised his eyebrows. "Don't get excited because it's nothing big."

"You didn't need to bring me anything," he said quietly.

"I was at the airport newsstand when I suddenly remembered all those newspapers you love to read. I know how expensive it is to get the big city papers here so I thought I'd save you some money." She zipped open her bag and lifted out a thick roll, bound with two elastic bands. "These are the two most recent Toronto papers. I thought some of the stories might be of interest. I didn't read them, though, so if they're duds, chuck 'em."

"I'm sure they'll make great reading. Thank you." Rick sounded as if he was losing his voice. He accepted the roll as if it was hot, tucked it under one arm and put his hand on the doorknob.

"Rick?"

"Yes." He finally looked directly at her. His green eyes swirled with thoughts Cassie couldn't understand.

"I just wanted to say thank you again for helping me realize I can trust you. It's a relief to know that after—" She paused, inhaled and continued. "Well, after I didn't think I could trust anyone. You've been so open and honest. That's something new for me."

"Well, that's…" He looked so uncomfortable with her praise, Cassie was about to ask him what was wrong when he exhaled deeply and said, "Cassie, I need to tell you—"

The door opened and Laurel entered.

"Hi. You're leaving?" she asked Rick. When he nodded, she said, "Probably a good idea if you want to sleep at home tonight. By the looks of it, this storm will be worse than predicted. The snow's already started."

"Then I'd better go." Rick paused. His gaze rested on Cassie for a moment longer. The hunted look she saw there confused her, but before she could ask, he pulled open the door and stepped into the swirling white world.

The door closed behind him. A moment later they heard the sound of his snowmobile roaring away.

"Rick wasn't very talkative. Is anything wrong?" Laurel glanced at Cassie as she slipped out of her coat.

"I don't know." Cassie excused herself, picked up her bag and carried it up to her room, unsettled by Rick's strange behavior. She left her bag unpacked and sat down on her window seat as old uncertainties came rushing back. Maybe she'd done something to upset him.

Her mind circled back to the newfound trust she felt for Rick. For the first time in a very long time, Cassie felt right about trusting.

"Rick's not like Eric and my father," she whispered. "He's generous and good. But—"

And that was the issue. But what came next?

Tired and confused, Cassie rose and unpacked. But she couldn't dislodge the wobbly uncertainty in her stomach that something was wrong.

Rick raced away from Lives, his mind replaying Cassie talking about how trusting him had changed things for her. The roll of newspapers burned like a hot coal where it lay inside his snowsuit. When he got home, he dropped Cassie's gift on the floor before shedding his outdoor clothes. He tried to calm the anguish her words had aroused, to no avail.

You should have told her the truth. She deserves that.

Yes, she deserved to know. But he needed privacy to tell her the whole story—how he'd renounced his old life of greed after losing money that belonged to her father and others, turned his back on wealth, dedicated himself to God and serving Him. He needed to explain those past mistakes.

Rick tried to pray about it. But the only voice he

heard inside his head reminded him, *be sure your sins will find you out.*

The truth was he'd deliberately kept his secret. Because if he'd told Cassie, he knew she would refuse to let him help Noah. The boy was finally emerging from his bitterness. He couldn't interfere with that just to appease his guilt.

A knock on his door interrupted his self-condemnation.

"What are you doing out in this weather?" Rick asked Kyle, drawing his friend inside and shutting out the snow.

"You left Lives in a rush looking pretty grim. I was worried about you." Kyle's gaze fell on the roll Rick had dropped on the floor. "Are those new?"

"Yes." Kyle gave a whoop of excitement and began unrolling them. Rick headed for the kitchen. "I'll put the kettle on—hot chocolate okay?"

When Kyle didn't answer, Rick turned. Kyle's gaze was locked on a one-page ad in the newspaper. After a moment he raised his eyes to stare at Rick.

"Yes. They're rereleasing my book." Rick swallowed.

"Is that why you've been so out of sorts lately?"

"Not exactly."

"What's going on, Rick?"

Rick took a deep breath and told Kyle about the strange connection that he and Cassie shared—that it was her father who'd saved Rick from the streets. And that Rick had gone on to lose all of her father's money for him, which he felt had caused tension between Cassie and her father after Eric had died.

"Does she know about this—?" Kyle flopped down, his eyes widening as he read the ad.

"She knows that I know John, and that John saved my life. But she doesn't know what I did to him. I was going to tell her the truth." Rick held up his hand, forefinger and thumb millimeters apart. "I was this close. Then Laurel came in. It's not the kind of thing I can explain in front of others," he defended when Kyle frowned. "I need to tell Cassie the truth in private."

"You need to tell her the truth right away," Kyle corrected. "She's going to struggle with knowing that you played a bigger role in their estrangement and kept it a secret."

"I know." Rick made the chocolate in two big mugs and handed one to Kyle. He placed his on a nearby table, unable to drink it.

"The truth always outs, pal. Always."

"I know. It's just hard to think of myself as that greedy jerk, even harder to explain it to someone else. Cassie's father was the only thing between me and death so many times."

"Did you tell her that?" Kyle leaned back, his mug in his hand.

"I told her some of it, but not all. After I hit bottom, Cassie's father was the one who introduced me to the Savior." Rick shook his head. "I'd never have made it but for John. I was hoping Cassie would see that maybe she misjudged her father, that maybe she didn't know the whole story."

"And?" Kyle leaned forward.

"I'm not sure. She hasn't said anything about him for a while, and I haven't wanted to bring him up, for obvious reasons." He shook his head sadly. "The sad thing is, Kyle, John adored his daughter. He was so proud of the way she struggled to keep strong in her faith after her mom died. When I last saw him a year ago, I guessed there was some resentment between them, but I never imagined they would stop speaking."

"Money can do that to relationships. Sara told me Cassie's dad calls every week but she mostly doesn't speak to him. That can't go on." Kyle tipped up his mug, swallowed the last of his hot chocolate, then rose. "For Noah's sake, if not for her own, Cassie needs to rebuild that relationship. She might not admit it but she needs her father. You're a minister. Your job is to help facilitate Cassie's healing."

Rick hadn't known about the phone calls, but now that he did, it only added to his guilt and fueled his determination to find a way to tell Cassie the truth.

Kyle didn't hesitate. He led out in a plea for God's leading, direction, preparation of Cassie's heart and for Rick to find the words he needed to say. Finished praying, he clapped a hand on Rick's back. "I know this will be a delicate talk. She might be furious at you. Any number of things might happen. But don't put this off, Rick. Tell her the truth. If you don't, it will only get worse." Kyle glanced at the newspaper and then at Rick. "There's something else we need to discuss. Are you falling for Cassie?"

Rick paused to consider his answer. The wind outside howled, rattling the windows with fury, causing a tinkling sound as it threw icy particles against the glass.

"I care about her," Rick admitted finally.

"Care, how? Like a pastor? Like a friend? Or more than that?" Kyle rose. "You don't need to tell me but I do think you need to figure out what you expect from her."

"I know." Rick glanced out the window. "It's gotten

much worse out there," he said. "Are you sure you can make it home?"

"Are you kidding? I've been getting around Churchill since I was a kid. I could find my way blindfolded." Kyle pulled on his snowmobile helmet. "Thanks for sharing," he said, his voice muffled.

"Thanks for listening. Have Sara call when you get home. I want to know I won't have to go searching tonight." Rick waited until Kyle nodded.

"Such a worrier," he teased. Then he yanked open the door and strode into the storm.

Rick listened for the roar of the snowmobile's engine, then closed the door. After Sara called to say Kyle was home safely, Rick turned off the lights, sank onto his sofa and stared into the storm that swept across the bay.

"I care about her," he whispered, looking toward the heavens. "A lot. More than an objective pastor should. But I know what I promised You. I'm not going to act on my feelings because nothing can happen between us and I don't want to hurt her."

But Rick couldn't see a way around causing pain to the woman he cared about. In fact, after he told her that he was the reason her father had no money—either for her or for himself—it was very likely that Cassie Crockett would hate him.

Rick tried to pray for strength and the right words to confess. But as the storm outside raged, all he heard was Cassie's sweet voice, and those words that caused him to hang his head in shame.

I trust you, Rick.

Chapter Nine

"Cassie this is stunning. I've never seen such creativity with yarn."

Alicia Featherstone lifted the piece Cassie had just finished, her fingers deft but inquisitive as she examined the sweater once meant for Eric. "Did you bring anything else?"

"An afghan. I was inspired by the Northern Lights' display we had a couple of weeks ago." She waited anxiously while Alicia examined the throw. "Are they suitable?"

"Suitable? They're amazing." Alicia tilted her head to one side. "Can you do some kids' things?"

"Sure." Cassie looked into Alicia's dark eyes and wished she could unburden her heart.

"You seem troubled. Is something wrong?"

"I'm just confused and mixed up." Cassie prepared to leave, but Alicia persuaded her to stay and share a coffee at the tiny table in the rear of the store.

"Please tell me what's wrong. I'd like to help if I can." Alicia handed her a steaming cup. "Is it Rick?"

"Why do you say that?" Had everyone noticed that she couldn't seem to stay away from him?

"Just a guess. You help him a lot with the choir and now the band he's started." Alicia smiled. "Besides, he's a very nice guy. I can understand why you'd care for him."

"I think I care," Cassie admitted. "But I don't really trust him. I want to but—" After a gentle prod from Alicia, Cassie poured out her story. "Dad, Eric, God—I feel like they all betrayed me and I don't want to be tricked again," she ended.

"God will never betray you, Cassie. I don't believe Rick would, either." Alicia frowned. "I don't know anything about relationships so maybe I'm off base, but it seems to me that it isn't that you're afraid to trust Rick. It sounds more like you don't want to trust him in case you get hurt again."

"I think you're pretty smart about relationships," Cassie murmured.

"Well, my friend Sara says that if you love someone, you have to be willing to expose yourself to hurt because people are human. But she says loving and getting hurt are better than not loving at all. Do you know what I mean?"

"I think so." Cassie smiled at her. "Thank you, Alicia. It was good to talk to someone."

"Pray about it. God will give you the answer. And don't worry that I'll tell anyone," Alicia said. "It'll be a secret between friends."

"Thank you." Cassie hugged her, finished her coffee and left. Then she visited the bank. Thanks to Alicia, her savings account was growing by leaps and bounds.

She drove back to Lives, bellowing out a praise tune she'd learned when she was a little kid, her heart somehow lighter.

She owed Rick big-time. In the past week since she'd come back from Winnipeg, she'd seen glimpses of a different Noah, thanks to the special bond that Rick and Noah seemed to have going.

Rick had brought up the subject of her father twice, but Cassie cut him off both times. This was her new life. She didn't want to be dragged back into her painful past and those feelings of being blamed. Yet, Noah was asking about his grandfather more often now, making Cassie wonder if reconciling would help her son shed whatever still plagued him. And, face it, she missed her dad. Alicia was right, loving was better than not.

When Cassie drove into the yard at Lives, her heart jumped inside her chest at the sight of Rick's snowmobile. She scolded herself for behaving like a teenager, but she knew it wouldn't change a thing.

Every time Rick was around, her emotions ran amok. She prodded her brain to remember her promise never to let anyone get that close again, but her brain ignored that. As Cassie walked to the door, her step grew a bit lighter in anticipation of seeing him.

Inside, noises from the family room intrigued her. She took off her coat and followed the sounds, helpless to stop her smile from widening when she saw Rick. Thankfully he didn't notice because he was busy trying to show Daniel some dance steps. And failing miserably. She couldn't help chuckling out loud.

"Ah." Rick's eyes gleamed. He held out a hand. "Just the person we need to get you fellows up to speed for the Valentine's Day dance. Now you guys watch and Cassie and I will show you how it's done."

Dance with him? Her mouth went completely dry. But Rick gave her no time to refuse.

"Start that music over, Rod," he ordered. He grabbed her hand, drew her close and grinned. "Ready?"

Cassie nodded, falling into the movement and rhythm of the music with an ease that surprised her. She'd loved to dance from the moment her mother had taken her to her very first ballet class. Dancing was something she'd shared with Eric when they were first married, until he became too busy to keep their weekly date night. It had been years, but as Cassie followed Rick's lead around the room, the joy of moving to music surged back. Worries and burdens melted away as she reveled in his strong yet gentle arm at her back.

"This is how it's done, guys," Rick said. His green eyes met hers. "You dance beautifully," he murmured.

For days now Cassie had felt some hesitation in Rick, something she couldn't quite put her finger on. But now she sensed that Rick was into this perfect moment as much as she was. The music carried her into a daydream world where she and Rick shared and laughed and enjoyed, a world that stretched into a future of possibility. She wanted it to go on and on, but the music ended too soon.

Cassie looked up and got trapped in Rick's searching gaze. It bored deep inside her, asking questions to which she had no answers, telling her something she couldn't quite grasp.

She was loath to move away until a burst of applause broke the spell. Then Rick released her. A draft of chilly air took the place of his warm embrace. He stepped back, bowed to her and then turned to the boys.

"So that's your goal," he told them, his voice slightly raspy. He looked her way, but the emotions she'd glimpsed in his eyes mere seconds ago were now hidden. "Would you mind helping the boys, Cassie? They seem to believe a few pre-lessons at home will make them look less awkward on the dance floor."

Cassie nodded, unable to speak. How Rick could seem so unaffected by their dance was a mystery. Cassie was thankful that he partnered her first with Noah. She needed some time to get her senses under control. Noah caught on to the steps quickly, despite his cast. Perhaps the impromptu dances she'd drawn him into when he was younger—times when Cassie desperately needed to feel alive and vital and carefree—had paid off. After a few minutes, Noah stepped away from her.

"I g-got it now, M-Mom. You'd b-better help, R-Rod. He l-looks like a g-geek."

"Hey!" Rod glared at him, his face dark red.

Cassie obliged, trying not to wince after Rod stepped on her toes for the hundredth time. When she glanced at Noah, she saw him peering out the window, his face gloomy and shadowed with his thoughts. She was going to ask Rod if he knew why when Rick broke them up to pair her with Daniel, who was also not happy.

"This is slow and pokey," he muttered, his hand fisted against her waist. "Nobody dances like this but old people."

"Don't you want to learn to dance, Daniel?" But Cassie knew it wasn't that. She could see in his eyes that he was battling a craving for drugs. He needed something to work it off. "Rick," she called. "Can you put on something faster?"

Rick's gaze met hers. He nodded, and a moment later an energetic tune filled the room.

"Okay now, Daniel. Concentrate." Cassie grabbed his hand and swung him into a two-step. Daniel floundered for a moment or two but he was a quick study and before the end of the song he was fully into it, moving easily, his face aglow.

"You, my boy, are a natural dancer," Cassie puffed as she caught her breath while the other boys clapped for them. "You've got a sense of rhythm that a lot of people don't possess. You should do something with it."

"Really?" Daniel looked startled.

"Cassie's right, kid. You've got the moves," Rick told him with a grin. "Now, how about you give someone else a chance?"

Daniel nodded and sat down with a proud smile as he watched the other boys clumsily learn the basic steps. Michael, whom she'd welcomed back this morning, was the last one. He shuffled toward Cassie, looking listless.

"Are you feeling okay, Michael?" she asked as she took his hand.

"Fine," he said, moving slowly to the jazz tune Rick had chosen. "But I'd rather be playing the sax to this than dancing."

"I know. Rick and I haven't given up on that. We'll find you one, I promise."

At one point Cassie glanced at Rick and found him staring at Michael, his forehead creased, his eyes narrowed. She was fairly certain his thoughts matched hers.

"I'm sorry I got called away." Laurel's voice drew their attention to the doorway as the music ended. "From what I just saw, I think we owe Rick and Cassie a big thank-you," she said and led the others in a burst of applause. "I don't think any of you will embarrass Lives Under Construction at the Valentine's Day dance," she teased. She then invited everyone to come for supper.

Cassie hung back with Rick and Laurel as the boys rushed to the table. "I'm worried about Michael."

"So am I," Laurel murmured. "But I don't know what else we can do."

"I might." Rick smiled at their surprise. "Leave it to me, okay? I've got an idea I want to try."

"Your ideas are a blessing to us." Laurel wrapped her arms around him in a brief hug. "I don't know what we'd do without you."

"Hopefully you won't have to find out," he joked. He turned to Cassie. "Will you be able to make choir practice tomorrow?"

"My schedule's clear so far." Cassie thought she'd heard a trace of desperation in his voice. "I'll be there after school."

"Excellent. I'd better go. I've got Bible study tonight."

"You won't stay for supper?" Laurel asked.

"I'll have to take a rain check," he said. "Thanks, though."

"You're always welcome," Laurel assured him. After a sideways glance at Cassie, she walked toward the kitchen.

"I need to thank you, too," Cassie said. "I deposited a lovely check today and that's thanks to you for suggesting I see Alicia. I'm gradually building back my savings."

"Good." But Rick's green eyes looked troubled as they rested on her.

"Is anything wrong?" she asked.

"Cassie, I—"

She waited, breathless, for what she didn't know. He shook his head. "Never mind. This isn't the time."

Frustrated, Cassie followed him to the door. "I'll see you tomorrow at practice then," she said.

"You will." He smiled absentmindedly then left.

Cassie stood in the doorway, watching him drive away until the cold air forced her to shut the door.

Something's going on with him, something he doesn't want to tell me about.

Later that evening, Cassie sat in the window seat in her room, knitting. The moon, round and full, illuminated the glistening snow. She could see for miles across the tufted tundra as she relived what it felt like to be in Rick's arms. She remembered the tender way he'd whispered in her ear, felt the sweet pressure of his hand against her back when they'd danced. Oh, how she'd wanted it to continue.

I love him. How had it happened? How had Rick Salinger made it past the barriers she'd erected after Eric's death?

Cassie had no answers. All she knew was that Rick had pushed the pain and sadness out of her heart. She felt alive, ready to take on her future. Maybe it *was* time to talk to her father, to try to rebuild their bond. Not just for Noah, but for herself, too.

Cassie took out a piece of stationery and her favorite pen. Worry gripped her. What if her father didn't want to reconcile? What if he only wanted to talk to Noah?

When I was a child I talked like a child, I thought like a child, I reasoned like a child; now that I have grown up, I am done with childish ways and have put them aside.

The old familiar passage from First Corinthians pushed out the doubts. Wasn't it time she grew up?

Wasn't it time to have some faith in God's love? For the first time in ages, Cassie bowed her head.

"Please help me," she whispered. "I need my dad. I need my family. I need You."

I need Rick.

Cassie wanted to beg God to take away the sprout of love that had taken root inside her heart. She wanted to, but she couldn't. Rick had become too big a part of her world, too important to her happiness.

She'd told him she trusted him.

It was time to trust God, too.

Dear Dad. She paused, then began to write, pouring out her heart on paper.

Chapter Ten

"Boy I'm glad to see you." Rick heaved a sigh of relief the next afternoon when Cassie rushed through the church door for the first rehearsal with the band and the choir together. Seeing her lovely face made him so happy, he felt like a giddy teenager.

"I'm sorry I'm late." She sounded breathless as she unwound her scarf and pulled off her jacket and gloves. "Would you believe Laurel's van wouldn't start?"

"Yes, I would." He grinned. "That vehicle needs to be replaced." He waited until she was seated at the piano. "Do you want to run over it before we begin?"

"I think I'll be okay," Cassie said. "I'm ready whenever you are."

"Good." Rick tapped his music stand to gain the kids' attention, waiting until all eyes were on him. "Ready? Here we go. Wait for Cassie's introduction." He nodded to her to begin. "Now."

Most of the choir managed to hit the first note but the band members straggled in late so he started again. It was only marginally better the second time but Rick pressed on, leading them to the end without stopping.

As the last note died away, the kids remained silent for a moment. Then everyone rushed to speak.

"We did it!" they exclaimed in proud surprise.

"Of course you did." Rick shared a grin with Cassie. "We have to remember those pauses where the choir sings without the band. But if we practice, I know we can have it perfect in time for Easter morning. Doesn't it make a difference having Cassie play for us?"

The kids concurred, eager to try again. After they finished the third run-through, they drooped, exhilarated but obviously tired. Rick praised their efforts effusively, reminded them of the next practice and then dismissed them. Cassie rose as if she, too, would leave.

This was the moment.

"Can I talk to you for a few minutes?" he asked. "Privately?"

Cassie's eyebrows rose in surprise but she nodded and began to put away her music. Once the last boy had wandered out, she looked at him, a question in her eyes.

"You've done an amazing job," Rick said. Her eyes still shone with the passion she'd poured into her playing. "I think this Easter is going to be very special."

"Me, too. I can't believe how much you've done with them," Cassie said. Rick's pride surged at her praise. "Noah sounds amazing. You were right—his stutter completely disappears when he sings."

"He's remarkable." Rick sat down in the front pew facing her. "They all are. I wish I could do more."

"More? Like what?" Her pretty smile flashed. "Get them doing a full-scale opera?"

"I doubt they'd agree to that," he said, laughing a little. "No, I meant I need to find something for Michael other than those bells. I need to find a saxophone and so far I'm hitting a wall."

Quit prevaricating. He exhaled. He opened his mouth.

"I wrote my dad, Rick." Cassie said it softly, quietly, studying him as she spoke. "I did what you said and told him how I felt abandoned by him."

"How do you feel about that?" he asked, relieved to put off his confession a little longer.

"Good. Calmer. As if a big block in my life has dissolved." Her surprise was obvious. "I guess I never realized just how much my anger about him was bothering me."

"It is surprising when we let go of something and then realize the hold it had on us," he agreed. "God answers prayer, Cassie. And He knows how to work this out."

"I haven't had much success with talking to God lately," she admitted, her eyes avoiding his.

"That's not unusual. When you haven't talked in a while, it takes some time to regain the closeness you used to share." He saw that mystified look on her face. "You have to purposefully rebuild your relationship with God, just like you do with your dad. Eventually you'll get to a point where you'll be able to declare something."

"Like what?"

"Like declaring that you'll trust God." He said it deliberately, knowing how shaky her trust was but wanting her to take another step. Cassie frowned.

"Even if I'm not sure I can?" she murmured. "I keep going back, Rick. I keep thinking maybe, if I'd been a better wife, paid more attention, if I'd seen Eric's desperation to impress his board, maybe I could have prevented his suicide."

"Looking back is useless. There's nothing you can do to change what happened, Cassie." He paused, waiting for some heavenly direction. But it wasn't there. Was it because his attraction to Cassie meant he was betraying his promise to God? "God knew what would happen," he said, struggling to find the words. "And He gave you the strength to get through it."

"I don't understand." She shook her head. "If He knew how much it would hurt, why did He let it happen?" A tear spilled down her cheek. "Why did I have to go through all that pain?"

Rick hesitated. He was a pastor. He was supposed to be able to help her, lead her so she could find God's love again. Yet he felt weighed down by his own guilt.

"I don't know why it had to happen that way, Cassie. But *why* doesn't really matter now, does it?" His own words sounded hollow as he moved from the pew to hunker down in front of her. He took her hand in his. "I see your struggle as a test. You've come this far. Now you need to decide if you're going to lose your faith or if you're going to fight for it."

"How do I do that?" Her eyes implored him for help.

This is why God placed me in Churchill.

Rick blocked out every emotion. He was determined to help Cassie through this.

"Whenever you talk about the past, your body language changes," he began. "Your shoulders hunch, you tighten up and your smile disappears. Your words are tight, tense and short."

"I know. That's how I feel," Cassie admitted.

"But if you could see yourself when you're with your

patients," he continued. "Your face is relaxed, your voice is soft. You're open and trusting." Rick smiled as images of her just like that filled his mind.

"How is that connected to my faith?" She frowned.

"I think you need to treat yourself like you treat your patients," he said. "You need new words to reframe the way you talk about the past and help you look to the future." Cassie's eyebrows rose high, as if that was the last thing she expected from him. "You need to be gentle with yourself. Because that's the way God feels toward you."

"Go on." She was still frowning, but he could see that he had her attention.

"Words are powerful and whether we realize it or not, what we say impacts the way we live our lives. I'm suggesting you start reframing your life and your faith with the way you speak."

Cassie slowly withdrew her hand from his. Rick rose, stepped back and sat beside her on the front pew.

"That sounds reasonable."

"It is. But if you're going to do that, you need to start with a basic premise," he added. "How about God is love?"

Cassie took a long time to think about it before she nodded.

"So because God is love and wants only the best for us, we trust Him." Rick forced his mind off the way her curls tumbled onto her face like shavings of gold, illuminating her lovely skin. "He teaches us to do that by giving us tests that will help stretch our faith. We might not like it, but we know that God has something good in mind. He's answering our prayer and we just haven't realized it yet."

"You're talking about the power of positive thinking," she said.

"Oh, no." Rick shook his head. "I'm talking about speaking the truths God gave us in His word and being confident in Him instead of letting the storms we go through control our emotions and thoughts."

"I'm not sure I follow."

"The best way to keep our trust in God is to remember His promises. 'I can do all things through Christ who strengthens me.'" Rick paused—he needed a moment to absorb the beauty of Cassie beginning to claim her faith. "'All things work together for good to those who love God and are called according to His purpose,'" he quoted.

"'I am more than a conqueror through Christ who strengthens me,'" Cassie quoted in return. The gold in her eyes began to glow. "'I will not fear, for God is with me.'"

Rick could only nod as realization of her position with God dawned on Cassie. He'd always thought she was beautiful, but now she was stunning as she radiated God's love. She repeated verse after verse, her voice filling the sanctuary, growing stronger as her faith grew.

When she stopped speaking, her eyes met his. Rick couldn't move. There could be nothing between them—he knew that and mourned it—but that didn't stop his heart from surging with joy at her renewal as a child of God.

"I'm beginning to understand," Cassie whispered as a smile spread across her face. "I get it."

This woman was a jewel beyond compare. Rick could no more ignore the affection he felt for her than he could have ignored her pleas for help.

Until he realized his own test was going to be giving her up.

"Just keep your thoughts and mind centered on God and His love for you," he said, knowing he couldn't put off telling her any longer.

"Sounds easier than it is," she said shyly.

"Yes, but you can do it." He inhaled deeply. "I wanted to talk to you about something else," he said.

The back door of the church slammed. They both turned to see Noah standing there.

"Are you f-finished, Mom?" he asked. "I've g-got a lot of h-homework."

"Sorry, Rick. Another time?" Cassie asked.

He held her coat while she slipped into it. For the merest fraction of a second he allowed his hands to linger on her arms, wishing he had the right to draw her close, knowing she'd never want that after he told her the truth.

"Can I take you out for coffee tomorrow?" he asked, hearing the desperation in his voice.

"I'm on nights tonight and tomorrow so I'll be sleeping during the day," she explained, searching his gaze. "Friday is the dance. I said I'd help the boys get ready in the afternoon, and I'm chaperoning at the dance that night. Maybe we can figure out another time."

"I hope so." The need to straighten things out so that nothing but the total truth lay between them nagged at Rick. But he would have to wait. For a little while longer he could enjoy their friendship.

Friendship?

"I loved playing today." Cassie leaned forward to touch his arm. "I know I told you I didn't want to go inside a church again, but I'm very glad I did. Will you pray for me?" she asked, keeping her voice too low for Noah to hear.

"Of course." Rick yearned to reach out and brush his fingers against her cheek, to hug her close, just for a moment. Instead, aware of Noah watching, he contented himself with a platitude. "Keep trusting, Cassie. Have faith in God's love."

"That is at the root of everything, isn't it?" She studied him, then gave him a smile. "Gotta go. Bye."

"See you." Rick watched Cassie leave the church with a myriad of emotions swirling inside, the strongest of which was a soul-deep yearning to be with her.

If only—

Rick stared at the cross hanging at the front of the church. God had sacrificed so much for him. How could he ask God to forget his vow to never get romantically involved? How could he forget the debt he owed?

He couldn't. But oh, how he wanted to. Certain now that Cassie and Noah could never be the family he'd longed for all these years, Rick knelt and prayed for strength to make the confession he needed to make.

But he also asked God to be with Cassie, to smooth the way so she wouldn't see him as the scoundrel he was when he told her he had lost all her father's money.

And made it nearly impossible for John to be there for his daughter in her moment of greatest need.

"How come you're not getting ready for the Valentine's dance, Noah?"

Cassie stood in the doorway of the computer room. She frowned when her son quickly shut down whatever he was looking at.

"What were you looking at?"

"Just eBay. I wanted to ch-check something out."
He stood up and tried to get past her to leave the room.

"You want to buy something?" Sensing this was important, Cassie held her ground, refusing to move out of the doorway. "What?"

"N-nothing." he said. When she still didn't budge, he shrugged. "R-Rick's guitar."

"Rick's guitar is on eBay? For sale?" Noah nodded. "But he loves that guitar. A friend in seminary gave it to him. Why would he sell it?"

Noah lowered his voice. "I think R-Rick is t-trying to get a s-saxophone for M-Michael."

"By selling his guitar?" Her heart swelled with different emotions—pride that Rick was concerned enough to give up his beloved possession, tenderness over the fact that he wouldn't ask for help but instead found a way on his own, and sadness that she and the boys would no longer be able to watch him play as he led the group in praise.

Rick, the perpetual giver, had spent much time with Michael since he'd returned to Lives, trying to help him break through his depression. He'd said he had an idea of a way to help. But to give up his most precious possession…

"He's selling it because he doesn't have enough money to buy a saxophone, you mean."

Noah nodded.

A sense of loss filled her. She shook her head. "That is a very generous thing for Rick to do."

"I know." Noah nodded. "C-can we buy it, M-mom?"

"Buy it?" As Cassie studied Noah's earnest face, understanding flowed. "And give it back, you mean?

That's such a lovely idea, Noah, but we can't afford it, honey. It would empty our savings."

"S-so? We can s-save again," he said. "I d-don't need anything."

"It's very kind of you to say that and I'm so proud of you for thinking of it." She reached for him, and suppressed the sting of rejection when he rejected her embrace. "But I have to be responsible, honey. If I bought that guitar, it would leave us with no money. What if something happened?"

Noah's disappointment was written all over his face.

"I'm so sorry, Noah," she said, laying a hand on his shoulder. "I want to help Rick as much as you do, but I simply can't do this."

"Y-yeah. I f-figured." He shrugged off her hand. "D-Don't tell a-anyone. R-Rick doesn't kn-know I know." Then he bolted from the room.

Alone, Cassie thought of Rick strumming his guitar, lost in another world, a place where he found solace and peace...

Be bold and strong. Banish fear and doubt! For remember, the Lord your God is with you wherever you go.

The words she'd read from Joshua just this morning convicted Cassie. Rick asked so little for himself, yet he gave so much. Who gave to him?

"Okay, God," she murmured. "This is trust in action."

Cassie sat down in front of a computer and searched eBay until she found what she wanted. Then, holding her breath, she made a bid.

I hope you haven't made a mistake, whispered the voice inside her head.

Cassie shut it down. In her innermost heart, she knew buying back Rick's guitar wasn't a mistake. She could always knit another sweater, work another shift. She was good at finding ways to build up a nest egg.

But it wasn't every day that an opportunity came along to do something wonderful for Rick.

And Rick definitely deserved wonderful.

Rick stood in the shadows of the school auditorium, unashamedly listening to Cassie's conversation with Lucy as they manned the punch bowl at the Valentine's dance.

"So you're playing for the Easter cantata with the choir," Lucy said. "Does that mean you'll be coming to church regularly?"

"I'm not sure," Cassie said with some hesitation. "I'm not really much of a churchgoer. I believe in God but I prefer to meet with Him on my own."

Rick winced, knowing Lucy was not going to like this answer.

"What good does that do?" Lucy demanded.

"I don't know what you mean." Cassie sounded confused.

"The Bible tells us not to forsake the assembling of ourselves—in other words, church!" Lucy was ramping up. Rick had to intervene and rescue Cassie.

He stepped forward and grinned at them. "What kind of punch do we have here?"

"Red," Lucy told him unhelpfully. She handed him a glass. "I was telling Cassie that it's part of a Christian's duty to be faithful at church."

"Lucy, everyone has to come to church in their own

way, in their own time," Rick said gently, trying to defuse Lucy's hard-nosed approach.

"Well, when will that be?" Lucy asked Cassie.

"I, um, don't think I'm ready yet." Cassie glanced at Lucy, her face thoughtful. "Some church members accused me of being involved in my husband's wrongdoing. I thought they should have known the truth because they knew me so I didn't dispute their claims. Now I'm wondering if maybe I should have."

"Why?" Lucy asked.

"Because I realize now that doing so might have made things easier for Noah," Cassie admitted. "If I'd publicly disputed their claims instead of avoiding confrontation, he might not have kept everything pent up inside. Maybe he wouldn't stutter now. I don't know."

"That's the thing. You never know. You do your best and you leave it in the Lord's hands. But you can share it with your Christian friends. We'll understand." Lucy clasped Cassie's hands between her own. "That's why we all admire Rick so much. He helps make our burdens lighter."

Rick felt his cheeks heat.

"I've often wished I had Rick's faith," Cassie admitted to Lucy.

"Rick gained his faith by learning from his mistakes," Lucy said.

"Hey. I'm right here, you know."

They ignored him.

"That's the way we all learn," Lucy told her.

"I don't think Rick's made as many mistakes as I have," Cassie murmured.

If she only knew, he thought.

"Come on," he said, grabbing her hand. "Let's dance. Okay?" he asked Lucy.

She grinned her know-it-all grin and nodded.

"The doubts are back, huh?" Rick asked as he threaded his arm around Cassie's waist. Cassie fit in his arms so perfectly. Their steps across the floor matched as if they'd rehearsed.

"I'm afraid my failure to defend myself was what damaged Noah," she whispered. "I wonder if it did so much damage he'll never get over his speech impediment."

"Your dad once lent me a book about a man named Sidney Cox. He wrote a song you probably know," Rick said, ignoring the guilt that rose up in him at the mention of her father. He paused a moment, then said the words in a very soft voice, "'My Lord knows the way through the wilderness. All I have to do is follow. Strength for today is mine all the way and all that I need for tomorrow.'"

"I remember that." Cassie sighed. He tried to ignore the feel of her head resting on his shoulder. "You're telling me to keep the faith, is that it?"

"Basically, yes." He felt her shoulders shake and knew she was laughing. "What?"

"Do you ever stop being a pastor?" Cassie asked.

Rick couldn't answer. Because if he had, he would have told her that the moment she'd begun to move with him to the music, he'd forgotten his vow, his determination to keep her at arm's length. He'd have said that with her he was simply a normal guy, thrilled to have the most beautiful woman in the world in his arms.

And then he would have told her why nothing could ever come of that.

Because she deserved the truth.

Rick opened his mouth but the words wouldn't come. When the music ended, Cassie thanked him for the dance and went back to her work at the punch table.

His arms felt painfully empty.

Suddenly aware that he was alone on the dance floor, Rick sought out Noah, who was standing on the sidelines, watching.

"How's it going?"

Noah stared at Rick for a long moment. The silence stretched between them until another song began to play, a loud, noisy one that had the kids laughing and twisting to the beat. Then Noah grabbed Rick's arm and leaned near.

"Will y-you teach me t-to box?" he asked. "P-please?"

"Let's go talk about it." With one last glance at Cassie—looking more beautiful than his heart could stand in her black velvet suit with her golden hair framing her lovely face—Rick led the way out of the auditorium.

Chapter Eleven

Two weeks later Cassie played with her coffee cup, on tenterhooks as she waited for Rick's arrival at the restaurant. He'd called her several times to arrange a coffee date, but she kept getting called into work.

Fussing isn't going to get him here any faster, she told herself. *Calm down.*

Saying that didn't help, either. She felt anything but calm when her thoughts centered on Rick Salinger. Her feelings for this man had grown and changed. Every time she talked to him she grew increasingly certain that this man was *different,* that she could trust him as she trusted no other.

Cassie caught her breath when he strode through the door. When he called a greeting to the owner and then grinned at her, a part of her heart melted. He sat down across the table from her, his green eyes expectant. Cassie struggled to control her response to him while they waited for the server to bring his coffee.

How should she begin?

"Cat got your tongue?" Rick teased.

"I'm allergic to cats," she said, then rolled her eyes at the inane remark.

"So?" He leaned back, crossed his booted feet and waited. "You called me," he said.

"I—" She regrouped. "You said you wanted to talk to me and I need to talk to you. About something." She rolled her eyes at herself.

"About Noah?" His eyes darkened with concern on behalf of her son, but Cassie didn't stop to analyze that. She couldn't. She needed to get this said.

"About your guitar." Sorrow flashed briefly across his face before he concealed it.

"I—uh, I don't have it anymore." He blinked. "Actually I sold it."

"I know. I bought it, Rick." Cassie waited for her words to penetrate. "I'm your online buyer."

"You? But…" Dismay filled his face. "You need the money for your savings. You told me how important that is to you."

"Saving pennies isn't as important to me as you having that guitar, which you love. That instrument is part of you. The way you use it to bring joy and peace to so many—" She shook her head. "I couldn't let you sell it."

His jaw hardened as he looked away from her. "I won't take your money, Cassie."

"The deal is done." Cassie reached out to cover his hand with hers and thought how strange it was to comfort him for once. "You have to take the money, Rick. You need it to get Michael his saxophone."

"You know?" His green eyes widened. "How—"

"Shame on you for not consulting me. This is our project. So I did my part." Cassie couldn't stifle the rest any longer. "You've already sent the guitar to Toronto, to a Mrs. Nancy Carr, right? She's my dad's next-door neighbor. Dad will bring your guitar when he comes for a visit sometime in the next few weeks."

"You've reconciled with him." He made a movement forward, as if he was going to hug her, but then he checked himself, substituting a smile instead. "Cassie, that's fantastic!"

"It is, isn't it?" she agreed, trying to ignore the silly feelings of loss that rushed over her at the missed opportunity to be in Rick's arms again, even if for a brief moment. "I got his letter yesterday. You were right, Rick," she admitted shyly. "I did misunderstand what my dad was trying to say. He was warning me not to get caught in the blame game and become bitter."

Rick squeezed her hand, then slowly let it go. "I'm so happy for you, Cassie."

"Thanks. It's not all sweetness and light, but we're both committed to working through the tough parts. There are still things I don't understand, but I realize now, thanks to you, that there's a lot about my dad that I don't know."

Rick leaned back, away from her. Something strange passed across his face, something she didn't quite catch.

"Are you pleased about your guitar, Rick?" she asked, suddenly feeling strangely shy.

"You shouldn't have done it, Cassie." His soft, low voice brimmed with respect and admiration. "I love that guitar, but I could have managed without it."

"I don't believe you should have to," she said, surprised by how strongly she felt. "That guitar is part of who you are, part of your ministry. And don't worry, Rick. Consider the money partial payment on the tithes

I owe God for the past few years. Alicia will help me replenish my account in no time."

He looked dubious.

"I want Michael to have his saxophone as much as you do," she reassured him. "That's what's important. Now you can buy one, can't you?"

"I already did." She laughed as Rick grinned at her. "I'm praying it will help."

"It will, Rick. Of course it will."

"Thank you, Cassie." His words were filled with such tenderness that Cassie couldn't catch her breath for a moment. "We should go—it's nearly time for choir practice."

"Wait—weren't you the one who kept trying to make a coffee date with me? Well, here we are." She was confused by his sudden rush to leave. "Wouldn't now be a good time? We have a few minutes to spare."

That look crossed Rick's face again as he swallowed the last of his coffee. "Let's do it another time."

Bewildered, Cassie gathered up her things. As they walked along the street toward the church, she was aware of speculative stares directed their way. The fact that people might pair them as Alicia had didn't bother her. In fact, she felt proud to be walking beside such an admirable man.

But she wondered if those curious eyes and whispered comments bothered Rick. Was that why he was maintaining a certain distance from her as they walked, careful not to brush shoulders or tease her the way he usually did?

Was he worried about his reputation, being seen with a woman who'd been married to a man who lost church funds? No matter how long the list of Rick's attributes, her past was a black mark that would work against him.

The doubts about Rick's behavior rose in Cassie's mind and would not be silenced.

Rehearsal did not go as well as previous ones had. Even Noah's normally clear, pure voice faltered in the midst of his solo. He actually missed several notes he'd never struggled with before.

Cassie wasn't sure if the problems stemmed from the fact that Rick didn't seem as focused, or because the kids were getting excited about the prospect of performing in public at the Easter morning service, which was now posted all over town. Whatever the reason, they looked as disheartened as she felt by the end of their practice session.

"Don't sweat it, guys. Everyone has a bad rehearsal now and then," Rick consoled them. "We'll do better next time."

"But Easter is only a month away," Rod said, disgruntled. "If we sound like this then everyone's going to laugh at us."

"No one's going to laugh," Rick said firmly. "We're going to be perfect for every note."

"Let's try it again," Michael said.

Rick shook his head. "We've done enough for today. We'll pick it up again next week. Stop worrying. It will come together." He smiled at them. "Go home now. It's almost time for supper."

As the kids left the sanctuary, Cassie studied Rick. He folded the pages of music he'd spread out, pausing every so often to call out a farewell. Though he'd pretended nonchalance, his eyes were dark with concern. Lines grooved deeper around his eyes. He glanced at her once, then quickly looked away, keeping his gaze averted as the kids left.

Only when Noah approached him and said something did Cassie see the faint vestige of a smile. Rick seemed to be shutting her out again, and she found herself wondering exactly what it was he wanted to talk to her about.

As she gathered her things and prepared to leave, her phone rang.

"Cassie, Laurel's trying to get hold of you," Sara said. "She rushed Daniel to the hospital. She's hoping you can meet her there."

"I'll be there in ten minutes." Cassie felt a shiver of dread walk up her spine. What now?

"Y-you'll be where?" Noah asked from behind her.

"The hospital. There's been an emergency with Daniel." She wouldn't say more until she knew more. She called to Rick. "I'm sorry to impose on you, Rick, but I wonder if you could take Noah home. Daniel's at the hospital."

"Sure, no problem. We'll go on my snowmobile. I had it tuned up this morning."

"Helmets?" she asked.

"I'm n-not a b-baby," Noah protested, his face red with anger.

"I insist everyone who rides my snowmobile wears a helmet," Rick said. "We'll be fine. We'll have supper together before I take him back."

"Thank you." Cassie turned to Noah. "Help with the dishes," she murmured sotto voce. "And remember, you need to get that geography assignment done tonight. No computer time until it's finished."

"I kn-know the r-rules," Noah snarled.

"I have to go." Cassie leaned forward to brush a kiss against Noah's cheek. It hurt so much when he reared back, avoiding her touch. She gulped down her tears and said, "I don't know when I'll get home. I love you."

Noah didn't respond.

Cassie turned to Rick. "Thank you for your help," she said quietly. Then she headed for the foyer.

"That wasn't very nice, Noah," she heard Rick say. "Your mother loves you."

"D-does she?" Noah didn't sound convinced.

There wasn't anything Cassie could do about it now, but when she got back to Lives, she would have a long, stern talk with her son and make sure he knew exactly how deeply she cared about him. And one way or another, she was going to have that private conversation with Rick, too.

Something was going on with him. It was time she figured out what it was.

"You want to go a few rounds?" Rick asked, nodding toward his spare room after they'd eaten a mostly silent meal and cleaned up. He'd hung the punching bag there, turning the place into a kind of mini gym, and he sensed that Noah could use some time with the bag to help with whatever was boiling inside him.

Noah's blue eyes sparkled as Rick helped him put on his boxing gloves. It was the first positive sign the boy had given all evening.

Noah worked out on the bag first, then they sparred. It was at least half an hour before Noah spoke.

"D-do you ever g-get so m-mad you want t-to h-hit everybody?" Noah grunted, his face red with exertion.

"Is that how you feel?" Rick felt practically victorious when Noah nodded, finally engaging in conversation with him. "Why?"

"N-nothing's going r-right." He smashed his fist against Rick's glove. "I h-hate it h-here."

"Because?" Rick parried and feinted, moving fast to keep up with the boy's explosion of energy.

"P-people think I'm w-weird."

"What people?" Rick could sense Noah's fury like a red-hot fever. "Kids at school?" Noah nodded. "Your teachers?" Another nod. "Your mom?"

Noah gnawed on his lip. "I'd l-like to s-smash th-them all," he snarled.

The sheer animosity in those words stunned Rick so much he was unprepared for Noah's fist and it connected with his nose. Blood spurted out and pain exploded across his face.

Rick grabbed a towel and pressed it to his nose awkwardly with his gloved hand. It took a long time to stem the flow. Eventually it slowed down enough for him to toss away the towel and use his teeth to untie his gloves. Only then did it dawn on him that Noah hadn't said anything.

Rick looked at the boy. Noah had paled to an unhealthy shade of white. He began to shake, his whole body twitching.

"It's just a nosebleed, Noah. I'm fine. I should have ducked, just like I've been teaching you." Rick summoned a grin, though moving even those few muscles hurt like crazy. But Noah didn't respond.

Ripping off his gloves, Rick grasped Noah's arm and peered into his eyes. "I'm fine. No big deal."

"I'm s-sorry," Noah gulped as tears coursed down his cheeks. "I'm s-so s-sorry."

"I know." Rick unlaced the boy's gloves and removed them. He slid off the protective headgear he'd insisted on, wondering wryly why he hadn't thought of it for himself. Then he wrapped an arm around Noah's shoulder. "Let's go get a drink."

"D-don't you h-have to g-go to the h-hospital?"

"For a nosebleed? You want them to laugh at me?" He held Noah's gaze, refusing to look away as the boy searched his gaze. "I'm not made of sugar, you know."

"I d-didn't m-mean—"

"Noah." Rick stopped him. "People get hurt in boxing sometimes. I warned you about that before we ever started, remember?" He waited for Noah's nod. "Anyway, I'm fine. Almost."

Noah flopped down on a chair in front of the windows. Rick sat down across from him.

"Want to tell me what makes you so angry you're beating up kids at school?"

Noah's head jerked up. "You know?"

"I've suspected for a while. Something's clearly eating at you, Noah. Let's get it out in the open." He prayed silently for God to give him the right words. "Talk to me. I only want to help."

"I'm not going to be hurt anymore," Noah said in a tight voice. "I'm not going to be made fun of ever again. If someone tries, I'll stop it."

Aghast at the admissions he was hearing, Rick sat silent, knowing Noah needed the release this honesty would bring. But the more he heard, the more he wondered— Why? What lay beneath the boy's pain?

The phone rang.

"Rick, is Noah still there?" Cassie's voice, breathless and worried came across the line.

"Yes." Just hearing her voice sent his every sense into high alert. *Get in control.* "I was about to take him to Lives," Rick told her.

"No! Don't do that." She inhaled. "I need a very big favor. Can Noah stay with you overnight, Rick?"

"Sure. What's the problem?"

"Meningitis." That one word drove all other thoughts out of his head. "Daniel has symptoms of bacterial meningitis. If that's what it is, it's very contagious. I don't want Noah to return to Lives and risk any more exposure than he already has. He's okay, isn't he?"

"He's fine." Rick caught Noah watching him. The kid rolled his eyes and shook his head, as if annoyed by his mother's concern. "You take care of yourself and your patients. I'll watch out for Noah."

"Thank you." Silence stretched between them for a moment, and then her voice dropped. "Rick?"

"I'm here."

"Can you pray? Hard. All the kids were probably exposed, but if Michael catches it..." Her voice trailed away and in that moment the severity of the situation hit him full force.

Meningitis was serious. Noah and Michael had both been exposed.

But so had Cassie.

Rick felt as if the world stopped. She was around sick people all the time. Hospital viruses were often the most dangerous. She could catch this thing herself and—die?

God, no.

"I know it's a lot to ask you," she whispered in a broken tone. "You probably had plans for tonight and I'm ruining them and—"

"Cassie," he said softly. "Noah and I will be praying.

You can count on that. And on God," he added, hoping to bolster her fledgling faith. "God knows what's at stake. He's right there with you."

He scolded himself for falling back on a standby platitude and thought what a sham he'd become. He was supposed to be ministering to her, yet his own doubts were derailing him.

"Thank you, Rick. I mean that."

Rick held the phone long after she'd hung up. Tenderness rushed over him in a wave of appreciation for this precious woman who took to heart the welfare of the boys at Lives and her patients while she worried for her own son.

How can I shut her out, God? How am I supposed to ignore her when my heart wants to be with her always, when every day that I don't talk to her seems empty and dull? How can I keep my vow to You?

Why won't You take these feelings away?

"Doesn't Mom kn-know I'm fine?" Noah's face contorted in a glower. "She t-treats me like a b-baby."

"Actually she's treating you like an adult, Noah," Rick said. "She asked us to pray for Daniel. They think he might have caught a very serious disease."

"Oh." His blue eyes narrowed. "Am I g-going to g-get it?"

"I hope not, but I can't say for sure," Rick explained quietly. "If you get a fever or start to feel unwell, I'll take you to the hospital right away. But for tonight your mom wants you to stay here. Okay?"

Noah nodded. "W-will she b-be okay?" he asked, uncertainty lacing his voice.

"Let's ask God to protect her," Rick said. But though

he prayed as hard as he could, he felt as if his prayers simply bounced off the thick barriers between him and God.

Later, when Noah was asleep, words that Cassie's father had once spoken to him returned, a strong admonition he'd given after Rick had asked for his help to get into the ministry.

"Don't make any vows you can't keep, son. If you're going to promise God to do His work, to let Him use you, you'd better be prepared to deny yourself. Keeping your promises could cost far more than you ever imagined."

For the very first time since he'd accepted Christ as his Savior, Rick regretted his promise to remain single. Worse than that, doubts about God's purpose for him had taken root. Maybe he wasn't supposed to be in Churchill.

You don't deserve her. How could she ever love you, the man responsible for the childhood she spent without a father? The man who cost her father his precious savings, savings that could have helped her when she was desperate for help?

This is the payment to be exacted for your greed.

Rick was willing to pay, to give up every dream he'd ever dreamed, if that was what God wanted, if it would help Cassie. But how was he to stop the sweet burst of joy that filled his heart whenever he saw her face? How was he to ignore the rush of love that burst inside like fireworks when she laughed or said his name or asked his help?

Love?

His heart stopped as the knowledge flowed through every cell of his body.

He loved Cassie Crockett.

Strong and beautiful, sweet and giving, Cassie was

altogether lovely, in spirit and in action. She was everything he'd imagined a woman he'd love would be, from the moment he'd started seeing her face in his dreams so many years ago, not long after his first glance at her picture on her father's desk. It was Cassie's face he'd used as a model whenever he'd dreamed of being loved. Though he hadn't known her then, it was her he imagined by his side.

Now, knowing Cassie, Rick could imagine a future brimming with joy and love, caring and giving.

And yet...

He'd made a vow. That vow meant Cassie—precious, beloved Cassie—could never be his, no matter how much his heart longed for her. All the glorious possibilities Rick had glimpsed through the years shrank and faded away as he sat shrouded in darkness and faced the truth of his future.

There could be no love to finally fill that vacant spot inside him. No wife, no family to protect and plan for, no chance to nurture and love. He could have none of that because he owed a debt.

Hours passed as Rick struggled to surrender the love that beckoned him to forsake his faith and follow his heart. Finally, aching and empty, he let go of it all.

Your will, God. I will do Your will.

Chapter Twelve

"Daniel's going to be fine. It isn't meningitis, it's a virulent flu," Cassie told Rick over the phone.

The reassuring knowledge that Rick was there to listen, to care, to help, sent sweet joy to her heart. How she treasured the bond of sharing with him.

"Thank God," he said, and she knew he meant it.

"Yes. We've seen a lot more cases come in through the night, however. Did you get your flu shot this year, Rick?"

"I did."

Cassie paused, seeing his face in her mind. Precious face, precious man. "How's Noah?"

"He's fine," Rick assured her. "School has been canceled so he's working here."

"He had his flu shot last fall so it's fine for you to take him back to Lives. Apparently, Daniel was the only one of the boys who hadn't had it." A flush of warmth suffused her. "I can't thank you enough for stepping in last night. I appreciate all you've done for Noah."

"No problem." Rick paused then asked, "When will you finish there?"

"Not for a while. This virus has taken out a lot of staff. I'm filling in where they need me. It's been crazy busy." She stopped to yawn. "I'm going to grab a couple hours of sleep here and then I'll get back on duty."

"Is there anything I can do?" he asked.

The words were kind, but Cassie heard distance in Rick's voice. Maybe he was tired of having a kid around, especially a cranky, grumpy one.

And yet, she couldn't quite make herself believe that was the reason. She'd been hearing the distance in his voice on and off for a while now.

"Cassie?"

"Sorry, I zoned out for a minute." She got her brain in gear. "You could get the boys to check on your elderly parishioners. This virus hits seniors very hard. The sooner they come in to the hospital, the better."

"Good idea. Noah and I will pick up the others if Laurel agrees. How are *you* holding up, Cassie?"

"A little rest and I'll get my second wind back." She hesitated. "How did you fare after a night with my son?"

"Actually, it was fun." His voice dropped. Cassie figured Noah must be nearby. "We played some games after dinner. He beat me, as usual."

"It was a lot easier to do my job knowing you were there for him," she said. "Thank you for being such a good friend."

Would Rick hear in her words how much *more* she wanted than friendship?

"You're welcome. Now is there anything I can do for you personally?" The briskness of Rick's voice was at odds with what he was asking. "Anything?" he repeated.

"If I phoned Laurel and asked her to pack a bag, could you pick it up when you get the boys and drop it here on your way past?" Cassie asked after a moment's thought.

Rick agreed and then quickly got off the phone. Cassie worried that maybe by asking him to care for Noah, she'd asked too much. And yet, Rick loved kids. He'd become a pro at coaxing Noah out of whatever mood he was in. No, something else was bothering him.

And Cassie now felt sure it was whatever he'd been trying to tell her about for a while now, but never quite managed to say.

Confused, Cassie went to sprawl on a cot in the staff room. Too tired to puzzle it out, she finally closed her eyes and let sleep claim her.

But it wasn't the restorative sleep Cassie needed. Instead, she dreamed of the handsome preacher. Though she tried to reach him, he kept backing away, insisting he couldn't care for her, that she wasn't the kind of woman he needed for a wife. She hadn't helped her husband through his crisis, nor was she having success with her son. She was a failure.

Cassie woke feeling as if a gray cloud hung over her. She couldn't shake the disquieting thought that trusting Rick so completely was a mistake.

She rose and went down to the cafeteria for a cup of coffee and something to eat before she went back to work. Thanks to the odd dream she'd had, she felt strangely subdued when Rick entered, carrying a small bag.

"I brought your things. What is *that?*" he asked, looking askance at the half-full bowl in front of her.

"Porridge. Somehow I don't seem to have the energy to eat it," she admitted wearily.

"Leave it. I'll get you some real food." He walked

over to the counter, flashed a smile at the woman behind it and soon returned with a fluffy, steaming omelet. "Try that," he said setting it before her.

"The cafeteria doesn't make omelets," Cassie said,
unable to stop staring at him as her soul soaked in the
beloved lines of his tired face.

"They do today. Eat up. You need some protein."
Rick leaned back in his chair, crossed his arms over
his chest and raised an eyebrow. "Well?" he demanded
when she didn't pick up her fork.

Cassie obediently placed a forkful of the omelet in
her mouth. Her eyes widened as the delicious flavors
woke up her senses. Rick got up and refilled her coffee cup, and got one for himself. He waited until she'd
finished everything on the plate before he spoke again.
"Thanks for suggesting we visit the seniors," he said
quietly. "We've lost Mr. Saunders but we managed to
get help for others who were in trouble."

"I heard about Mr. Saunders," Cassie said. "I'm so
sorry."

"Thanks." Rick's chin drooped to his chest, his eyes
downcast. "He was an amazing man. His integrity never
wavered. What he said, he did." Rick said the words
slowly, thoughtfully.

That feeling that something was going on with him,
something she didn't understand, nagged at Cassie.

"I hope people remember me as fondly as everyone
speaks of him." Touched by Rick's dejection, Cassie
reached out to rest her hand on his shoulder to express
her sympathy. He didn't immediately pull away. For
a moment, the pastor leaned into her touch, as if he
needed it to deal with his sorrow.

But a moment later Rick drew back. He lifted his

head to look at her and Cassie realized something had changed in their relationship. Something had come between them.

"What's wrong?" she whispered as fear built inside. "You can tell me, Rick. In fact, I think you've been trying to tell me for some time now."

He looked directly at her. "You've been a good friend, Cassie."

Emphasis on *friend*. She'd been right. He was distancing himself. But why?

"And you've been a good friend to me," she said very quietly. "What's bothering you, Rick? Can I help?"

"Now *you* want to help *me?*" Rick gave a soft chuckle. "Don't you have enough to do, woman? You're working overtime, you're dead tired and you want to help me?"

"If I can." She held his gaze and her breath, waiting.

"You're quite a lady, Cassie Crockett." Respect laced his voice. She also thought she heard a note of caring in his kind words. But if he did, why was he trying so hard to build distance between them?

She wanted so much to help him, to give back just a bit of the help he'd so unstintingly offered her. But more than that, she wanted to share the burden of whatever troubles made his shoulders bow.

Most of all, she wanted to love him, and have him love her.

Love. I love him.

For a moment that knowledge paralyzed Cassie. All she could do was stare at him, filling her senses with his presence, letting the rush of joy suffuse her body.

She loved him. But he was hurting.

"Please let me help you," she whispered.

Rick gazed at her. The pure emerald-green of his

eyes laid bare his emotions—sadness, grief, helplessness, but worst of all a despondency Cassie had never seen in him before.

"I can't."

Stung, Cassie drew back.

"I need to tell you something," he said, his voice raw, ragged, as if he was having trouble breathing. "Something important."

Her pager went off. Cassie wanted to scream at the interruption. She needed to know what was wrong between them so she could fix it.

"I'm sorry," she said, rising slowly.

"I know." Rick rose, too, carrying her bag. "I'll leave this at the desk for you. You can pick it up later."

"Thank you." She couldn't make herself go, couldn't leave him like this. The pager went off a second time. "Rick, let's make sure we talk later, okay?"

"Take care of yourself, Cassie," Rick said, his voice hoarse and strained.

Why did it sound as if he was saying goodbye?

Aching for the pain he seemed to be in, Cassie stood on tiptoe and pressed a kiss against his cheek.

"You take care of yourself, too, Rick," she said, then hurried away with no understanding of what had just happened between them.

Lord? I trust You. Please help him.

Cassie halted, and took a moment to amend her prayer.
Please help us.

For seven long days the flu epidemic raged through Churchill. Rick drove himself to be the pastor his community needed. He prayed by parishioners' bedsides through long, lonely nights and worry-filled days. He fetched and carried whenever he was asked. He drove countless people to the hospital. He made sure those who were fighting the flu at home had all they needed.

He made himself as useful as he could around Lives, too. He and Teddy Stonechild helped Laurel take care of the boys' meals so Sara could stay home and keep her baby safe.

In a way, the long nights and wearying days were a panacea, allowing Rick to avoid the painful acceptance of what he knew God was asking him to give up—what he now accepted as a soul-deep love for Cassie. He told himself he kept up his frenetic pace because his job was to minister to people.

But that wasn't the whole truth.

As day after weary day passed, each time he caught a glimpse of Cassie in the hospital, all thoughts of his ministry fled. The vibrancy that had always characterized her bouncing gold curls and melting brown eyes faded. Her beautiful face grew thin and drawn as she lost weight from working so hard. The only thing that cheered Rick was seeing her never-faltering smile that was always at the ready for patients and staff alike. When she smiled at *him,* he wished for the privilege of seeing it every day for the rest of his life.

But Rick knew that could never be. No one could wreak the kind of pain and havoc he had and get away scot-free.

She smiled at him now, as she sat across from him in their now-familiar meeting spot in the cafeteria. He could hear the harshness in his own voice and knew concern underlay it.

"You need to get out of here," he said, hating how

pale she was, and worried by the way her hand trembled
when she lifted her coffee cup.

"A few more hours," she murmured, closing her eyes
to savor the brew. "Fresh staff will arrive then and I'll
be able to leave."

"Can you last that long?" He struggled to stem his
irritation at whoever had asked her to keep working
when she was obviously so exhausted.

"Oh, Rick, how can you ask that?" She shook her
head at him and for a moment her lovely brown eyes
sparkled with a hint of mischief. "Don't you know 'I
can do all things through Christ who strengthens me'?"

He had to smile. In spite of all the difficulty she'd
endured, or perhaps because of it, Cassie's faith had
grown by leaps and bounds this week. He'd overheard
her quoting an encouraging verse to another staff member. She'd even told him yesterday that seeing the pre-
cariousness of life had made her realize she needed to
keep her faith strong. For that Rick gave praise.

"I'm not the only one who's overworked," she said.
"You've been run off your feet looking after everyone,
haven't you?" Her big brown eyes peeked through the
stray strands of blond curls that tumbled onto her forehead. "I hope you're taking care of yourself."

"Don't worry about me." Rick had made up his mind
that today, he would finally tell her what he'd done to
her father. And yet as he sat here, looking at her, feeling what he felt for her, he realized he couldn't do it.

The knowledge shook him to the core. How could
he be so weak, so selfish?

"I *do* worry about you, Rick." Cassie's eyes sent his
a silent message that made his skin hum. His fingers
itched to push that tendril of gold off her face. "I'm

going to go finish my shift." She stood and looked at him for a moment longer, clearly giving him an opportunity to say something more. When he didn't, she gave him a tired smile and turned.

"I'll talk to you later," he called to her.

She waved a hand and kept going.

Rick left the hospital moments later. He needed to pray for strength to tell the truth. The fact that he had been tempted to keep quiet, to let the silence about his past continue, was unbearable.

Because he now realized that Cassie cared for him. The look in her eyes, the way she'd touched him—suddenly everything was clear. She felt about him the same way he felt about her.

Not my will, but Thine, he repeated in his mind over and over again, feeling his heart crack as he drove to the church.

Cassie stood outside the hospital and drew the frosty March air into her lungs. It felt so good to finally escape the sickness and loss, to let the sunshine warm her skin.

She saw a dark-haired man bend to lift a child from a car and her heart stopped. Rick. She opened her mouth to call out, then realized it wasn't him at all.

She laughed out loud. Rick was so much a part of her, in her mind and her heart, that she thought of him constantly. Those moments in the cafeteria—when she'd finally realized that she loved Rick as she'd never loved before—had been the start of exploring a new vision of what her future could be, a future that she'd never dreamed was possible.

Rick filled her mind and her senses, her dreams and her waking moments. He was everything a man should be: strong without being overbearing, gentle but firm when necessary, caring, committed, thoughtful. The list could go on and she'd never fully describe the man who'd come to mean the world to her.

And he cared about Noah.

Thank You for giving me this love, she prayed as she walked toward her car in the staff parking lot. *Please help me now.*

She needed help because she was going to tell Rick how she felt. She was going to bare her heart to him and trust that he returned her love, that God would work it out.

Cassie kept a steady stream of prayers flowing as she unplugged her car's block heater, then sat inside and waited for the engine to warm up. Doubts crept in, making her wonder if today was the right day, if this was the right time, if Rick would reject her. But Cassie resolutely pushed away her uncertainties and recited verses she'd memorized, verses designed to build her trust in God.

As she did, an idea flickered through her mind. So often she asked God for things, just as Noah often asked her. Before the flu epidemic, he'd pestered her about taking boxing lessons. Cassie had staunchly refused. She'd attended a boxing match once with Eric and had been appalled, so she'd remained adamantly against her son being subjected to such violence.

Did God feel the same when He refused things His children pleaded for, things He knew would be detrimental to them? He was her heavenly Father, He loved and cared for her. Sometimes He said no to her requests because He knew what was best.

Wouldn't God, like any other parent, appreciate being thanked?

Enter into His gates with thanksgiving and a thanks offering, and into His courts with praise! Be thankful and say so to Him, bless and affectionately praise His name.

When was the last time she'd thanked God for anything?

With a grimace, Cassie shoved a CD in the player and let the heart-lifting melodies soak in. After ten minutes, immensely cheered by her private worship service and with the car giving off a toasty heat, she pulled out of her parking spot.

As she drove to Rick's home, she couldn't help noticing the brilliance of the sun. The days were longer now. Easter was just two weeks away. She wondered how the choir and band were doing. Rick had said nothing about practice, probably because he didn't want to worry her when she was so involved with her patients. But Noah had told her during their daily phone call that the group kept practicing.

Singing was the one thing she and Noah could consistently talk about without arguing.

Cassie's mood continued to lift the closer she got to Rick's house. It stood isolated, alone on the cliff top at the end of the street. His car was there, as well as his snowmobile, so she knew he was home.

The full realization of what she was about to do— bare her heart to this man she'd come to trust—made her pulse thrum with excitement and hope. She pulled into his drive and parked her car.

This was it.

"Be with me, Lord," she murmured as she walked

over the snow, footsteps crunching loudly in the silence of the afternoon. "Soon Rick will know how much I care for him. Please, please let him love me back." She inhaled then pressed the doorbell.

There was a long delay. Cassie was about to press it a second time when the door was suddenly flung open.

Cassie stared at her son, standing there in some kind of unfamiliar workout clothes with boxing gloves on his hands and a helmet covering his head. She stepped inside and pushed the door closed behind her, frowning.

"Noah? What are you doing?"

"B-boxing with R-Rick." She could hear the challenge in his voice as he told her, "We p-practice lots. Rick s-says I'm g-getting g-good."

"Who is it, Noah?" Rick appeared behind her son, also wearing gloves. His welcoming smile bloomed when he saw Cassie. "Hi."

She ignored the greeting.

"You're teaching my son to box?" she asked in disbelief. He nodded as if it were a perfectly normal thing to do. "Why?"

"Because he asked me to." Rick motioned to a chair. "Do you want to sit down? It won't take a minute for him to change."

"No, I don't want to sit down." Cassie blazed inside. "How could you do this, Rick?"

He blinked, confusion clouding his eyes. "I don't understand—"

Furious with him, Cassie turned to her son. "What I want to know is why you specifically disobeyed me, Noah." She held his defiant gaze. "I refused when you asked me the first time and I kept on refusing," she reminded. "I know you heard me. So why?"

"Cassie, I didn't know you'd forbidden it," Rick interrupted. "I'm truly sorry. I had no idea I was going against your wishes."

"But you didn't bother to ask my permission, either, did you? The first time you ever mentioned boxing to Noah, I know you could see that I didn't like the idea." That same old wall of distrust began building inside, brick by impenetrable brick. "You should have asked me," she said.

"D-don't blame R-Rick!" Noah shouted.

She stared at him, shocked by the fury he directed at her.

"I n-need to d-defend myself." Scorn filled his bitter words. "Y-You turned your b-back on m-me and everyone else. You c-closed down instead of f-fighting for what you b-believe. I'm n-not g-going to be l-like you, M-Mom."

"How can you say that?" Bewildered, Cassie could only stare at the son she would gladly give her life for. "Your father—"

"D-dad would n-never have let people diss us l-like you d-did. You g-gave them b-back their m-money, but they k-kept on s-saying we s-stole it and y-you l-let them. You d-didn't s-stand up for us. Y-You didn't s-stand up for *me*." Tears welled but he dashed them away angrily. "Y-you didn't even n-notice what I w-was going through."

"That's not true."

"I think we're finally learning what's been bothering Noah for so long," Rick said in a very gentle tone. His arm slid around her shoulder as if to impart strength. Cassie, confused and brimming with suspicion, tried to pull away. But Rick drew her to a chair and urged her into it.

"Listen," he urged in a whisper. "He needs to say this."

Cassie could not tear her gaze from his. The tenderness she saw there was a balm to her injured heart. She stared into his green eyes, her confusion growing. Had she been wrong to trust this man? *No,* her heart whispered. Rick would help her, whatever was wrong. Somehow she knew that one thing was true in spite of the doubts that flooded in.

Finally she nodded.

"You have the floor, Noah." Cassie saw something unspoken flow between them. "Get it off your chest, but when you're finished, you're going to listen to what your mother has to say."

Noah drew in a deep breath, then turned to her. In unforgiving, bitter language he blamed her for everything that had happened since his father's death. "I w-was the school f-fool," he said, his tone blistering. "My f-friends c-called me n-names, said I w-was a crook. They s-said we were u-using the church's m-money."

"We weren't," she said, unable to remain totally silent under the assault.

"I d-didn't know th-that. All I knew was that w-we didn't g-go to ch-church anymore," Noah said in a cold, hard tone. "Y-you were always w-working. I h-had nobody t-to talk to when it g-got r-really bad. N-nobody believed m-me when I s-said we didn't t-take the m-money." His face tightened. "Th-they would h-have believed y-you. B-but you w-wouldn't s-say anything. I g-got b-beat up b-because you w-wouldn't t-tell the t-truth."

A part of Cassie was nearly ecstatic that Noah was finally talking. She prayed that he would finally find healing. Another part of her reeled at his accusations. But as he spoke, her son's blame, his censure and most of all his feeling of being alone gutted her. All she could do was listen.

At last Noah finished, pale but still defiant. Cassie couldn't speak.

"So because you were mad at your mother, because you blamed her for the pain you suffered when your dad died, because you needed to feel strong and invincible, that's why you started picking fights?" Rick said.

Noah bowed his head.

"Picking fights?" Cassie said, her voice raw. "Noah was bullied."

"No." Rick shook his head. "Tell her, Noah." When Noah didn't respond, Rick continued. "You deliberately picked on other kids, pushing them around until they couldn't take it anymore and they hit you. Isn't that true?" Rick asked. After a long pause, the boy nodded. "You lashed out to get rid of the hurt and in doing so, you hurt other people."

Cassie saw the truth of Rick's accusations on Noah's face.

"H-how d-did you know?" Noah mumbled.

"It was just a hunch, something you said the day you gave me a nosebleed."

"He gave you a—" Cassie began.

Rick cut her off, his focus on Noah. "Thank you for admitting the truth, Noah."

"I feel like I don't know you at all," Cassie whispered, aghast at what she was hearing.

"You don't know m-me," Noah growled.

Rick's glower marred his handsome face. "I'm not sure I do, either. You conned me into teaching you boxing because you needed a way to get the upper hand with kids who wouldn't back down from your threats."

"Yes." The admission hissed from Noah's lips.

"The thing is, I never realized your mother had forbidden it." Rick's voice was hard. "I don't like being used, Noah. I especially don't like being used against your mother."

"I'm s-sorry," Noah said without remorse.

"Are you?" Rick held his gaze. "You had lots to say about the people in your former church and how they treated you so miserably. You accused your mother of not standing up to them." Rick's severe tone held Noah captive.

"Sh-she didn't," Noah sputtered.

"No, she didn't, because your mother is the strongest woman I've ever known. She stood tall, did what she could to make amends for your dad's mistake and then picked up and moved here to help *you*." Rick shook his head when Noah tried to argue. "I think *you're* the one who isn't standing up to the problem. Instead of facing the issues and dealing with them, you're hiding behind anger." Rick's tone softened. "You hurt kids who only wanted to be friends with you, Noah. You did to them exactly what people did to you. You've got a lot of burned bridges to repair if you want to have real friends here."

Cassie could stay silent no longer. "I'm not sure I understand everything you're saying, Rick." She frowned at him. "But I wish you'd come to me with what you suspected about Noah. I feel like you've kept things hidden from me."

Rick met her gaze and held it. "I'm sorry. I wanted to wait until you were more rested before I opened this wound. Now that everything's come to light, I'm sure Noah can clear up any questions you have."

"I have quite a few." She looked at her son. "You've made a lot of assumptions about me. You judged me and condemned me, but whether you believe it or not, everything I've done has been for you." When Noah had no response, she said, "We'll talk at home. Get your things and let's go."

"Cassie, I'm sorry—"

"Not now, Rick." Cassie waited while Noah pulled sweatpants and a shirt over his training clothes. She couldn't shed her feelings of betrayal—Rick should have told her, should have clued her in. "Let's go, Noah."

Rick walked them to the door. When Cassie looked into his eyes, she could think of nothing to say. Finally, she stepped outside into the snow, leaving Rick behind her as she wondered how everything had gone so horribly wrong.

She'd come over here to tell Rick she was in love with him. And now here she was, feeling betrayed, crushed, heartbroken.

How quickly things could change and fall apart.

What a fool she'd been.

Chapter Thirteen

Cassie had been gone all of two minutes when Rick grabbed his keys and dashed out the door to his car. He'd put off talking to her for so long now it was embarrassing. What kind of man hides from the truth the way he'd been hiding? And he called himself a pastor?

His heart was pounding as he drove to Lives. He was driving too fast, recklessly even. At the rate he was going, he'd probably get there before her, if he didn't end up crashing his car.

Breathe, he told himself. *You're almost there. The truth is almost out. Just breathe.*

When he pulled into the driveway, Cassie and Noah were about to go inside. Cassie nodded at her son as if to tell Noah to go ahead without her, and then she waited, arms crossed, for Rick to approach.

And when he did, she gave him a piece of her mind.

"I trusted you," she said quietly. "I let go of all my inhibitions and I put my faith in you because I was certain you had our best interests at heart."

"I do," he said, chagrin under his quiet words.

"Do you?" she asked. There was a hard edge to her

voice that Rick had never heard before. "It doesn't feel like you do when you're keeping Noah's deceit to yourself."

"I didn't know it was deceit! But I was going to talk to you. I was waiting for the right time—"

"I was, too," she whispered. "Do you know why I came to see you today, Rick? I was going to tell you that I thought we had something special between us. Now I'm wondering. I want so badly to trust you. I'm trying to trust you but you keep putting this distance between us."

Rick couldn't deny it, and he offered no defense. With a heavy sigh, Cassie turned to go inside. He gripped her arm, halting her movement.

She turned, frowning at his hand on her arm, and said. "I feel like I don't know you or Noah."

"You *don't* know me, Cassie. You shouldn't trust me because I don't deserve it." Just saying those words made him feel lighter. He was getting closer. Closer to telling her everything.

"Why?" she asked, hesitantly.

It was time.

"Cassie, I am a much bigger cause of the trouble between you and father than you realize. Because of me, your father lost…everything. He lost his life savings, and money he had put aside for you and Noah. I'm the reason he couldn't help you when you needed him most."

Cassie's face registered many emotions as she processed what Rick had just told her, but all she said was "Tell me."

Rick took a deep breath, air rushing into his lungs for what felt like the first time in months. "You know

I grew up on the streets," he began. "I was alone. Until I met your dad."

"You told me about that."

"John helped me graduate from high school, and he helped me get a scholarship to go to college where I majored in finance. I became a stockbroker. I was good at it. I took risks and they paid off. Hugely." The irony of it all washed over him once again. "I had money enough for two lifetimes. I should have been satisfied, but taking risks became a game to me—how far could I go? The more risks I took, the wealthier my clients got and the more I needed to risk to get the high I craved. I was the golden boy of brokers." He paused a moment, remembering those heady days with chagrin.

"What did you do to my father?" Cassie's voice snapped him back to the present.

He stared at her, his soul dark with guilt. "One of my clients was a publisher. I made him very wealthy with some high-risk investments. That gave him the idea to publish a series on high-risk, high-return investing for do-it-yourself investors. He asked me to write one book in a series he was publishing. My topic was risk-taking in the market." Rick ran a hand through his hair as he tried to figure out how to continue.

"Okay." She stared at him in confusion.

"It was a game to me, Cassie, a way to show off. I included every risky maneuver I'd ever tried in it and some new ones I was trying on my clients just so I could write about them. My name wasn't on the cover, so I thought, where's the risk?" He shook his head.

Cassie sat silent, her eyes widening with every word.

"I used your father's money for the riskiest move I ever made because I wanted to repay him for everything

he'd done for me. His account built like crazy and I figured my approach was paying off. I put it in the book
and it sold like crazy."

Cassie's face said everything he knew she was thinking. If he was so wealthy, what was he doing here in
Churchill, living in a dinky house, having to sell his
guitar to raise funds for Michael's saxophone?

"I'm sorry but I don't see—"

"I thought I was invincible and I took one gamble too
many," he said, hating the words even as he said them.
Guilt crushed him over the pain he'd caused with his
arrogance. "I lost everything I owned and everything
my clients had entrusted to me. I had a fiancée at the
time—I lost her family's benevolent fund." Rick swallowed. "And I lost the money your father had spent a
lifetime saving."

He waited as moments passed and his words sank
in. Horror filled Cassie's face.

"That's why he wouldn't help me," she said, understanding dawning.

"Yes. Because he couldn't. Because of me. Because
of my greed." Rick felt sick at the words. But he plowed
on, desperate to confess everything. "Overnight I went
from top of the heap to the bottom. I became the in-
vestment guru brought down by his own folly. I was a
laughingstock. My friends didn't know me anymore.
The woman I loved left me."

"I'm sorry, Rick." Cassie's brown eyes shone with
tears.

"Don't be sorry for me, Cassie," he ordered, angered
by her tender response. "I got exactly what I deserved.
I was showing off, showing them all that a kid from the
street could beat the rich folks at their own game." *Oh,*

Lord, forgive me for my pride. "I used other people's life savings to get approval and acceptance. I cost families their homes, their futures. For God's sake, don't feel sorry for me."

The sadness on Cassie's face—the tenderness—remained. It was almost more than Rick could bear.

"The worst thing is, *I* deserved to lose everything, but they didn't. Your father didn't. They all trusted me and I abused that trust."

"You don't have to tell me this, Rick. It's none of my business," Cassie whispered.

"Yes, it is! You're one of the people I hurt with my greed. My actions caused irreparable damage in your life and for that I am profoundly sorry." Rick swallowed.

"What did my father do?" Cassie asked gently.

"I'd decided to end my life when your dad found me. He should have hated me for what I'd done to him." The wonder of it was as profound now as it had been when it first happened. "Instead, your father helped me sober up. Then he told me that even though I'd made such a colossal mess of my life, God still had plans for me, good plans. I stayed with him and he helped me get straightened out. Every day he taught me about God. And when I decided I wanted to commit my life to Him, your father helped me get into seminary."

"I'm glad he was there for you," she said simply. There was no regret in her voice, no blame.

There should have been.

"The day I was ordained, I made a promise to God." Rick summoned his courage—this was the last thing he had to confess to the beautiful woman standing in front of him, her gorgeous face radiating compassion he didn't deserve.

"Say it, Rick," she whispered.

"I knew I could never make up for the lives I'd ruined. So I made a vow to give up my dreams and goals and dedicate my entire life to His cause." He lifted his head and looked directly into Cassie's eyes. "That's why I've gotten so involved at Lives. Your dad helped me understand that my showboating, my high-living, my risk-taking was all a plea for someone to love me, to see past the kid who'd lived in the gutter and accept me as worthy of love. I was trying to fill a hole in my heart that no one but God could fill."

She nodded as if she understood.

"That's why I work with the boys at Lives," he said quietly. "I want them to know that no matter how bad it was, no matter what they did, they are loved, that I am there for them always."

"The boys know that," she said gently, her eyes shining.

"I hope so." He struggled to resist the urge to reach for her, to pull her into his arms. He would never have the right to do that again. "I'm very touched that you care for me, Cassie. But you can't waste your love on me. I promised God I'd atone for my guilt by giving up the one thing I've always longed for—a family of my own, someone to love. Someone who loves me."

Cassie was silent for a very long time, studying him. He held her gaze, forcing himself to stand up to her scrutiny. "You're saying that you're trying to make up for your mistakes by never letting yourself love, is that it?"

In the depths of her brown eyes, Rick could suddenly see unfathomable pain. "So instead of filling that empty spot in your soul with money, now you're going to fill it with duty."

"If you want to put it that way."

"Tell me something, Rick. Do you love me?"

The words crashed over him like a tidal wave. Every fiber of his being wanted to tell her *yes*. "It doesn't matter," he said.

"It does to me. Answer the question."

He knew that he owed her the truth, as painful as it was to admit. "Yes, Cassie, I do." He watched as her eyes filled with tears. "But nothing can come of it. I'm in debt to God," Rick said somberly.

"A debt of love, which you are trying to repay with sacrifice," she murmured.

"Cassie, I don't deserve to love and be loved. Keeping my vow is the only way I know to atone for what I've done." He raked a hand through his hair, wishing he could make her understand.

She simply looked at him.

"I wish I could erase it all. I wish I could be the man you need, the man you think you love. But even if I could, what I've done would always stand between us." Rick desperately craved the sound of her voice, her touch on his hand, something. But she remained still and silent. "I have to keep my vow. That's why there can never be anything between us. I'm sorry, Cassie."

"So am I, Rick." With one last look at him, Cassie silently turned and disappeared inside Lives.

Rick stood there a moment, stunned by the overwhelming waves of loss that swamped him. He ached to hold this woman he'd come to love. He hadn't meant to love her, but it had happened because he'd lost sight of his promise. Once again he'd failed God.

In that moment, Rick knew the time had come to leave Churchill.

His spirit felt lost, cast adrift, decimated at the thought of never again seeing Cassie and Noah.

Lord? Where are you? Help me, please. No response. Had God abandoned him because he'd forgotten his vow?

After Easter, after the kids had presented their cantata, he'd leave this place he'd come to love, this place that seemed like home.

And once he was away from here, maybe Rick could find a way to end this desperate need to have Cassie in his arms, in his heart, in his life.

Cassie entered Lives feeling as if she'd been knocked to the ground not once but twice. First Noah's demoralizing tirade had rocked her world. Then Rick's bombshell explanation that his love for her could never be realized had doused the joy she'd reveled in earlier. Life had seemed full of possibilities this morning—now it seemed empty.

Noah stood waiting in the hall.

"My room," she said to him quietly. "You and I are going to talk."

Noah shot her a dark look, but did as she asked. Cassie closed the door, suddenly overwhelmed. Tears that could not be suppressed rose in a great tide of sadness and she let them fall, unable to stem her sobs. "Mom?" Noah gazed at her uncertainly. "D-don't cry, Mom."

The tears kept flowing. "All I wanted when I decided to move us here was for you to be happy. But you're not. I've done everything wrong."

"No, y-you haven't," he said.

"Then how do you explain the fact that you've been hurting other people intentionally, Noah?" she demanded, dashing away the tears from her cheeks. "The worst thing is, you hurt them to make yourself feel better. Do you realize you could be sent to jail, just like the boys at Lives have?"

"It's m-my fault." Noah closed his eyes. "I kn-know it d-doesn't h-help now, b-but I'm r-really sorry, Mom."

"Why are you sorry?" she demanded, afraid to believe in him.

"I d-didn't realize what I was doing t-to you and to R-Rick." Shame suffused his face and he looked down at the floor. "I n-never meant t-to hurt him. I n-never realized—" He choked up. Several moments passed before he could speak again. "H-He's always been g-good to me. I d-didn't think—"

"That's the thing, isn't it?" Cassie said. "You didn't think how your actions would affect Rick or anyone else, including me."

"Y-You?" He frowned.

"Think about it. What happens if you get into trouble? Do you think the government will want the mother of a kid with a criminal record working with troubled kids?"

Shock covered his face. "I d-didn't—"

"Think that far ahead? Everything we do in this life has ramifications, Noah. You throw a stone and the ripples spread out far and wide." She closed her eyes. "I thought you were mature enough to realize that, especially after what happened when your father died. I guess I was wrong."

Noah sat down on the side of the bed as if a heavy

responsibility weighed him down. "I'm s-so sorry," he whispered. "I was angry b-because you didn't treat me like the m-man of the family, but I d-don't deserve that. I was s-stupid."

"Nobody gets everything they want in life," Cassie said, the sourness she felt inside tingeing her voice. "We all have to deal with hard things."

"L-like you l-loving Rick?" he asked very quietly.

"What do you know about that?" she asked him, startled.

"I can see it wh-when you look at him," Noah said in a soft tone. "And when he l-looks at you."

"Well, you don't have to worry about it now, Noah," she said, pressing down the surge of sadness as she accepted the truth. "Nothing's going to change."

"Because Rick m-made a vow," Noah said with a nod. "He t-told me about it. He s-said he has to pay for his p-past. I think th-that's wrong."

"Wrong?" Cassie frowned at him. "What do you mean?"

"Rick's always t-talking about f-forgiveness, how God forgives our s-sins and remembers them n-no more. He s-said that's what Easter's all a-about." He shrugged. "If G-God doesn't r-remember them, why would He w-want Rick to pay for them?"

Cassie stared at him, stung by the wisdom in the words that had come out of her young son's mouth. A smile took over her face and she tentatively put an arm around him. For the first time in a long time, he didn't flinch away.

"That is an excellent question, Noah."

A question Pastor Rick should have to answer.

* * *

His last days in Churchill slipped away from Rick like a skate blade across the glinting ice of Hudson Bay. Though it was late March, he found the still-wintry days dreary as he never had before.

He'd replayed his last conversation with Cassie a hundred times, but no matter how he wished otherwise, he'd had no choice. He'd had to push her away, even though it had cost him dearly. What puzzled him was that Cassie seemed to hold no grudge. She'd never said anything about that day when she came to the church on Sundays with Noah, or to choir practice.

Rick hadn't asked her to continue playing for them. She'd simply appeared and waited for his cue. It seemed to him that the kids were suddenly hitting each note exactly as he'd hoped, that they raised their voices in praise and worship as if they now fully grasped the meaning of Easter. For that he was grateful.

But rehearsal was bittersweet torture to Rick as he counted down each precious moment he had left with Cassie. He repeatedly reminded himself that God had brought him here, but that didn't mean God had brought him to Churchill to be with Cassie. It puzzled Rick that God would intentionally put him on this course when He knew Rick would fall for her. But at the same time, the joy he found in seeing her beautiful smile, in hearing her encourage the kids, in sharing a glance that said she still cared for him—that left him breathless.

He wouldn't have traded those moments for the world. And yet always, always, he faced the knowledge that he must leave here, leave her. Cassie's life would go on. She'd find someone else to love, to share her future with. She was too special for some other guy not to notice her. He wanted that for her.

But he would be alone. It was the way it had to be.

"Are you g-going to see Rick?" Noah asked, staring at Kyle.

"Yeah. He seems down lately." Kyle gave him a grin and grabbed the door.

"Wait. I need to t-tell you something." Noah summoned his courage. He had to fix things. "Rick l-loves my mom, you know."

"I kind of guessed." Kyle frowned. 'How does your mom feel?"

"She loves h-him, too, but Rick did something that hurt my g-grandpa." Noah felt his face get hot, but he didn't stop. "I know I shouldn't have d-done it, but I was listening at his d-door and I heard him m-make a reservation on the t-train. I'm pretty sure h-he thinks the only way to make it better is to leave. I don't want him to d-do that. Nobody d-does." He peered at Kyle through the falling snow. "Can y-you do s-something?"

"I don't know. But I'm going to try." Kyle slapped him on the shoulder. "Thanks for telling me."

"I w-want my m-mom to be happy. She w-won't be if Rick g-goes away."

"Got it." Kyle went inside.

"What were you saying to Kyle?" his mom asked as he climbed into her car.

"Just man t-talk." Noah spent the ride home praying.

"Rick?" Kyle stood in the now-empty sanctuary, peering at him with a puzzled look. "What are you doing?"

"Where is everyone?" Rick glanced around, realizing that while he'd been daydreaming, everyone had left.

"Gone home for dinner. Wanna share a pizza? Sara's at a baby shower." Kyle waited, his frown growing when Rick just stared at him. "You okay?"

The yearning to see Cassie, to hold her and tell her that he'd never love anyone as he loved her—all of it screamed at him to forsake his vow. He could feel the temptation to relinquish his faith, to abandon it and let himself revel in the love he felt for her.

"Thinking about Cassie?" Kyle asked in a knowing tone.

"You know?" Relief filled him. Rick poured out the whole ugly story. "I don't see a way out of this, buddy. I think I have to leave this place."

"Not so fast. I think we need to pray about that decision. How about if I lead off?" Kyle offered.

"I'd like that." He knelt with his friend and recommitted his life to God

Then Kyle insisted it was time to eat.

Rick went with him, but he wasn't hungry. All he could think about was the question that kept rattling through his brain. If loving Cassie was wrong, why didn't God take his feelings away?

Chapter Fourteen

On Good Friday Cassie went to church.

Rick had invited missionaries from Burma to speak in the morning. After sharing a lunch of soup and sandwiches to commemorate the Last Supper, he led them in a solemn foot-washing ceremony.

Cassie's heart swelled with pride for this man of God. She watched him humbly wash the feet of old and young alike, drawing their focus to the meaningful action Jesus had done, knowing he was to die. With tenderness and quiet respect Rick moved through the small group, his eyes glowing as he ministered. When he came to her, Cassie felt a jolt of response to his touch but Rick seemed unaffected as he poured warm water over her feet into the basin.

"'My protection and success come from God alone,'" he murmured as he dried her feet on a towel. "'He is my refuge, a Rock where no enemy can reach me. O my people, trust him all the time. Pour out your longings before him for he can help.'"

His head lifted as he finished speaking and for one timeless moment their eyes met. Cassie saw a tender, gentle love in his gaze. How she ached to respond, to reach out and embrace him, willing him to forget everything but caring for her.

For a moment she thought he would. But then he closed his eyes and, without looking at her again, moved on to the person beside her.

Why God? her soul cried. *He loves me. I know he does. And I love him. Is that wrong?*

"Your will be done," she heard Rick say.

Us loving each other—that's not Your will? Tears slipped between her lashes. *I can't have him, can I?*

A soft rush of certainty filled her. God was saying no. Oh, how that hurt. She took deep breaths then dabbed at the wetness on her cheeks.

God had something for Rick to do, a mission that was more important than loving Cassie Crockett. She couldn't stand in the way of that. Not after she'd seen his extraordinary gift for ministry. His heart was for God and he took his vow seriously. She could not diminish his dedication by asking him to break that vow.

She didn't think she could turn her back on the joy and the rightness of being with him. But as Rick stood in their circle, reminding them of how much God had sacrificed to have each of them as His child, Cassie suddenly understood. She'd finally learned that no matter what happened, God came first. Somehow He would help her give up the desire of her heart if she trusted Him completely.

As one the group rose, joined hands and sang the first verse of the hymn "Old Rugged Cross." Cassie was struck anew by the depth of Rick's abilities. She wasn't the only one with tears drying on her cheeks. Others in the congregation had been as deeply moved and a few, like her, lingered in the sanctuary to absorb or perhaps prolong the glory they'd experienced.

It took a long time to resolve the turmoil in her heart. Part of her longed to ignore God's will, to grab hold of her happiness and hang on, to beg him to give up his vow. She wanted what she wanted.

And yet how much more guilt would Rick feel? Cassie couldn't do that to him. For Rick's sake, she released everything into God's hands. It would cost her dearly when she saw him and heard his voice, and when her heart argued that she had a right to happiness.

But she had a right to nothing. She'd given up the right to run her life the way she wanted when she'd renewed her faith and trusted God.

It had to be complete trust.

She gazed at the mural of the good shepherd on the wall. It had been painted many years before. The colors were faded and worn except for the eyes. Dark brown, gentle and beckoning, she stared into them and at last found the peace she craved.

He's yours, Lord. Soft and tentative, peace flowed over her soul. She wiped away her tears. "Your will," she murmured at last.

She rose and walked to the exit, but earnest voices stopped her from leaving. Rick was standing in the foyer, talking to George Stern, who looked upset.

"I'm tendering my resignation, George. Effective immediately." Rick's words hit her with a decimating force. "I'll be leaving Churchill Tuesday morning."

The moment she heard the words, Cassie knew two things instantly and with a certainty that filled her soul. First, this was where God wanted Rick. Churchill needed his love and understanding and patience. This town was his ministry.

And, second, he was resigning because of her, because she was causing him to struggle against the vow he'd made. The weight of it almost crushed her.

Rick could not leave. Churchill was where he belonged.

So she'd have to go.

She'd talk to Laurel and resign. They could find someone to replace her.

But who could replace Rick?

Cassie waited until the two men left. Then she made a beeline for her car. Her dad was arriving tomorrow on the train. She'd tell him her decision, she decided as she drove back to Lives. Maybe after they cleared the air once and for all, she and Noah could go back to Toronto and live with him. It wouldn't be easy on Noah, but she knew he'd understand if she told him about Rick's resignation.

She pulled into the yard and took a good look at what made up Lives Under Construction. But the exterior, the skating rink, the shed—that wasn't the essence of the project. What mattered were the lives inside, boys who needed a man like Rick to guide them into their future.

Your will be done. With resolute determination Cassie left the car and walked into the house. "Laurel?"

"In the kitchen." Her friend greeted her with a smile that quickly faded when she saw Cassie's face. "What?"

"I have to resign, Laurel. Noah and I have to leave." Then, despite her best intentions, she broke down. Weeping, she explained what had happened.

Laurel listened, but she didn't try to talk Cassie out of her plans. Cassie knew that was because Laurel understood that Rick's presence in Churchill was a necessity. Anyone could nurse a sick boy, but not everyone could be the spiritual leader these kids needed to rebuild their lives.

God needed Rick in Churchill, not Cassie.

It was time to go.

"Dad!" Cassie threw her arms around her father's neck and hugged him tightly. "I'm so glad you came."

"Me, too, honey." He squeezed her and brushed a kiss against her hair. "Where's my grandson?"

"Hey, G-grandpa." Noah rolled his eyes at Cassie as the older man hugged him, but he said nothing, clearly happy to be reunited.

Cassie drove them back to Lives, bubbling with excitement as she and her dad caught up. Noah pointed out landmarks. Once they'd arrived, she introduced her father and they gathered to eat lunch. When it was over, the moment she'd been waiting for finally arrived.

"Can we talk, Dad?" she asked.

"It's about time, don't you think? I need to apologize to you for not supporting you enough after Eric's death."

"I understand now why you couldn't." She clutched his hand in hers. "But why didn't you tell me?"

"Shame. Embarrassment. Maybe some anger." He shook his head. "What kind of father doesn't have enough money put aside to help his own daughter? I felt like a failure."

"Because Rick lost your money," she said.

"He told you." John sighed.

"Yes. Dad." She hesitated. "Are you okay?"

"I'm fine, Cassie. I earn a good salary teaching at the seminary. I don't have a lot of expenses and the government sends me a pension check every month. If you need to borrow—"

"No, no. I was going to lend you some." They grinned at each other.

"Rick's a great guy, isn't he?"

"You can say that after what he did?" Cassie said.

"I was mad at him at the time, but I always knew he was a risk taker." He chuckled. "Rick is the son I never had. Just like I've always prayed for you, I've prayed for him for so many years. I believe God sent him to me to help and I tried my best." Her father's eyes narrowed. "Cassie, I've sensed something in your letters. You care for Rick, don't you?"

"I love him." She wasn't afraid to say it anymore. "It's because of Rick that I learned to trust God." She explained about her decision to leave Churchill.

"You'll live with me." John studied her. "How does Rick feel about you?"

Cassie explained her belief that he loved her.

"He gave his resignation—that's why Noah and I have to move. Rick belongs here, Dad. This place is his ministry, just like yours was always in Toronto. I can't let him give it up for me."

"So he's still determined to keep that vow." John's eyes narrowed. "I brought his guitar. I think I'll pay him a visit tomorrow," he said thoughtfully.

"I love you, Dad." She nestled in his arms, praying that somehow God would help her father help Rick.

"It's so good to see you, John." Rick held his office door wide, then embraced the stooped, gray-haired man who seemed to have aged twenty years since he'd last seen him. Obviously the result of losing his life's savings. He pushed the thought aside. "I'm glad you came for Easter. And doubly glad to see this again." He took the guitar from John, glad to feel the weight of the case in his hands again. "I wish Cassie hadn't done it, but I'm glad she did."

"She knows how important that guitar is to your ministry," John said.

Rick asked about mutual friends and the seminary where John still taught classes, even though he was supposed to be retired. Rick tried to dodge John's personal questions. No way did he want to discuss his feelings for his mentor's daughter. But John was as wily as ever.

"I've been thinking a lot about you recently, son." John tented his hands under his chin, his face thoughtful. "The Lord keeps telling me to pray for you so you'll see more clearly."

"See what more clearly?" Rick asked in puzzlement.

"His love." John leaned forward. "Or, more specifically, His forgiveness."

"Have you and Noah been talking?" Rick asked. "He was in here this morning, asking about me questions about God's forgiveness."

"Cassie told me how my grandson was struggling, and how you helped him see the light. I don't know how to thank you for doing that," John said.

"I only did for him what you did for me." Rick leaned back in his chair. "It's about time I started paying back my debt to you."

"There is no debt, Rick." John frowned. "I told you that long ago. I love you like the son I never had. If I helped you, then it was a God-given privilege, not because I wanted payback." He shook his head. "Are you still trying to keep that vow you made to God in seminary?"

Rick had known it was coming. He exhaled. "Yes. It's the only way I know to repay God."

"So you're still trying to buy your salvation."

Rick blinked. "Buy salvation?"

"What else can you call it? You think if you do enough, strive hard enough and help enough kids that you'll be able to repay God." John leaned forward. "I told you then and I'll tell you now. You can't earn forgiveness from our Lord. It doesn't matter what you do or don't do, He's still forgiven you for the mistakes you made."

"But—"

"Isn't that exactly what Easter is about?" The old man smiled. "The day Jesus died, your sins were forgiven. Period. There's no way you can earn or be worthy of that forgiveness. By trying you negate God's sacrifice."

Rick frowned at the words as they began to sink in.

"If we can be worthy of forgiveness, if we can deny ourselves in order to earn it, then Easter doesn't matter, son." John sighed. "I should have said this a long time ago, the day you made that vow, in fact. But I thought—"

"You're saying we shouldn't make vows to God?" Rick asked.

"I'm saying your vow isn't about God. It's about you, about easing your guilt."

"Me?" Rick shook his head, aghast. "No, I'm trying to make up for my mistakes."

"You can't." John tented his fingers, then peered at him. "You're not in control of the world. If you try to be, you make yourself ineffective for God. You're fixated on the past and what you can do to make amends, but God doesn't want your amends or your guilt. He's already forgiven you. Now He wants you to move on, to do the things He has planned for you."

Rick struggled to wrap his mind around what John was saying, but the next sentence drove all thought from his mind.

"My daughter loves you," John said quietly. "She said you told her you feel the same. But you won't act on those feelings, you won't see that God brought you together, because you're too busy trying to make God see how worthy you are."

Stunned by the condemnation, Rick reeled.

"This vow you made—have you ever asked God what He thinks about it?" John asked. "That's the thing about being in the ministry. We have to constantly measure our motives against God's expectations. Easter is about forgiveness for everybody, regardless of what's in their past. There's no mention of earning it or making repayment because we can never atone. And when we try, we hamstring God." John let that sink in for a moment, then rose. "I have to go, Rick. Noah and I are going to go ice fishing. My grandson and I have a lot of catching up to do."

Rick shook hands with the man he'd revered for so long, his mind in turmoil as he watched John leave the church. Alone, he stared at the cross hanging above the altar. He thought of all the people he'd hurt and of the time he'd spent trying to make up for it.

My grace is sufficient for Thee.

What did that mean? That he'd been wrong to make his vow?

"Rick?"

Cassie's quiet voice drew his attention to the back of the church. Love welled in him like an ocean tide as he soaked in her loveliness. Would he ever get over the yearning to wrap his arms around her and hold her close, to protect her and never let her go? "Cassie," he managed to croak.

"I just wanted to tell you something." She fiddled

with bright pink gloves that he knew she'd made. That vibrant color personified Cassie—she brought light and life with her wherever she went. "Noah and I are leaving Churchill. On Tuesday. With my dad."

"What?" Feeling sucker punched, Rick stared at her. Her brown eyes glittered with determination. "Why?" he whispered.

"I know you gave your resignation and I know you did it because of me. But you can't leave. This is your mission field, Rick. This is where you belong." Her voice grew stronger as she spoke. "The kids at Lives, Churchill's seniors, the people who live here—they all need you. This is where God sent you. Because He has a purpose for your life here." She smiled.

"If you leave, who will love the kids in your band and choir? They need to be part of something wonderful. Who will make sure the seniors are okay when the next problem hits? Who will show them that God is a God of love? You can't give up your calling here. I won't be responsible for ruining God's plans."

"But—"

"Because of you, I found God again. I understand now that His will comes first and I know that His will is for you to continue to minister here." She stepped forward. Her fingertips skimmed across his face, cupped his cheek and followed the line of his jaw. She touched her forefinger to his lower lip as if to press a kiss there.

Rick nearly lost it. Every good intention, every resolve, even his vow—they nearly caved in under the rush of longing that wailed through him. His instincts urged him to grab hold of her and hang on for dear life.

"I love you with my whole heart, Rick," she whispered, her smile affectionate yet sad. "But I understand that you have your vow, that you need to keep it and you can't do that if I'm here. So I'll leave wishing you God's very best. I'm so thankful that one of the people you helped heal was my son."

"I'm so sorry, Cassie."

"You don't owe me any apologies, Rick. I just want to say one thing more. It's actually something Noah asked me," she said. "You preach forgiveness. You've repeated it to the boys, to me and to Noah. You say it over and over."

He nodded.

"But if God is a God of forgiveness and second chances, why can't He forgive you for your past? Since when does God expect atonement for what's already been forgiven?"

She gazed at him a moment longer, then turned and walked out of the church, leaving him with her questions ringing in the air.

Rick stood there feeling broken and lost. "I love you, Cassie," he whispered. But his words fell into the emptiness of the sanctuary.

He returned to his office to work on his sermon for tomorrow, Easter Sunday. But there was no joy in his heart. Nor could he find joy in the glorious music the kids made in their afternoon practice. There certainly was no joy in watching Cassie walk out the door after practice without even looking at him.

Easter was all about joy. But all he felt was loss and guilt.

God doesn't want your guilt. John's words echoed inside his head.

Then what does He want?

Chapter Fifteen

"What are you thinking about, honey?"

Cassie was still adjusting to being around her father, and to his kindness. As he put an arm around her shoulder and hugged her close, sharing her wonder at the Easter morning sunrise, she sent up a quick prayer of thanks.

"Isn't it beautiful?" she whispered. The sun's rays made the snow gleam like a diamond, as if in jubilant praise. "I'll miss this place."

And Rick.

"You don't have to leave."

"Yes, I do. Rick's needed here. I can be replaced." She turned her head slightly, letting a smile tug at her lips. "Most women would fight like crazy for the chance to love a guy like him. He's one in a million."

"But?"

"But this place is his calling. How can I interfere in that? How can I ask him to turn his back on something he believes is his duty?" Cassie clapped her hands together. "Let's not talk about it anymore, okay? Let's just enjoy the time we have left here."

So they did. They shared a riotous breakfast with the boys. While Cassie cooked waffles, her dad insisted on frying mounds of bacon. Laurel got carried away whipping cream enough for twenty people, and yet somehow it all disappeared.

Joy filled the air at Lives Under Construction. From time to time the boys paused in their feast to remind each other of something in their choral presentation. Cassie smiled at the syrup that dotted Noah's T-shirt as he joined in the conversation. His stutter was almost gone and the dark clouds of anger had lifted, leaving behind the child who, because of Rick, was finally able to genuinely interact with the Lives' boys.

"You'd better wait till you're at church before you put on your new shirts," she said. Each boy had a brand-new white shirt, black pants and a black bow tie. "We don't want any spots on this performance."

As she laughed and smiled with them, Cassie could only keep Rick out of her thoughts for minutes at a time. The idea of never seeing Rick again, of never hearing his burst of laughter or the music he could coax from his guitar or his amazing voice—

I'm doing the right thing, aren't I, God?

What else could she do?

It took a lot of work to get the kitchen cleaned up and the boys ready to go. Cassie pulled into the packed church lot with only a few moments to spare before the service began. In a way she was relieved that there was no time to chat—she didn't want any awkwardness in her relationship with Rick.

Later she'd think about all they'd shared, all she'd lost. Today she'd concentrate, pour her heart and soul into her accompaniment and make sure Rick and the kids had the best music she knew how to provide.

She'd do it out of love, for him.

Cassie walked into the church. To her surprise, the church burgeoned with flowers. In the entry, a huge basket of fragrant hyacinths welcomed everyone. A dozen pots of pure white Easter lilies with big glossy yellow bows lined the front of the stage. On either side at the front, someone had arranged two massive vases of bright pink tulips.

One glance at her father's face and Cassie knew he'd done it.

"They must have cost you a mint," she said. "But they're beautiful. They remind me of the flowers Mom always got for our church. It really feels like Easter now."

"Then they were worth every penny." He squeezed her hand, then handed her her music bag. "Break a leg, sweetheart."

After whispering much the same thing to Noah, Cassie walked to the front of the church, laid out her music for the choir then began to play a prelude to quiet the congregation. She deliberately chose hymns she'd learned as a child, words that spoke of the resurrection and the life given by God. As the boys filed into the first two rows, silence fell, allowing the music to soar to the ceiling of the small building. Along with the lovely scent of the flowers, a feeling of joy permeated the packed room as Rick walked through the door to the left of the pulpit.

Please bless him. Let him feel Your presence today.

When Rick moved into position, Cassie let the last few notes die away. Her senses couldn't get enough of him, his dear face and gentle smile. His voice quiet yet edged with authority, he asked the congregation to rise.

How I love him...

Cassie forced herself to look down to hide the rush of emotion that threatened to break through. This was Rick's day to show his community what his ministry was about. Today they would see how God had used him.

"He is risen," he said, his smile wide as he gazed out over the group.

"He is risen indeed," the congregation responded.

Cassie waited as he welcomed everyone. Her heart thrummed with anticipation when at last he nodded to the choir and they took their places on stage. Then Rick looked directly at her.

Spellbound by his stare, Cassie saw anxiety flicker through his green eyes. She knew he was second-guessing himself, wondering if he'd been right to encourage the kids to do this, worrying he'd asked too much.

Yes, he'd rejected her love. And come Tuesday, she would leave Churchill with her heart breaking. But today—today she was going to make sure that this man she loved with her heart, soul and mind would not regret this day. She lifted her lips in a huge smile that she hoped told him that she believed in him, that she knew today would be a success.

Faith, she mouthed at him.

Slowly, surely, his beautiful smile transformed his face. He nodded at her. *Faith.*

Then, with the choir's full attention, he lifted his hand. Cassie played the somber opening chords, thrilled as the dark low notes echoed through the sanctuary. Choir and band hit the first note in perfect unison.

Thank You, Lord.

Then Cassie threw herself into playing the music, for Rick.

Rick had arranged a Scripture reading to give the choir and band a break halfway through the Easter cantata. While they sat, John rose. Standing amidstst the congregation, his baritone voice authoritative and yet personal, he began to recite verses about that first Easter morning.

Rick got caught up in thoughts of the next part of their presentation until a pause in John's speech caught his attention. He looked up and found John staring directly at him, his dark eyes focused and intent. Then in a clear ringing tone he quoted, "'There is forgiveness of sins for all who turn to me.'"

Every cell in Rick's body homed in on that sentence. Jesus died to forgive sins, *his* sins. Hanging on to them diminished the very sacrifice he celebrated.

Light filled Rick's soul, cleansing, clarifying, chasing out the guilt and refreshing it with the joy of the Easter message. Bemused by the wonder of freedom that flowered inside, he waited until John sat, then motioned for Noah to prepare.

Forgiven. I am forgiven. His soul chanted the glad refrain.

Cassie played the entrance to the song, this time a booming, triumphant series. Rick lifted his hands and their voices responded, soaring in hallelujahs that blended and harmonized in a perfect tribute.

Then Noah's pure voice rang out, the words of redemption clear. His face shone as his solo echoed through the rafters. *Redemption. Deliverance. Freedom.*

Still lost in the wonder of the gift that took away his guilt, Rick led them to the end of their Easter cantata, every note exploding with praise for the Easter gift God had freely given.

As the last note died away, as the crowd rose and applauded, Rick bowed with the choir, his choir, then motioned for Cassie to take a bow. In that second the truth of what others had been trying to tell him finally hit his heart. God didn't need or want his vow or his sacrifice for something He'd already wiped out. God needed a heart ready and willing to serve.

Churchill was where God wanted him.

But God had also sent Cassie here.

For him?

Hope flickered to life in a part of his heart that Rick had shut down. He needed to talk to John, to make sure his thinking wasn't off, that he wasn't making another mistake.

Can it be that You planned this, God? Love? For me?

His heart began to sing a new song—for Cassie.

Cassie snuck away from the church right after the service. She knew Noah and her father would catch a ride with Laurel. Before their Easter dinner, she needed some time to get her emotions under control, to make her heart stop hoping and yearning for something it couldn't have. By the time the boys and Laurel appeared at Lives, she thought she was in control.

Then Rick walked through the door.

Control and rational thought fled, along with her voice. Her eyes couldn't get enough of his spiky hair and his lopsided grin, and the low musical rumble of his voice. Each one seemed to resonate through her.

"Thank you for your amazing playing, Cassie," he said, his smile stretching across his face. "You made us sound great."

"That was all the boys. I just provided background noise."

There was something different about him. But though she studied him surreptitiously throughout the meal, Cassie couldn't figure out what it was. And it was hard to be so near him, to tamp down the love that burgeoned inside.

Oh, Lord, her heart wept.

So when everyone went to the family room to play games, Cassie crept away. She pulled on her coat and gloves, and left the house. Outside the sun beat down with intensity, moderating the afternoon's chill.

She was lost in her thoughts of Rick and prayers for the courage to hold fast to her decision when a hand touched her arm.

"Cassie."

Oh, that voice. She turned and rested her gaze on his beloved face, stunned by what she saw glowing in the depths of his eyes. His face shone, his voice held a depth of joy that took away her breath. "Rick?"

"I've been redeemed, Cassie." The words rang in the crisp air. He tipped back his head and laughed. "Redeemed. I don't know why I didn't see it. I'm a minister! I shouldn't have made such a stupid mistake, getting caught up in my wrong thoughts, but I did."

What was he talking about?

"God forgave me, Cassie. 'There is now no condemnation for sin,'" he recited, green eyes shining. "I've been trying to pay off a debt that wasn't there. My mistakes were all forgiven the first time I asked God. That's what Easter is all about."

"I know," she whispered, uncertain as to what this meant, and afraid to hope.

Afraid? Had she not yet learned to trust the One who loved His children enough to make the ultimate sacrifice? *I trust You. Help me, Lord.*

"Your father helped me see that my vow was wrong, that the guilt I've been clinging to is not part of His plan of forgiveness." He wrapped his arms around her and swung her in a circle, his head thrown back as he gazed into the blue sky. "I'm free!"

Startled and off balance, Cassie grabbed hold of his shoulders. Their faces were mere inches apart.

"I love you, Cassie Crockett. I love you with all my heart. Please don't go. Please stay and help me reach Churchill for God. Together we can do wonderful things for Him. We proved that today."

Inside her something released. For the first time since that awful day at his house her spirit lifted and she knew, she *knew* God was giving her the go-ahead. But just to be certain it wasn't her own will, she closed her eyes.

Are You saying yes, God?

Cassie felt Heaven's nod with every fiber of her being.

"Cassie?" Rick set her on her feet. His hand cupped her chin, his breath caressed her cheek. "What's wrong?"

"Nothing's wrong. For once everything is perfect. I love you, Rick. You're the man of my heart. I thought I'd never trust anyone again. I thought if I put my trust only in myself that I'd be safe, but God is teaching me that trust is an integral part of any relationship. I trust Him completely and that's because of you, because of what you've taught me about Him."

She had to stop, catch her breath. But she couldn't because Rick was kissing her. He started with her forehead, then her cheek, then the corner of her lips. Their breaths mingled in a cloud of vapor and then his lips met hers. He clasped her tightly to him and for a timeless moment the world stood still. Cassie reveled in the sweetness of his kisses, the rightness of being in his arms.

"I'm sorry for hurting you," he whispered. "Please forgive me."

"Of course." She rested her head on his shoulder. "I need your forgiveness, too, for misjudging you."

"Done." He sighed, pulling her closer. "Forgiveness. How is it I got so totally confused about that word? It means 'remembering no more.' And yet I kept dragging the past back, focusing on it instead of on what God has done. It took me a long time but I finally see what God's been trying to show me."

He drew back enough to see into her face. Cassie tensed with worry for a moment before she remembered that God was in charge. *I will trust Him.*

"I come with baggage, Cassie," Rick told her. "Maybe that's the wrong word, but you must know that I am dedicated to doing God's work. There's no fame, no glory and not much money."

How she loved him, loved his dedication to his Lord.

"Look around, Rick. We live in the most beautiful place in the world. Fresh, untouched, with God's handiwork all around. How could fame and glory ever compare to this?" She smiled. "Besides, you're laying up treasure in Heaven with your work. God honors that."

"So that means you'll stay in Churchill? You'll help me, share my work here?" He paused. "Will you marry me, Cassie?"

"I'd be honored to," she said. "Because I love you."

He kissed her back with heartfelt abandon. Cassie's soul sang with joy she'd once thought lost forever.

"Perhaps together we can use our mistakes to help others heal, as you've done with Noah and the boys," she murmured and pressed a kiss against his cheek. "I can never thank you enough for Noah, Rick. You reached past his angry heart and helped him begin to heal. Because of you I have my son and my dad back. And I'm building a better relationship with God."

"So am I," he said with a cheeky grin. "Isn't this a happy Easter?"

"The happiest." She turned in his arms and together they stood and admired God's handiwork. "We're going to be very happy," she said with certainty.

"I already am," Rick replied.

Epilogue

In Churchill the ice melted, the snow disappeared and the tundra bloomed as Rick's church grew, in part thanks to John's help. He'd moved to Churchill to be near his daughter and grandson, and had worked with Rick through the summer on a book for kids about getting rich with God.

In early autumn Churchill's splendor changed again to vivid red berry bushes, golden moss and bright yellow grasses. The air grew crisp, the sun blazed in the richest blue of the sky. Geese honked overhead as the land prepared for winter.

On the brightest of these days, Rick's little church teemed with activity as the boys from Lives Under Construction joined with local kids to ready themselves for the wedding of Cassie Crockett to Rick Salinger. Everything had to be perfect so they arrived well before the first guest to practice their part in the wedding.

Thus it was that when Cassie arrived at the church with Laurel, Alicia and new-mom Sara, the band welcomed her inside. She followed her two bridesmaids down the aisle as Michael played a solo on his saxophone. Her eyes rested for a moment on Kyle, who stood tall as best man, then moved to Noah. She smiled and her son smiled back, his blue eyes twinkling. Then her gaze locked on Rick, the man who filled her world and her heart.

Her father led them in their vows to each other.

"I love you, Cassie. I love the promise I see in you, the heart you lavish on those in need, the joy you bring to my days. I look forward to our future because I know God has great plans for us. I'll be by your side always as we place our faith and our trust in Him." His gaze holding hers, Rick slid the wide gold band onto her finger, then kissed it in place.

Cassie smiled through a gloss of tears, her heart lifting. God had brought her so far.

"I love you, Rick. I love your joy in people. I love your God-centered life and your dedication to do His will. I love you for loving me, for moving beyond the past to embrace our future. I will love you until eternity." She smiled into his eyes as she slid a matching circle of gold onto his ring finger.

"As much as these two have pledged their love to each other, by the power of God I declare Rick and Cassie to be husband and wife." John grinned at them. "You may kiss your bride."

A hush fell inside the little church as Rick and Cassie kissed. Then Noah's voice rose in a joyful a cappella solo giving praise to God for His gifts of love. Cassie's heart almost burst with pride.

What a long way they'd come. All of them.

"Ladies and gentlemen, may I present Mr. and Mrs. Rick Salinger."

Her arm looped in her husband's, Cassie took her

first steps as Rick's wife while the band played the Hallelujah Chorus.

"They aren't perfect," Rick murmured in her ear as they made their way down the aisle to stand in the receiving line outside.

"None of us are. But love covers mistakes, don't you think?" Cassie shared her husband's smile.

"Love and forgiveness," he agreed.

Love and forgiveness. The two could change the world. That was the message Cassie and Rick would share with Churchill for as long as God wanted them here.

* * * * *